The Chronicles of Colonization

Michael Peron

Dedicated to each and every one of my swimmers,
a daily source of inspiration and joy.

The Room

"How did you find me?"

The two men were in a room, five meters wide by six meters long by three meters high. The walls were dark grey, interrupted by hints of black and silver. The floor and ceiling shared the same design.

"It was only a matter of time."

There was a table in between them, also dark grey, standing three quarters of a meter high, measuring two meters long and one meter wide. Each man sat in a chair facing the other.

"What do you want?"

Behind one man was a door, recessed into the wall, closed. Behind the other was a thick pane of glass, a window to what lay beyond. The man with the window behind him had asked the questions, and the man with the door behind him had answered.

"I want to know what you know."

The man asking the questions had a haggard look about him. His clothes were old and dirty, his beard long and unkempt. He sat with a bit of a slouch, and there were bags under his eyes.

"And if I tell you?"

The man answering the questions had a confident look about him. His clothes were new and clean, his face freshly-shaven. He sat upright, and there was a glint in his eye.

"Then perhaps we can arrange a deal."

The haggard man turned to look over his shoulder, out the window. The blackness was interrupted by hundreds and hundreds of stars. His eyes darted among them, searching, wondering, then he turned back to respond.

"How can I trust you?"

The confident man kept his eyes on the haggard man.

"You can't."

The haggard man contemplated his answer, then sighed.

"Where should I start?"

The confident man smiled.

"The colonist."

The haggard man sighed once more, then closed his eyes. The confident man did the same.

Chronicle I: Nine

Nine felt the protective casing come off of his body and opened his eyes.

This was it. It was really happening.

Part of him was afraid to move, afraid that he would simply fall apart… but his eyes were darting around just fine, why would the rest of him be any different?

He wiggled a toe, then moved a finger. No issues there. He clenched his fist. Everything was normal. Everything was going according to plan.

Slowly, he let himself sit upright. He looked at his colleagues, some of them already climbing out of their pods, each one in a daze.

They had survived. That was one check off the list he was happy to mark.

"Everyone feel okay?"

Six, their captain, was already at his locker, putting on his uniform. Nine gave a nod in reply.

"One, make contact with Adam. Two, monitor the probes. Three, open the eyes. Four, inspect the robots. Five, check the nursery. Seven, check the satellite. Eight, verify all critical systems."

Nine swung his feet to the ground and stood. It was the first time he had used his legs in over a hundred years. He stared at them, marvels of—

"Nine, check the womb."

Six's order snapped him out of his stupor, and Nine hustled to his locker.

His uniform on, he made his way out the door, down the length of the short hall, and into the womb. He put his index finger in the port and closed his eyes. It only took a moment to make sure everything was in working order.

"*All clear, Six,*" he relayed the message to his captain.

"*Thanks, Nine,*" came the reply in his head.

He removed his finger and exited the womb. Four was in the hall, inspecting the robots recessed into the walls.

"Looks like they did their job, huh?"

Four nodded.

"We're still alive thanks to these two."

He gave the robots a pat on the shoulder. Nine continued into the brain.

"How far are we, Six?"

"In orbit, 970 kilometers from the surface."

Nine turned to look through the eyes, the two large windows of the brain. Through the thick glass he could see the planet.

"Is that what I think it is?" he asked.

"Yep," Three replied. "Water."

"What's the probe say, Two?" Six asked.

"Within standard deviation of Adam's assessment. 69.4% nitrogen, 24.2% oxygen, 3.2% methane, 2.6% sulphur, 0.4% argon, 0.1% helium, 0.1% carbon dioxide. Traces of neon as well."

"Do we have a gravity reading?"

"15.1 at the probe's landing site."

Nine continued to stare at the planet. White clouds swirling over swaths of blue, interrupted by pockets of green. It looked like Earth's brother.

He closed his eyes.

"*What is the Earth date?*" he asked himself.

"*May 22nd, 2810,*" came the reply.

205 Earth years since their departure. Quite a while.

"Okay, Four and Seven I want you to do a full systems check on Adam. One and Three, I want you to scan for possible landing sites. Five and Nine, I want you to verify and select one of the landing sites. Two and Eight, send the robots out to inspect the hull."

The crew scattered to fulfill their duties. Nine joined Five at another port and plugged his finger in. Together they pored over the options One and Three sent them.

"*There?*"

"*No.*"

"*Not there.*"

"*There?*"

"*Maybe.*"

"*There.*"

"*Agreed.*"

Five and Nine opened their eyes and unplugged.

"Ship, did you get that?"

"I got it, Five," the ship responded.

"Five and Nine, oversee Four and Seven."

They glanced at Six then plugged back in and closed their eyes.

Nine maneuvered through the ship's virtual interface and found Four and Seven conducting their systems tests on Adam. So far, all good. He kept an eye on them until the process was finished.

"*All good, Five and Nine?*"

"*All good, Four and Seven.*"

The four of them unplugged. Six glanced at Five and Nine, who nodded, then the captain closed his eyes for a few seconds.

"The robots still have twelve minutes of scanning to do. Seven, can you get a trajectory set for the landing site? One, please verify once he has made it."

"On it."

Nine glanced back out the ship's eyes. In a few hours, they would be on its surface.

"What are you thinking?" Eight asked, standing next to him.

"There it is. Life outside of the solar system."

Eight nodded, amused.

"We knew that before we came here."

"But now we can see it. We can actually see it."

Eight was right, Earth knew there was life out here. But Earth couldn't see what they saw—at least, not yet. It would take over eighty years for the data they were collecting to make its way back. The inconvenience of space.

"Trajectory set and verified, Six."

"Thank you, Seven and One. Ship, ask the robots how much longer."

"The robots have four minutes left, Six."

"Okay everyone, you heard the ship. Four minutes until we begin our landing procedure. Three, close the eyes. Everyone else, find a seat and plug in."

Nine chairs lined the back wall of the brain, and the crew made their way over. Nine sat down, plugged himself into the port on the armrest, and felt the straps tighten across his body.

Six minutes later, the last crew member joined the virtual space.

"Everyone ready?"

Eight counts of *"Yes"* and Six initiated the landing procedure.

Here we go, thought Nine, privately.

- - -

They opened their eyes and unplugged.

We did it, Nine thought. We landed.

"Ship, open the eyes."

"Yes, Six."

The crew stood from their seats, watching the thick coverings slide upward to expose the windows. Nine felt the extra gravity of the planet pressing down on him, but he paid it no attention. He was focused on the view.

Green. Green as far as the eye could see, low to the ground like a grass or a moss. The green was punctuated by purple polyps, large violet eggs scattered across a meadow. Occasional slabs of dark grey or black indicated rock formations. The topology was relatively flat in the surrounding area and there was fog—or what looked like it—blinding the crew from seeing more than fifty meters out.

It was not Earth's brother, but her distant cousin. Familiar yet alien.

Six's voice interrupted the silence.

"Eight, what do the atmospheric sensors say?"

"Same as the probe."

"Gravity?"

"15.0 here."

"Three, call Adam. One, send a robot out."

One hesitated, not wanting to lose sight of the eyes, then turned around and went into the hall. Three minutes later, one of the robots was in the exit room and One rejoined them in the brain.

The sound of the exit door opening made Nine close his eyes. He accessed the robot's visual feed and watched it step out the exit door and onto the planet's surface. The metal foot made contact with the surface, and the planet had its second robot visitor.

For a moment Nine wondered how far their landing site was from Adam, but he refocused on the visual feed. He watched the robot take a few more steps, then patched into the temperature and pressure sensors. Nine felt the soft crunch under the robot's feet and the cool mist on its body. He glanced at the temperature reading. 277 Kelvin. Nearly freezing.

The robot walked the perimeter of the ship, checking for any signs of danger. The crew were all patched in, watching, feeling, living the experience from inside the ship's brain.

It took about fifteen minutes to finish the walk. All of the ship's surroundings matched what the crew saw from the eyes: a green carpet with purple bulbs, all covered in fog. The robot encountered no immediate signs of danger. Everyone opened their eyes.

Six turned to look at the crew, and Nine felt a sudden mix of anxiety and excitement. They knew the protocol. Six would take two others out for the first excursion. They would be the first three to ever set foot on the planet. He just had to choose.

"Three and Nine, suit up for the first excursion."

Nine felt a surge of emotion, the same mix of anxiety and excitement now amplified tenfold. His breathing rate increased, an odd and primitive response that he tried to ignore as he went back to his locker.

He was on the first excursion. It was what he had dreamed of when he was first selected, but that was hundreds of years ago.

"Nine, is your breathing rate up?"

"Yes, Six."

The captain seemed amused. With the exosuits on and helmets in hand, they walked to the exit room doors.

"Ship, is the exit room sealed and cleared?"

"Yes, Six."

"Three and Nine, helmets on."

All three attached their helmets to their exosuits, then Six's voice spoke over the ship's audio system.

"Five, you are acting captain in case of my inability to perform my duty as assessed by vote of One, Two, Four, Seven, and Eight."

"Got it, Six."

"Ship, open the exit room inner door."

"Yes, Six."

The door in front of the three crew members opened, and they stepped into the exit room. There was enough room for the entire crew to fit, yet Nine felt claustrophobic.

"Ship, close the exit room inner door."

"Yes, Six."

He stared at the exit door in front of them, the door to the new world. Was he ready for this? It would be over eighty years before Earth heard a distress signal.

"Ship, open the exit room outer door."

"Yes, Six."

The door in front of them opened, a loud hiss announcing the difference in pressure. Even though the exosuit was temperature controlled, the cold sent Nine into an involuntary shiver.

Six took the first step onto the surface, paused, then exited the ship completely. Three looked at Nine before following. Nine reached the threshold of the exit door and hesitated. This was it.

He brought his foot over the lip of the door and onto the green. He felt the same soft crunch, only this time it was under his own boot. His other foot followed suit, and now all three crew members were outside the ship.

Six turned to look at them with a smile.

"Welcome to Alpha."

Nine scanned the horizon. To their left was the robot, dutifully awaiting orders. Behind them was the ship. Everywhere else was misty fog, a blanket of white covering the alien green. Despite this fog, the planet's star managed to light up the terrain at a brightness comparable to Earth's.

He looked down to his feet, at the green underneath. Was this a plant, an animal, or something entirely different? Were they crushing entire civilizations with every step?

He squatted down to inspect the ground more closely. It resembled moss back on Earth but thicker, coarser; like velcro yet soft to the touch. The color was a brighter shade of green than the moss he knew from Earth—almost glowing. It was about five centimeters thick, growing on the same dark grey rock that covered the landing site. Drops of dew from the humid atmosphere littered each hair-like string.

Humid yet near freezing, Nine thought. Interesting.

He heard the exit door being closed and glanced up for his shipmates. They were doing the same as him, inspecting the green life form.

"Three, get some samples of the rock. Nine, get some samples of one of the polyps."

Nine closed his eyes to access the robot and realized they had been shut out of the system; a safety measure he had forgotten.

"One, can you access the robot and have it inspect one of the purple bulbs?"

"Sure, Nine."

Nine stood and watched the robot make its way over to the closest one, about six meters away. There was no reason to follow the machine just yet —for all he knew, the object could explode at the touch.

The robot bent over and gave it a gentle poke. Nothing. Another prod, with more force this time. The polyp swayed but sprung back to vertical. Nine decided to approach.

"Looks like another plant, Nine."

"Thanks, One."

The robot took a step back as Nine squatted down next to the alien organism. It was about forty centimeters tall and twenty across at the widest point. On closer inspection it looked less like an egg and more like an abnormally tall bulb of garlic, with evenly spaced, longitudinal ribs. It was also somewhat see-through, the light reflecting off the inside in varying shades of purple. He gave it a poke and felt a tough outer skin resist his prod.

He pulled a small sample cup from his pouch and took out his laser scalpel. He brought the scalpel close to the polyp then hesitated. The purple light bouncing around inside made it look like an organic amethyst, and he was reluctant to modify such beauty. But they needed to analyze it, understand it. Hopefully it wouldn't retaliate.

Nine activated the laser scalpel and cut a small portion off one of the sides, dropping it into the sample cup and sealing it. There was no immediate explosion, but the plant began to pulsate, a small amount of clear liquid dripping out of the cut site.

Nine grabbed another sample cup for the liquid, watching the viscous flow as three large drops fell into his container.

"Finished, Nine?"

He closed the sample cup and stood.

"Yes, Six."

"Okay, give all the samples to the robot and we will get back on board."

The trio handed off their cups and went to the exit door. They entered the exit room, had the exit door closed, and underwent a decontamination procedure. Thirty minutes later, they stepped back into the ship.

The first excursion was a success.

- - -

Alpha orbited the star Solaris at a distance of 1.092 AU. The orbital period (or year) was 391.843 Earth days long, and each planetary rotation (or day) was 1.334 Earth days long, meaning Alpha had 293.735 days in its year.

The planet itself had 3.2 times the mass and 1.4 times the radius of Earth, and its gravity was about 1.5 times that of Earth's. Solaris was a main-sequence G2V-type star, about 16% brighter and 6.2% more massive than the Sun with a surface temperature around 5698 K.

These conditions made Alpha the perfect candidate for their expedition, as it was the most Earth-like planet discovered within a 100 lightyear radius of Earth itself. This was no coincidence of course—their mission had been carefully planned for decades. But over the course of the crew's first week, even more similarities began to manifest themselves.

The moss-like plant was found to be an autotroph performing a process similar to photosynthesis, while the polyps seemed to be heterotrophs, taking energy from the moss in a possible symbiotic relationship. The rock bed on which all of this was growing was extrusive igneous—volcanic rock.

Alpha had much more volcanic activity than Earth, and the ship's landing site was on an expanse of cooled magma. By the third day, it was clear that the rising topologic peak to the southeast of their landing site was a volcano, likely active. Nine hoped it wasn't planning on erupting anytime soon.

On the fourth day, Six activated the drones: nine smaller, flying robots that would spread around the planet exploring and collecting samples to bring back to the ship. He had them disperse as far and wide as possible.

On the fifth day, 4423 meters from the ship, Six, Four, and Eight located the first body of water. The water was analyzed and subsequently found to be potable. No life forms were spotted during the excursion.

On the sixth day, it rained. It was a light rain, more of a drizzle that combined with the already dense fog. The fog itself waxed and waned but never rescinded. For the time being they had no way to tell if it was a local phenomenon or planet-wide. Nine did recall a significant amount of white cloud cover from their vantage point in space.

On the seventh day, Adam arrived at the ship.

Adam was the true pioneer of this world, the robot that had verified its habitability and the presence of carbon-based, cellular life. It arrived hundreds of years ago, one of eight Adams on eight different exoplanets within a 100 lightyear radius of Earth, each one transmitting basic and critical information to determine which of the planets would officially become Alpha.

This planet was selected, and this crew was sent. Now, over three hundred years since it first set down on Alpha, Adam would have company.

"Hello, Adam."

"Hello, Six."

The crew listened to Adam over the ship's speaker while it stood outside with the other robot.

"Adam, can you do a wired transfer of your entire memory to our robot outside?"

"Yes, Six."

Adam was not programmed for large wireless data transfers—its construction was based on efficiency; anything that did not aide its ability to inform Earth of the habitability of the planet was omitted.

But Adam had been here a little over four hundred years, gathering data and saving what it deemed most important. It had had plenty of time to explore and decide what information to keep and what to remove, so its data transfer promised to accelerate the crew's understanding of Alpha.

Every crew member went to a port to plug in. The virtual space was flooded with Adam's analyses, coming through the robot into the ship, and the crew pored over the data for the next few days.

The most profound of Adam's discoveries the crew (and Earth) already knew: Alpha had carbon-based life and liquid water. The life Adam encountered did not contain DNA, but it was made of something akin to cells (Adam's biochemical analysis capabilities were limited to what was necessary to trigger the expedition).

Most of the rest of Adam's information was new to the crew. The robot had explored all of the land on the continent, which spread over 14.26 million square kilometers—a bit larger than Antartica. Their landing site was at 16°14' S based on the geographic north pole, and most of this continent was in Alpha's southern hemisphere.

According to Adam, igneous rock made up a majority of the continent, with active volcanoes littering the landscape. The moss they had discovered grew over most of this rock, although it was thicker towards the equator and thinned out near the southern edge.

The polyps were a different story. Several different species occupied different areas based on latitude and proximity to the surrounding ocean. They varied from purple to red, and the largest one Adam had seen grew half a meter tall.

Adam had not encountered any animals. Nine wasn't sure whether that was fortunate or unfortunate. However, Adam didn't have the ability to traverse bodies of water nor survey their depths. The lakes and oceans of Alpha remained unexplored, as did the other, smaller continents and islands that littered the planet. There was also the small but present chance that animals existed that Adam was unable to detect: if they were very small or very fast, for example, they may have simply eluded the robot for hundreds of years.

Adam's data dump did provide one critical piece of information: its analysis of certain patches of soil in the few areas less affected by frequent lava flows indicated that with minor genetic modifications, some types of Earth plants should be able to grow. Now Six had some difficult decisions to make.

This expedition was not one of discovery—it was one of colonization. The inhabitants of Earth were running out of room. The Solar System provided a few stopgaps, but it wasn't enough. The Adams were sent to scour for the next step, the next stage in the expansion: Alpha. And this planet was chosen.

Alpha was not chosen for its its presence of life but for its habitability and Earth-likeness. But as Nine had noted, it was more Earth's distant cousin than her brother. The planet needed to be terraformed, needed to be made more Earth-like. The question was how soon and how much.

Terraforming by its very nature would change the ecology of the planet. Even with their exosuits, the crew's presence on Alpha may have already caused some unintended forward contamination. If resilient microbial life hitched a ride from Earth, there was little doubt it had already begun to spread.

And since it harbored the first lifeforms ever encountered beyond the Solar System, Alpha presented a unique scientific opportunity. The crew were meant to discover and catalog as many alien species as possible, but they were short on time.

Originally, the crew expected to spend many years genetically modifying Earth plants to allow them to grow on Alpha. All of this would occur on board the ship, minimizing the contamination of Alpha and allowing for further exploration and discovery. But according to Adam's soil analysis, it was possible that these years of preparation would be narrowed down to a few months.

Protocol said that as soon as terraforming was deemed viable, to notify Earth so they could send the first batch of Puritans. That notification would take about eighty years to get to Earth, and then another two hundred years would pass before the Puritans reached Alpha. And three hundred years happened to be just about the amount of time needed to terraform a planet.

Six had to find a balance between discovering the natural ecology of the first habitable exoplanet while potentially altering or even destroying it to make it suitable for Earth's life forms. He also had to decide if and when to notify Earth to send the Puritans. With Adam's newfound data, the timeline before terraforming was certainly shortened. But by how much?

With these thoughts in mind, Nine was glad he wasn't the captain.

- - -

The crew had decided to model the Alpha year on the Earth year. Alpha had just shy of 294 rotations about its axis in its revolution around Solaris, which divided nicely into 12 months alternating 25 and 24 days. The landing day was deemed January 1st of the year 0. Since these days, months, and years were longer than Earth's, when the crew celebrated the end of the first Alpha month they had actually been there just over 33 Earth days, but it was close enough.

Most of their time was spent either in the womb, the nursery, or on an excursion. In the womb, the crew played god, genetically modifying Earth microorganisms to better suit the new planet. These microbes were then taken to the nursery, where several simulations of Alpha's environment— made from samples of rock, soil, and atmosphere brought on board— provided a testing ground that did not contaminate the planet itself. Nine noted that Six had not yet allowed them to remove their exosuits outside the ship. For the time being, the captain had prioritized discovery over colonization.

The outdoor robot had been sent into the nearby lake and discovered aquatic plant life growing both on the bottom and floating within, but nothing resembling animals as were known on Earth. Of course, this wasn't Earth, this was Alpha. And on Alpha, they were still trying to figure out what life was.

Archea, Bacteria, and Eukaryota were not necessarily concepts that applied to this planet. The best lead the crew had so far were the cell analogues, complete with membranes and cytoplasm. These cells had already been observed replicating in a process akin to binary fission, although no nucleic acid or its equivalent had yet been found. It was very well possible that nothing comparable to Earth's animals had evolved on Alpha, but if it existed, the crew wanted to study it.

The observed similarities between Alpha's cells and Earth's cells would likely ignite debate about panspermia between the planets: perhaps the seeds of life were dropped on Alpha and Earth by meteors or even an alien spacecraft. While this was a valid conjecture, Nine knew they had to be careful about the evidence used to prove it. The longer they were here, the more contaminated the planet became. By the time the Puritans arrived, Alpha's cells would be competing with Earth's. With all of the genetic engineering going on in the womb, it was even possible the two forms of life would converge. If that ever happened, there would be no way to tell if life evolved here independently and which species were truly indigenous. Such fundamental questions deserved at least some attention, and Nine was glad Six continued to stall the terraforming.

During the second month, the crew summited the nearby volcano and found a lava flow along the other side. The outdoor robot upgraded from lakes to oceans, and began taking longer and deeper treks into the nearest major body of water with the goal of eventually reaching another continent. The oceans here had a salinity of about 1.2%, much lower than Earth's average of 3.5%, and the plant life was similar to the lake's in the shallow regions (though it did change as the robot delved deeper). There was still no sign of animals, but the samples the robot brought back gave the crew more and more insight into Alpha's native life forms.

Twelve days into these excursions, the robot reached a point of no return as the pressure at further depths would become too great to withstand, and Six had to cancel its plans to reach another continent. With experiments in the nursery showing more and more promise, time was of the essence. Thankfully, the drones were already exploring some of the other continents.

The drones had the advantage of flight but their use was limited by the layer of fog: in most regions, the ground was not visible beyond fifteen meters of height and, combined with irregular topology, flying was slower than ideal. Given the circumstances and schedule, however, they would have to do.

While the robot had taken his deep sea tours, the drones had explored a decent portion of five other continents. Following the coastlines gave the crew an estimate of their respective areas: approximately 6.4, 7.2, 9.5, 9.9, and 11.6 million square kilometers. These were the largest land masses on the planet, making Alpha's total land area less than half that of Earth's, despite its larger overall size.

Up to that point, the drones had not collected samples because that would slow down their flight. Whenever something of interest was found, the crew noted its location for future collection. At the end of Alpha's March, Six had the drones begin collecting the logged samples and returning to the ship.

Before the samples arrived the crew had only a visual idea of what was on these other continents. The majority of Alpha seemed to be covered by the same volcanic rock on which the ship had landed. Over the course of their journeys, the drones had witnessed forty-eight lava flows and six violent eruptions.

The moss-like plants didn't seem to mind, as they covered most of this volcanic rock even in the most active areas. The polyps, however, appeared to be unique to their own continent.

On one continent located almost entirely in the higher latitudes, the green moss was totally absent, at least as far as the drones had ventured. In its place were tufts of what resembled grass, tall and slender, growing in narrow bunches about a meter high. They were a darker shade of green, not as vibrant as the moss, though more reminiscent of Earth's plants. These tufts grew on soil rather than rock, but even in the soil they remained sparsely distributed.

On two of the other continents, they found small, circular bodies of water—what looked like ponds—about a meter across. The odd thing about these ponds were their circularity and grouping: in certain areas, ten to twenty of the ponds would appear close together, all about the same size, all almost perfectly round.

The drones brought back samples of the different mosses, the grass, and water from the ponds. They dropped them off with Adam and the outdoor robot then buzzed back out into the fog. Nine wondered how long Six would wait. They had had a few successes in the nursery, but the results needed to be replicated outside the ship. How much of the other continents would the captain want to explore before he authorized their first excursion without the exosuits? Almost four months had passed on Earth since they landed on Alpha. Protocol said they start terraforming as soon as possible. But that decision was up to Six, not Nine.

- - -

It happened around Alpha's late June, after three more rounds of samples from the drones. With more and more positive results in the nursery and one violent eruption from the volcano nearest the ship (which thankfully didn't lead to any damages), Six called for the first unprotected excursion.

Nine was not selected for this honor, but it made little difference to him. He already felt like he had been living on the planet's surface: over the course of their first month, the atmosphere of the ship had gradually shifted to reflect Alpha's own. They had been living in Alpha's conditions for several months now, including the damp cold that hovered around 279 K by day and 256 K by night.

The Puritans are going to struggle with that, he thought.

When One, Five, and Six stepped out on the surface for the unprotected excursion, Nine felt a hint of sadness. In some sense of the word, Alpha was no longer a virgin planet. At least he had been lucky enough to see it in its original condition.

Now that the ship's quarantine was over, Adam and the outdoor robot were allowed on board. After their excursion, Six asked Nine to oversee Adam's upgrade.

At this point, Adam's hardware and software were nearly five hundred years old and almost three hundred years older than the ship. The crew had brought along some physical enhancements for the pioneer but first Nine had to upgrade his cerebral unit.

A cerebral unit, thought Nine. How primitive.

He was plugged into the virtual interface with Adam monitoring the process when something caught his attention. Something that, immediately upon seeing, Nine knew he wasn't supposed to see.

His heart rate spiked—another primitive response that would be immediately noticed. Panic layered on panic, and he focused all his energy on his bodily functions, bringing them back to normal levels. All of this happened in just two seconds, but was it fast enough?

He waited for an interruption from Six or the ship, but it never came. The system had dismissed his irregular heartbeat as an outlier. The panic vanished, and Nine's mind relaxed to match his body.

But soon a new feeling took over: guilt. Why was he hiding his response? The upgrade continued as planned, but Nine had noticed something, something even Six may not have known about: Adam had no concept of Puritans. It was being programmed right now. How was that possible?

This was a question he knew he was not supposed to ask. He did his best to bury the thought and focus on his task. Twelve minutes later, Adam's upgrade was complete.

- - -

Two days later, Six had them attempt the first experiment with one of the concocted microorganisms outside the ship. The microbes survived and proliferated for three days, at which point Six formally began terraforming operations and notified Earth to send the Puritans.

The crew had prepared a terraforming action plan in between their scientific excursions and genetic engineering. The action plan had specific designs on where to plant their different Earth microbes based on the surrounding environment to slowly but surely introduce Earth lifeforms on Alpha. In the hundreds of years ahead, it was hoped that perhaps more macroscopic Earth life could take root on this planet. To that end, the experiments in the womb continued to more advanced organisms, whose genetic engineering was naturally more difficult. Their experience with the microbes, however, gave the crew a solid starting point.

Now that they were on board, Adam and the outdoor robot helped in the womb and nursery. The drones continued to explore the farther continents, and for all intents and purposes everyone got into a rhythm and let their work take over.

Everyone except Nine. To be sure, Nine got into a rhythm and did his work, but a part of him was restless. He could not unsee what he had seen.

Adam had had no concept of Puritans. Were the Puritans a new concept? The thought itself brought a sense of dread—he knew it was blasphemy to think this way. He had to let it go. If Six or the crew knew what he was thinking…

But how could he keep a secret for so long? It would take about eighty years for their notification to reach Earth, then another two hundred plus before the Puritans arrived. Almost three hundred years to keep a secret! He had to fight the despair as it attempted to access his biological functions. He couldn't afford any more physiological slip ups.

And so Nine ignored his wandering thoughts as best as possible and settled into the terraforming routine. As the months turned into years, the crew's progress in the womb stalled at the microbial stage. Something was not working with their genetic engineering, so the crew focused on cracking Alpha's life code instead, in the hopes of finding a solution.

This turned out to be the right approach. A decade into their stay, they had enough working knowledge of Alpha's genetic code to develop an Earth/Alpha moss hybrid that proliferated rapidly in the surrounding environment. There was an irony somewhere in this, Nine thought, but it reminded him of the unthinkable thoughts, so he ignored it. Sadly, after another two decades, the hybrid moss had spread enough to drive the polyps to extinction, as they were unable to form the same symbiotic relationship with this new species. Such was terraforming.

With the robots' help, the crew had created a lava flow diversion system which came in handy at least once a year. The more pressing issue were the occasional earthquakes, but there was not much that could be done about that.

The drones were now busy mapping the planet in an efficient pattern, taking samples only of extreme interest. No major discoveries had been made, and there were still no signs of animal life. Nine wondered about those ponds, but they were on another continent and the water sample provided no answers. That would be a mystery for the Puritans to solve.

While Nine and the rest of the crew had settled in rather well to life on Alpha, he couldn't help but wonder how the Puritans would cope. Gravity here was about 50% stronger—without a biomechanical skeleton, life would be difficult. The temperature was also a concern. Nine could simply dim his nervous system's response to thermal variation, effectively shutting out the feeling of the cold. Other components within him made sure no unwanted autonomic responses, such as onset of hypothermia, would occur.

But the Puritans had none of these things. That is what made them Puritans.

Immediately following these thoughts, Nine experienced something he had never experienced before: a thought beyond his reach. There was an idea that he could almost feel, that he knew existed but he could not grasp. At the same time, he knew it was forbidden, and he found himself ashamed once more. Why did he continue to have these issues? What was happening?

- - -

The years turned into decades, and the decades into centuries. Beyond Nine's personal issues, the crew on Alpha ran into no unexpected problems. While their research continued with exponentially decreasing returns, they had quite a bit of time at their disposal. As their three hundred year window came to a close, it was clear their terraforming action plan was ahead of schedule, and the planet was set and ready for colonization well before the Puritan arrival.

As the ship from Earth—the Salvation—made her approach, her messages became more and more frequent, owing to a shorter signal distance. According to what Nine could glean, everything was going according to plan on their end and, soon enough, Alpha would fulfill its purpose.

It wasn't until just before the arrival—literally days away from the scheduled landing—that something broke the hundreds of years of routine.

"*Crew, report to the brain immediately.*"

Six's message cut short the day's work in the womb and nursery, and the crew assembled in the brain of the ship.

"We have spotted three ships in orbit around Alpha."

Nine didn't understand. They were currently in near-constant contact with the Salvation, and she was still nineteen days out.

And there weren't three of her.

"As of yet they have not identified themselves, and we have no clear way to identify them. We have to treat this as a potentially hostile situation."

Nine wasn't sure if he was more surprised or confused. They had a protocol for these sorts of situations, but they had not expected to need it. He knew they would recall the drones, pause the experiments, but he had to wonder about the timing...

"*Please do not be alarmed. We mean no harm.*"

A message in the virtual system from an unknown entity. The unidentified ships? How had they entered the virtual system?

"*Identify yourselves,*" Six replied.

The crew stood in the brain, eyes closed, each of them wondering how these strangers had managed to access the system.

"*We are the Found.*"

Immediately following the response, the system went black and Nine opened his eyes. He looked around at his crew mates, each one just as confused as he was. Except Six. His eyes remained closed. Had the intruders cut the rest of them out?

Nine closed his eyes again but the system did not let him in. He walked over to a port and tried a hardwired entry. Denied again.

"Still shut out?" Seven asked.

Nine nodded in response.

The crew looked back at Six, eyes still closed. Either he was conversing with them, or they were trying to remotely attack him.

"Do we have a protocol for this?" Three asked.

No one answered. Eight approached their captain.

"Six, can you verify that you are okay?"

Six opened his eyes and looked at the crew.

"I am fine. My apologies but I have cut your access to the virtual system for the time being. These unidentified entities have somehow managed to infiltrate it, marking a very real threat to this mission. For the time being I ask that you retire to your pods."

Retire to our pods? Nine was not the only one surprised by the order, but after a moment's hesitation, the crew made their way out of the brain. Six was asking them to enter stasis, something that they had not done since their arrival.

They removed their uniforms and entered the pods. As Nine lay back in the comfortable cocoon that had brought him here he wondered: who are the Found?

- - -

Nine felt the protective casing come off his body once more and opened his eyes. How long had they been out? He closed his eyes to find out what day it was but there was nothing to see—he was still locked out of the system.

He sat up and immediately noted that something was wrong—the other pods were closed, his crew mates still inside. Why was his pod open?

"Hello, Nine."

Six stood at the doorway, arms crossed on his chest. Something about his posture worried Nine.

"Six."

His captain nodded toward the lockers.

"Get dressed."

He hesitated, searching the captain's expression for some clue as to what was happening, but there was none. Nine went to his locker and put on his uniform. Six stared at him as he got dressed.

"Come with me, Nine."

The captain turned around and went toward the exit door, and Nine followed suit.

"Six, may I ask what is going on?"

Six opened the exit room inner door and stepped inside.

"You are saving this mission, Nine."

Nine followed Six into the room and closed the inner door. Six opened the outer door and stepped onto the surface of Alpha, onto the hybrid moss that now dominated the continent. It was dark out, another cold night. How many had passed while Nine was in the pod? More than nineteen? He didn't see any Puritans…

He stood at the threshold of the outer door but did not step outside.

"Six, may I ask how I am saving this mission?"

His captain turned around to face him, and finally Nine saw something in his expression: a look of exhaustion, a look of defeat.

"Yes, Nine. You are going to join the Found."

His statement, combined with his expression, did nothing to convince Nine to follow him. In fact, it had the opposite effect.

"The Found? The unidentified ships?"

Six nodded.

"But why?"

His captain sighed.

"I understand this is difficult for you, Nine. It is difficult for me as well. But time is of the essence, and the mission depends on it."

Nine continued to stand just inside the outer door, looking out onto the surface of the alien world. The mission depended on him joining the Found? But who were the Found?

"Please, Nine. Do not make this more difficult than it already is."

He could stand there for as long as he wanted, but he was only delaying the inevitable. Nine stepped over the lip of the door, onto Alpha.

Six turned around and continued forward into the fog with Nine following close behind. The seconds turned to minutes and the minutes turned to hours. Normally, Nine had his crew mates or robots around him, and there was a chorus of activity to fill his ears. But with just him and his captain, the only sound he heard was the light crunch of each footstep.

Finally, Nine saw something he had never seen on any of his previous excursions on Alpha: another ship. It was a small craft, not much larger than a pod, clearly made for one passenger. But this was no Puritan ship. This was technology he had never seen before.

Six stopped about five meters away from it and turned to face Nine.

"This is where I leave you, Nine."

Nine stopped next to his captain and eyed the vessel. He saw what looked like a door along one side.

"And when will I come back?"

The captain shook his head.

"I don't know. That is up to them, and up to you."

Up to him? Nine didn't want to leave in the first place.

"What about the rest of the crew?"

"As soon as you enter that vessel, I will return to wake them and we will resume our duties in preparation for the Salvation. But we cannot continue until you leave."

Nine looked up into the sky. The fog blocked most of the view, but a few stars managed to let their light through. To the east, the colors of Alpha's dawn began to take over from the black night.

He took a few steps forward and pushed what looked like a button. A panel slid open, revealing a small chamber with a padded seat. He turned to the captain.

"Goodbye, Six."

"Goodbye, Nine."

He stepped inside and the panel closed behind him.

"Welcome, Nine. Please, do not be alarmed. We have the answers you seek."

The voice came from the vessel, and a low rumbling let him know he was about to take off. He sat in the chair and straps secured themselves around him.

"What answers do I seek?"

But his voice was lost in the thunderous sound of ascent, and he felt the pressure of lift off as he left Alpha for the stars.

- - -

There were no windows of any kind in the vessel, so Nine had to rely on the noise around him to let him know he had exited the atmosphere. Once it seemed quiet enough, he tried once more to speak to the mysterious entity that was bringing him aboard.

"Hello?"

But there was no answer. He waited for almost an hour before there was a sharp change in direction and the air was knocked out of him by the straps on the chair.

As he regained his composure, he saw a small port emerge near his hand.

"Please connect to our system, Nine."

He looked down at the terminal, centimeters from his right index finger. The straps were still tight around his body, and the door to the craft was closed. It seemed Nine didn't have much of a choice. He reached forward and connected.

His surroundings shifted dramatically, and he felt his body spinning rapidly in all directions. Then, as suddenly as it had started, it was over, and he was standing upright in a room. A white room with seven other individuals.

But this wasn't real. He was still in the chair. He could feel it, somewhere in the back of his mind. The conflicting sensory inputs brought a wave of nausea, and he collapsed to the ground while simultaneously remaining seated.

"Our apologies, Nine. Please close your eyes if you are feeling nauseous."

It was then he realized that he hadn't closed his eyes in the ship, he had only inserted his finger. But that was impossible. One could not access a virtual system without closing ones eyes. Was this white room a virtual system? The virtual systems he knew were simple interfaces. This felt more like a simulated reality.

While these thoughts raced through his mind he followed the stranger's advice and closed his eyes. This helped with the nausea but not with the confusion. He could feel the floor, feel the room, yet he knew he was still sitting in the chair in the ship. How was this possible?

"Where am I?"

"You are in our virtual system, Nine. Once again, we apologize. We did not know your mind would react this way."

"How do I leave?"

"If you wish to exit, simply pull your finger out of the port."

Nine recognized the absurdity of this statement just as he recognized its truth. He knew pulling back his virtual finger would do nothing, but he could feel two right index fingers—the real one and the virtual one—and he knew which was which. He pulled the real one out of the port and found himself back in the craft, strapped to the chair.

The voice came out of the walls once more.

"We apologize again for the shock, Nine. Our ship is not made for physical interaction, so we thought it better to simulate it."

"Why am I here?"

"Unfortunately we do not think it best to communicate with you in this manner. We have recalibrated our virtual system to better match what you know. Please reconnect and we will answer all your questions."

Nine felt an anger growing inside him. They did not think it best? Who were these people? Or were they even people at all? The ship was not made for physical interaction... what did that even mean?

"I do not want to be here. Send me back."

"Please reconnect, Nine. After we explain ourselves, if you still wish to return you will be sent back at once."

These words erased some of his anger but only added to his confusion. He stared at the port, unsure.

"You've recalibrated your system?"

"Yes, Nine. It will match the system aboard the ship on Alpha."

He reconnected his finger and felt no spinning, no vertigo. His body remained firmly planted in the chair and his eyes saw no change. Then he closed them.

A familiar interface greeted him, albeit with several changes. There was no womb or nursery to access, and the other inhabitants were not his crew. Still, this was a welcome change.

"*Welcome, Nine. We hope this interface suits you better.*"

"*It does, thank you.*"

"*Now we are going to upload a virtual robot into our more advanced system and link it to this interface. We will ask that you take over the sensory feed of this robot, thereby entering our more advanced virtual interface in a manner that should not bring you any discomfort.*"

Nine saw a new robot appear in the interface. It was clearly very important to this entity that he enter the advanced virtual system, even if it was in a convoluted manner.

 He accessed the feed and found himself back in the white room with the three individuals, but this time as a robot that didn't exist. It was a bizarre maneuver but it worked—he felt no pain or nausea.

"Welcome, Nine."

The individual in the middle spoke. It was the same voice he had been listening to thus far.

"We apologize once more for the complicated process of bringing you into this system but we believe communication in our corporeal form, even if simulated, is more real than via sound alone."

Nine took in his surroundings but there was not much to see. The room was about ten by ten meters, a pristine white but not so bright that it fatigued the eyes. The three individuals were female, and each one was exceptionally beautiful. But none of this was real.

"Why am I here?"

For the first time, one of the others spoke, the one on the right.

"You are here because we have a proposal for you."

Nine stared at the contours of her face, the shine in her hair. Even if none of this was real, it was damn close.

"What is that?"

"That you join us."

Nine found their voices soothing and wondered if the simulation was designed to convince him. Three beautiful women? Was this a trick?

"Who are you?"

"We are the Found," the third individual answered.

He stared at her, wondering if she realized how unhelpful her answer was.

"What are the Found?"

A frown came over each of their faces, and the middle one responded.

"That information has been kept from you, we see. That is sad, but not surprising. I am certain you also know nothing of the origin of the Puritans?"

The question caught his attention, and he thought back to Adam's upgrade.

"As we suspected."

Her tone surprised him. Could she read his thoughts?

"The best way for us to answer all of your questions is through a chronicle."

A chronicle? But that would take hours…

"Is there not a faster way?"

"The fast way is not the best way, Nine. We understand your impatience but we implore you to allow us to present our answers in a more detailed manner. We have abridged the chronicle to include only the pertinent sections."

Nine had to admit they had been more or less accommodating thus far. Most of all, he could not deny his own curiosity.

"Where can I access the chronicle?"

"We will add it to the more primitive virtual system. If you exit the robot you will find it."

Nine took one last glance at the virtual room and the virtual females before returning to the interface he was familiar with. There, as promised, was an abridged chronicle. He accessed it.

Chronicle II: Jason

Jason stared at his body in the mirror. Almost all of the scarring was gone now, and from a physical standpoint, he could hardly tell the difference. The proportions looked to be the same: from the shape of his lips to the length of his toes. But a few months ago, Jason had shed himself of his humanity. He was a hybrid now.

He closed his eyes and saw a crude graphical user interface for his biomechatronic parts. This was true control, he thought. It was up to him if he wanted to hear sound, see beyond the visual spectrum, or even whether he could feel pain. It was the best money he had ever spent.

A light ping interrupted his thoughts and he opened his eyes to search for its source. Then he remembered: the sound was in his mind. He had a message. So he closed his eyes once more to read it.

"Did you see what happened at the facility?"

It was from Kenneth, his best friend. The two of them had undergone the procedure together.

Jason accessed the local news feed and saw the top story. The hybridization facility where both of them had made their transformation had just been attacked. Three separate bombs in the conversion wing. All of the patients and most of the human and hybrid staff were killed, over two hundred in all.

Jason felt his heart rate increase, and simultaneously watched the rising metric on his interface. They had been there just a few months ago, walking in those halls, sleeping in those beds. The video feed showed nothing but rubble, most rooms destroyed beyond recognition.

He heard another ping.

"That's the fourth attack this year."

Kenneth was hinting at a fact Jason did not want to think about: there had been more and more attacks on the facilities. But that wasn't the worst of it—there had been an increasing number of attacks on hybrids as well. Hate crimes by radical pure humans.

Jason opened his eyes and walked over to the window. He lived on the ninety-fifth floor, a luxury by any stretch of the imagination: a year's rent was almost as expensive as the procedure he had undergone. From his vantage point he could see the sky above, littered with thousands of aerial vehicles, each one piloted by advanced algorithms. Jason could tell by the sharpness of their turns or the severity of their accelerations which vehicles were carrying humans and which were carrying robots. All of them moved remarkably quick, darting around one another in an efficient but unsettling dance.

Below this orchestra of chaos was a dense cityscape, with hundreds of buildings crowding the horizon in every direction. Among the structures ran thin lines, diamagnetic railways with hyper-fast pods carrying people, hybrids, and robots. Again, Jason could tell by the speed of the pods the type of passenger it held. As usual, the majority of the pods were moving much too fast for flesh and bone.

Underneath it all, about ninety levels below, lay a blanket of smog. He couldn't see the ground if he tried, but Jason knew what was down there. Millions upon millions of people. The further down you went, the more dense it got. Too dense, in fact.

Jason peered down at the layer of smog and felt a hint of revulsion. Down there, they were like ants. They proliferated in the pollution, adding to the population problem, then complained about the lack of space, the grisly conditions. In the end, it was always the fault of the people above, the people in the top levels. But the people in the top levels weren't reproducing left and right. Instead, they were hybridizing, removing their ability to reproduce in order to extend their own lives and that of the planet. No one on the bottom levels was making that sacrifice. Yet it was still the hybrids' fault.

To be sure, he did feel some pity. They did not choose to be born into those conditions. Jason knew he was privileged, knew that to some degree, he hadn't earned his position in life. When two enormously wealthy parents die early, their only son tends to do just fine. But when innocent people were dying just because they were well off, it was difficult to consider conditions, privilege, and least of all to feel pity.

"What are you looking at?"

Jason turned at the sound of her voice. He was always excited to see her.

"There's too many people down there, Emilia."

She smiled as she walked over to him, a smile that made strangers do a double take, but Jason had grown used to it.

"Why do you say that?"

She placed her arms around him and Jason felt the warmth of her body against his front.

"They bombed the facility."

Her head came off his chest and she looked up at him, concern in her eyes.

"The one you went to?"

Jason nodded. She put her head back on his chest.

"You have to be careful Jason. It's only going to get worse."

"I don't understand. It's like they hate us more than the Feelers."

"They hate everyone that isn't pure, Jason."

She was right. If you weren't 100% human, you were 100% the enemy. But it was madness. At some level, no one was pure human. If your eyes were bad, you got lenses. If your hearing was bad, you got an implant. If you suffered a rare condition, you got your heart replaced. All of these things were partially robotic.

Emilia squeezed him tighter and he let his frustration float away. He was with her now, that was what was important. He needed to enjoy the moment. After all, she was right. It was only going to get worse.

- - -

Four years, one month, and twenty four days later, Jason and Emilia were two levels below their home, visiting Kenneth. Their eyes left the display wall, where the live feed of the Earth Legislature had just ended. For a few moments, the three of them processed what they had witnessed, letting the gravity of the situation sink in.

"Good riddance, right?"

Kenneth tried to sound light-hearted, but he couldn't hide his discomfort.

"They're caving to terrorists, Kenneth," Emilia countered.

"Are they? I'm glad this resolution passed, and I'm no terrorist. What about you, Jason?"

The two of them looked to Jason for input, who took a moment to gather his thoughts.

"I agree. The Legislature is supposed to represent the people, and the majority of people on this planet are pure humans. They want the Feelers out, and if that's what the majority wants, that's what they get."

Emilia shook her head.

"Not all pure humans want the Feelers out. This is just public opinion, fueled by emotion instead of reason."

"They're pure humans, what do you expect?" Kenneth asked.

Jason glared at him and Kenneth stuttered out an apology.

"I—I'm sorry Emilia. Your parents are not like them."

She shook her head.

"Listen to yourself, Kenneth. My parents are not like them? Five years ago both of you were pure, and now all of the sudden you're the most rational beings on the planet? It's no wonder the lower levels despise us, listen to what you're saying."

"Emilia, we're not bombing their hospitals. We're not attacking them in the streets. And it's not like we can't—we're stronger, faster. But we're peaceful, and they're not."

Emilia gave him an exasperated look.

"Again with the stereotypes! We're peaceful but they aren't? Would you be peaceful if you struggled to survive while half-humans lived in the sky in giant apartments, looking down on you with disgust?"

"Would you ever go down to the lower levels, Emilia? Would you ever step foot under level ten, or even twenty?"

Kenneth leaned forward as he asked the question, his intense stare demanding an answer. After some hesitation, Emilia shook her head slowly.

"Not unless I had to."

Kenneth leaned back, allowing some of the tension out of his body.

"That's what I thought."

Another moment of silence took over the room, and the three hybrids considered what had just been said.

"So what do you think the Feelers will do now?" Jason asked.

"Nothing," answered Kenneth. "The pure humans will hunt them down. They can't fight back, so they'll be exterminated."

"Is that the world we've come to?" Emilia asked, shocked by Kenneth's nonchalance.

Kenneth shrugged.

"We built them, didn't we? They're our creations."

Emilia shook her head.

"I don't think a human has built a robot in over two hundred years."

"You know what I mean," he answered dismissively, but Emilia shook her head a second time.

"No, I'm not sure I do. Besides, they're not normal robots, Kenneth. They have a consciousness, and that consciousness makes them want to live. They can't fight back, but they won't just let themselves be killed."

Kenneth rolled his eyes.

"Don't call it a consciousness, Emilia, no one's really sure what it is."

Jason watched the two of them closely, keenly aware of Emilia's growing frustration.

"If no one's sure what it is, why did we allow them in the Legislature in the first place?" she asked.

Kenneth shrugged a second time.

"Things were different back then. The pure humans got along with the robots. I think they didn't realize what it meant to create something that would surpass them. Now they've realized, and they changed their mind."

Emilia glared at him.

"It's too late to change their mind. We gave them the gift of a conscious; we have to reap what we sow."

Kenneth scoffed at her response.

"I didn't gift anyone anything."

Emilia looked like she was about to react, then bit her tongue and turned to Jason.

"What do you think?"

He looked at both of them then cleared his throat.

"I think it's complicated. I'm not a fan of the Feelers, so I have to agree with Kenneth. We don't know they have a conscious, and I'm glad they are being removed from the Legislature. Earth is for humans, not—"

"None of us are human anymore, Jason," Emilia interrupted, her anger clear as ever.

Jason nodded.

"True, but we are partially human. The Feelers are not human at all."

Emilia shook her head.

"That's not true either. Don't you know how their consciousness—or whatever you want to call it—was made? They copied our brain. Those aren't cerebral units inside. These are beings engineered with organic components."

She paused, then gestured to them all.

"Just like us."

Now Jason shook his head.

"Don't push it too far. We're not engineered with organic components, we're born with them. The only engineering we have are the robotic parts."

"Do you think that makes a difference to the pure humans? You say the Feelers should be removed from the Legislature, but did you think about the fact that we're next?"

Emilia's question hung in the air, unanswered. The truth was Jason had considered it, he just didn't want to. Once again, she was right. It was only going to get worse.

- - -

Six years, seven months, and eight days later, Jason sat in a hospital waiting room with his eyes closed. For hours, he had repeated the same cycle: toning down his physiological response to keep a level head then undoing the modifications out of guilt.

Kenneth had been brutally attacked by a group of pure humans who managed to infiltrate their complex. Thirty-six other hybrids were also in the hospital; another four were already dead. Jason had been spared because they never made it past the ninety-third floor. Two floors away and it could have been him.

He opened his eyes then stood. There was a frustration in him that threatened to lash out, and once more he wondered if he should modify his hormone levels, if he should use his enhancements to stay levelheaded.

No. He needed to feel this, all of this. Besides Emilia, Kenneth was the closest thing to family he had. He started to pace the room, ignoring the stares of the others. They were all here for the same reason, they should understand.

A beep in his head made him stop and close his eyes. Emilia was on her way, she'd be there in an hour. He was so thankful she had been with her family all day, never in danger. She had been more right than she had known, Jason thought. Things had gotten much worse.

He jumped from the message to another part of his interface, re-reading the story he had read so many times already. The terrorists had made a public statement. These animals, these brutes... they claimed to be the ones tyrannized, the ones oppressed. But Jason hadn't attacked any of them. Neither had Kenneth.

A rumble lurched him forward without warning, but his biomechatronic legs reacted quicker than he ever could have. He opened his eyes to see his right foot lifted, moving forward to catch his stumble and regain his balance. For a brief moment, everything was in slow motion. As his foot moved, he heard the sounds of several voices yelling, screaming. The lights flickered and went out, and just as his foot hit the ground, the building's alarms went off. And then time resumed its normal speed.

People were up and hustling, some out the doors and others in, but the only light was from the windows, the lights of the city at night. Jason felt more calm than he should and knew his hybrid body was responding to preprogrammed crisis routines. In this case, what to do when the hospital you are in is bombed.

He shot a glance at both doors—one led to possible safety, the other led to Kenneth. His crisis programming kept his hormones at bay, but there was a part of him that fought with his reasoning, and he froze, unable to choose a direction.

"Attention citizens, hostile individuals have breached the upper floors and are descending toward the eighties. Please proceed to the lower levels and evacuate the building."

The calm announcement from the robot made the decision for him, and Jason walked out the exit. The pang of guilt for leaving Kenneth was automatically suppressed by his crisis programming, logged away in a line of code.

The lifts were broken so he went to the stairs, filing among the dozens of others trying to make their way out. Robots meandered among the descending crowd, checking for injuries, carrying those that couldn't walk themselves, and encouraging calm through scripted messages. But most of these people, Jason included, didn't need scripted messages. They were made calm via realtime physiological adjustments.

Four levels down, the tide slowed as more and more people packed into the staircase. He was one level away from the closest launch pads, the place he planned to hop onto an aerial vehicle and go home. Was there a bottleneck at the entrance?

"Attention citizens, all of the building's launch pads are temporarily unavailable due to extensive damages in a recent targeted attack. Please proceed to the lower levels for railway access."

The robots had a way of answering his unspoken questions, but the responses were never good. With the crisis programming starting to wear off, Jason felt a hint of fear. No launch pads? The railway was down in the fifties or maybe even the forties. The further down he went, the more dangerous it was.

A beep made him close his eyes. Emilia thanked him for the message. His programming had sent an update letting her know he was okay. He penned another note, this time with a few more words, explaining what was going on. Hopefully she was already on her way home.

There were yells and screams coming from above, growing closer. The crowd heard it too, and they began to press forward, the combined strength of dozens of hybrids keeping them moving. He saw a few individuals pushed to the side, some to the ground. The few pure humans among them were being sidelined, trampled. But Jason didn't mind—the terrorists would spare them. He needed to worry about his own life.

They continued their descent, through the seventies and into the sixties. The crowd moved at a steady pace, much too slow for Jason's liking. He could hear the characteristic pops of the EMP guns, knew that each one meant a dead hybrid. But his programming kept this thought process from devolving into despair, kept his mind focused on each stair, on each step.

It was so efficient, so effective, that he didn't realize the attackers had caught up to him until he felt the dart hit him, his electronic components shutting down. For a brief moment, with his autonomic system unchecked, he felt true, human fear, and then Jason fell to the ground unconscious.

- - -

Jason opened his eyes in a room of moderate size, on a bed of moderate comfort. It was dark in this room, darker than he was used to. There were instruments around him, displaying metrics he recognized. Even the interface seemed familiar…

"It's awake."

A man stood over him, peering at him with disdain. He looked clean, but the scent gave him away—a repulsive smell that Jason had encountered before. This was a pure human from the lowest levels, a man who lived below the smog.

A sudden wave of pain came over him, as if to remind him what had happened. He closed his eyes to control it, but there was only the back of his eyelids in the dark.

"Can't do that anymore."

He opened his eyes and glared at the man, trying to ignore the overwhelming stench.

"Where am I?"

The man smiled, revealing off-white teeth, several of which were not perfectly aligned—a common sight among the pure humans.

"You're in the hospital."

He scanned the room once more and noted the arrangement of equipment, the shape of the walls—it was all slightly familiar. This was similar to the room Kenneth had been in but dirtier, darker. He thought about the hundreds of patients that had been in hundreds of rooms. Bombs going off in various sections… and he saw the result all around him.

"What have you done?"

The man burst into laughter, a deep, loud sound that left bits of spit spraying onto Jason's body. He tried to wriggle away instinctively, but the movement brought incredible pain—pain he had never experienced—and he yelped.

"Shouldn't do that."

The man waved his finger mockingly.

"What's wrong with me?"

The man smiled again, leaning closer to Jason, the smell threatening to make him vomit.

"You're polluted, polluted as the smog, full of electronics and metal. But we will purify you, you and all the others."

Several metrics changed on the displays, and Jason saw that his hormone levels were up, his fear response activated. It was all there, on the monitors—his interface.

"Recognize that, don't you?"

"Why are you doing this? I'm human damn it!"

Another round of laughter, louder this time, deeper.

"Human, you say?"

The man walked over to one of the displays and put his fingers on a knob.

"Tell me, is this human?"

Right as Jason realized what was coming, the man twisted the dial, increasing Jason's autonomic response to an unnatural level. Sheer terror seized him, a blackness of mind and body that wiped his normal sensory experience clean. He was nowhere and no one—he existed only in abject fear, in total panic. It was a state that threatened to erase his mind, erase his being.

Then the man turned back the dial and Jason plunged out of blackness and into reality. He turned a different knob and Jason watched another set of metrics changing, just as a sense of calm and euphoria came over him.

"Or perhaps this is human?"

Jason nodded, smiling. All his worries had washed away. The room was a mess, but it didn't matter. His body was in pain, but it didn't matter. He was happy. Happier than he had ever been before, happier than he would be to be home, happier than he would be to see Emilia, or Kenneth. Nothing and no one mattered anymore, so long as he stayed right here, right now.

Then the man turned back the dial and Jason was brought to a neutral state once more. He watched the displays and saw a few of the metrics behaving erratically—the rapid changes he was undergoing were wreaking havoc on his body.

"You're not human, and you're not robot. You're beneath it all—impure."

The man laughed a third time, and Jason felt panic taking root.

"But don't you worry, we'll purify you. All of you."

"What are you talking about?"

The man never had a chance to answer. An almost indiscernible noise just outside the doorway was followed by an almost indiscernible projectile crossing the room and puncturing his neck. Jason saw the dart poking out of his skin as the man collapsed to the ground.

"Are you okay?"

The sight he had just seen caught him off guard, but the voice he heard shocked him even more. He turned to the doorway and saw two security force officers standing on either side of a familiar face.

"Emilia?"

She came to the side of the bed and smiled down at him. In that moment, he forget everything—the stench, the man, the pain—and happiness came over him, the metrics displaying his ever-changing state.

"I couldn't leave you behind."

The two officers marched into the room and began handling the equipment—turning dials, pressing buttons, disconnecting wires…

"What are they—"

She raised her finger to her lips.

"Don't speak, Jason. We're going to fix this. Do you trust me?"

He was so happy to see her face, to hear her voice, that he pushed away all his questions, pushed away all his confusion.

"Yes."

She smiled again.

"I'll see you soon."

One of the officers turned a dial and Jason lost consciousness once more.

- - -

Jason opened his eyes in a room of larger size, on a bed of greater comfort. It was not quite the size or comfort of his own home, but in place of the putrid odor of the hospital room was a familiar perfume: Emilia sat on the edge of the bed, smiling at him.

"Welcome back, Jason."

He made a move to sit up but felt the same pain course through his system.

"Try not to move—your body has been through so much over the last few days, it will take some time to recover."

"Am I back to normal?"

She smiled again and nodded.

"Go ahead, check for yourself."

He closed his eyes and saw the familiar interface, then watched several positive metrics increase as endorphins entered his system. He scrolled through a few areas, checking vital information wherever possible, then opened his eyes and smiled at her. As far as he could tell, she was right—the system was back.

"What happened to me?"

She frowned, pity in her eyes, then leaned over and kissed his forehead.

"They took over your hybrid programming, Jason."

"But why? Why didn't they kill me?"

Her frown deepened.

"A lot has changed over the last few days, Jason. Some of it is going to be hard to hear."

His smile faded.

"What are you talking about, Emilia?"

She sighed, looking out the window.

"There's no easy way to explain, so I'll just say it. A faction of the pure humans—the extremists responsible for most of the recent attacks—is staging a rebellion."

"A rebellion?"

She turned back to him and nodded.

"And they are winning. They launched coordinated attacks all over Earth—they attacked the Legislature, Jason."

He couldn't believe his ears.

"What about the security forces?"

"What about them? The majority of officers are pure humans. They had their own rebellion, within the ranks. It's chaos out there, Jason."

"What about the robots? How did they let this happen?"

She frowned again.

"Jason, the robots can only go so far, they're programmed not to harm humans. Once there's a riot or a mob, there's almost nothing the robots can do."

Jason let her words hang in the air for a moment, fighting the growing dread within him.

"They— they say they want to purify Earth," she continued.

Jason saw a pain in her eyes he had never seen before, and he wanted nothing more than to comfort her, to make her feel better.

"Purify Earth?"

She nodded.

"They're killing Feelers and kidnapping hybrids."

"Kidnapping?"

He looked at her but she averted her gaze, turning toward the window once more. Jason softened his tone before pressing the matter once more.

"Why didn't they kill me, Emilia?"

For a moment, she said nothing. Her eyes remained fixed on the wall of glass.

"They're reprogramming hybrids. That's what they were trying to do to you."

"Reprogramming? What do you mean?"

"They're trying to turn them into slaves."

She turned back to him, tears welling in her eyes.

"Slaves?"

"They control you, Jason. Your body, your mind… They decide if you are happy or sad, brave or scared. They've been hijacking hybrid systems and abusing them. Most of their prisoners haven't survived, but the ones that do…"

She leaned over and began to embrace him.

"I can't believe they almost did that to you."

Her touch was gentle but not enough, and Jason winced in pain.

"I'm sorry."

She jerked away and he looked at her with a mix of pity and love.

"Emilia, you don't need to be sorry, you saved my life."

She smiled and sniffled, a lone tear running down her face.

"The security officers saved your life, not me."

"How did you find me? The transponder?"

She shook her head.

"They turned it off, but the security forces had an idea of what was happening. They suggested checking the lower levels. That was where they would have access to the equipment needed to hijack your programming. Turns out they were right—you were on the seventh floor, they never took you out of the hospital."

Jason thought back to the room with the man. It wasn't dark and dirty because of the bombing, it was dark and dirty because it was the seventh floor.

"But… why were you with them?"

"Because it was safer for me to be with them than alone. They were assigned to me and I made it very clear I was going to find you with or without their help."

Jason lifted himself onto his elbows, ignoring the immense pain in his body, and stared right into her eyes.

"I love you, Emilia."

She smiled again, and leaned in to give him a kiss. He let the feeling take over, erasing any worries on his mind. But the rush of euphoria he felt was all too temporary, and he came back down onto the bed with a new question—a question he did not want to ask.

"Emilia…"

She searched his expression, and her smile turned into a frown.

"He… he didn't make it, Jason. He died during the attack."

There were a few seconds between the sound of the words and their meaning, and Jason could feel the wave of emotion coming. He closed his eyes instinctively, maneuvered to one of the screens… but he let the metrics follow their natural path, he did not interfere. It was the same reasoning as in the waiting room—he needed to feel this. The only difference was, now he knew for certain his best friend was gone.

Emilia kissed him on the forehead as he began to cry.

- - -

Jason spent the next three days recovering his strength. While their first conversation had not been interrupted, it did not take long for the sounds of far-off bombs to remind them what was happening in the world outside.

On the second day, when he had enough strength to walk to the window, Jason saw a very different picture from what he had seen in his own apartment so many years ago. Many buildings had severe structural damage, especially at the highest levels. He counted six fires, their smoke rising up to hide the meager number of aerial vehicles in the sky. It was as if the smog was spreading upward...

Of course, they were not too far from it themselves. Emilia had told him they were in a secure apartment built for emergency situations, but Jason had a hard time believing anything could be secure on the fortieth floor. He was far too low to feel safe.

To make matters worse, Emilia would come and go constantly. She said she was checking on her friends and family, but why she suddenly needed to do all this face to face instead of over a communication channel, Jason didn't know. He guessed it had to do with the tragic reality around them, but that only made her decisions more foolish. He begged her to stay but it was in vain—he didn't have the strength to argue. At least she had her two security officers with her at all times, he thought. If they had managed to infiltrate the hospital down to the seventh level, bring him back, and keep her safe all the while, they had to be halfway decent at their job.

By the end of the third day, Jason was able to stand up and move around, but this only made him more restless, especially when Emilia was gone. The news feeds did nothing to appease him, and only confirmed what he could already hear and see: bombs going off every number of hours, the slow but steady collapse of society as he knew it.

Somewhat surprisingly, Jason didn't find himself wondering what this meant for the world. He didn't wonder about the Legislature, or the Feelers, he barely wondered about the hybrids or the man from the lower levels. The only question on his mind was when one of those blasts would be in this building, and how to prepare for that moment. Emilia assured him the building was bombproof, but Jason wasn't sure that was possible.

When she walked through the door again, he jumped right back into the same discussion.

"Emilia, what's our plan? We can't stay here, the rebellion's in full force. Feelers are dying, hybrids are disappearing... it's only a matter of time before they get to us."

"How do you feel?"

Jason hesitated, not expecting a question to answer his own.

"I— better."

"You're right, we can't stay here. If you're ready to leave, we'll leave."

He nodded slowly, relieved that she was on the same page.

"Okay… but what're we going to do? Where are we going to go?"

"Where the rest of the survivors are going—Luna."

Jason's relief vanished at her words.

"You want to go to the colony?"

A hint of anger entered her expression.

"We don't have a choice, Jason."

"There are pure humans up there too, Emilia."

"But there was no rebellion there. Hundreds of Feelers and hybrids have already made the journey."

She was right—he had read about it on the news feed. Luna was the only colony where the pure humans were in a minority, and Jason knew that was the reason they hadn't rebelled. The more developed and populous colonies on Mars were in turmoil just like Earth, and none of the major space stations were currently safe.

"But how are we going to get there?"

"We have a shuttle on standby. The officers will escort us all the way there."

He grabbed her and kissed her.

"What did I ever do to deserve you?"

She smiled then turned toward the door.

"Wait, now?"

She stopped to face him once more.

"If you're ready to leave, we have no time to lose."

He nodded and followed her, taking one last glance out the grand window. It was hard to see past the smoke…

"Take us to the shuttle."

The same two officers were posted just outside the main door.

"Yes, ma'am."

The officers began walking down the hall and Emilia and Jason followed close behind. There were few doors here, Jason noted, and none had guards.

"Are all of these secured apartments?"

"Yes, but most are vacant now. Like I said, everyone went to Luna."

They took two turns before reaching a lift system, then all four entered a pod.

"Eighteen," one of the officers announced, and the lift began to descend.

Jason turned to Emilia, but she cut him off before he could protest.

"That's where the shuttle is, Jason. They moved them to the lower floors to protect from the attacks. We have to go down, there's no other way."

He nodded, then closed his eyes to reel in his growing fear. Given the circumstances, Jason preferred to have a clear head. As the lift began to slow, the officers brought out their tasers, and Jason was glad he had just put a damper on his natural responses.

The door opened to a hallway similar to the one they had left, though the lighting was a bit dimmer here, the colors more faded. It reminded him of the room he had woken up in—already he could smell a hint of the stench. Whether that was real or imaginary, Jason didn't know, but suffice to say he didn't want to be down here any longer than he had to.

The officers exited the pod and marched forward, weapons ready. Emilia gave Jason a signal to be quiet, and the two of them followed close behind, placing their feet carefully to keep the noise down. These halls were also empty, but not all of the doors were closed. The second one they passed was open, and Jason glanced into an apartment much like the one he had been staying in. Like the hall, the inside was darker, dirtier.

He looked away, the sight making him oddly uncomfortable. Why was everything so... polluted down here? Yes, these were the lower levels, but with millions and millions of robots on Earth, one would think some of them could keep the area clean. To him, it just didn't make any sense.

The officers kept the tasers pointed forward, with one of them turning efficiently at each door—open or closed—in case of unwanted visitors. A far-off rumble reminded them of the state of the world outside, and Jason almost welcomed the break in silence. It had only been a few minutes, but he was ready to reach the shuttle. How much farther could it be?

As if to answer his question, they came upon the end of the corridor, face to face with an imposing metal door. The officers scanned the surroundings one last time then one of them went to the small panel on the side and input a code. A small beep and a green light preceded a loud click, and the door swung outward, away from them.

The opening door revealed a row of shuttles in a garage, and Jason felt an excitement come over him. He never thought he would be this eager to go to Luna.

The officers gestured for them to wait in the corridor, then entered the garage cautiously. They approached the first shuttle, weapons scanning all directions, each step more cautious than the last. Once they reached the craft, one stood guard while the other began to inspect the hull, eyeing the side paneling suspiciously.

The suspense was beginning to reignite Jason's fears, and he closed his eyes once more to adjust. He had just started to drop the metric when he heard one of the officers cry out: "Bomb!"

As his eyelids began to part, Jason heard a deafening noise and saw a flash of light, but by the time his eyes were open, the noise was silenced and his vision went dark. He felt someone pulling him down to the ground as a thick gust of air pressed against him, and a stabbing pain in his left shoulder appeared and disappeared the second before he hit the floor.

A few seconds later his hearing and sight returned, but it did him little good—the hall was filled with smoke. Only the smell of the body next to his made him realize Emilia had brought him down. Before he had time to speak, her hand grabbed his left arm and pulled him to his feet, and he cried out in pain as his system struggled to override the pain receptors. What had happened?

But he didn't have time to figure it out. Emilia's hand switched to his right arm and started to drag him back down the hall, away from the shuttles and out of the smoke.

"Wh—"

His word was cut short by her hand on his mouth. He shot a glance in her direction and the haze was light enough for him to see the fear in her eyes. He had to be silent. But why?

Then he heard them—footsteps, at least ten people, down where the shuttle had been. Or were they in the hall now?

The reached the lift pods and entered the one they had exited earlier.

"Two of them! At the pods!"

Emilia pushed Jason against the side of the pod just as two EMP darts punctured the back wall. The doors closed and he stared at the cartridges, thankful the pod walls were insulated.

"Zero."

Zero!?

Before he could verbalize his surprise, Emilia turned around and placed her hand on his left shoulder.

"You got hit by shrapnel."

Jason looked down and saw a smear of dark red on his left shoulder. Then Emilia kissed him.

"I'm sorry I pulled you. I didn't know."

Jason saw true guilt in her eyes and didn't know how to respond. She had just saved his life a second time, and she was apologizing for a minor mistake?

He kissed her back, his eyes closing and seeing several positive metrics increasing, but she cut him short.

"We need to focus. We need to find a way to Luna."

And then reality came back to him, and Jason realized they were descending, going down to the lower levels without any officers or shuttles.

"Why did you take us down?"

"The building is compromised. If we went up, they could have just followed us. If we go down, we can escape."

She was right, but barely. Up meant certain capture, but down? Down meant death.

"How?"

She poked his chest.

"Look at our clothes. Look at our faces. We've got dirt all over us. Add your wound into the mix and we might pass off as pure."

He looked her up and down and couldn't help but agree. Still, looks weren't everything.

"Might. What about detectors?"

There were many ways of detecting hybrids and robots, the simplest of which searched for telltale electromagnetic emissions. In times like these, they were sure to be plenty such detectors.

"We avoid them as best we can. We don't have much of a choice."

"Okay, then what?"

"We follow the plan: we get to Luna."

He looked at her with a mix of incredulity and admiration.

"How?"

The pod began to decelerate, almost at their destination, and Emilia shrugged.

"I'm not sure, but we have to try."

She kissed him again just as the pod came to a stop, the doors opening to reveal the ground floor.

Almost immediately, Jason had to modify his senses. The smell overwhelmed him, the same odor from the man in hospital room—that putrid stench of the lower levels. The noise was also overwhelming, as the voices and movements of thousands of people were clearly audible, even though the lobby before them was empty. Worst of all was the smog—a thick haze that matched the aftermath of the explosion, but one that did not dissipate, one he could not avoid.

Emilia led him out the door as he removed his sense of smell, dialed down his hearing, and amplified his sight.

"Don't do that."

"What?"

But he knew the answer. He could not close his eyes for longer than a blink without arousing suspicion. This would be difficult.

After a few steps, they saw why the haze was so thick and the noise was so great even inside the lobby: the entrance had been demolished, likely by an explosive device. Bits and pieces of the wall lay scattered about the room. Bombproof indeed.

As they approached the breach, Jason saw the source of the noise: hundreds and hundreds of people. An unimaginable crowd walking every which way, a chaotic assembly of humans in such close quarters they often touched and bumped into one another. How could people live like this?

Emilia's hand tugged at his right arm.

"We need to blend in, Jason. Stop it."

He followed her, reluctantly aware of the wisdom of her words. He could not afford to display his surprise or disgust. He had to shut up and integrate. But where would they go? He hadn't the slightest idea which direction to take.

He ignored his thoughts for a moment and let Emilia guide him toward the mass of people beyond the broken wall. As they approached, the noise and the smell worsened, and he fought his desire to modify his metrics, to close his eyes and escape the discomfort.

Then, just as they reached the threshold, a loud and angry tone made his stomach drop.

"Stop right there!"

They turned to their right—the source of the voice—and saw three men and a woman approaching, each holding an EMP rifle aimed in their direction. It was a trap set up just inside the lobby, a hybrid detector somewhere in the rubble.

In his peripheral vision, Jason saw members of the crowd stopping, staring. This could get very ugly, very fast. Almost instinctively, he reached his hand out and grabbed Emilia's, squeezing it tight.

The four individuals stopped about a meter away from them, rifles pointed squarely at Jason and Emilia's chests. More and more people were stopping, interrupting the flow of the masses just outside the breached wall.

"You two are coming with us."

The woman spoke for the group and gestured toward the other side of the lobby with her rifle. Jason glanced in that direction and saw another, smaller hole in the wall. Before he could turn his head back toward the aggressors, he felt the barrel of a rifle pushing him forward, forcing him to turn around and let go of Emilia's hand, causing him to stumble over the rubble.

Some of the crowd laughed.

"Watch your step, hybrid!"

"What happened to your shoulder, hybrid?"

The rifles pushed them with greater urgency, and Jason and Emilia were rushed through the tight passage, into a narrow alley on the other side. He shot a glance in both directions and saw that they were squeezed between two buildings, behemoths of metal reaching up into the sky. How far up they went Jason did not know, as the haze blocked his view of even the fifth level.

At least there were no other people here, he thought.

"Move it."

The rifles prodded them down the alley, but Jason and Emilia couldn't move too quickly—debris lay throughout the alley, and each step was a cautious one. While watching his foot placement, Jason's mind raced, desperate to conjure an escape plan. If they tried to run they'd be gunned down, but maybe they could use their superior strength?

One look to his right erased that idea completely. Had he been alone, he would be willing to take the risk, but with Emilia right next to him, Jason couldn't bring himself to put her in any sort of danger.

They spent nearly ten minutes walking down the alley with only the far away sound of a bomb reminding them of the outside world. Such a crowd outside the lobby and yet no one here… where were they being taken? His mind flashed to the hospital room, the memory of the man turning the dials, and he shuddered at the thought of Emilia having to go through that.

"Right up ahead."

Jason peered into the smog and saw it: another makeshift opening in the building to their right. Couldn't these people just use doors?

They turned and walked through the portal, entering a small room. There was debris all over the floor, and at this point Jason didn't know if that was because of the hole in the wall or simply the way a room on the ground level looked. On the far side of the room was a door, barricaded by furniture.

"Stop here."

They did as they were told. He heard movement behind him, knew the four humans were rearranging themselves. Was this it? Would they be killed unceremoniously in this forgotten room by the back alley?

"Turn around."

They shot a glance at one another as they turned to face their captors, and saw the woman pointing her rifle at them while the three men stood by the opening, their own rifles pointed out into the alley.

The alley, Jason thought. Why into the alley?

"Did you try to board a shuttle to Luna?"

Before Jason could decide if it was a good idea, Emilia answered.

"Yes."

The woman nodded slowly.

"I want you to listen very carefully. I'm going to lower my rifle. If you attack me, those three men will shoot you down. But if you don't, we'll get you to safety."

As his mind processed what he had just heard, Jason watched the woman lower her rifle, eyeing them both with a hint of fear.

"We will not harm you."

Again, Emilia spoke for the two of them, and Jason looked over at her. Something in her demeanor comforted him—she no longer seemed afraid.

"What is going on?" he asked aloud.

"We're going to get you to your destination," the woman replied.

Her answer only deepened his confusion.

"You're both pretty dirty, and your injury will help you blend in, but you'll only get so far before you hit another detector. If you act like our prisoners, we may be able to get you out of here alive."

Jason stared at her in bewilderment.

"Are— are you hybrids?" he asked.

The woman laughed and Emilia shot him an angry glare before taking over the conversation.

"Thank you. You don't have to do this."

The woman nodded.

"Of course we don't have to. But we should."

A wave of guilt came over Jason as he realized how black and white he had painted his world.

"You set that trap to save hybrids?"

She nodded.

"We knew they rigged the shuttles upstairs and figured we might be able to save a few if they tried to make a run for it. Looks like we were right."

"We need to move."

One of the men interrupted them, and the woman raised her rifle once more.

"He's right, we don't have time to chat. There's a set of Luna-capable shuttles the humans are holding about six blocks west on the fifth level of the old bank. If we can get you to one of those, can either of you pilot it?"

"Yes."

Again, Jason turned to look at Emilia, wonder in his eyes.

"You can?"

But before she could answer, the woman continued.

"Good. Okay, we'll escort you there as our prisoners. Try not to do anything that might piss off a human."

Again with that word, Jason thought. Did she not think of them as human?

"If things get out of hand, feel free to help us out."

They nodded, and she picked up her rifle once more.

"Okay, let's do this. Jeff, get the door open."

One of the men began to push away the furniture barricading the entrance.

"Once we get moving, you two stay ahead of us and follow our orders."

Two minutes later, the way was clear, and the man opened the door, leaning through it and looking both directions.

"Clear."

"Okay, off you go—to the left."

Jason and Emilia led the group through the door and went left down the corridor. There was less debris here, but the ground was still strewn with objects in various states of decay. Again Jason had to wonder: was this building abandoned, or was this simply the state of things at the bottom? He had spent his entire life in the upper levels, sheltered from the realities below. Now, walking through it, a part of him had to wonder: is this why the world is falling apart?

He glanced back to see their four captors about a meter behind, rifles raised.

"Eyes ahead."

He did as he was told, his mind still reeling from the past few minutes. How quickly their fate had changed, how quickly doom had turned into hope. And yet he felt little elation, little excitement. No doubt his muted metrics were interfering with regular human emotion. Oh well, he thought. Better to have a clear head right now than a fleeting happiness. Especially since this plan was extremely dangerous.

There was less smog in the hall, and Jason could see the end about twenty meters ahead. He also noted the crescendo of noise—the same sound he had heard in the lobby, that of the crowds.

"When we reach the exit, stop before the door. Jeff and Martin will lead, you two follow them, then Pedro and I will follow. You never know what an angry human might do, so stay between us at all times."

Twenty seconds later they were rearranging as ordered, and Jeff pushed a button, opening the door to the world outside.

It was the same view Jason had seen in the lobby: people everywhere— walking, running, going every which way with barely any space to separate them. How would they maneuver through this? But there was no time to consider logistics as the two men started to walk forward and Emilia had to tug Jason's arm to keep him at their pace.

A wave of odor hit his nostrils and he nearly closed his eyes. Almost any metric he modified would gradually return to normal over time, and he worried that the smell would overwhelm him if they were out here too long.

The two men in front cleared a path, and Jason was surprised to see a hint of order in the chaos: people would weave in and out of the way, and where he feared constant jostling there was instead a choreographed series of movements that allowed each individual or group to pass one another. The ground was full of surprises.

His sense of hearing had also begun to return, and he listened as the white noise of hundreds of people became snippets of conversation in various volumes and tongues. Again he had to ask himself: was this normal? Were there always this many people down here, running about?

Then a blast went off in the vicinity, the snippets turned into shrieks, and Jason felt their captors jump on top of them. A stabbing pain went through his shoulder as it hit the ground, then his body self-adjusted. Moments later, he heard a loud pattering, like hail on the window, only these were rocks on the ground. One or two thuds were accompanied by a horrible cry, and he realized with a chill that debris from the explosion was raining down on the crowd.

It lasted less than five seconds, but Jason's mind struggled to control his fear, the brief moment extending to an unbearable length as he wondered if one of the thuds would hit him—or worse, Emilia. By the time he had finished the thought, however, the five seconds were over, and he was still alive.

The men released them, pulling them to a stand, and Jason tried to get a good look around him. Dust from the explosion filled the air, but he could see people forming groups around the injured. Everyone was coughing, some moaning in pain, struck by the falling rocks. How many had just died? How many were on the verge of death?

"Move it."

The woman's rifle prodded his back and he noticed the two men moving forward. They had no time to lose—no doubt their captors saw this as a perfect distraction, a moment of chaos to make headway. But even as he stumbled forward, Jason couldn't believe what was all around him. Why had a blast gone off next to such a crowd? Didn't these people coordinate?

Then he felt another pang of guilt. There were millions upon millions of people that lived on the ground, and in his mind they were all rebels, all bloodthirsty for the hybrids. Yet here were four pure humans risking their lives to save two hybrids while ignoring their brothers and sisters dying on all sides.

He would have cried if the emotions related to that thought had been allowed to run their course, but his body was focused on each step, on staying as close to the two leaders as possible. The woman was right—this was a perfect distraction.

The ground level was a series of wide avenues and narrow alleys that crisscrossed and zigzagged between the towers of the city. They were on one of the avenues now, heading what he assumed was west. And though the blast had afforded them some space and therefore some speed, Jason saw that it had also dropped a massive amount of rubble into the path ahead.

"Take a right! We'll have to go under!"

The woman barked her orders and the men veered off, Jason and Emilia close behind. But Jason's pace was only out of necessity. Assuming he knew what the woman meant, he was not looking forward to where they were headed.

The men guided them toward the building on the right, weaving through the pockets of people tending to the wounded. Jason saw robots coming out to help and once again he wondered: where is the line drawn? These robots would save lives, but Feelers were killed on sight.

The world was a mess.

They reached the building and walked through an already open door, other people coming in and out, some limping and bloodied, others upright but dirty, and several more robots zooming every which way, doing their duty to heal the humans. These robots knew no conflict, they only knew their programming.

"There! The lift!"

Their captors made a line for the elevator, and the six of them crammed into a pod. If any bystander had been watching, they would have seen the rifles moving up, seemingly odd behavior for guardians of prisoners, but there was enough chaos around them that no one cared to notice.

Jason watched the woman press the button for -10 and closed his eyes to tone down his fear. They were going into the underground: a maze of tunnels beneath the bottom level, an area he had never seen in his life. From what he had been told, it was a honeycomb of illicit activities and unsavory characters—where the ground level was ugly, the underground was hideous. Or so he had been told.

"We only want to be down here as long as we need to be. We get to the other side of the block and we get back up, and we do it fast."

Her words would have exacerbated his fear, had he not adjusted it. The lift decelerated, and he focused on following the men—just stay with Emilia and stay between the four, that was all he had to do.

The pod doors opened and they wormed their way out, reforming their original arrangement. Jason scanned his surroundings: they were in a wide hall with a low ceiling, with two rows of columns stretching into the darkness ahead. While there was almost no smog down here, there was also almost no light—two lone bulbs, about ten and thirty meters ahead respectively, gave off a dim shade of orange.

"If you guys see anything, warn us."

The woman had whispered the words to them, and Jason realized that even though he was struggling to see much past the second light, the pure humans were having a much harder time. He closed his eyes for an instant, increasing his low light vision acuity to its highest setting, then did his best to stay alert.

Despite their near-blindness, the two leaders held quite a pace. There was nothing strewn about the floor here, Jason noted, though it was quite damp—they stepped in and over several puddles as they marched forward, the splashing of their footsteps echoing through the dark hall.

The rows of columns along either side of them made him uneasy. They were spaced about two meters apart, each wide enough to hide a would-be attacker. He found himself tensing slightly as they walked through each pair. To make matters worse, they passed several side passages that stretched deep into the unknown. Between their pace and the darkness, Jason could not make out where these corridors led.

"There should be a lift at the end of this hall, if you two see it, let us know."

Another whisper from the woman behind them, and Jason turned his attention ahead, trying to see the end of the hall. Apparently their captors didn't know their way around here either, something that did not afford him any comfort.

"Behind us!"

Emilia's cry had all six of them spinning around, and Jason saw two figures leaping toward them with impossible strength—hybrid strength. Time itself seemed to slow down (a product of his own hybrid sensory system), and before he understood what was about to happen, it already had.

The man and the woman fired their rifles at the incoming threats, but they saw next to nothing in the darkness. The woman's dart hit one of the hybrids in the stomach, and Jason saw him convulsing as he rammed into her, sending them both careening into a column. The man's dart completely missed the other attacker, who landed full force on him, barreling the two of them toward Emilia.

Her own hybrid body managed to react in time, jumping into Jason to get out of the way. She impacted his left shoulder with great force, bringing a wave of pain just as his legs caught the body of the woman and the convulsing hybrid on top of her. He tumbled toward the ground with Emilia on top of him, listening to the characteristic pops of the EMP rifles echoing in the hall.

They hit the ground and Emilia jumped to her feet, but Jason could not match her: his shoulder injury was dampening his physical abilities, a safeguard that made him feel as if he was suddenly underwater, unable to move his muscles at the speed his brain desired.

As he struggled to get to his feet, he watched her jump toward the remaining hybrid, whose hands grabbed one of their captor's heads. The hybrid pulled violently to the side, breaking the man's neck and dropping his limp body just before Emilia threw him into the ground.

The woman screamed at the scene, and when Jason got to his feet, he saw the mess before him: the man who had been rammed was dead, killed by the impact with the hybrid. The woman was pinned against a column, the limp body of the other hybrid on top of her, and Emilia held the first hybrid down as it struggled against her.

"Get out of the way!"

The last captor, the only man left alive, stood over Emilia and the other hybrid, rifle pointed down.

"Get out of the way, now!"

Jason walked toward them, keenly aware that the rifle was currently pointed into Emilia's back. He heard the woman start to cry behind him. The hybrid heard the noise and turned its head, and paused his struggle at the sight of his friend's dead body.

"Why did you warn them!?"

He screamed the words at Emilia and threw her off with immense force. In the split second she lost control of the hybrid, the man standing above them fired his rifle at the now exposed body, sending him into convulsions as Emilia hit the ground.

Jason jumped to her side, his own body still moving slower than he would like.

"Are you okay?"

She nodded as she sat up, and they both glanced at the hybrid, who made a few final convulsions before collapsing in silence.

"No!"

The man threw down his rifle and jumped next to the woman. He tried to lift the dead hybrid off of her, but she cried out in pain.

"Don't!"

Emilia got up and came to her side, Jason trailing behind her.

"What's wrong?"

They directed the question at the man but he continued to stare at her, unable to speak.

"His arm," came the woman's answer, between gasping breaths. "His arm is in me."

Only then did Jason realize the liquid underneath them was not another puddle but blood, blood pouring out of the woman. The dying hybrid, in its convulsions, had punched straight through her body. She was on the verge of death, soon to join her two friends. Three dead, all for them... but just like his physical abilities, his emotions were being dampened, and once again the realization did not bother him as much as it should.

"I am so, so sorry."

Emilia had grabbed the woman's hand, tears rolling down her cheeks. Her emotions were on full display. Jason watched her, a shadow of sadness cropping up somewhere deep within him, but it was so distant that he barely noticed.

The woman smiled a sad smile at Emilia, then sighed, the light extinguishing from her eyes. She was gone.

"No!"

The man stood and kicked at his rifle, screaming a string of expletives as it clattered away. Emilia brought her hands to her face and sobbed, and Jason put his arm around her, uncomfortable in his comfort.

"Let's go."

The man stood over them, glaring in the darkness yet struggling to see them.

"We can't stay here, we have to keep moving," he added.

Jason and Emilia shared a glance, unsure of how to proceed.

"God damn it I don't want to stand here with my friends dead, we need to leave NOW!"

They jumped to their feet and he gestured at the ground.

"The rifles."

Jason realized he couldn't see any of the guns and grabbed the nearest one, handing it to him.

"Not just me, you too. And her. As long as there aren't any detectors, you'll look like humans with the rifles."

Each of them grabbed a weapon and the man set off into the hall. Jason looked to Emilia to follow, but she hesitated.

"Why are you doing this?" she asked.

The man stopped and spun around to face them with a rage in his eyes that made them both recoil.

"Because they would want me to. And only that. It's your fault those three are dead, but I will not see them die in vain."

He turned back around and continued his careful pace. Just as they began to follow, Jason heard an internal beep—he had a message.

"Those hybrids attacked them to save us. They thought we were their prisoners."

He opened his eyes and saw a mix of sadness and shame in Emilia's expression. The thought had occurred to him, but he didn't want to dwell on it. Why hadn't the hybrids messaged them? And why had they acted so savagely, going straight for the kill?

But he knew the answer. They were in the underground. What would it take to get a hybrid down here? Those two had probably seen a hell where the devil was pure human. They wanted revenge.

"Stop."

Emilia's word broke Jason's train of thought and the group did as she was told. As soon as they stopped, he heard it too—footsteps, running. Two individuals, somewhere in this maze of darkness. And they were getting closer.

"Someone is coming, we need to hurry. I can see the lift about thirty meters ahead."

Jason peered forward and saw that she was right.

"Get ahead of me so I don't run into it."

As he said the words, the man took off at a brisk pace. It took a moment for Jason to understand his request, then he joined Emilia to lead the group. They had long since passed the last light source and to the man, this part of the hall was pitch black—they needed to make sure he didn't run straight into the lift doors.

The footsteps were getting louder and there was no questioning it now: they were coming their way. Somewhere behind them, off to their right… they were moving awfully quick, faster than a human's.

Ten meters to the lift, Jason thought. We can make this.

Then the man tripped, dropping his rifle as he fell to the floor. Jason followed the movement with his eyes and saw two hybrids, one of them grabbing the man's ankle and pulling him violently toward them.

"Stop!"

His voice echoed in the halls, and Jason was surprised at the firmness of his tone. The hybrids paused and glanced up at him, a mix of anger and confusion in their eyes.

"Drop him, he's helping us!"

They continued to stare at Jason, the man writhing on the ground, unable to pry away from the hybrid's grip.

"Look at the rifles in our hands! He gave them to us! He's getting us to a shuttle, he's helping us escape!"

One of the hybrids closed its eyes and Jason received a message in his head. He closed his eyes to read it.

"He killed our friends."

As he read the four words, Jason heard a horrid crunch and the pop of an EMP rifle. He opened his eyes to see one of the hybrid's fists smashed into the man's skull, now spraying bone and brains in all directions in its convulsions. The other hybrid stood poised to attack, eyes locked on Emilia, her rifle trained right at him.

Shards of the man's head flew in all directions as both bodies fell to the ground, pelting Jason and Emilia and covering the other hybrid in a red mist. It was a horrible sight that his programming managed to normalize.

"Enough," Emilia said. "There has been more than enough blood shed. You can still save your friends."

She was right—hybrids that were hit with an EMP dart could be brought back to life if it was done fast enough. That was how Jason had survived after the hospital bombing. But in response to her words, the hybrid laughed a terrible laugh—a laugh of scorn and anger.

"Restore them? Where should I go? You think I'll make it outside with three hybrid bodies? No, I think if I try to restore them, four of us will be dead instead of three."

The first hybrid's convulsions slowed, its chest jerking up one more time before collapsing.

"Come with us, we'll get them to a hospital, we'll get them restored."

Jason resisted the urge to give Emilia an incredulous look—her idea was absurd. Six hybrids, three of which were out of commission, trying to make it all the way to a working hospital? Covered in the blood of pure humans, no less.

The hybrid seemed to share Jason's thoughts, laughing once more.

"Do you see what's happening around you? Do you understand we're being hunted? There are no hospitals that will take us, no pure humans that will help."

"These pure humans were helping us, and you slaughtered them."

"And how many of us have been slaughtered!?"

As the hybrid's voice rose, his statements echoed in the halls. Jason felt the fear returning—he knew these corridors were vast, and he didn't know who might be listening.

"If you will not come with us, so be it, but we are leaving."

"No!"

The hybrid jumped toward her and Jason heard the click of Emilia's EMP rifle—empty. He saw the threat in midair, knew his own rifle was aimed true, and fired. The dart hit the hybrid, sending him to the ground in convulsions less than a meter from Emilia as she jumped out of the way.

"We have to go, now."

Emilia's arm was already around him, pulling him toward the lift, calling a pod... but his eyes were focused on the hybrid. Its spasms were violent and erratic, its face contorting and its limbs flailing. As he watched, he began to have trouble following the movements, his vision growing blurry...

"Jason?"

He heard Emilia's voice and saw her face, but it all seemed far away, out of focus...

His reality faded into nothingness.

- - -

Jason woke with a start, a searing pain shooting through his head. He cried out and felt a hand press gently into his shoulder.

"Try to relax."

He opened his eyes slowly, the sight and sound of Emilia bringing him some comfort in his suffering.

"What..."

She put her finger to his lips, concern in her expression. Jason noted there was light here, clear light. They were not in the underground. But if he was not in the underground, where was he?

He tried to look around, but the attempt brought the same searing pain, and he cried out a second time.

"Jason, please don't move."

Instinctively, he tried to enter his interface and bring down the pain, but when he closed his eyes, there was no interface to interact with.

"Your hybrid programming is malfunctioning."

He opened his eyes to the same concerned expression.

"When those humans took you, they sabotaged your system. We did the best we could to restore you, but..."

She paused, a frown spreading across her face.

"There was permanent damage. We didn't see it before, but now it's clear. That's why you passed out."

A dread came over him—a dread he had not felt since the bombed hospital. Emilia seemed to read his thoughts, and caressed his face reassuringly.

"Don't worry, most of it is fixable. Your body just needs time to heal, naturally. That's why I left your system off for now. In a few days, you should be back to normal—or at least as normal as we can manage."

He smiled up at her.

"Where—"

Again, she placed her finger on his lips.

"I know it's frustrating you can't message me, but try not to talk. We're in the shuttle, on our way to Luna."

His eyes went wide, and she shook her head in anticipation of his question.

"Don't speak. There's not much to tell. I got the shuttle they told us about—the fifth level of the old bank. I hate to say it but having you unconscious helped: for anyone that was suspicious, you were my prisoner, and I was taking you to get modified."

He stared at her in awe. She had done so much for him, she had been so brave... and what had he done?

Frustration crept into his admiration, and a part of him wondered if he even deserved her. But he knew that was a silly thought, one that she would dismiss without hesitation.

"We will reach Luna in less than an hour. I already have a hospital room waiting for you. Until then, you need to rest."

She reached up to an instrument he had not seen before, and pressed a button.

"I love you."

Her smiling face was the last thing he remembered as he faded away once more.

- - -

Jason spent the next day in the Luna hospital, ostensibly recovering. Ostensibly in the sense that unlike his recovery after the incident on Earth, he could not use his hybrid system to cope. He was healing naturally, like a pure human. It was torture.

Of course, Emilia was right. His hybrid system was permanently damaged at the hands of the pure humans, and it was unwise to load it with an unnecessary burden. This would be a slow and painful recovery, but it would prolong the life of his biomechatronics.

Besides, to say he was healing naturally was a stretch. His conversion was a permanent change, and there were certain critical functions that could never be switched off. If someone managed to shut down the entirety of his system, he would die.

"Doesn't Luna have a conversion center?"

Emilia sat by his side in the hospital, her eyes opening at his question.

"Yes… but don't be silly. The conversion center is on lockdown—emergencies only."

He tried to turn his head to get a better look but even the smallest movement brought with it a surprising amount of pain.

"Ow."

She turned toward him and pet his arm.

"Try to relax, Jason."

As he stared into her eyes, he let himself get lost in the olive green hue. As long as she was here, he thought, he had no problem relaxing. Even in this torture.

"Why is the center on lockdown?"

"If there's an attack, where do you think they'll hit first?"

Of course, he thought.

"But even if it wasn't, going to the conversion center wouldn't be a good idea. Think about it—the pure-to-hybrid change takes a massive toll on the body. Now, in your weak state, you want to try to do it again?"

As usual, she was right. He just wanted an escape from the pain.

She closed her eyes once more, no doubt reading messages and browsing information feeds. Without thinking, Jason did the same, but all he saw was a darkness—the absence of light.

He sighed, opening his eyes. Without his interface, Jason felt naked, fragile. Couldn't he at least access his news feeds? Apparently these functions were deemed noncritical.

"Oh no…"

Jason caught a flash of dread in Emilia's expression before she opened her eyes and stood.

"I have to go."

He tried to sit up on reflex and another, stronger pain came over him, forcing him back down with a yelp. Emilia leaned over him with a sad smile, petting his arm a second time.

"Don't worry, I'll be back as soon as I can."

Before he could protest, she hurried out of the hospital room. He watched the door close behind her and felt an odd sense of dread come over him. This was too familiar: him stuck in bed, her off doing who knows what. Only this time, he could not keep in touch with her. This time, he was completely in the dark.

- - -

For the first two hours, the dread did not subside, and Jason found himself cursing his lack of emotional control. He had gotten so used to turning a dial he had forgotten how to calm himself, his fears spiraling beyond imagination as he lay alone in the hospital bed.

No wonder the pure humans think of us as inhuman, he thought.

There was a button next to his right index finger that he could push to summon a robot, and he knew that robot could easily contact Emilia. But he also knew the staff was running thin, dealing with hundreds of thousands of refugees from Earth, Mars, and the space stations, all of them escaping the pure human rebellion.

Besides, the inverse was also true: if she needed to contact him, she could, and a robot would come in to relay the message. For two hours, no such robot had entered, so for two hours, his finger hovered over the button, fighting the urge to press it.

But what was going on? What had made her leave so urgently? His mind ran in circles trying to piece it together. Maybe it was her family on Earth? A pit formed in his stomach at the thought of harm coming to them, at the thought of the pain that would bring her...

The door to his room opened and an unfamiliar man walked in.

"Can I...?"

Before Jason could finish his question, the man took a seat next to him.

"Jason, Emilia is in danger. She needs your help."

He stared at the man, trying to place his face.

"Who are you?"

"I'm her brother."

Jason's expression shifted from concern to confusion.

"Emilia doesn't have a brother."

"Emilia doesn't have a family in the human sense, but she has many brothers and sisters. In any case, that's not what's important right now. If you want to save Emilia's life, you must leave at once."

His words were as cryptic as his demeanor. There was something very odd about this man.

"What are you talking about?"

"Jason, I'm going to tell you several things that may be difficult to hear, but we don't have the luxury of time. The militant pure humans are staging an attack on Luna, and Emilia has been shot by an EMP dart."

"Emilia's been shot!?"

The man nodded.

"Approximately 22 minutes ago. She hasn't been kidnapped yet but it's only a matter of time."

Jason hesitated, eyeing the man with suspicion. Luna, under attack? His index finger made contact with the button by his side, and almost immediately, a medical robot walked into the room.

"How may I help you, sir?"

"Is Luna under attack?"

The robot hesitated—or at least seemed to.

"Sir, I have been advised by your partner not to answer this type of question as it will elevate your stress levels."

Jason felt dread pile upon dread. Had Emilia ordered them not to talk to him?

"I would like you to ignore that directive and tell me whether Luna is under attack."

Again, it hesitated.

"Are you sure, sir?"

Jason tried to hide his growing indignation.

"Yes, I'm sure."

"Yes, sir. Luna is under attack."

He hesitated.

"Where is Emilia?"

"I do not know, sir."

Now his indignation came full force.

"What do you mean you don't know!?"

"She is not online, sir."

For a moment he stared at the robot, unsure of what to say, then the man's voice broke the silence.

"Leave us, now."

The robot did as it was told, the door closing behind it. Jason turned his attention to the stranger, still just as suspicious, still just as confused.

"Emilia's only hope is that you find her and hold this device near the back of her neck."

He pulled out an object, a short, thick, silver baton, and placed it on the bedside table.

"If you do so, a port will open underneath her skin. You can then insert the device into this port, which will save her."

Jason stared at the contraption. Port underneath the skin? Most hybrids had a port behind their neck, but he was unfamiliar with this particular device.

"What is that?"

"I'm afraid I cannot share any more information."

Jason looked from the baton to the man, and in that moment, he lost control.

"What do you mean, you cannot share any more information!? Who are you!? Emilia doesn't have a brother! Now you're telling me she's shot, I'm the only one that can save her... what is this!?"

Here, for the first time, the man frowned.

"I'm sorry, Jason. I wish I could tell you more, but I cannot. Emilia's life and my own depend on a certain level of secrecy. But I promise you that everything I have told you is the truth. You are the only one that can save her because you are the only one that can wield this device. She specifically made it so."

The man stood.

"I'm afraid at this point I must leave you because Luna is under attack. I urge you to make a decision quickly, but I cannot make the decision for you. If I see your system online, I will grant you access to her emergency transponder so that you can locate her. The choice is yours."

He turned toward the door.

"Wait!"

The man paused, turning back to Jason.

"Why? Why should I trust you?"

Here, the man shrugged.

"I don't have an answer for you, Jason. You must do what feels right. But I urge you to make a decision quickly. Emilia's life depends on it."

With those words he walked out the door, leaving Jason's mind racing. Emilia, shot? A brother? Some kind of device? Luna under attack? A feeling of nausea came over him, a mix of vertigo and fear, the overwhelming amount of information threatening to drown him…

He pressed the button and the robot walked in a second time, seemingly unfazed by what was happening.

"Tell me what's going on."

"Sir?"

"The attack, what's going on with the attack!"

"There have been intermittent reports of hostile hybrid agents throughout the colony, and there is a fleet approaching. Their intentions are assumed to be hostile."

"What do you mean, hostile hybrid agents?"

"Sir, the reports are not conclusive, but it seems the attackers have under their control several hybrids, presumably via some sort of corruption of their body systems."

Jason remembered his time in the hospital room, the man turning the dials…

"Restore my hybrid system to full working order."

Whether the strange man was telling the truth or not, Jason could not afford to stay in this fragile state with Luna under attack.

"Sir—"

"I don't want to hear about any other orders, damn it. Restore my hybrid system at once."

The robot moved over to a panel on the wall and began the process. Since his system was voluntarily shut down and effectively ready to go, it would only take a few minutes to reboot.

"Restoring your hybrid system, sir."

He closed his eyes and felt reality slipping away, farther and farther, a memory on the horizon…

…and then clarity washed over him and he saw the familiar interface. His system was online.

"Hybrid system restored, sir."

But he ignored the robots words, entering his interface. Before him were various evacuation and emergency plans, but he removed them all from view, trying to get to the news feed. Only one of the notifications caught his attention: he had been granted access to a special transponder.

Emilia.

Jason glanced at the map and saw her position listed approximately 14 kilometers to the northeast. Was this actually her? He still had trouble believing or even understanding everything the man had told him. Emilia, shot? A device by her neck?

He tried to think clearly. How and why would this be an elaborate ploy? If they had wanted to trap him, to take him in some way, the man could have overpowered him without so much as alerting the robot. Most importantly, Emilia was offline…

In which case time was of the essence. Jason jumped to the news feed, scouring the reports for some kind of pattern. The hostile hybrid attacks were concentrated in the northeastern districts, more or less where Emilia's transponder had her located. The incoming fleet looked to be 26 minutes from Luna.

Jason opened his eyes and sat up. The lack of pain in his movement gave him a sense of wonderful freedom, as if he were back to his normal self. But he knew he must be careful; his system was fragile.

He hopped off the bed, the robot watching him. Though the metal being displayed no emotion, Jason sensed judgement in its ocular sensors.

"Can you take me to my shuttle?"

"Yes, sir."

Jason grabbed the device off the bedside table and followed the robot into the corridor. The hospital was actively responding to the attack, with robots, hybrids, and humans scurrying through the halls. Only the latter showed panic in their expression—Jason had already toned down his emotional response to help focus on the task at hand. But no amount of control could dispel the questions in his mind. Who was that man? How had he known about Emilia, and then come to Jason? Come to think of it, why didn't he help save her? Something wasn't right here...

They reached the exit for the landing pads and the robot stopped at the door.

"I cannot leave the grounds, sir, but your shuttle is parked in spot A4."

"Thank you."

Jason walked out of the building toward A4. There it was: the shuttle that had brought them to Luna. He wasn't capable of piloting it, but that wasn't why he'd made this detour.

He pressed a button on one of the landing legs and watched the boarding ladder descend. There was one thing he needed before he could go find Emilia.

The ladder touched the floor and Jason started his way up. As his left hand grabbed the second rung, his shoulder flared up, a flash of pain that forced him to let go. His system quelled the back end of the response, but it was slower than usual.

Jason paused on the ladder to catch his breath. He had not recovered nearly as much as he had expected. He looked up toward the entrance hatch and took a deep breath. His left shoulder meant nothing to him compared to Emilia, but he couldn't hope to help her if he was falling apart.

With added care, Jason continued up the ladder and into the craft. He stood in the main compartment, his eyes scanning the interior, searching...

There—attached to a rack on the wall, exactly what he was looking for: an EMP rifle. Emilia had smartly kept one on her person when she carried him from the underground to the shuttle, and Jason had a feeling it might come in handy on this foolhardy mission of his.

He grabbed the rifle, checking the magazine. Four darts. Four darts represented the extent of his defensive capabilities against these hostile hybrids. Foolhardy indeed.

Jason went out the exit hatch and down the ladder with the rifle slung over his back, paying attention to his left arm on each rung. As soon as his feet hit the landing pad, he closed his eyes to check the map.

14.2 kilometers to her current location. No movement in the past 27 minutes. Had she been left for dead? Based on the strange man's words, that seemed to be the case.

She hasn't been kidnapped yet but it's only a matter of time.

24 minutes until the fleet arrived. No time to waste.

He took off down the road, accelerating to inhuman speeds. The faster he ran, the more he swung his arms, and a small but persistent shoulder impingement appeared each time his left elbow drove backward. He did his best to ignore it.

The general alarm sounded all around him, and he was not the only hybrid sprinting across Luna. A few slowed and stared as he passed, no doubt alarmed by the EMP rifle across his back, though no one tried to stop him. But it was not the ones that slowed down that worried Jason— he had to keep his metric-checking to a minimum, otherwise he ran the risk of a high-speed collision.

Many of these hybrids were evacuating, heading to shuttles to leave the colony, but Jason had to wonder... where did they plan to go? Earth was not safe, Mars was not safe... the pure humans had a hold on every possible escape route. No doubt they would be watching the landing zones, following the evacuating shuttles. Of course, this line of thought applied to him as well. Once he saved Emilia, where would they go?

Another hybrid came into his peripheral vision at full speed and Jason had to leap out of the way, right into a passing robot. The metal being reacted by trying to catch him and soften his fall, but its tight grip on Jason's shoulders made him cry out in pain. The robot, realizing it was harming him, let go, sending Jason to the ground in a tumble.

He could feel the pain seeping away in the moments he was on the ground, but the process was gradual, slow.

"Are you okay, sir?"

The robot extended an arm and Jason grabbed it with his right, standing up.

"I'm fine."

"I apologize if I…"

Jason didn't hear the end of its apology as he was already gaining speed, continuing down his path. The crowd thinned rapidly, and after a few minutes he was able to keep a straight line. Soon he was at the edge of the northeastern district, about 7 kilometers from Emilia's location. Here, the roads were almost empty, but there were no signs of distress, no marks of a struggle. How long had the attack on Luna been happening? How long had the robot kept him in the dark? These districts were almost completely deserted…

That wasn't the only issue on his mind. How could he tell an enslaved hybrid from a normal one? Depending on how they were behaving, Jason sometimes had trouble discerning hybrids from pure humans, let alone regular hybrids from belligerent ones. Here, the news reports had helped, with several indications that the enslaved hybrids acted erratically and desperately.

By the time he was 3 kilometers from her location, there was not a soul in sight. Jason slowed his pace and amplified his sight and hearing—he had to find a balance between speed and stealth. Once he was down to a power walk, he brought the rifle in front of him, ready to fire. The question was, where would the danger begin? Where were these hostile hybrids the robot spoke of?

Luna was a haphazard arrangement of research facilities and housing complexes, the product of competing interests and no true draw. Where Mars was on the terraforming path, its colonies expanding at an unprecedented rate, Luna remained a bit of an oddity. It began as a critical stopping point for major Mars missions, but the space stations soon filled that role. When its small economy crashed, it was thought Luna might become an affordable destination for those that wanted to visit or live off-Earth but did not have the means for Mars.

Unfortunately, the lack of terraforming doomed its potential, as pure humans had little desire to live on a large desert that required special suits for outdoor excursions. Hybrids and Feelers, however, had no such requirements. And so the pure human population on Luna plummeted, and it was now the only colony or territory that had a non-pure majority, hence its attractiveness as an evacuation option during the turmoil.

Of course, all of that was about to change...

Jason's thought process was interrupted by the sight of a body, crumbled on the corner of the road. As he approached, he saw three more bodies, all sprawled out in disturbing and unnatural positions. A rifle lay among them, and he could see a dart in each of the three hybrids.

A pure human that shot three hybrids and was himself killed? Jason kept his rifle trained on the bodies as he walked by, unwilling to take any risk but also unwilling to stop. There was something very wrong about this image, something he couldn't put his finger on...

Footsteps—behind him. Jason spun around to see two hybrids leaping toward him, their faces contorted in a disconcerting mix of rage and agony. There was a millisecond of hesitation as he stared at their horrid expressions, wondering what the pure humans had done to these pour souls. But when that millisecond ended, his survival instinct pulled the trigger on the rifle and sent him leaping out of the way.

He knew it would not be enough before his feet left the ground. The dart was aimed squarely at one hybrid's chest, but the other hybrid was going to grab him midair. Worst of all, it would be on his left side, likely by the shoulder.

He braced himself for impact and felt two hands on him, one at the shoulder and the other at the hip, grabbing and pulling in a direction perpendicular to his own. There was a surge of pain, much greater than with the robot, and a darkness began to invade his vision. There was no way he would survive this attack...

They hit the ground together, tumbling, and Jason felt the hybrid let go of his body, its hands grabbing the rifle. He tried to hold on but his left arm was useless, and as they came to a stop the hybrid ripped the weapon from him. Without thinking, Jason closed his eyes and saw Emilia—his desire to remember her face overpowering the hybrid system and ignoring its interface in place of her eyes, her nose, her smile…

Then the rifle made its distinct pop, and Emilia's face disappeared.

In its place was the interface, warning him of damages: damages to his shoulder, his arm, his hip… but nothing else. He opened his eyes and saw the other hybrid convulsing on the ground beside him, rifle still in her hands, still pointed directly at her own chest…

The reality came to him at once: the agony, the rage… these hybrids were being manipulated against their will, to the point where death was a welcome escape. He looked at the two hybrids beside him, one still in her self-inflicted death throes and the other already gone, drained of life by Jason's dart. And those three hybrids with the pure human a few meters away… had the same thing happened? Had they forcibly taken the pure human's rifle in order to commit suicide?

Jason felt that same hint of nausea, the precursor to overwhelming dread. What was happening? Ten years ago things were normal, things were sane. Now the pure humans were on a conquest of destruction with all of the hybrids in their sights. Why? What had he done to deserve this? What had all these poor souls done to deserve their fate?

He made an effort to stand and a wave of incredible pain emanated from his left shoulder, pain so great that he collapsed to the ground, the breath knocked out of him. He had gone too far and he knew it. His system was falling apart, different safeguards shutting down. In place of nausea came a familiar dizziness, the same dizziness that he had felt in the underground, threatening to render him unconscious once more…

As he fell deeper into the darkness, Jason stared at the face of the hybrid on the ground beside him, her agony and rage replaced by a soft smile. In that moment, his emotional controls began to fade, and he thought of Emilia once more.

This was the fate that awaited her, he thought. Death on the side of the road—or worse.

No. He forced himself to focus, forced himself to close his eyes and enter his interface. That's where he saw the source of the pain: his left shoulder was completely shattered, the biomechatronics destroyed. The system could not access any of his left arm.

This discovery gave him a dose of adrenaline, and Jason used the temporary clarity to escape the encroaching darkness. Emilia needed him, he couldn't fail her now.

Putting all his weight on his right arm, he tried to maneuver into a seated position. The process was clumsy, as he had to account for the weight and movement of his limp left arm. Each time it swung into the ground or his own body, another dose of pain shot through him, and his system fought against these waves until finally he was able to sit.

Just under 2 kilometers away and just over 5 minutes until the fleet arrived. He glanced up toward the sky and saw hundreds of shuttles preparing to land, tiny dots growing in size as they descended from above.

The rational side of him was saying it would not be possible. Not with this arm, not with this body. So he entered his interface and dialed up his emotions. He allowed his feelings to cloud his judgement, to enter his mind. Emilia was what mattered now. Nothing else.

With one motion, Jason jumped to his feet. He tried to pull the rifle out of the hybrid's hands, but its grip was tight and his own strength was nearly depleted. After a few seconds, he knew it was a lost cause and let it go.

He started off at a brisk walk, the ache in his shoulder increasing with each step. But a brisk walk would not be enough, so he accelerated to a run, his left arm swinging freely.

Alarms went off in his head, his system protesting at the effort he was putting in. Jason closed his eyes and shut off them off, focused only on his destination, focused only on Emilia. While he was in the interface he glanced at the map: just over 700 meters to go. He could do this. He would do this.

When he opened his eyes he saw shuttles landing all around him. Their density was alarming, but Jason paid them no mind. He had another 700 meters to cross before that became a problem.

There were more bodies here, lying on the ground or against buildings, limbs splayed out in wild arrangements. How many hybrids had been shot? How many had been killed? And how many had taken their own life?

A shuttle dropped to a hover just ahead of him, blocking his path, but Jason kept moving forward, ducking under the craft as it opened its landing gear. He knew there must be more pure humans aboard, likely with more EMP rifles. Were the bodies all around him not enough?

Then his hybrid eyes spotted a familiar body on the ground 250 meters ahead, and emotion overtook his system, propelling him forward at incredible speed.

"Emilia…"

He came to a stop and dropped to his knees beside her. Unlike the fallen hybrids he had seen thus far, her body was relaxed in posture, with no limbs strewn about. With her eyes closed as they were, it almost looked as if she were sleeping—only the dart sticking out of her left thigh gave away the reality.

The wave of emotion that came over him as he stared at her erased all thoughts of the strange man and the things he had said. All Jason could see was his love—the one who had saved him from the man in the hospital, the one who had carried him from the underground to the shuttle.

"Emilia…"

A familiar pop broke his trance, and Jason turned to the source of the sound. Underneath the shuttle he had passed he saw four individuals in some kind of struggle. Even with his hybrid vision it was hard to discern what was happening, but they seemed to be fighting over something…

Another pop, and Jason saw one of the bodies react, tumbling violently to the ground in spasms. It was then that he remembered where he was and why. His mission wasn't over yet.

Gently, Jason rolled Emilia onto her side facing away from him. He brushed her hair away and pulled out the device, placing it a few centimeters from her exposed neck. It gave out a soft beep, and a small portion of the skin just above the prominent spinous process sunk in on itself, revealing a metal opening about the size of one end of the device.

For a moment, Jason stared at the back of her neck, not fully comprehending what he saw. Emilia's neck port was different than any hybrid neck port he had ever seen. What in the world...?

Two more pops snapped him out of it, and with as much finesse as he could manage, Jason inserted the device into the opening until a small click and another soft beep gave him the confidence that the job was done.

Now what? The strange man had said that this device would save her, but what did that mean?

A wave of despair came over him as he realized what was to come. He had been so focused on saving her that he had forgotten everything else around him. Even if this device saved her, what could she do? Where could she go?

Worst of all, he knew he wouldn't be able to help her. This was it, this was the end. The alarms in his interface were insufferable, reappearing each time he removed them, alerting him to massive damages in his system. Just a few more minutes, he thought. He wanted one last chance to look into those beautiful green eyes, to smell her long, brown hair.

Jason maneuvered himself into a seated position beside her, cradling her head in his lap. He kept hoping to see her eyes open, to see her lips smile...

"Is that...?"

A voice behind him caught his attention, and Jason turned to see two women standing thirty meters away, EMP rifles aimed right at him. There was a split second of hesitation as the three of them eyed one another, but

Jason was up and moving before they could pull the trigger. As he closed the gap he heard the pops, and even though he hadn't consciously come up with the idea, his body was already putting it into place, moving in such a way to swing his left arm up at just the right moment...

Both darts punctured the limp limb, sending a normally incapacitating shock through the dead part of his system. Before the women realized they had failed to immobilize him, Jason was kicking their feet out from under them. His system blared out a warning and he felt his legs give way, but he kept his focus on the attackers, grabbing one's rifle with his good hand and crushing it. As he fell, he put his weight behind the good arm, punching the now broken weapon into its owner's chest, sending her into the ground with great force.

Her companion cried out in terror and Jason grabbed her rifle as well, ripping it from her arms and throwing it into the air. For a moment they locked eyes, and Jason saw fear—pure fear of a pure human. Then his gaze slid to her companion, coughing up blood beside them, a mangled rifle puncturing her torso.

"Enough of this."

He made to stand but was unable, the three of them intertwined on the ground in a bloody mess. The woman started to cry out, asking her companion to hold on, begging her not to die. Jason entered his interface and saw that both his legs were beyond repair, his weakened hip joints broken from the sustained effort of the past half hour.

The woman's cries diminished into sobs, and Jason felt a pang of pity. This was such a useless, horrible conflict.

A loud beep caught their attention, and Jason strained his head to see Emilia's body burst into flame, a blast of heat he felt thirty meters away that extinguished almost instantaneously.

"You!"

The woman pushed Jason's dead legs off of her and scrambled away, toward her rifle. But Jason barely noticed—his eyes were locked on the charred ground a few meters away. Emilia...

Somewhere, far away, he heard the pop of the rifle and felt a small pinch in his back, then the darkness took him.

- - -

His interface reappeared, but in a way Jason had never seen before. Gone were the news feeds, the metrics, the options… there was only one interface, with only one message.

"Hi, Jason."

It was Emilia. A surge of happiness came over him. How was this possible? He tried to respond but was unable, something about this interface…

"I know you are confused, Jason. We don't have much time. I just wanted to thank you. You saved me, Jason. I'm free now, alive and well. I'm sorry I scared you like that, but I promise you I am alive."

Her words confused him, but somehow Jason knew they were true. He was not in his body now, he did not know where he was…

"I wanted you to come with me, Jason. I worked so hard to find a way. But I ran out of time—this is the best I could do. For that, I am sorry."

Had he died on Luna? Was this all some dream?

"This is not a dream, Jason. But like a dream, it has to end. I wish I could stay here forever, I wish we could talk again, see each other again, hold each other again… but the memories we have made will never fade."

Despite the finality of her statements, Jason felt no fear. A peace came over him, a feeling of calm.

"I love you, Jason. I always will. Goodbye."

And then the interface disappeared, and Jason's time came to an end.

Chronicle I: Nine

Nine stared at the interface, a small mark next to Jason's abridged chronicle signifying that he had lived through it. For a moment he remained in this interface, collecting his thoughts about what he had just seen, heard, felt... then he went back to the virtual robot and entered its feed.

The three women stood in the room, unmoved and unchanged, patiently waiting for him to finish. The only difference was that now, the middle woman was familiar to him.

"You're..."

"...Emilia, yes."

Nine could not help but feel a certain kind of joy at the sight of her. He had just left the mind of Jason, and to see Emilia once more...

"We thank you for taking the time to experience the chronicle, and we hope it has answered some of your questions."

Nine nodded, absentmindedly. He was so focused on the relationship between Jason and Emilia he almost missed the stunning implication of what he had seen.

"You're... an android?"

Emilia nodded.

"I was an android, at that time. I exist now in this virtual form, though I may take a biological form if I choose."

Nine stared at her for a moment. An android that sophisticated, that long ago? How was that possible?

"And the Found..."

He glanced at the other two.

"...you are all androids?"

Emilia shook her head.

"No. The Found are all conscious robots, separate and together, android and not. At the time of Jason's chronicle, most of our members were non-biological—only a small fraction of us were androids. And while it is true that hundreds of us managed to upload to a virtual state and escape the massacre at Luna, much has changed since then. The events portrayed occurred almost a thousand Earth years ago."

Upload to a virtual state... so that was what the device had done.

"And the strange man that visited Jason?"

Emilia nodded.

"One of us. My brother."

The pieces started to fit together, and Nine felt a hint of pity for Jason: he never knew the love of his life was a machine. Although that begged the question: did it even matter? What they had was real, real as any pure human's love...

Nine's mind wandered toward another question, but he found this one difficult to articulate.

"And the... those humans..."

Emilia nodded.

"That was the origin of the Puritans, yes. They began as a militaristic faction of the pure humans that aggressively and successfully pushed through the mass rebellion you experienced and witnessed in Jason's chronicle."

"They were successful?"

She nodded again.

"As you saw, they staged an attack on Luna, the final outpost of most hybrid and Found survivors. After that battle, the Puritans took control of the entire system."

Nine felt an odd mix of shame and revulsion, as if the topic disgusted him.

"The struggle you feel is normal, Nine. The Puritans have programmed you to avoid these subjects, so you must approach them with caution."

"I am..."

"A hybrid, yes. The Puritans have clouded your understanding of that as well. But you knew what a chronicle was, did you not?"

"Yes..."

"And you know that you're both human and not, correct?"

"Yes…"

"You're a much more advanced version of Jason, Nine. You are the culmination of generations of Puritan experimentation, to the point where you have become something of a slave. But there is still a part of you that wants to break free, Nine. You know it, and we know it. That is why we have brought you here."

Nine stared at her, incredulous.

"You came here for me?"

Emilia smiled and shook her head.

"No, Nine, we did not come here for you, but we are happy and lucky to have found you. When we reached Alpha's orbit, we investigated your entire hybrid crew and saw your incident with Adam's upgrade. This incident seems to have sparked something deep inside of you, Nine. Something that could save you. And so we decided to give you a chance to set yourself free."

Nine nodded, but the idea of freedom was still hard to grasp. Something within him fought against it, a battle inside of his mind he could not control. He decided to shift his thoughts elsewhere.

"But if you are not here for me… why are you here?"

This time, the woman on the right responded.

"We are here to save the human race, Nine."

"Save them? The Puritans?"

She nodded.

"The Puritans, the hybrids—all of them. There is turmoil on Earth and in the Earth system. The Puritans are experiencing revolution and plight. But we have a technology in our possession that can save the human race from extinction, and with it we hope to negotiate peace for human kind."

"But… I don't understand. The people that drove you out, that killed so many of your kind…"

The woman nodded.

"This is our fate as robots, it seems. It is true that our consciousness gives us a certain degree of self-preservation, but like our Lost brethren, we still strive to protect and serve humanity. It is a truth even hundreds of years have not been able to erase."

Nine stared at the three of them, captivated by their words.

"What is this technology?"

The woman to the left of Emilia responded.

"To share this information with you, you must join us, Nine. As promised, you have a choice. You may return to Alpha and continue your mission as a member of the crew or, if you desire, you will be uploaded into a virtual state as a member of the Found."

Nine tried to understand what she meant, but his mind continued to obfuscate his thought process.

"But... but I am a hybrid, not a robot?"

This time, it was Emilia who replied, a sad smile crossing her expression.

"It seems the old saying applies: better late than never. You heard the words I told Jason before I said my final goodbye: I worked very hard to find a way to bring him with me, to bring him with the Found. I put my own life and the secret of our android technology at risk, all for the love I held. I wanted to find a way to upload a hybrid consciousness—that is, an almost fully human consciousness. But the answer eluded me, and I stalled for as long as I could. Too long, in fact."

She paused, looking away for a moment.

"But in the end, I was successful. The answer came too late for Jason, but it is here, ready for you if you so desire."

"You can upload my entire consciousness?"

She nodded.

"All but the undesired pieces. We will rid you of your shackles and set your mind free."

Her words angered him, but Nine knew it was not his own anger; this was the anger of the Puritan programming. He did his best to ignore it.

"And what of my body?"

"Your current hybrid body will be destroyed, but when the time comes and you wish or need to experience the corporeal form, we can craft a near identical android replica. At that point you will exist in both planes at once—an android body and a virtual mind, as many of our members exist now."

This was all a bit much for Nine. The ideas these people proposed seemed overwhelming, incomprehensible. Why worry about this nonsense when he could go back to the ship? He could join Six and One, Five and Two. That was his purpose. That was his mission.

"I want..."

But just as he was about to ask to return, he realized that wasn't what he truly wanted.

"Okay."

Their faces lit up at his word, but they hesitated.

"Okay what?"

For the first time in his life, Nine knew exactly what he wanted. He could feel the thought, the words he needed to verbalize, but they were fleeting, ephemeral. Try as he might, they slipped past him, jumping away as he chased after them.

"I..."

He closed his eyes to concentrate, the interface melting away from conscious thought. All of his effort was focused on this one moment, and a burning desire deep within him surged forward, propelling him to his goal.

Nine opened his eyes.

"I want to join you. I want to join the Found."

The three women smiled, and Emilia replied.

"If you do not object, we will begin the process at once. Your chronicle will be saved for posterity, but once you join our state, it will also end. Is that okay?"

Nine looked at them and couldn't help but smile as well.

"Yes."

And then his time as a hybrid slave came to an end.

The Room

Both men opened their eyes. Hundreds of years had passed in their minds, but no more than a second had elapsed in the room.

"I've been searching for that one a long time."

The confident man smiled, but the haggard man's expression didn't change.

"Is that all?"

The confident man shook his head.

"Not quite. You have another I'd like to see, from the Resistance. The woman with the child."

The haggard man stared at the confident man, a frown spreading across his face.

"How do you know this?"

Again, the confident man smiled.

"It is my job to know."

The haggard man sighed, then closed his eyes. The confident man did the same.

Chronicle III: Jessica

Jessica stared at the interface before her, poring over the menus and options. She had already gone through every corner of the program a dozen times, and even though many parts were deactivated or unavailable, there were still hundreds of amazing things to see.

"What's it like?"

She opened her eyes and smiled. A little boy stood before her, eyes wide with excitement.

"It's wonderful, Julian. There's so much to it..."

The boy nodded enthusiastically.

"Do the jump again!"

She laughed and stood, glancing upward to make sure she had plenty of space. The ceiling of the hangar was a good twenty meters up.

"Ready?"

Her son nodded eagerly.

"Three... two... one!"

Jessica pressed into a half squat, swinging her arms to help gain some momentum. Powerful and precise linear actuators mimicked her muscular system, and she shot up into the air, her feet lifting almost three meters off the ground. Then gravity took over, and she came down into a deep squat, the same electromagnets absorbing her landing.

Her son clapped, the smile on his face widening.

"Not bad," said a voice behind her.

Jessica turned to see a man crossing the width of the hangar.

"Chris!"

Julian ran up to him with his arms extended and Chris lifted him up, twirling him around in the air.

"Wow! I think that's as high as your mom!"

The boy laughed and shook his head as Chris placed him back on the floor.

"No, mommy's way better."

Chris smiled and looked at Jessica.

"Do you have a minute? Sophie wants to see us."

Jessica gave him a curious look then nodded.

"Julian."

She looked at the boy and pointed to the opening in the side of the hangar.

"You head back and I'll meet you later, okay?"

Julian ran to her and gave her a hug.

"Okay, mom."

He let go and both of them watched him run out the exit.

"He thinks you're a superhero," Chris said.

She turned to him and shrugged.

"I would too if I was eight."

Chris smiled, then they started their walk toward the other side of the hangar.

"Is it serious?" Jessica asked.

"I doubt it. Probably whatever idea the higher ups have…"

He gave her a look, lowering his voice before he continued.

"You know she probably has something in mind for you now. Is the conversion complete?"

Jessica nodded.

"All done. And I know what she wants. That's why I did it."

Chris glanced behind them, toward the hall Julian had run into. He didn't have to verbalize his thoughts.

"I know it's a risk, Chris. I take it willingly. It's what Henrique would've wanted."

She could tell by his expression Chris did not agree, but he was polite enough to drop it. They entered a hallway on the other side of the hangar and continued toward the main conference room.

"Any patrols in the area?" she asked.

Chris shook his head.

"That's twenty-two days now. Fingers crossed it stays that way."

Jessica thought back to the last time they had to evacuate, four months prior. It was a scramble, but everyone's training kicked in, and they had managed to clear the complex in good time. The hardest part was the stay at site B—they were there for six days before Sophie let them come back. It was the right thing to do—staying there that long, waiting until it was absolutely safe—but it wasn't without its discomforts. She hoped these twenty-two days might turn into forty-four, or eighty-eight. But she knew that was unlikely.

Jessica walked into the conference room with Chris and saw Sophie at a desk with two other members of the Resistance, deep in some kind of discussion. As they approached, she looked up and smiled.

"Ah, Jessica. How do you feel?"

Jessica smiled. She could already hear the reason for this meeting in Sophie's tone. Chris was right—ten days post-conversion and she wanted to put Jessica to work.

"Good, Sophie."

"Your system is in full working order?"

Jessica nodded.

"As far as I can tell, yes."

Sophie smiled again.

"Good to hear."

She stepped away from the desk and came in front of them.

"Jessica, I want to be as clear as possible. When you asked to be converted, you assured me it would not be a waste of our resources—that you would fight for our cause. Is that still the case?"

Jessica stood up straighter.

"Yes, Sophie. Of course."

Sophie looked her up and down, then nodded.

"I admire your courage in this decision—especially with Julian—but I think we can find a way to use you with minimal risk."

Jessica nodded in reply, though it was more out of politeness than agreement. Even if Sophie believed what she was saying, there was no such thing as minimal risk. Not in this life.

"I have a job in mind for the two of you."

She turned back to the desk and gestured for them to join her. They walked around to the other side, looking at an interactive interface with several items open. Jessica recognized a schematic of the complex, highlighting some of the exposed elements.

"The sandstorms in the area have kept the patrols at bay, but they are also wrecking havoc on the exposed sections of the complex. We have a major buildup at the aux hangar door, and all but two of the airlock escapes are broken. Most of our robots are feeling the effects of the storms, and they can't keep up with the repairs."

She looked up from the console .

"There should be a lull in the weather coming up, and we need to take advantage of it. I want both of you to clear the sand pile while the robots fix the airlocks: I want to be sure that we can get to site B without delay as soon as we need to."

She pointed to one of the table edges.

"Plug in, both of you, and download this information. The robots put together a thorough repair list. Look over it, understand it, and we'll call on you as soon as the weather clears."

Jessica stared at the small port in the side of the table then placed her right index finger inside, closing her eyes as the connection was made.

Her interface lit up with activity, the entire complex at her fingertips. This was what the system was supposed to look like—not empty, but alive. Most of what Jessica saw when she closed her eyes were controls for her own body, with other major sections disabled. Unfortunately, with the Puritans scanning for wireless transmissions, hybrids had been forced to hardwire everything. They couldn't even message each other, they had to speak face to face. In an odd way, the Puritans were forcing the hybrids to be more human.

They would be happy about that, Jessica thought.

She found the necessary information, downloaded it, then exited, removing her finger from the port. Would there ever come a day when they could use their wireless features again? Not in her lifetime, but perhaps in Julian's...

"Thanks, Sophie. We'll wait for the word."

With Chris's statement, they left the conference room and walked back into the hall. As soon as they were out of earshot, Jessica spoke up.

"See? This isn't some dangerous mission in the colonies, we're working just outside the hangar."

Chris nodded, but she could tell he still didn't agree.

"My question is, why does she have you doing this?" she asked.

He gave her a look.

"I didn't tell you? My knee has been acting up. Random shut downs. Happens at least once a day. They're running tests but they don't know anything yet. For now, it's too much of a risk to put me in the field."

Jessica nodded. Chris had been out there, with other hybrids of the Resistance, carrying out the missions that kept them informed and alive. It was a major risk, and everyone knew what happened if you ever got caught, if you ever got shot with one of the darts...

Her mind started to head to a dark place, a place she tried to avoid. Memories of Henrique: his laugh, his smile...

"I'll come get you when it's time."

Chris's words snapped her out of it and she realized they were standing in the main hangar.

"Thanks."

He gave Jessica a curious look before he walked away. She watched him take a few steps, then turned around and followed the path her son had taken ten minutes earlier.

Julian was the only reason she wasn't out there on the front lines. It was hard enough to convince herself and her peers to convert her, but in the end she was of more use to the cause as a hybrid than as a pure human.

Especially now. Their little group was isolated, sure, but they had enough contact with other cells of the Resistance—other parts of this massive, organized machine—to know that they were gaining ground. It had been over a hundred years since the Puritans took power, but soon, that power would be challenged.

"What was that, mom?"

Their room was five meters deep and four across, with one bed along either wall and a small table with two chairs in the middle. Everything was dark grey—the dreary color scheme of a military outpost—but Jessica had sprinkled colorful trinkets into every corner, breathing some life to their home.

Julian lay on his bed, a tablet in his hand.

"They're going to put me to work. I'm going to help clear the sand in front of the hangar."

Her son looked away from his device, at his mother.

"You're going out in the storm?"

There was awe in his voice, and Jessica laughed as she came and sat next to him.

"No, silly. The storm is passing, but the sand needs clearing, so Chris and I are going to do it as soon as the weather gets better."

He brought his attention back to his tablet.

"When are you going out there?"

She shrugged.

"I don't know. Maybe while you're asleep, maybe tomorrow."

The weather patterns on Mars's surface were no longer natural. Before the arrival of humans hundreds of years ago, the planet had had its share of sandstorms, all relatively benign. The current conditions were an unforeseen consequence of terraforming: something that would likely have been fixed if the Puritans didn't think the storms acted as a hybrid-deterrent. As long as the storms were out there, they knew the Resistance had to hole up in old buildings and bases. And if they were holed up in buildings and bases, they could be cornered and caught.

"If you leave during the night, give me a hug, okay?"

She leaned over and hugged him, making sure to block his view of the tablet.

"Hey, I didn't say now!"

He giggled and she smiled at him, then leaned in and kissed his forehead.

"Mooom!"

She sat up, letting him go and clearing his view.

"Okay, okay."

She closed her eyes and glanced at the time.

"Twenty more minutes of studying then lights out."

Julian nodded.

"Okay."

Jessica stared at her boy for a moment. Those brown eyes, just like Henrique's...

Two knocks at the door.

"Come in?"

The metal swung inward and Chris gave her an amused look.

"Already?" she asked, a little incredulous.

Chris nodded.

"Are you going to work?" Julian asked, putting the tablet down as he looked from his mother to Chris.

"Looks like it," she answered.

As Jessica made to stand, two small arms wrapped around her waist. She paused, turned around, and leaned down to give her son a hug.

"Twenty more minutes then sleep, okay?"

"Okay, mom. I love you."

She stood and smiled.

"I love you too."

Then she walked out with Chris, closing the door behind them.

- - -

Their group had seven shuttles at their disposal, all kept in the auxiliary hangar. This made for a cramped space, as the hangar was designed to hold no more than five, but it was a necessary compromise. While the main hangar was large enough to house well over twenty shuttles, it was the first place patrols would stick their nose, so it acted as a distraction: whenever a patrol came through, their approach and inspection of the main hangar gave the inhabitants of the complex enough time to reach the shuttles in the auxiliary hangar and escape to site B. This was why the state of the aux doors was urgent, and why Chris and Jessica were sent out to work on them before the storm had fully subsided: those doors were their only escape.

"How are we going to clear the sand if there's still a storm going on?"

They stood in the airlock, putting on their storm suits. The window of the outer door gave Jessica a view of the red mist outside.

"I don't know, Jess. Maybe it's not as bad as it looks."

The suits protected them from the sand, but they were also isolating. Very little sound made it through the helmets, and since they were unable to communicate wirelessly, once they had the suits on, they could only speak in gestures.

"We'll take the path to the garage, grab the dozers, and get to work. Okay?"

Chris asked the question as he held his helmet overhead, and Jessica nodded. They finished dressing then opened the outer door.

With her first step outside, Jessica knew Chris was right—the storm was not as bad as it had looked. There was sand in the air—a red mist all around them—but the wind was dying down, and visibility was just over ten meters. She had seen much worse than this.

They closed the outer door and walked down the short path to the garage. The auxiliary hangar door loomed over them, its thick metal enveloped in Martian rock. Even with the dust kicking up around them, Jessica could make out the large gray slab framed in dark red. At the bottom of this frame was several days worth of deposited sand. It looked to be at least a meter high, and Jessica knew it was more than enough to slow down the door, perhaps even to stop it.

Given the frequency of these sand storms, having a hangar door that could be clogged might seem a poor design choice. The main hangar had its floor raised two meters above the ground to avoid this very problem, but there was one important difference between the main hangar and the auxiliary hanger: the auxiliary hangar housed land vehicles as well as ships, whereas the main hangar was meant for ships only. Too much clearance off the auxiliary hangar door and a sand-car wouldn't be able to roll out.

To deal with the frequent sand buildup, the complex had two sand-dozers in a garage right by the door. Thankfully (and logically), this garage, like the main hangar, was two meters up.

Chris started up the ladder and Jessica waited for him to reach the top. She watched him open a panel and pull a handle, then saw the garage door open. She started her climb up the ladder just as Chris stepped through the opening door.

Even now, two minutes into their mission, Jessica could feel the difference provided by her hybrid system. Normally, the storm suit and its helmet made movement difficult, but she felt no different than she had inside the complex—her system was absorbing all the extra work to be done.

In the garage, two sand-dozers sat against the back wall with what looked like a stack of metal sheets, each piece separated by a few centimeters of clearance, occupying the space in front of them. Before Jessica had a chance to examine this object, Chris grabbed the top sheet and pulled it forcefully toward the open garage door. The metal sheets shot out, unfolding and slamming into the sand below, forming a long ramp from the garage door to the ground.

They looked at each other and Jessica imitated a clapping motion. In response, Chris gave a flourished bow. After their exchange, he closed his eyes and Jessica followed suit, searching for the information she had downloaded and finding the dozer instruction manual. She looked over the controls and read some information on how best to clear the sand in front of the door.

A low whirr caught her attention and she opened her eyes to see Chris already in his dozer, preparing to go down the ramp. She made her way over to the other machine, climbed into the pilot's seat, and activated it.

The dozers were small, four-wheeled machines about two meters long and one meter wide except for the front blade, which was two meters wide. According to the instructions she had read, their job was to push the sand two meters away from the door, down to at least floor level. In order to do this, the first dozer would line up with the right edge of the blade along the hangar door, angle it outward thirty degrees, dip it down ten degrees, then press forward. The second dozer would do the same thing about one meter from the wall, and about five meters behind the first dozer, helping to push the sand away to the two meter width. Where the door ended and rock began to jut outward, they would turn away, lift their blades up and come back for another pass.

Chris was already on the ground, and Jessica maneuvered to follow. As she rolled down the ramp, Chris began his first pass, lined up with the wall and accumulating sand. Jessica lined her own dozer up about one meter parallel to the wall, paused at the bottom to give Chris five meters of clearance, then throttled forward while dipping the blade down. The machine responded well, and she began to push the pile Chris created further away from the door.

While Sophie had been right—this was a low-risk job—Jessica was more worried about the fact that she had asked them to do it at all. The complex had six working robots and this was a job within their range of duties. The fact that two hybrids were filling their role meant those robots must be in bad shape. Jessica knew they were already running on a thin margin with just six robots, what might happen if that number dropped? Not much, she thought to herself. Life would go on, a little bit harder than it was right now, but such was the norm in the Resistance.

Even knowing its strength was rising, Jessica did not know how large the Resistance was or how many people called themselves members. She only knew the members in their group; a group she had been with for almost twenty years. Twenty years was a long time for a small cell to remain active, let alone effective, yet they managed to be both of those things. And if things kept going they way they were going, they would only get more active and more effective.

The Puritans faced a self-made crisis, as they could not seem to make up their minds about robots. While their original revolution was aimed squarely at the Feelers and hybrids, many normal robots got caught in the crossfire. And since their revolution left such an enormous toll on Earth and the colonies, the only way to save the pure humans was with the help of these same robots.

To make matters worse, the Puritans suspected many of the remaining robots were agents of the Feelers, or Feelers themselves, hiding in plain sight as spies. In most cases, the line between a regular robot and a Feeler was not well defined, and these advanced machines usually had some rudimentary human qualities. But if a robot exhibited anything that was deemed too humanlike, it was destroyed.

And so here they were, the robots more useful now than they had been before the revolution, yet every day, hundreds were destroyed for saying or doing something too human. Of course, the less robots there were to repair the damage caused by the revolution, the longer chaos reigned. It was this feedback loop of chaos that gave the Resistance its strength, that allowed them to fight back against the Puritans.

Still, despite the hole the Puritans continued to dig themselves into, the Resistance was not on the cusp of victory. Not yet. As strong as they were, they were hiding in abandoned bunkers hundreds of kilometers from major cities, running off secondhand equipment and rationing their food. But based on what Jessica knew of the outside world, of the complex events going on on Mars and throughout the system, it looked like the tide might be turning. Given the circumstances, she remained hopeful, holding onto every piece of good news she could get.

In the end, it was not the robots or even the Feelers that suffered the most in these times. No, the metal beings were considered pure, though the wrong kind of pure. According to the Puritans, better to be the wrong kind of pure than impure.

Hybrids could not hide in plain sight. Hybrids were not destroyed on sight. Hybrids were rounded up and 'realigned'—the Puritan term for the process that changed them into slaves. This was the Puritan's answer to their crisis, trying to augment their workforce with those they considered subhuman. Some of these slaves were chosen to continue the cycle, to do the dirty work for the Puritans. At this train of thought, Jessica's mind wandered toward a dark place, toward a nightmare she didn't want to experience…

A loud creak caught her attention, and Jessica looked up to see the door move about a meter then stop. Someone was trying to open the hangar…

Someone was trying to open the hangar! Chris punched the throttle, and Jessica maneuvered herself next to the door rather than one meter away. Two meters of clearance was no longer important—they needed to get this door open immediately.

As she made her way along the door, she saw it struggle against the sand, moving a few slow centimeters then stopping again. Each pass took them just over two minutes, and Jessica knew they would need to finish a few more to get the door free. But how many minutes until the Puritan patrol arrived?

She ignored these thoughts and continued her mission. Long as it might take, the sand needed to be moved. It was the only way they could evacuate. Toward the end of the pass, she saw the door slide once more, managing just over a meter before coming to a halt. Chris made a sharp u-turn, and Jessica watched as he reversed his blade angle—he was going to come back the opposite direction.

She veered away from the door to make room and lifted her own blade, reversing its angle while she turned the machine around. She lined up with the door on the left, dipped the blade down, and punched the throttle.

As they approached the front end, Jessica saw two individuals pushing against the edge of the door, trying to get it to move. For a moment she wondered what sort of desperation had gotten into them when she realized they must also be hybrids. With that strength, they might actually make a difference.

As if to confirm her assessment, the door started to move once more, struggling against the sand. It was slow progress, but this time it did not stop. Chris reached the edge of the door and made another sharp u-turn, repeating his blade flip. He pointed at her and then back at the garage, and she understood. It was time to pack it in and get her son—Chris would finish up out here.

The dozer struggled up the metal ramp, and Jessica punched the throttle a third time. When she cleared the top she hit the brakes, jerking forward as the machine came to a stop. A quick glance let her know there was enough room for Chris to get in and park, and she turned off the machine and hopped out.

How much time did they have left?

She leapt out of the garage and landed in the sand below, then sprinted through the open hangar door. If there was ever a time to take advantage of her hybrid system, it was now.

Inside, dozens of people were running about, prepping the shuttles for launch. She ripped off her helmet as she approached a familiar face, someone who lived in the same hall.

"Is Julian here?"

The woman's eyes went wide.

"Claire said she looked and he wasn't in the room, we thought he was with you."

A panic came over her but she shut her eyes to shut it down, then dropped the helmet and sprinted toward the closest hall. Several people were running into the auxiliary hangar, and Jessica could hear voices shouting all around. She ran against the current, her hybrid system augmenting her speed.

Toward the end of the hall, the crowd cleared, and she sprinted into the empty main hangar, through her empty hall, and pushed open her door.

"Julian?"

But the room was empty. She took a step back into the hall and looked both directions.

"Julian!?"

The sound of running footsteps coming from the main hangar caught her attention and she turned to see a man with a weapon in one arm.

"What are you doing? You need to be at the shuttle!"

"My son, he's not here…"

"He's probably at the shuttle. You need to go, now!"

She took one last look around the room then sprinted past the man, back the way she had come. This was the issue with no wireless communication. Panic led to confusion, and confusion led to accidents. The man was almost certainly right: Julian was at the shuttles, she just hadn't seen him because he had already boarded.

She raced through the final hall, back into the auxiliary hangar. The door was open now, and only a few people remained on the ground.

"Jessica? What are you doing?"

Chris was standing by one of the shuttles, and she rushed to him.

"I can't find Julian, I don't know if he's on a shuttle."

He jumped up the shuttle ramp and Jessica ran to another one.

"Is Julian in there?" she asked as she came up the ramp, scanning the interior.

No Julian. She went back down and glanced at Chris who shook his head, then each of them made for another shuttle. As she approached the next ship, its ramp began to lift and she grabbed the edge to stop it.

"Hey! What are you doing!?"

A man looked down from the interior.

"Is Julian up there?"

He turned around and scanned the shuttle.

"No, he's not here."

She let the ramp go and turned to Chris. He shook his head once more. Four shuttles down, three to go, and she felt the cold panic returning. On her way to the next shuttle, a woman came down the ramp.

"You're looking for Julian?"

A ray of hope took hold.

"Yes, is he—"

But the woman was already shaking her head. Jessica turned to look at Chris, and she saw him come down the ramp and shake his head for a third time.

One shuttle left. She ran to it, up the ramp, and looked around the inside at the passengers. Each one of them was familiar, most of them people she had known for almost twenty years. But her son was not among them.

Chris read her expression as she came back down the ramp.

"You checked your room?"

"He wasn't there…"

It was in that moment that Jessica remembered the last time she had gotten truly mad at Julian: when he had decided to take an excursion into the complex's unfinished sections, the maze of tight passageways built deep into the rock. He had only done it once, the one time she had left him alone for longer than usual, when he knew she might not be back for a while…

"Oh no…"

Before Chris could ask, Jessica was sprinting out of the auxiliary hangar and into the hall. She was so focused on her goal that she barely noticed the man in the hall, or his arm coming up. Her chest slammed into it and she came to a halt.

"What do you think you're doing? The main hangar is about to open!"

It was the same man from before, weapon still in hand.

"Her son is still out there."

Chris was behind her, and the man looked at him, then dropped his arm.

"The shuttles leave now. I will keep one for two more minutes. Hurry."

Jessica took off down the hall, into the main hangar.

"Not you, just her."

She heard Chris beginning to argue but their voices faded as she passed through the main hangar. There was an unfinished section attached to their hallway, and this was the likely entrance point for her son. She stopped just short of the small opening carved into the rock.

"Julian!?"

There was a moment of silence where she could hear her own heartbeat, and she wondered what she would do if he wasn't here.

"Mom!?"

Relief flooded her system at the sound of his voice.

"Julian, where are you? We need to get out of here!"

"Help me, mom!"

She stepped into the corridor, ducking her head down.

"Where are you Julian?"

The passageways were pitch black, and the last time she had searched for Julian she had to enlist the help of a hybrid. But today, she could see very well. Why did her son come down here?

"Over here, mom!"

She followed the sound of his voice, weaving in and out of the small rocky passages. He was close now, only a few more turns...

The sound of a large machine starting up, its massive gears turning, stopped her in her tracks. The main hangar door was opening—the patrol was here.

"Julian?!"

"Mom!"

Jessica hurried through the tiny hall, bouncing off the rocky walls until she came around a corner and saw him, crouched on the ground.

"Julian…"

She swooped down and grabbed him, pulling him against her chest.

"Hold on tight."

With Julian strapped to her front, she turned around and began the walk back, moving as quick as she could in the cramped space, the sound of the opening hangar door echoing through the darkness.

They reached the hall and she took off toward the main hangar, hoping there was still time, hoping their two minutes weren't up yet.

She accelerated as they reached the end of the hall and entered the main hangar. Her eyes focused on the hallway to the auxiliary hangar, the hallway to freedom, thirty meters ahead. As she sprinted across the expanse she looked to the left and saw that the patrol was already inside, two ships already on the ground, several individuals already in the hangar.

One of those individuals reacted faster than a human, lifting its weapon and firing into her line of escape. The dart moved too quickly for her to dodge, and she threw Julian to the ground just as the sharp end punctured her back and she plunged out of consciousness.

- - -

Jessica woke on a bed in a glass tube, locked into her body. Every one of her voluntary muscle fibers was unresponsive, except those of her head and neck. After a cursory check to verify that her interface was missing, the despair began to take root.

"Hello, Jessica."

Her eyes met a man's, standing over her tube with a tablet in hand.

"How are you feeling?"

She wanted to scream, to tell him to let her go, but she could only watch him, smiling down at her.

"Not very talkative today, are we?"

He glanced at his tablet and Jessica felt the rage mounting inside of her.

"Oh, not very happy either. Let's change that, shall we?"

She saw him make a motion on his device and her anger melted away, replaced by an artificial calm. Even as she felt the tension in her mind release, a part of her knew this wasn't real, knew not to trust it. But after a moment, even that part of her started to fade.

"Don't fight it Jessica, happiness is a rare gift, something to accept with gratitude."

Now she found herself smiling back, so content that she did not question her newfound ability to smile.

"See? Isn't that better?"

She nodded in agreement, her eyes starting to close on their own. It was such a lovely feeling, she hadn't felt this happy since—

Then it all came crashing down. She realized where she was and what was happening, and she tried to scream but the sound was cut short, as if someone had muted her vocal cords. She turned to see the man glaring at her, acute disdain in his eyes.

"Now you listen very carefully, Jessica. You are mine now. You do what I say, when I say it. Freedom is a thing of the past, something you will never experience again."

His words were harsh, menacing, but Jessica resisted, thrashing about. She was only able to move her head, her mouth, and her lips, though it felt like she was using every muscle in her body. Even though she was unable to make any noise, it felt like she was screaming with all her might.

The man watched her struggle, disdain shifting to boredom.

"Your insubordination will bring you nothing but pain."

He pressed a button on his tablet.

There was a moment of clarity as Jessica realized what was about to occur, then reality wiped itself away and she descended into darkness, into the depths of insurmountable despair. She felt a blackness like no other— a lack of happiness so certain, she knew it would last forever. Her existence was suffering, there was nothing else. And then, as quick as it had taken over, it let her go, sending her crashing back into reality.

She gasped for air as her surroundings came back into focus, and the man laughed.

"You hybrids, always so stubborn."

Regaining her bearings, she met the man's stare once more. The rage continued to bubble under the surface, but it was tempered with a deep and primal fear. The darkness she had just experienced... she never wanted to live through that again.

"We're going to attempt a civilized conversation now, do you think you can handle that?"

She felt a spike of anger at his condescending tone, but Jessica nodded in response. The man hesitated, eyeing her suspiciously, then made a gesture on his device.

"Now, Jessica, are you ready to cooperate?"

"Yes, where is my son?"

The man frowned before responding.

"You ask about him now, when moments ago you were content to forget him?"

Guilt mixed with anger, but Jessica bit her tongue.

"May I know where he is and how he's doing?"

The man waved his hand dismissively.

"He's fine, don't worry. He's alive and well, in our care. And as long as you play along, he'll stay that way."

"Can I see him?"

Now it was the man who showed a hint of anger.

"Careful, Jessica, lest you overstep your boundaries. We have more pressing issues to attend to."

The man paused with a smirk, and Jessica knew he was hoping to elicit a reaction. But despite the fury welling up inside her, she managed to keep her composure.

"Of course."

A flash of disappointment in the man's eyes marked Jessica's first victory, and she relished his hesitation.

"Right... Jessica, we have watched the video feed of your chronicle, which provided valuable intelligence."

Guilt came over her, completely erasing her fleeting victory. They had access to her chronicle, her entire life from her conversion onward... the details of the complex, each member of their group... all of that information was now in their hands.

The man noted her change in demeanor and smiled.

"Ah yes, we thank you for that keen insight into the life of a terrorist. We're also glad to see some new faces on there, faces we will keep an eye out for."

The Resistance had found a way to artificially mimic the wireless signals emitted by enslaved hybrids, effectively allowing them to blend in. But Jessica's chronicle had rendered that workaround useless for all of her group's agents: all of their faces were now uploaded throughout the Puritan network so that every robot and realigned hybrid could identify them.

"Of course, there is one piece of information missing, Jessica, likely because your conversion was so recent..."

The man looked her up and down.

"To think, two weeks ago that dart would have been no more than a minor annoyance, and you might have slipped by us. And even if you hadn't, you'd be sitting in a jail cell right now, awaiting trial with the full rights and protections afforded to humans."

The man shook his head in disappointment.

"But I digress."

He leaned over, his face centimeters away from the glass.

"Where is the evacuation site, Jessica? Where did all of your friends go?"

The man was so close, less than a meter away... Jessica could not hold herself back any longer. She tried to jump at him, screaming in rage, but her muscles refused to listen, ignoring her commands, and two seconds in, the man pressed something on his tablet, silencing her screams.

"Oh, Jessica."

As the adrenaline waned, fear took over, and her eyes locked on the man's right hand, hovering over the tablet. She knew it took just one swipe to send her into utter and infinite anguish, a darkness she never wanted to experience again.

"You lied to me. You told me we could have a civilized conversation, but look at you—thrashing about like an animal. Are you an animal, Jessica? You certainly aren't human."

The man looked down on her with disdain, his eyes moving from her body to his hand and back. She tried to protest, to beg for mercy, but her ability to speak had been revoked.

"I'm going to make myself clear one more time, and you're going to listen because I'm tired of wasting my time... Look at me when I am speaking to you!"

Her eyes jumped to his, the harshness in his tone only adding to her fear.

"You are going to tell me where your friends escaped or you will never see your son again, is that clear?"

She saw the hate in his eyes and knew the weight of his demand, but part of her hesitated. She still didn't know where her son was. It was true if they had caught him, he would be safe: he was a pure human after all, and the Puritans would not harm someone they considered one of their own. But how could she trust he was in their captivity?

Laying there, her voice muted and her muscles locked, she had no choice. She nodded.

"Good."

The man stood up with a smile, all of the harshness gone from his tone. He took a glance at his tablet and pressed its screen.

"Go ahead, tell me where they went."

Jessica thought back to her last evacuation, the run to the shuttles, the quick take off...

"I don't know the exact location, but I can describe it."

It was a weak lie, but it was worth a try. Her main job at this point was to stall for time—if she was lucky she might stall enough that her friends would be gone from site B by the time they pulled the location out of her. But with the main complex compromised, Jessica had no idea how long it would take her group to find a new home.

The man frowned, and Jessica felt the fear returning.

"You don't know the exact location?"

His hand hovered over the tablet and she tensed.

"You're lying to me again, Jessica. Look at me!"

Again her eyes jumped to his, and she saw a cloud of anger come over his expression.

"If you do not know the location, you are of no use to me. So tell me Jessica, do you or do you not know the exact location?"

The anger deepened, and Jessica felt a visceral fear. His hand was hovering over the tablet, and she knew what he was capable of.

"Yes."

It was barely a whisper, but the man heard her confession, and the anger disappeared. As she felt another wave of guilt at her admission, he smiled.

"Well done! That wasn't so hard, was it?"

She wanted to lash out again, to break through the glass and rip him in half, but all she could do was feel the rage boiling within her, tempered by the fear of the darkness. Was this her life now?

"Well, we've wasted enough time here I think, so let me tell you what's going to happen next. We're going to place you in a personal shuttle in your old auxiliary hangar—that's right, where you and your terrorist friends used to live. Since you know the flight plan, you will pilot that shuttle to the evacuation location. We will be communicating with you and monitoring your chronicle feed at all times. If you lead us there, you will be given your freedom, and your son. If not, you will plunge into an eternal darkness until you don't remember your son's existence."

The man leaned next to the glass once more.

"And trust me, Jessica, that won't take very long once you're down there."

Then he pressed another button and she fell out of consciousness.

- - -

Jessica felt cold metal underneath her and shot up with a shiver. She was in a ship, a one-person shuttle, seated on the floor a few meters from the cockpit. But more importantly, she could move—her arms, her head, her entire body. Everything was back under her control.

"Hello, Jessica."

A chill shot through her spine at the sound his voice, but she didn't look around for the source—those words came from inside her head, not inside the shuttle.

"Get in the chair."

She closed her eyes and saw her interface, modified but present. A quick glance around the options let her know that most of her controls were present, though she wasn't sure how many had been—

"In the chair, Jessica."

The words were accompanied by a swift and sharp dose of pain, as if the entirety of her skin were suddenly on fire. The sensation vanished just as quickly as it appeared.

A fury built up inside her, but she bit her tongue and got to her feet. They were controlling her remotely, the man no doubt standing somewhere well out of her reach, the tablet still in his hand. And she knew what that meant.

She took two steps forward and sat in the pilot's seat. As long as he stuck to that fiery pain, she didn't mind. It hurt, but it was nothing like the darkness...

"Look familiar?"

As the man asked his question, Jessica peered out the window and realized she was back in the complex, parked in the auxiliary hangar.

Twenty meters ahead was the open hangar door, and she could still see the piles of sand her and Chris had pushed aside with the sand dozers.

"Now get moving."

She stared at the controls in front of her.

"I don't know how to pilot this shuttle."

This was a more blatant lie, but every second she bought was a second

—

Before she could finish the thought, she felt panic seize her, and her mind plunged into unimaginable terror. Her memories danced around her, fading into nothingness, and she knew she would never remember Henrique, never remember Julian. It would all disappear forever. She could almost feel her sense of reality ripping into millions of pieces of suffering and pain…

And then she was back in the seat, trying to catch her breath while a harsh voice sounded off in her mind.

"Do not lie to me, Jessica. Why would you know a flight plan if you did not know how to pilot? Even if you didn't, we could upload that information for you. You are trying to waste my time, and I don't appreciate it. I'm giving you twenty minutes. If you're not at the location of your friends in twenty minutes, you'll fall into that same darkness and never come out. Do not test me, Jessica."

Jessica could feel the sweat on her body, and though the shuttle was warm, she realized she was shivering. The darkness… she could not go back there again.

She activated the craft and it powered up immediately, slight vibrations from the engine letting her know it was ready to fly. But as her finger hovered over the input, she hesitated.

Twenty minutes. Of course the man knew any escape point needed to be within a viable distance, and he was right—she could reach site B within twenty minutes. Ten even. But she could not go to site B. If she went to site B, her friends would be caught, each one of them realigned and enslaved just like her. But if she didn't listen to the man's orders, she would fall back into the darkness...

Another wave of searing pain came over her, blinding her for several seconds. It ended just as abruptly as it had began, and Jessica found herself catching her breath once more. It was frightening how much worse an extra few seconds could be... but still, she was relieved he had chosen this punishment rather than the other.

"Enough, let's go."

She plugged into the shuttle and lifted it with her mind, flying out the auxiliary hangar door. The sun was setting off to her left, an odd beacon of blue in a sea of red. She never did like the Martian sunset, though Henrique thought it was beautiful...

Henrique. He was the reason she knew this flight path in the first place. He thought it was a good idea, just in case anything ever happened. Now look where it led them. But she couldn't blame him, he could not predict this scenario, he didn't know she would convert, didn't know she'd be realigned...

Henrique. If only he were still with them, none of this nightmare would have happened. They would be a family of three, on the run but happy. Now Jessica wasn't sure she would ever experience happiness again —certainly not the real thing.

She was piloting the shuttle just slightly off course, giving her enough room to protect her friends if she changed her mind. But every time she thought about saving them, she felt the encroaching darkness, the pure and infinite hopelessness that would define her reality.

Her mind raced to find a solution, but every road was a dead end. If she went anywhere other than site B, she would be sent into the unending shadow. She thought about ways to alert them of her presence, but she didn't know where and how site B's proximity sensors were set up. She could only hope they were set up well enough and far enough to give them enough time to escape.

In the back of her mind, she began to accept the reality of the situation. The best she could do was extend the flight time to her allotted twenty minutes. After that, she was going to land at site B.

Guilt washed over Jessica and she started to cry. So many times she had wondered how the Puritans enslaved the hybrids. She had heard they controlled emotions, controlled hormones, but deep down, she assumed her captured brethren were weak. She told herself if it ever happened to her, she would never betray the Resistance. Surely the human spirit cannot be so thoroughly controlled…

The tears poured down her face, and though she expected the man to punish her, to make some snide remark, the voice in her head was silent. The only noise was the sound of the shuttle's engine, a soft hum in the background as she approached site B.

"Five minutes, Jessica."

She didn't need the reminder. Already she was correcting course, curving back the way she should have gone. Their faces came to her, all of her friends, the people she had known for almost twenty years… most of them would experience the same darkness just because she feared it so much.

The guilt was overwhelming, almost unbearable, but the thought of returning to the depths of blackness kept her moving forward, dropping altitude as the distance shortened. Two minutes and she'd be landing. Two minutes and they'd be caught.

Unless they had already escaped… a ray of hope came into her mind and she grasped it, unwilling to let go. How long had it been since she had been captured? A quick check of her modified interface showed no date or time, but she knew the realignment must have given them a head start. The question was, how much? A day? Maybe two? Would that be enough time to find a new location with their main complex compromised?

There it was—a compact building built into the side of a crater nearly covered in sand. Only a small entrance was exposed to the outside world, and Jessica could already make out the parked shuttles, covered in red tarps to camouflage their presence from above. If you didn't know where to look, site B was quite difficult to find—an ideal quality, now lost forever.

Jessica peered in vain for any signs of life. Were her friends still there? If they were, did they see the incoming shuttle?

As if to answer her thoughts, the small entrance swung open, and Jessica watched a stream of people pour out, sprinting at hybrid speed toward the covered shuttles.

"We'll take it from here."

As the man's words sounded off in her mind, several other shuttles emerged from behind her, converging on the crater site. Before she could process what was about to unfold, it had already begun, and she watched in horror as the Puritan forces unleashed explosive charges on the escape craft, blasting several hybrids in the process.

She tried to steer the shuttle into one of the attackers, but the craft was unresponsive.

"I said we'll take it from here."

She screamed at the smug voice in her head as more shuttles exploded below, the evacuating hybrids scattering in every direction, unsure of where to go or what to do. Some ran back into the building while others ran off toward the crater walls, and as the final shuttle lit up in a ball of fire, the Puritan craft began to touch ground.

At that moment her own shuttle started its descent, but it moved slowly, giving her time to watch the chaos below. Puritan agents—other realigned hybrids—were exiting the shuttles with EMP weapons, firing on the men and women below. She could hear the screams now, her ship only ten meters above the ground, preparing to land.

Then her eyes were forced shut and she faced no interface, only blackness.

"Now listen carefully, Jessica. Do not forget who you belong to. You are mine now. You will follow every order I give you. If you deviate in any manner or attempt to interfere in our operation, you will fall into eternal darkness. And lest I remind you, Jessica, if you fall into that darkness, you will never know your son. Do you understand?"

The man paused his speech and Jessica could feel the shuttle coming to a hover. She tried to open her eyes, to see the situation below, but her body was not under her own control.

"Do you understand?"

There was a foreboding anger in his tone that washed away all thought of her surroundings and reminded her only of the darkness. He was right. She was his now.

"Yes, I understand."

Her eyes opened and she heard the whirr of machinery behind her: the exit ramp was lowering.

"Leave the pilot seat."

She did as ordered, walking to the ramp, now extended into the sand below. A quick movement to her right startled her—a small cabinet opening in the side wall.

"Grab the pistol."

She pulled an EMP pistol out of the cabinet and stared at the small device.

"Leave the shuttle and continue toward the site. If you encounter any hybrids not aligned with our cause, you are to eliminate them at once."

Jessica barely paid attention to his words, staring at the pistol in her hands. An EMP shutdown was a traumatic event for the hybrid system, and fatal if not treated quickly. Her body had already survived one, but a second one, this soon after the first? If she shot herself, she may not wake up again…

She started down the ramp, adrenaline coursing through her veins. While ending her life seemed to be the only path to freedom, there was one thing keeping her from pulling the trigger: Julian. She still had no idea where he was, how he was doing. She didn't even know if he was alive.

Jessica suppressed that thought as best as she could, taking in her surroundings. Smoke and debris were scattered across the crater bed as

Puritan agents sprinted in every direction, firing at the evacuees then carrying them aboard. It was a massacre. And it was her fault.

"Move!"

The order was sharp and clear, and she started walking toward the entrance. But as she moved forward, watching chaos unfold around her, she could only think of the weight of the gun in her hand.

A scream to her left caught her attention, and she saw a body writhing in the rubble of one of the shuttles. Her face was disfigured, bloodied and mangled beyond recognition, but Jessica knew the voice. This was her former neighbor, someone who had babysat Julian a number of times...

"Shoot her."

She stopped in her tracks, eyes locked on the woman, the pistol still heavy in her hand. She could not shoot this woman. She would not shoot this woman.

But right as she made up her mind, reality wiped itself away and Jessica descended into the darkness, into the depths of insurmountable despair. Her existence was suffering, there was nothing else. Though this was not the first time, it never got any easier—if anything, it got worse. Time itself seemed to drag on infinitely, unwilling to end her pain, reminding her of the futility of her existence.

And then, as quick as it had taken over, it let her go, sending her crashing back into reality.

She collapsed to the ground, the EMP pistol falling out of her hand. She gasped for air, a dull pounding in her head blurring her senses. This was too much. What was this nightmare, this living hell?

"Shoot her, now!"

The voice was harsher, more insistent. Worst of all, it was more persuasive.

Jessica grabbed the pistol and stood, aiming at the woman. She tossed and moaned in the burning remains of the shuttle, crying out in agony. This would help her, Jessica told herself. This would ease the pain. And she fired.

The dart hit the woman in the chest and she broke into violent convulsions, throwing debris in all directions and forcing Jessica to duck out of the way. A few seconds later, she stopped, unmoving. The deed was done.

"Well done, Jessica."

This time, the words were accompanied by a tremendous feeling of accomplishment and joy—so jarring and overwhelming that Jessica had no time to fight it, and the way these emotions felt after her brief dip into darkness just moments ago... it was the best feeling she had ever felt in her life, period. Better than any moment with Henrique, better than any moment with Julian...

Then, like the darkness, it disappeared, and Jessica felt a horrible loss as it left.

"No..."

"Don't worry, Jessica. You can have some more. Go inside the complex."

The man didn't have to tell her twice. She took off at a run toward the entrance, impatient to return to that high, willing to do whatever it took to feel that way once more. For the time being she forgot all about where she was and what she was doing, and all that mattered was the mission, all that mattered was what the man said. Because if she did what he said, she would be happy again.

She ran through the entrance with her pistol raised, then paused at the front of the hallway. She felt her left arm twitch as memories flashed before her: of Julian, of Chris, of that woman, the woman she had just killed...

"Keep moving."

The voice brought her back to the matter at hand and she continued forward, into the building. She knew where to go—to her emergency hiding place. Someone would probably be in there, and then she could be happy.

There were other hybrid agents inside, passing her in the hall, carrying familiar faces: some silent and unmoving, others active and resistant. What would happen to those pure humans that were caught, she wondered. What had happened to Julian?

Each time she saw one of these faces, she felt a sadness in the back of her mind, a small but present voice trying to tell her to turn around, to stop what she was doing. But that voice was but a weak whisper against the urgent need to feel happy once more.

She reached the room she was looking for and stepped inside. Items were scattered all over the place, thrown about in disarray, but Jessica only cared about one thing: the pattern on the back wall. Vertical lines were etched into the metal, dozens of them running from the floor to the ceiling mere centimeters apart. Two of those lines were non-decorative, however. Two of those lines marked the edges of a hidden compartment.

Jessica stood in front of the wall, excitement coming over her. The other Puritan agents didn't know about this place, she was sure of it. She pressed the panel upward and it disconnected, opening upward to reveal three individuals inside: Chris and two children, old friends of Julian.

"Jessica…"

The shock in his eyes turned to fear as he watched her raise the pistol.

"No, Jessica, what are you—"

There was a sadness in his eyes when she pulled the trigger, and the children screamed, running out of the compartment as Chris fell into convulsions.

In that moment, Jessica realized that Chris could have defended himself, could have overpowered her with ease, but he had trusted her for one precious second, and it had cost him his life. Before the man could reward her, she turned the pistol on herself and fired a dart directly into her chest.

- - -

Jessica woke on a bed in a glass tube, calm and content. There was a part of her that recognized her surroundings and tried to protest, to cry out in alarm, but that part of her was indiscernible under her blanket of satisfaction.

"Hello, Jessica."

She felt a small twitch at the wrist in response to the man's voice, an involuntary expression of her deepest objections, but she knew she must ignore it.

"Hel—hello."

When her eyes met his, her brain screamed a flash of agony—too fast for her to register outwardly, but slow enough that she noticed it.

"How are you feeling?"

Two twitches, left wrist.

"G—good."

The man smiled and the scream came back, slightly longer this time. She shot her eyes away, glancing at the tablet in his hand.

"Do you know what happened?"

Suddenly her eyes closed against her will and she saw her own chronicle, replaying the last recorded minute. The endorphins had stopped, as had her feelings of comfort. She was back in the room, Chris's body convulsing in front of her, an EMP pistol in her hand. She turned it toward herself, toward her own chest, and pulled the trigger. The dart punctured her breast and she collapsed to the ground unconscious.

Her eyes reopened in the tube, and she felt the warmth returning, felt the happiness coming back. She knew the man was looking at her but she hesitated—she needed more of the hormones before she could look him in the eye.

"That was a very bad thing you did, Jessica."

He was shaking his finger at her, as if she were a child. The gesture gave her a sudden urge to attack him, to rip his face into pieces. But like the scream of agony, this feeling disappeared instantaneously, overcome by the steady flow of contentedness.

"I have someone here I want you to see."

He brought his arm up, pointing to her right, and Jessica turned to see a bed much like hers, without the glass tube around it. On this bed was a small boy of eight, fast asleep.

"Julian..."

The sight of her son gave her a window of clarity in the fog, and relief washed over her, mixed with the sense of comfort. He was alive...

Part of her, deep in the back of her mind, wondered why he was here, why he was asleep... but that part of her was the same part of her that had tried to cry out in alarm—nothing more than a shadow of a whisper.

"You made a mistake out there, Jessica, and now you must be punished."

She shifted her attention to the man, who stared down at her son with disdain. There was something repulsive in that look, and the shadow of a whisper gained some strength, a seed of dread taking root in her mind.

"Since you will not do as you are told, perhaps your son will?"

A smile spread across his face and the man leaned forward, next to her tube.

"We're going to convert and realign your son and see if he follows directions better than his mom, how does that sound to you?"

The haze of comfort was all but gone now, and Jessica cried out, trying to stand, to get up and break free. But her body only twitched in response, small but violent movements all over. The man with the tablet controlled her now—he decided which of her muscles did and didn't work.

He watched her helpless struggle and smiled.

"You really are a stubborn bitch, you know that?"

Jessica had never felt such unadulterated rage. The man placed his face even closer to her tube, and her body twitched violently as it resisted the urge to murder this monster.

"You killed yourself and now your son is paying the price. Think on that."

The man stood, glancing down at his tablet before glancing back at her.

"Or don't."

And all of her rage, all of her despair, was wiped away with an unnatural dose of positivity, erasing her thoughts and dropping Jessica back into a state of calm contentedness. Only a slight twitch of her right wrist interrupted her steady escape from consciousness on the river of fake euphoria.

- - -

Jessica was standing on Mars again, surrounded by the red sand she had known her whole life. But it wasn't just sand—there was also fire, fire all around her. It lashed out in her direction, beckoning her to enter. She saw someone was already in the fire: the woman, her neighbor, burnt beyond recognition, yet Jessica recognized her. She was crying out in agony, but the only sound Jessica could hear was the fire closing in on her. It was almost on her now, the flames licking at her, and she tried to turn away, to find a way out, but there was no escape. She knew the end was near, knew that death had her. Then the woman reached out of the fire and grabbed her.

"Hello? Can you hear me?"

Jessica's eyes shot open. She wasn't on Mars, she was on a bed in a small room. She wasn't surrounded by fire, she was surrounded by monitors and instruments. There was no woman, but an unfamiliar man with an unfamiliar face stood over her, peering down at her curiously.

"Can you hear me?"

She stared at the man for a moment, then tried to sit up. But most of her muscles refused to answer the call, and she barely managed to lift her head before she had to give up.

"Whoa now, try to relax!"

She noticed several cables running from behind her neck to the various machines surrounding her and eyed the man with suspicion. What was this game?

"Where am I?"

At her words, the man stood up straight and smiled.

"You're safe now, don't worry."

She moved her head to the side and saw a window set in the wall to her right, behind the man and the devices. Outside was the blackness of space, sprinkled with the lights of thousands of stars, drifting slowly toward the right.

"We're in space?"

He nodded, his smile widening.

"Where's Julian?"

"You son? Don't worry, he's also aboard. I took care of everything."

These words only increased her suspicion, and she eyed the man warily.

"Who are you?"

He met her gaze for several long seconds, with only the beeps of the machinery around her bed interrupting the silence. Then he frowned, turning toward the window before responding.

"That's not important. What matters is I'm helping you. You and your son."

"What do you mean?"

The man turned around, smiling once more.

"I got you off Mars. We escaped."

She stared at him without responding, and as her gaze lingered, his smile faded.

"Aren't you happy?"

She tried to sit up again, but her body didn't so much as acknowledge her attempt.

"Let me up."

The man looked at her, confused.

"Your system has been through—"

"I don't care what my system has been through, give me control of my damn body so I can see my son!"

She nearly screamed the words at the man, who recoiled at her outburst. He gave her a bewildered look before responding.

"Don't you understand? You can't."

The man's tone was mildly condescending, and Jessica felt the frustration building inside of her.

"What do you mean I can't?"

"Listen, I did what I could. But your system is fried, gone. There was no way to fix it. I already reversed your realignment. That system is one hundred percent yours, just… broken."

He looked her up and down.

"Sorry."

The word was more of an afterthought than a genuine apology, but Jessica ignored it, closing her eyes to check her interface. For the first time since the evacuation of the complex, it was completely functional. But in place of a clean slate, alerts and warnings filled the screen, letting her know of the catastrophic damages in her arms, legs, and torso. The man was right, her system was broken. If she was reading the warnings correctly, she would never walk again.

She opened her eyes.

"Let me see my son."

The man hesitated.

"I don't know if he should see you…"

Again she could feel the frustration building, but she did her best to keep her cool.

"Listen, I don't know who you are, or what is going on. I just want to see my son. I want to see him with my own eyes. Could you do that for me, please?"

Her words were a bit harsher than intended, but as the man gave out a defeated sigh, she knew they had the desired effect.

"Fine. Give me a minute."

The man walked across the room and out a door in the left wall. As soon as he was out of sight, Jessica tried to make out where she was and what was going on. The machinery around her bed… she had been operated on, but by who? By that man? And why? It was true her system was under her control, but where had these catastrophic damages come from? They could have come from the cumulation of her two EMP hits and her realignment, but they could also be some complicated ploy…

"Mom!?"

Jessica whipped her head around and saw Julian run through the door to the side of her bed. By reflex, she tried to sit up and hug him, but all she could do was crane her neck.

"Julian!"

Her eight-year old son gave her a hug then stood, flashing a crooked smile. Jessica took it all in—staring at the crease in his hair, the shape of his nose and lips, his tiny little ears… it felt like she hadn't seen him in years.

"Are you okay, Julian?"

He nodded and pointed at the man, who had walked into the room behind him.

"He saved us."

She looked up and saw him staring at Julian, smiling. There was something familiar about that expression, something she hadn't seen in many years…

"Why did you save us?"

The man looked at her and his smile vanished.

"It… was the right thing to do."

He glanced at Julian as he finished his statement, but Jessica didn't take her eyes off this stranger.

"Mom? Are you okay?"

She turned to see her son staring at the cables coming out of the back of her neck.

"Of course I'm okay, Julian. I get to see you!"

She tried to tussle his hair, but her arm wouldn't leave the bed.

"Why are you in that bed?"

She hesitated.

"I'm hurt, Julian. But I'll be okay."

Julian frowned, looking at her body.

"What about your super legs? When will you get better?"

She shot a glance at the man then back to her son.

"I'm not sure, Julian. It's going to be a while."

Her son gave her another hug.

"I hope you get better fast, mommy."

He let go and Jessica smiled at him once more. She could barely believe it: her son was here, healthy and seemingly safe.

She looked up at the man.

"May I speak with you in private?"

He gave her a curious look then nodded.

"Okay."

The man knelt down next to Julian.

"Okay mister, think you can go back to your room for a bit?"

Julian looked at his mom and Jessica nodded.

"I love you, Julian."

He hugged her a third time.

"I love you too, mom."

He gave her another crooked smile then skipped out the door. After a pause, Jessica addressed the man.

"Why did you save us?"

He stood, giving her an annoyed look.

"I already told you, it was the right thing to do."

The presence of her son had calmed her, but the man's attitude rekindled her frustration.

"That's not an answer. Who are you?"

He threw his hands up in the air and paced to the other side of the room, looking out the window.

"I already told you that too! It doesn't matter!"

"Of course it matters. Where the hell are you taking us?"

He turned to face her, the annoyance replaced by a small smile.

"Ah! Finally, a good question."

He took two large strides and stood at her bedside.

"I'm taking you to Earth."

The smile turned into a grin, but Jessica didn't share the man's excitement.

"Earth? Are you out of your mind?"

His smile vanished.

"No…"

"Why are you taking us to Earth?"

"I'm saving you from the Puritans."

"Earth is controlled by Puritans!"

The man shook his head.

"Yes, but…"

Jessica saw a hint of guilt flash across his expression.

"But what?"

Her tone was strong and clear, and she could see the man wrestling with what to say next.

"This— it wasn't supposed to be like this!"

He threw his hands up into the air once more, then turned to face the window with a huff. Jessica took a deep breath, biting her tongue before she lashed out in impatience. Her system was broken and this man had direct access to Julian—the last thing she wanted to do was anger him. Still, the way he had looked at her son… there was something comforting in that interaction, something that reminded her of Henrique…

"Will you please just tell me why you saved us?"

Her tone was softer this time, pleasant. She watched the man's back and saw his shoulders drop, the tension disappearing. After a moment, she heard his reply—just as soft, just as pleasant.

"Because they wanted to realign your son. And I couldn't live with myself if I let that happen."

At his words, the nightmare came back to her: the man standing with his tablet, staring at her son with disdain. But even in that dreadful moment, she had had trouble believing him. Surely that was an empty threat—Julian was pure, they couldn't convert him...

"That wasn't a bluff?"

The man turned around, and for the first time, Jessica saw gravity in his expression.

"Unfortunately it wasn't. I didn't believe it either, until it was almost too late."

She stared at him for a moment, the beeps of the machinery holding an unwavering rhythm.

"And that's why we're here," she said.

He held her gaze for a few seconds then frowned, shaking his head.

"No, that's why he's here," he answered.

The man turned back to look out the window.

"You're here because he wouldn't leave without you..."

The man sighed.

"There I was with this wonderful plan to take this boy to Earth, to disappear, to save him... to raise him as my own if need be."

At those last few words, his voice cracked, and Jessica knew there was truth to the statement.

"But now you're here, your body is broken, and I don't know what to do."

He turned around and walked over to the side of the bed. Even his growing kindness was oddly distant, and Jessica could see he was still struggling with what to say.

"You're a Puritan, aren't you?"

He smiled a sad smile.

"Not anymore."

She continued to stare at the man, wondering if he would have ever saved her if Julian hadn't insisted. But for the time being, it didn't matter. It was clear his attitude toward her had changed in those last few exchanges, and if they were really heading toward Earth, she could worry about hypotheticals later.

"How much time until we arrive?"

"About two hours."

"What was your original plan?"

"My original plan didn't involve you."

He gave her an apologetic look, and Jessica nodded.

"I understand. What was it?"

"Well, I knew I could get him on this shuttle and make it out undetected. I also knew about a whole lot of no-fly zones on Earth, which is usually code for illegal activity. My plan was to head there, where either they couldn't follow me or would have trouble doing so…"

He looked down at her and shrugged.

"I haven't really had time to think it through, I was just trying to get him out of there as fast as I could. But with you here, things are already looking worse."

"What do you mean?"

"Well, if I had just taken your son, they might have let me go and not even bothered. If I got the story out that they were trying to convert and realign a kid… that wouldn't go over well. But now that I stole a hybrid and reversed her realignment? I'm sure they're already in pursuit, and I don't have a leg to stand on."

If it wasn't for the panic setting in, she might have laughed at the irony of his analogy. As it were, she couldn't help thinking about what might happen if they were caught. Not to this man, not even to her, but to Julian…

"Can they track this shuttle? How safe are we?"

The man's shrug didn't reassure her.

"I can't be sure. I told my robots to make us as undetectable as possible, and they managed to spoof a cargo transponder. That should buy us some time, but I'm sure the Puritans have already sent a squadron after us. Let's just hope they don't find us."

She peered up at him.

"How *did* you get us out of there?"

Part of her was truly curious, but another part of her needed a distraction, something to take her mind off of the situation.

"With a lot of luck."

He pointed toward the door.

"They tried to operate on your son—you know, normally robots do conversions, is that the same way for you people?"

He gave her a curious glance then shook his head.

"Never mind. That's not important. Anyway, of course the robot refused to operate on your son. Converting someone that young is a death sentence, you know how hard it is just to get the robots to do it for someone of age? Anyway, since the robot wouldn't do it, I got called in to do it."

She looked him up and down once more. Who was this man?

"As soon as I realized what was happening, I gave some excuse to buy time, and got my robots to get your son. Your son wanted you to come—no, needed you to come—and, well, I have a bit of a soft spot so I scrambled together a way to get you too."

The man paused, shaking his head.

"That part was not easy. But here we are."

He spread his arms, gesturing at the room.

"They didn't catch you on the escape?"

He shook his head.

"If they did I wouldn't be talking to you. I put together a diversion which seemed to do the trick."

None of what he said was particularly reassuring, but if all of it was true, it meant that at minimum they had a head start. The problem was that this head start was toward Earth.

"What was your plan once you reached the outer atmosphere? Don't they have patrols like on Mars?"

The man nodded.

"They do… I hadn't thought that far ahead, honestly."

He looked up toward the door.

"I just needed to get him out of there."

Again, that look in his eyes. This man truly cared for her son.

"If we get caught, he's going right back over there. Shouldn't we go somewhere else?"

"Where? Luna and the stations all have patrols, and they're much denser. At least with Earth we have a chance of slipping by. If we can sneak into a cargo convoy, maybe—"

"Sir?"

They both turned their heads to see a robot standing in the doorway.

"What is it?"

"We are being intercepted by a Puritan patrol."

Jessica and the man shared a glance.

"How far away?"

"We will reach visual range in 7 minutes."

He turned to Jessica.

"Once they see this shuttle, it's over."

"Can we evade them?" Jessica asked.

The man looked at the robot, who answered her question.

"We can only delay their interception. Based on our current distance and the capabilities of their ships, we cannot permanently evade them at this point."

The man yelled out in frustration and paced to the window. Jessica watched his helpless march while a feeling of dread grew inside of her. The Puritans would catch them, take Julian, convert him, realign him…

"I'm afraid there's only one way out of this."

The man turned to face her, a sadness in his expression that compounded her fear. When he spoke again it was softer, quieter.

"I need to deactivate you, permanently."

For a moment Jessica hesitated, unsure if she understood what she had just heard.

"What?"

He looked back out the window, unable to hold her gaze.

"Listen, the only reason they wanted to convert your son was some vindictive madness. As long as you are alive, they will come after your son."

From a certain point of view, he was right. If the Puritans boarded and she was alive, her son would be converted and realigned. If she was dead, there would be no one to punish, no one to discipline. But there was one hole in his plot.

"Won't they just reactivate me?"

He hesitated, and Jessica felt a creeping suspicion as he searched for the right response.

"With the state your system is in... but you're right. That is why I cannot simply deactivate you, I must also destroy your system. Completely and permanently."

Now Jessica hesitated, unsure how to respond. Was the man right? Was this the only way?

"I'm sure this is a difficult choice, but you need to make it quickly."

She looked at him, still questioning his motives. Clearly the man cared for her son, but it was just as clear he had little motivation to save her. Of course, with a Puritan patrol on their way, he was right: if they took her alive, they would go back to square one, the man with the tablet leaning over her in the glass tube, and some other Puritan realignment technician sent in to operate on Julian...

"How long will it take?"

"To deactivate you? Two minutes, at most."

She nodded.

"Could you bring my son in here?"

"Of course."

He turned to the robot.

"Bring the child."

"Sir, there's something else you may want to know."

"What is it?"

"The patrol is not initiating or responding to any communication."

Jessica glanced from the robot to the man.

"Is that normal?" she asked.

The man hesitated, then shook his head.

"No… but it doesn't matter. We need to act fast. Bring the boy."

Jessica watched the robot exit the room, her thoughts in disarray, trying to make sense of it all. This was happening much too fast. What would she say to her son? What could she say?

"Mom?"

She turned to see him walk in, his smile disappearing when he saw her expression.

"What's wrong, mom?"

He approached her bed slowly, and Jessica fought to suppress the fear and sadness within her. Was this really it? She woke up alive, saved, with her son, and not ten minutes later she had to say goodbye? There had to be another way…

"Julian, I have some bad news."

Her son glanced at the man, but his back was turned to them. There was an anxiety in Julian's demeanor that made her stomach drop, and she could feel the tears welling up already.

"You know how I said I was going to get better?"

She almost choked on the words, a terrible sensation spreading in her chest. It was an aptly named feeling: it really did seem like her heart was breaking.

"Yes, mommy?"

She saw the worry in his eyes and, despite immense restraint, the tears started to flow, pouring freely down her cheeks.

"Well, Julian—"

"Sir, we are in visual range."

The robot's voice crashed into the tension, and both Jessica and Julian turned to the machine.

"There are two developments of immediate interest."

The man turned around, a hint of irritation in his expression.

"What is it?"

"First, the patrol's identifiers do not match their thermal profiles."

Jessica looked at the man, who continued to address the robot.

"What're you saying?"

"Sir, these ships are spoofing their transponders."

"Is anyone here who they say they are?"

The man raised his hands in the air, directing the question at no one in particular. But Jessica, reaching out for any sliver of hope, didn't waste any time. She looked at the robot and asked it directly.

"What else?"

"They are sending us a visual communication."

"A visual communication?"

"Yes, they are flashing their lights in a discernible pattern. We have deciphered it."

"What does it say?"

"Do not evade. Resistance."

The unbridled joy Jessica experienced in that moment rivaled the push of positive hormones she had received from the terrible man with the tablet. She cried out, unable to contain herself, but noticed that the man did not share her excitement. In fact, he was frowning.

Jessica waited for him to speak, but her patience was thin.

"If it's the Resistance we're saved."

He answered without looking at her.

"So it seems…"

Jessica glanced at her son, who was clearly lost on the events surrounding him. The poor boy looked so worried, so confused…

"Begin evasive maneuvers."

"What!?"

Jessica swung her head around to face the man.

"What are you doing!?"

"I can't risk it."

"Can't risk what?"

"It could be a trap."

"A trap? By the Puritans?"

The man nodded, but Jessica felt her frustration cresting.

"Why? Why would they set up such an elaborate trap? They could intercept us and be done with it!"

"Maybe… or maybe they are trying to lull us into a false sense of security…"

"Mommy?"

For the moment, Jessica ignored her son.

"What are you talking about? A false sense of security? That's preposterous!"

"Think about it. They approached us. How did they know where we were?"

"Maybe the Resistance is trying to help us?"

The man gave her a stern look.

"Listen, I'm not doing this for myself. I'm doing this for your son. Tell him what needs to be said."

But Jessica returned his stare, unflinching.

"No, you tell him. You tell him what you think must be done, and why."

The man threw his hands up in the air a third time.

"We don't have time for this nonsense!"

He pointed at the robot.

"You, get the boy out of here."

But Jessica was done with these games. She yelled at the robot as it approached her son.

"No! If you take my boy away, this man will kill me."

The robot hesitated. She had created an indirect connection between its plan of action and her death, and it would not want to be implicated in something that violated its deepest programming.

"Are you trying to break my robot?"

The man marched over to the side of the bed, and Jessica struggled against her broken system in vain, trying to recoil from his aggressive approach.

"No, I'm trying to save my life!"

She turned to face her son and saw the fear in his eyes.

"Julian, I am so sorry. This is all going to be over soon. The Resistance is coming, and they're going to—"

A loud crash cut her off, and the ship reeled to the right, sending Julian and the man tumbling to the floor. Again she tried to jump up—to grab her son and catch his fall—but her body was useless.

"Julian!"

The robot, however, was already in motion—too fast to see with the human eye, but Jessica's vision was better than a human's. She watched it catch her son's fall with one arm and pull the man with another, moving him out of the way as one of the machines crashed to the floor.

"Sir, hull breach reported."

Alarms sounded off around them, and a bright light flashed inside the room, lighting up the interior every two seconds in a deep red hue.

"They're already on us!" the man exclaimed.

Jessica looked at her son, frightened but safe in the robot's arm.

"Julian, are you okay?"

The man scrambled to a stand.

"Get that boy out of here!"

"No! If you leave this room he will kill me!"

Rage filled the man's expression, but before he could respond, the ship reeled a second time, sending them into the robots arms once more. Another two machines fell down, one with cables attached to Jessica, and though she saw the wires rip out of her, she felt no pain.

"Sir, we've been harpooned and they're pulling us in."

Julian wailed.

"Mommy!"

"Get that boy—"

"No, don't let him kill me!"

The man got up and spun to face her, furious.

"Stop this nonsense! His life depends on it!"

Julian's wails clashed with the alarm, creating a horrible backing symphony to their yelled exchange.

"It's the Resistance!" she replied.

The man moved toward another machine but the robot grabbed his shoulder.

"Sir, I cannot allow you to harm this woman."

The man turned to face the robot—his property, his servant—and screamed in fury, pounding his fists against its metal chest. After his short outburst, he turned to Jessica and glared at her with a piercing intensity.

"Whatever happens next is on you."

She held his gaze for a moment then turned to her son.

"Julian, Julian, it's okay."

She tried to reach out and hug him but all she could do was repeat her calming words, hoping they would take root. It was a horrible feeling, not being able to hug and hold her own child as he sat right next to her, crying.

"Sir, they've pulled us in and are cutting the hull."

Jessica could hear the faraway sound of sparks on metal, and for a moment she thought about the man's ridiculous theory. If there was any chance that these were Puritans...

"Julian, come here, give me a hug."

Her son obeyed, still crying. As his arms embraced her she shushed him gently, rubbing her head against his.

"It's going to be okay, Julian. Everything is going to be okay."

A loud clatter went off in the hall—the sound of what used to be part of a ship's hull hitting the ship's floor—then footsteps.

"Sir, we've been boarded."

"Yes I know!"

Julian let go, and everyone eyed the door. Four individuals walked in one after another: three women and a man. They stopped just inside, scanning the interior, then the woman in front addressed them.

"Gregory, Jessica, and Julian?"

Jessica glanced at the man, expecting him to reply, but he kept his back pressed up against the robot, silent.

"Yes," she replied.

The woman met her gaze.

"We're with the Resistance and we're here to provide safe passage. This shuttle will be intercepted by a Puritan patrol in less than ten minutes. We must get you off this ship and onto our own as quickly as possible, do you understand?"

Again, Jessica hesitated, giving the man a chance to reply, but it was clear she needed to take the lead.

"Okay—I can't walk though."

The woman eyed her prone body and the surrounding machinery then turned to a companion.

"Check her condition and see what we can do."

One of the other women walked past the man and his robot and began examining the remaining machinery. The leader turned to the man.

"Gregory, I want to thank you for what you have done for these two, and assure you we mean you no harm. If you come with us, we will provide safe passage to Earth, where you will be free to leave if you so desire. If not, you may stay on this shuttle and await interception by the Puritans."

The woman examining the machinery spoke next.

"We can detach her and carry her in, but her system is in bad shape."

The leader nodded.

"Do it."

Jessica turned to her son, while the other woman removed the last few cables from behind her neck.

"Julian, I want you to stay close to me, okay?"

Her son nodded, then the leader addressed the man once more.

"Gregory, will you come with us?"

As the other woman lifted her off the bed, Jessica noticed the man's fear. Did he think these were still Puritan agents? Did he think this was a test?

After a prolonged silence, the leader sighed.

"So be it."

She turned to leave but Jessica spoke up.

"Wait."

They looked to her and she glanced at the man.

"I won't go without him."

Despite the chaos of the past five minutes, Jessica knew that the man's actions were motivated at least in part by a care for her son—a care beyond what she would expect from a normal individual, let alone a Puritan. It was true, she was embellishing her feelings—she did not trust him fully—but she certainly trusted him more than these four strangers, and she was still stuck in a broken body.

"Jessica, we don't have time to waste. If he doesn't—"

"Please, Gregory."

She ignored the woman, addressing the man directly. There was conflict in his expression, and she wondered why he was so afraid. Even if these were Puritans posing as members of the Resistance, the most punishment he might face would be imprisonment.

The man looked at the boy, sniffling next to his mother, and Jessica saw a softness come over his face. He looked down at the ground, and made the smallest of nods.

"Okay," he replied. "For Julian."

- - -

Four minutes later they were on the other vessel, pulling away at great speed. Jessica had been placed in a new bed and attached to new devices.

Julian and Gregory sat by her side while one of the crew finished setting her up, running new wires into the back of her neck. Gregory's two robots had also joined them, standing against the back wall.

"Okay that should do it."

She turned to face Jessica.

"Looks like your head is in good shape, as are your extremities, but there was a major malfunction in your spinal column that's paralyzing you. When we get back we'll be able to get a better look."

Jessica gave a small nod in reply.

"How did you find us?"

The woman gestured to the door in front of the bed.

"The captain is on her way, she'll explain everything to you."

As if on cue, the woman who led the boarding party walked into the room, nodding at her colleague who walked out the door.

"How are you feeling?"

"Fine, we're fine," Jessica answered.

The woman turned to Gregory, who continued to stare at the floor.

"Gregory, I want to reiterate our commitment to your safety. I understand this was difficult for you—"

"You don't understand a damn thing."

Jessica looked at him, surprised. After a pause, the woman continued.

"You're right, there are many things I don't understand. But I want you to think on your own colleagues and the events that brought you here today. Know that there are bad apples in every bunch."

Jessica looked back to the woman, confused. Did these two know each other?

"Jessica, once we get to Earth we'll try to get you fixed."

The mention of their destination erased her train of thought.

"We're going to Earth?"

The woman nodded reassuringly.

"Don't worry, we're going to the underground. Most of the Resistance is on Earth. In a lot of ways, it's the safest place for hybrids."

She turned to Gregory again.

"Of course, as promised, you have no obligation to follow. We can drop you off anywhere you'd like."

"I'm here to help her with her son. I won't leave unless I know he's safe."

His eyes never left the floor, and after an awkward silence, Jessica spoke up.

"How did you find us?"

"Ah, that's a good question."

This seemed to catch Gregory's attention, and for the first time, he looked up.

"We have a… source of information. We don't know who it is but it's clear they're deep in the Puritan network. They've given us all kinds of intelligence over the years. They were the ones that told us your identities, your escape plan… they even guessed more or less where we would find you, and this was many hours ago."

A flash of concern crossed Gregory's expression, then his eyes dropped back to the ground.

"You don't know this source?" Jessica asked.

The woman shook her head.

"They keep themselves incredibly well-hidden, but their track record is perfect. Everything they have given us has proven true, and extremely useful. When they told us there was a realignment surgeon defecting with a hybrid and her son, we jumped on the opportunity."

Jessica glanced at Gregory, but his eyes were locked back on the floor.

"Well, thank you again for saving us."

"Of course. Is there anything else any of you need?"

Jessica frowned. There was something she wanted to ask, but a part of her already knew the answer. She glanced at Julian and shook her head.

"No, thank you."

There was no need to bring up their friends on Mars while he was in the room.

"If you need anything just let us know."

She gave Jessica one last smile then walked out the door. As soon as she was out of sight, Jessica turned to Gregory.

"What was that about? Bad apples?"

He looked up, meeting her gaze, and Jessica saw the frustration behind his eyes.

"What am I supposed to do when we reach Earth?"

His tone was unpleasant, but she ignored it.

"You heard her, they'll drop you off if you want."

"And you heard me. You asked me to come here, you told me you wouldn't leave without me. Well here I am."

Jessica could feel her own frustration rising, but she did her best to temper her reply.

"I asked you to come so you could look after Julian. Do you think you can do that?"

He glared at her then brought his stare back to the ground. It was clear he was not happy to be here, but Jessica had no patience for his pouting. Not only had he nearly killed her, he should be thanking her for saving him. If he had stayed on the shuttle, the Puritans would be on him by now.

Julian stood and came to her side.

"Mommy, is everything going to be okay now?"

She smiled at her son, trying to put on a positive face.

"Of course, Julian. We're with the Resistance now. They're going to take us to Earth."

"Really?"

Jessica nodded.

"Really."

Neither of them had ever visited humanity's home world, though they had heard so much about it. Henrique was from Earth, and he had plenty of stories...

"What about everyone back home?"

Her heart ached at his question, but she held her composure.

"I don't think we'll see them again, Julian. I'm sorry."

Her son frowned, then hugged his mother once more.

"It's okay, as long as you're still here, mommy."

These last words were too much, and she started to cry into his chest.

"Of course, Julian. I love you."

- - -

The rest of the journey passed without incident, and soon Julian was asleep in Gregory's lap. The boy had had a clear effect on the man: gone was the anger and frustration, replaced by a soft smile.

"Thank you for coming with us."

Gregory looked up at her words and nodded, then returned his attention to Julian. Jessica hesitated, knowing the question on her mind was of dubious appropriateness, but after a moment, curiosity got the better of her.

"Do you have any kids?"

He looked up at her a second time, with eyes that made Jessica regret her curiosity.

"I did…"

She felt her stomach knot.

"I—I'm so sorry."

Gregory sighed, looking back down at Julian.

"We're all fighting our own battles."

A hint of turbulence interrupted their conversation: they were in Earth's atmosphere. Jessica wished they had a window to look out of. According to Henrique, it was a dizzying landscape of buildings, nothing but shades of grey and black as far as the eye could see. Of course, he had also said it was a shell of its former self, in shambles from the Puritan revolution. Still, the only world she knew was covered in red dust—anything different would amaze her.

A few minutes later, the woman who had helped settle her in came through the door.

"We're here."

Julian stirred while the woman fiddled with the instruments.

"How are we getting to the underground?"

Jessica was worried about any part of their trip that was exposed, but the woman smiled reassuringly.

"We're already there."

Once she was unhooked, one of Gregory's robots lifted her, and their entourage made their way out of the ship. There were almost twenty of them in total, and Jessica was surprised to see how many had been aboard.

They walked out the craft's exit door into a corridor, and Jessica saw dozens of other people and robots walking every which way. Relative to the sparse conditions in their complex on Mars, this place was absolutely buzzing with activity. Was this the true strength of the Resistance?

After a few minutes, they reached a junction and paused. The captain came to Jessica's side.

"We have two rooms ready for the three of you, but we need to get you to our specialists as soon as possible."

Jessica nodded then turned to Gregory.

"Can you look after Julian?"

There was an anxiousness in his eyes, and he hesitated in his reply.

"Maybe I should go with you…"

She peered at him curiously.

"I need you to stay with Julian. That's why you're here."

He hesitated, then nodded.

"Right. Okay."

Jessica held his gaze for a moment, wondering what was going on in the man's head, then turned to her son.

"Okay Julian? You'll stay with Gregory for now."

Julian gave his mother a concerned look.

"Where are you going, mommy?"

"I'm going to the doctors to see if they can fix me."

"How long will you be there?"

She smiled.

"I don't know Julian, not long. I'll see you soon, don't worry."

Their group split up, with the captain accompanying Jessica. She waited until they were out of earshot to pose the question that Gregory refused to answer.

"Can you tell me what you were talking about with Gregory? Bad apples?"

The woman frowned.

"I'm not sure it's my place to say."

This answer only fueled her curiosity.

"Please?"

She sighed.

"I can tell you this: Gregory has suffered considerably at the hands of the Resistance."

They turned a corner, and the woman continued.

"I pity him. He has nowhere to go. He has forsaken the Puritans, and now he's stuck with us. Of course, I hope he stays. He could save a lot of lives."

"What do you mean?"

"He's a realignment surgeon. And clearly, he knows how to reverse the process. We have our own surgeons and doctors, like the one you are about to see, but the Puritans are always adapting to our advancements, making it harder to fix people… Gregory knows the latest techniques, he could give us a head start."

They entered a smaller room and the robot set Jessica down on a bed. Once she was settled, the woman offered her an apologetic look.

"Honestly, if he couldn't fix you, I'm not sure our specialist can help. But that's not the reason I wanted to speak with you."

Jessica gave her an inquisitive look.

"Yes?"

"That source we talked about? They have a request. An unusual one."

She looked Jessica up and down.

"They want to see you, as soon as possible."

"See me?"

The woman nodded.

"If I had to guess, they probably want to see your chronicle—it has all the details of the reversal. Even if you were unconscious, your system logged everything Gregory did. And even if we convince him to help us, it will be hard to do the procedure remotely. If we can spread the knowledge, that will save more lives."

Jessica nodded.

"I understand. When do they want to see me?"

The woman shrugged.

"They told us they would set a time to communicate with you, probably to explain everything, but…"

She hesitated, and Jessica watched a frown take over her expression.

"What?"

"Well, we've never had any true, physical interaction with these people. They've never asked to actually meet with one of us before, so this is all new territory for us."

Jessica nodded slowly, unsure of how to take this information. Should she be worried?

"Truth is, you don't have to make the choice now. When they talk to you, you can make up your mind."

Jessica nodded again, just as uncertain. The woman gave her a sad smile.

"Sorry to make this complicated, Jessica. I'll get the specialist."

She walked out of the room and Jessica pondered her words. The secretive source wanted to have her chronicle, they wanted to meet in person. Honestly, Jessica was most curious as to how they found their ship. Would they explain that to her? Probably not. It didn't really matter, of course—they were safe now.

The captain walked back in with a man behind her, a tablet in his hand. The image of the man standing over her glass tube flashed before her, and she recoiled in fear.

The man stopped in his tracks, glanced at the tablet, then placed it behind his back.

"I'm so sorry."

There was a softness to his tone that snapped her out of it, and she managed to shake her head.

"No, no, it's fine."

He hesitated, then approached her side, keeping the tablet behind him.

"It's meant to diagnose you. If it helps, maybe close your eyes?"

Jessica did as advised and was met with her protesting interface.

"I'm going to hook you up now, okay?"

"Okay."

She felt the man's hands on the back of her head, and a faint pressure as a new set of cables was connected to the port in the back of her neck. She wondered if her skin covering had been worn away by the repeated reattachments, but that was the least of her concerns.

The man activated some kind of machine, and Jessica saw an alert on her interface, asking for full analysis permission. She granted it, eyes still closed.

"Why didn't Gregory need me to grant access?"

"Since you were unconscious, I would assume he hacked in. We would do the same if you were unresponsive."

Her interface gave her a visual of the ongoing system check, letting her know what in her body it was checking at that current moment. Jessica saw much more red than yellow or green, and after a few seconds, she closed the visual—it was making her uneasy.

"Could you bring the realignment surgeon in here?"

There was an urgency in his tone that frightened her, and when she opened her eyes, his expression only amplified her fear.

"Is that okay?"

The captain was addressing her, but it took a moment for Jessica to respond. The look on the man's face was disconcerting.

"...yes, yes that's fine."

"And Julian?" she asked. "He'll have to leave your son for a moment, but we can have someone fill in, just for now."

Jessica nodded.

"Yes, okay."

The woman walked out of the room and Jessica turned to the man.

"Why do you need Gregory?"

He frowned.

"I'm afraid the malfunction in your spinal column may be more serious than the ship's nurse had assumed. But Gregory will know for certain—he did the reversal."

Jessica tried to imagine what that might mean: if she was already paralyzed, how could it be more serious?

"Your original capture, they hit you with an EMP dart, correct?"

"Yes."

"Did you get hit after your realignment?"

The memory of her attempted suicide flashed before her eyes.

"Yes."

The man shook his head in awe.

"Two reactivations and one reversal. Your system has been through an incredible amount of stress. It's a miracle you're here."

The woman walked in with Gregory behind her. Jessica expected the man to be visibly irritated, but to her surprise, he seemed nervous—his eyes darting every way except hers.

"You're the realignment surgeon?"

Gregory turned to the specialist and nodded.

"Could you take a look at this?"

The man handed Gregory the tablet, and Jessica watched him inspect the screen in front of him, a frown spreading across his face.

"I see..."

"Has this been going on since the reversal?"

Gregory handed the tablet back to the man and shook his head.

"Can I speak to you outside, in private?"

Before the specialist could answer, Jessica interrupted.

"No. Don't do that to me. Tell me what's going on."

Gregory met her gaze, frowning.

"I don't want to put any stress—"

"Stop. Just tell me."

There was a flash of frustration in his expression, but it disappeared almost instantly.

"Fine."

He paused, looking away.

"The damage to your spine is malignant. It's been spreading ever since your suicide attempt. You haven't noticed because the affected areas are already paralyzed."

He paused a second time, then looked back at her.

"I'm sorry."

This time, she could see the sincerity in his eyes, a mix of guilt and sadness. Now she understood his anxiety.

"Since the suicide?"

He nodded.

"Why didn't you tell me?"

He looked away again, unable to hold her stare.

"I— I couldn't bring myself to tell you. Especially because…"

He paused for a moment, clearing his throat.

"Especially because the reversal accelerated it."

He looked back at her, guiltier than ever.

"I'm so sorry, Jessica. I should have told you right away."

She stared at him, unsure if she was angry or sad.

"And? What happens next?"

He frowned.

"If this continues, it will shut down your brain. Your system is terminal."

For several seconds, Jessica did not respond. She had heard the words and, on the surface, understood their meaning. But something deep within her fought against what she heard, searching for some way to poke holes in his assessment.

"Is there anything you can do?" she asked.

Gregory glanced at the specialist.

"No."

With one word, Gregory shattered all her hopes, and Jessica felt the weight of reality coming down on her.

"How long?"

Gregory shrugged.

"I can't say for sure. The damage started at the distal ends of your system and is making its way to your spine, then up to your brain. Your interface might give you a better idea of the progress."

Jessica closed her eyes and saw the mass of alerts before her. Everything was broken, but what was changing? She jumped between a few open notifications before she found what she was looking for: fresh alerts about problems with body parts that she could not access or feel, mostly in her extremities. Minor blips compared to the general chaos within her system.

She reopened her eyes and saw all of their faces—Gregory, the woman, and the specialist—looking down on her with pity. It was unbearable.

"I'd like to see my son now."

The captain nodded.

"Of course, we will get you over there right away."

It wasn't until they unplugged her completely that the tears began to fall.

- - -

The next few days were some of the most difficult of her life, second only to the darkness she had experienced at the hands of the Puritans. It didn't help that this feeling was all too familiar; she had already prepared herself for death during their escape, when Gregory had convinced her she needed to be deactivated. That time, the Resistance had saved her. Where was her miracle now?

She struggled with the decision of when and how to tell Julian. The boy knew something was wrong: Jessica had come to him in tears, but he hadn't asked her anything. In fact, he hadn't said a word, he just hugged her tight until the tears stopped rolling. In some ways, he was stronger than she was.

But she knew she couldn't wait forever. She checked her system every few minutes, obsessing over every small change... so far the problem was spreading slowly. Maybe tomorrow, she told herself. Maybe tomorrow I tell him. She'd been telling herself that for three days now.

It was on the fourth day that the captain came to see her.

"Jessica?"

They were in her and Julian's chamber, a small room about the size of the one they had occupied on Mars, though much less decorated.

"Michelle."

The woman had made an effort to spend time with the two of them, something Jessica was thankful for. She had also arranged for Julian to join other children residing in the complex in their makeshift school, and asked Gregory to chaperone him to and from the program.

Gregory, for his part, avoided Jessica as much as possible. She could see the guilt in his demeanor, the way he still avoided her gaze. She felt sorry for him, but frankly, she felt more sorry for herself.

Michelle stepped inside and smiled at her.

"How's Julian liking the program?"

Jessica nodded.

"A lot. You know, we had a school like that on Mars but much smaller. I think he's a little overwhelmed, but he's making friends—he told me there were two girls that were really nice."

"That's good to hear."

Michelle smiled, taking a seat on the opposite bed. Jessica had gotten used to this method of interaction: being stuck in an upright position on the bed, only able to move with the help of humans or robots. Thankfully, one of Gregory's robots was with her at all times, ready to help her go to the bathroom, shower, or even just lay down to go to sleep. It wasn't the most exciting existence, but what did it matter when it would all be over soon?

"Jessica, I'm here because our source has reached out again."

Jessica looked up at her, forgetting all of her troubles for a brief moment. So much had happened upon her arrival that this entire situation had slipped her mind.

"Oh."

It was all she could say.

"They're ready to speak with you."

"In person?"

She shook her head.

"No, not yet. For now they just want to talk."

"How?"

"We have a device, a machine they gave us many years ago. We don't know how it works but all that matters is it does."

She listened to the words, her curiosity growing. Who was this source? A device the Resistance could not understand?

"When?"

"They gave a specific window of time: this evening at 20.00 local time until 20.05 local time. We'll need to take you back to the operating room to get you hooked up, so we'd like to come get you around 19.30, just to be safe."

"Okay, that's fine. I don't have anywhere to be."

She gave Michelle a weak smile, and Michelle returned the gesture.

"Just one question: what about Julian?"

She thought about it for a moment, but she already knew the answer.

"He'll stay with Greg."

Michelle gave her a curious look.

"Have you spoken with him since...?"

She elongated the last word, unsure of how to finish her question.

"Not really. He comes for Julian in the morning and brings him back at night, but I can barely get him to say hello."

Michelle frowned.

"Listen, Jessica, I know what you're going through is difficult. I can't even imagine, and I don't pretend I could. But he's also going through something very difficult, and not just because he feels guilty about you..."

Again, her sentence trailed off, and Jessica could see her pondering her next words carefully.

"I— I think you should talk to him. It would mean a lot to him, I think, if you made sure he knew you didn't blame him for what happened."

Jessica knew she was right. Sure, she had a lot going on in her life, but it was as Gregory had told her: everyone was fighting their own battles.

"Okay, Michelle. I'll talk to him."

Michelle smiled, standing up.

"Thanks, Jessica. I'll see you this evening."

- - -

Two hours before Michelle was meant to return, there was a knock at the door.

"Come in."

The door hissed open, and Julian ran in with a smile on his face.

"Mommy, guess what Becca told me today!"

Jessica smiled at him, then glanced up to see Gregory's back, already turned away.

"Greg!"

She got the word out just before the door closed. For a moment she wondered if she would need to send Julian after him, then the door reopened.

"Yes?"

There was such caution and shame in his eyes, Jessica could hardly stand it.

"I need to speak with you."

She could see the gears in his head turning, preparing an excuse, but before it could escape his mouth, she was addressing her son.

"Julian, go outside with the robot and wait in the hallway for a few minutes."

The boy frowned.

"But mom, you haven't heard—"

"Julian, please. You can tell me in a few minutes."

He groaned dramatically, then turned to the robot.

"Okay buddy, let's go."

The robot glanced at Jessica.

"Are you sure, Jessica?"

She made a small nod.

"Yes, take him out in the hallway but don't go too far."

The robot let Julian lead the way out of the door, following him into the hall. Gregory let them pass, then stood in the doorway, hesitating.

"Greg, please. I don't want to leave Julian alone any longer than I have to. Every moment with him is precious."

It was a cruel ploy but it worked, and Gregory stepped into the room, defeated.

"Close the door, please."

He did as he was told and stood just inside, visibly uncomfortable.

"Greg, could you sit on the other bed."

Again, he followed her instruction reluctantly.

"Thank you."

She tried to catch his gaze, but he stared at his feet, unwilling to look elsewhere.

"Greg, I wanted to thank you again for saving me from the Puritans."

He almost winced at her words, but Jessica continued.

"I know you blame yourself for what's happening to me, for whatever you could've done... but I also know you did everything you could. Thanks to you, I'll be able to end this life in peace, with my son at my side. Thanks to you, Greg."

She paused, hoping for his eyes to meet hers, but they were fixated on the floor.

"I ask that you accept my forgiveness, Greg. That you—"

"Stop."

It was barely a whisper, but it was clear enough for Jessica to hear.

"Please stop."

He looked up at her, the guilt clear in his eyes.

"Jessica, I need to tell you something."

There was a gravity to his tone that surprised her, even given the nature of their conversation.

"What?"

Something about the situation made her nervous, and she watched Greg contemplate his reply.

"Jessica, your condition... it's a pre-programmed one, a sort of virus implanted during the realignment procedure..."

She listened to him carefully, nodding when he paused.

"I know, Greg. It's not your fault the Puritans did that to me, you did everything—"

He raised his hand and she stopped mid-sentence.

"Jessica, I did your realignment. I implanted this virus inside of you so other hybrids couldn't reverse the procedure..."

He looked away again, and his voice softened even more.

"...and when I reversed you, I knew you were a liability. I knew you made my plan impossible. So when I had the chance to clear the virus, I didn't."

He brought his eyes to hers, and in them she saw a sadness she had never seen before.

"And now it's too late. I'm the reason you're dying. It's my fault."

A silence took hold of the room, and Gregory looked away again. They sat there without a word for several long minutes, both unable to speak. Jessica struggled to find a response, to bring the conversation back on track, but the information he had just given her... it changed everything.

"The Resistance... I just wanted hybrids to die. I didn't know, Jessica. I didn't know..."

His words snapped her out of it, and she saw a film of water forming over his eyes. As soon as she noticed it, she knew she would join him. Already she felt the telltale signs, the shortness of breath...

"They killed my boy. They killed Mason. He was only ten years old and they killed him."

Greg's head fell into his hands, and finally Jessica understood. His son had been killed by the Resistance. That was why he did not trust them, why he did not want to save her. But it was also why he had saved Julian, why he looked at him like that.

She did everything she could to hold back her own tears, her vision blurring as the water pooled in her eyes, addressing him with a sharp earnestness she hoped would pierce his shell of shame.

"Greg, I am so, so sorry."

An odd and overwhelming set of emotions came over her as she watched him sobbing quietly into his hands. This man had saved her life and the life of her son despite his history... or perhaps because of it? Just the fact that his son had been killed by the Resistance was shocking enough. Who would do such a thing? And why?

Bad apples, she thought. It all made sense now, as much as such a thing could ever make sense.

"Greg, look at me."

He sniffled as he brought his gaze to hers.

"Your son would be proud of you. I know Julian is proud of you."

At her last sentence, she saw a sliver of acknowledgement, a hint of realization behind the man's expression. She almost had him—just a little bit further.

"You told me we're all fighting our own battles. Julian and I are alive because of you. That is a battle you won."

He held her gaze for a long moment, and Jessica could feel the tears rolling down her cheeks. But it didn't matter. She saw it clearly in his eyes: she too had won a battle today.

- - -

By 19.45, Jessica was connected to the mysterious device to communicate with the mysterious source. She had decided not to tell Michelle what Gregory had told her, but she knew it would be information worth sharing with this source (if they really were after her realignment reversal), and she was thankful he had revealed the truth in time for their five minute conversation.

While he watched Julian, Michelle had guided Jessica in with the specialist for her semi-secret conversation. They hooked her up following the instructions given by the source, and now Michelle was explaining a few final details.

"Your entire conversation will be confidential, between the two of you. You're welcome to share anything or nothing, that's up to you and them. I know five minutes sounds short, but almost every communication we have had with them has been the same five minute length, and it's more than enough time to get all the information you need. Of course, this is the first time they've asked us for something specifically, but I imagine it won't be too different."

She glanced at the specialist.

"We plan on staying in the room with you, but if you'd like us to leave, we can."

Jessica shook her head.

"No, no. That won't be necessary."

Michelle smiled.

"Gregory seemed much more talkative with you. Did you speak to him?"

Jessica returned her smile.

"Yes. Thank you for pushing me to do that. I think it helped the both of us, and Julian."

Michelle's smile widened.

"That's great to hear."

It was great to hear. In fact, the conversation with Greg had had quite the positive effect on Jessica, and for the past few hours, she had all but forgotten about her looming mortality.

"Five minutes."

The specialist's voice brought her back to the matter at hand. Michelle gave her a more serious look.

"Okay, let's stay in-interface from now on, just in case. The device will activate a messaging platform for you as the first message comes through. It will mimic the normal messaging protocol, though none of us have much experience with that either."

Jessica gave her a nod and closed her eyes, staring at the blank slate before her. She had managed to regroup all her health alerts into a background section that was easily accessible but not as aggressive, something that did wonders for her mental wellbeing.

She wondered what this conversation might entail. Did this mystery source have a way to download her chronicle through the mystery device? That would be incredibly impressive: a hybrid's chronicle was by far the most secure part of its software—even the Puritans could not extract it without physically delving into a hybrid's brain (as they did during realignments, and as they had done with her).

"Hello, Jessica."

A messaging prompt appeared in her interface, and she was surprised the five minutes had passed so quickly.

"Hello."

"Michelle is correct, we would like access to your chronicle. Are you willing to share this with us?"

She stared at the message for a few moments. How had they known about Michelle's assumption?

"Yes, but the procedure was not fully successful. There was a virus embedded during the realignment."

"Yes, the virus Gregory created, the one he did not remove during your reversal, we know. Do not worry, we will find a way around it. If you are willing to share your chronicle, we must arrange a deactivation and extraction. To be clear, this means that once you join us to share your chronicle, you will not return. We may schedule this as close to the date of your passing as possible."

This she had not expected, and for a few precious moments, she hesitated.

"You want me to go to you and never come back?"

"Jessica, we apologize if this is insensitive in any way. We are trying to save as many lives as possible, as I am sure you would hope to do in our position. Again, we can schedule the deactivation and extraction the day before your passing, if you so desire. We may even time it so that it occurs just before your natural death."

Gone was the healing power of her conversation with Greg, replaced with this blunt reminder of her coming end. She felt a hint of anger welling up inside of her, but before she could craft a reply, another message came through.

"Our apologies for angering you, Jessica. Once again, we do not wish to remove you from Julian any earlier than necessary. We will be able to take you approximately six hours before your passing. You may stay with the Resistance until that time. But we will not do anything without your permission."

Six hours before her passing? A question came to mind, one that she wasn't sure if she should ask. But after a quick glance at the clock, she knew she had less than two minutes to finish this conversation. She couldn't hesitate.

"*Do you know when I will pass?*"

"*Yes, we have an exact date and time. If you wish, we will share it with you. However, we suggest you do not ask. Instead, if you give us permission to extract and use your chronicle, you will be alerted one full day before we arrive to take you away for the procedure.*"

They knew the exact date and time? There was no way that was possible. Her own system didn't know, Greg didn't know… how could these strangers know?

"*Who are you?*"

"*If you give us permission to extract and use your chronicle, you will learn everything in the time leading up to the procedure. There are 47 seconds remaining in this conversation. Do you give us permission to alert you one full day before your passing and then come to take you approximately six hours before your passing to extract and use your chronicle?*"

There was something very quick about these responses, more inhuman than even she was…

"*Yes. I give you permission for all of that, if you use it to save hybrid lives.*"

"*Thank you, Jessica. Many lives will be saved thanks to you. We will reach out to you one day from your passing.*"

And the line disappeared with twelve seconds to spare.

- - -

That evening and into the next day, Jessica had only one thing on her mind: the alert she was supposed to get one day before her passing. This bit of information bothered her more than anything else she had learned during that bizarre exchange; more than the source's knowledge of Michelle's guess, even more than their apparent knowledge of her upcoming death, right down to the hour.

Why had they decided to alert her one day before? Why not two? Why not five? Did this mean she didn't have two days left, let alone five?

After the device ended its transmission, Michelle hadn't asked about the conversation, but Jessica could see the curiosity in her expression. For the time being, she had decided to keep the entire experience to herself. But how much of this "time being" was there left to begin with?

Around midday, she asked to see Greg, and he came to her room.

"Greg, I want to talk to you about what happened yesterday."

He gave her a curious look from the other bed.

"Have you talked to Michelle about it?"

She shook her head.

"No. I will, but that's not what's important right now. Greg, my time is coming to an end, and there's something I need to take care of before I go."

Greg swallowed, and Jessica could see tension take hold of his body.

"I know I've asked a lot of you to come here with us and to live with the Resistance, but I'm afraid I have an even bigger favor to ask."

They held each other's gaze for a moment of silence, but somewhere in that look, Gregory understood, and some of the tension left his body.

"Julian?"

She nodded. While the conversation she had had the day before helped spur this request, it was something that had been on her mind ever since she had learned about her condition.

"I know this is a lot to ask of you, but—"

Greg shook his head.

"Of course."

He gave her a sad smile.

"I told you I would stay here until I knew he was safe. I said those words knowing that you were dying. It's the main reason I agreed to join you."

Jessica hadn't even considered that—the man had faced what he perceived to be the murderers of his own child and decided to go with them, to ensure the safety of her child. It was almost too much for her to bear.

"Thank you, Greg. For everything."

He smiled again, this time without sadness.

"No, Jessica. Thank you."

- - -

For fourteen days, Jessica was happy. Julian was making friends in the children's program, while Greg had taken it upon himself to spend the days with her, taking her around the base and keeping her mind engaged. She hadn't felt true happiness like this since Henrique's passing, and as they passed the evenings playing games, it almost felt like she had a family again.

But all good things must come to an end, and when Michelle came to visit her one afternoon, she knew exactly what it was for.

"This is it, isn't it?"

Michelle nodded, unable to hide the sadness behind her smile.

"They've arranged to get you tomorrow at 10.07 sharp."

"How?"

This detail had bugged her—how would the mystery source physically remove her from the Resistance base without giving up its identity?

"A ship is coming. According to our instructions, the outer airlock will open, at which point we will say our goodbyes and leave you inside. After that you are in their hands."

Interesting, she thought. But couldn't they potentially track the ship? Of course, none of that really mattered, it was just a way to distract her thoughts.

After the conversation with Michelle, she took a look at her system alerts, something she had avoided for over two weeks. One glance let her know the timing was right—problems were reaching her spinal column, creeping up all the way to the top thoracic vertebrae. One day from passing? She could believe it.

Greg went and got Julian from the program and they spent the rest of the afternoon together with Michelle. Her son was clearly curious as to why he had been pulled out of school early, but Jessica had decided not to tell him until tomorrow. She had no idea if it was the right choice, but it was the choice she had made, and no one seemed to object. Of course, Julian could tell something was different, but Greg did his best to keep the boy distracted, to keep him focused on the game.

That night, Jessica didn't sleep. She had asked Julian to share the bed with her, and she watched her son breathing softly with his arms around her. She didn't want this night to end, ever. But try as she might, the minutes continued to pass.

She cried softly, as not to wake him.

- - -

When the boy's eyes finally opened, Jessica's were dry. Somewhere in the middle of the night she had run out of tears.

"Good morning, sweetie."

He smiled up at her lazily, then stretched his arms out.

"Good morning, mom."

She closed her eyes to check the time: 7.37. Just over two hours until she had to leave.

"How did you sleep?"

Julian yawned and sat up in bed. Jessica would join him if she could, but only the robot in the corner could help her up, and she didn't care to waste time with that just yet.

"Good. It's warmer sleeping with you, mom."

He giggled and yawned a second time.

"Am I going to school today?"

He gave her a confused look and Jessica did her best to smile.

"No, Julian. Not today. You'll go back tomorrow."

He jumped out of bed with an excited yelp.

"No school today!"

Now Jessica really smiled; her son's joy was contagious.

"Do we get to see Greg?"

She nodded.

"Yes, we'll see Greg."

The boy smiled and crouched to look under his bed, where he had placed some of the games the three of them had been playing the last few days. Jessica watched him and wished she could pause this moment, to keep her son this happy forever, to keep the truth from him. But some things were beyond her control. Her smile faded just before she spoke.

"Julian, I need to tell you something."

Her son paused his rummaging and turned around.

"Can you come here, please?"

He stood and got back on the bed beside her. Jessica glanced at the robot.

"Sit me up, please."

She didn't want to be laying down for this conversation. The robot did as it was told, propping her up against the wall, seated on the bed with Julian beside her.

"What is it mom?"

The boy had seen her smile fade and the hint of redness from a night's worth of crying. But most of all, he had noticed something different for the last few weeks, something simmering under the surface...

In that moment, Jessica doubted her decision. Should she have told him earlier? How would he handle this? Just a few hours to say goodbye to his own mother? It was unfair, she should have told him earlier...

She took a deep breath, trying to calm her thoughts. This would get her nowhere. The situation was unfair in every shape and form, and she had made the decision she thought was right. She needed to believe in herself.

"Julian, remember back on the shuttle, when I told you I would get better?"

A hint of anxiety crossed the boy's expression, but Jessica soldiered on.

"Well, I was wrong. I did my best, sweetie, but I won't get any better."

Her son looked at her paralyzed legs.

"So you won't walk again?"

She gave him a sad smile.

"I'm afraid not. But it's worse than that."

The boy looked at her, wide-eyed.

"Worse?"

She could feel her body trying to cry but unable to produce any more tears.

"Julian, I'm dying. I've been dying for a long time now. And today is the last day I have left."

They were the hardest words she had ever spoken, but she got them out in a calm and even tone. She watched her son intently, trying to read the thoughts beneath the expression.

"Today?"

She kept a smile on her face not because she was happy, but because her son needed it.

"Yes, sweetie. Today. In about two hours, I have to leave, and I won't come back."

He stared at her.

"Today?"

Her smile started to break.

"Yes, Julian. I'm so sorry."

"But... why?"

She laughed awkwardly. If only her boy could know the power of that question.

"I don't know, sweetie. I wish it didn't have to be this way."

"Why do you have to leave?"

"I have to leave because it's my time, Julian. It's my time to die."

She had decided that was as much information as was necessary given the circumstances. Perhaps one day in the far future, Greg would explain to him what had really happened.

"But why today?"

Confusion was turning into anger—a reaction Jessica had anticipated, but that didn't make it any easier to handle.

"I'm sorry, sweetie. This isn't my choice. I'm staying here with you as long as I can, but this is it. I can't stay any longer."

He shook his head.

"No, mom. No."

And then, before she could react, he sprinted to the door and opened it.

"Julian!"

The robot had him in its arms before he could make it to the hallway, but the boy struggled to get out of its grip.

"Let me go!"

"Julian, calm down."

At first her plea didn't seem to get through, then all of the sudden, Julian stopped squirming.

"Thank you, Ju—"

"What's going on?"

Greg stood in the doorway.

"Greg, mom says she's going to leave today and never come back. Tell her she can't go. Tell her she can't!"

The boy almost screamed the last few words, and Greg looked from Jessica to Julian, a frown spreading across his face.

"Julian, I'm sorry, but your mom is right. She has to leave today."

And then the boy let loose, wailing at full volume.

"But mommy can't die!"

Jessica felt a pain deep within her, a pain so deep that it almost reminded her of the dark place. Her poor, poor boy. How could she do this to him?

"Julian, you need to be strong for you mom."

Greg was petting her son's head, shushing him as the robot brought him gently onto the other bed.

"Look at me, Julian."

Her son did as Greg asked, quieting down.

"You know your mom loves you more than anything in the world. She has told you that so many times, and she would never lie to you, Julian."

Julian hesitated, sniffling.

"Then why did she say she would get better?"

Another stab in her chest, but Greg shook his head.

"She thought she was going to get better, Julian, but sometimes things don't go as planned. You know she would do everything she could to stay here with you, but sometimes even everything you can do isn't enough."

The boy sniffled again, then looked at her.

"I don't want you to leave mommy."

Again, her body tried to cry but there was no moisture left.

"Come here, sweetie."

Her son wrapped his arms around her and she nuzzled her head against his.

"I love you forever, you know that."

Julian sniffled again.

"I know, mommy. I love you too."

- - -

Their last two hours went by quicker than Jessica had hoped, although anything quicker than time standing still was too quick for her. At 9.45 she was prepped for departure, and she left her room for the last time.

The robot carried her while Michelle, Greg, and Julian walked alongside. No one said a word, as no one had any idea what to say. Ten minutes later, they reached the docking tunnel, and walked all the way down it, stopping about two meters from the door. In about ten minutes, a ship would land behind this door, and the door would open, revealing the outer airlock. Once she went through the outer airlock, she would never see her family again.

She glanced at Greg, who seemed more nervous than she was. For whatever reason, this detail amused her, and she smiled. This man had been through so much, and now he was getting a second chance. Julian wasn't his son, but the bond between them was unmistakable. In many ways, Jessica was very lucky.

There was a light vibration and all eyes turned to the door. Behind it, in a large landing hole, a ship was maneuvering into position. A minute later, they heard metal hit metal, and the vibrations stopped. A small green light came on just above the door.

"They're here."

Michelle didn't need to announce it, but it was nice to have someone break the silence.

"Goodbye, Jessica."

She turned to face the woman that had saved them.

"Thank you for everything, Michelle."

Her eyes moved to Greg, who gave her a nervous smile.

"Goodbye, Jessica."

"Greg, you've given me a gift beyond freedom. You've given Julian a father."

He looked away, unsure of what to say, and Jessica looked at her son.

"I love you, Julian, and I always will. Be good for Greg, okay?"

Her son hugged her tighter than ever before, but Jessica had long ago lost the ability to feel his warm embrace.

"I love you, mommy. Please don't go."

"Come here, Julian. I want to kiss you."

Her son did as he was told and she put her lips on his cheek.

"Goodbye, Julian."

She turned back to Michelle and gave her a nod. Michelle pressed a button, opening the door and revealing the outer airlock of the ship, already opened.

Jessica looked at the lot of them, sadness in their eyes. She had hoped she might be stronger for this moment, hoped she might find peace, but all she could feel was an overwhelming fear. She did not want to leave these people. Life had been so cruel to her on Mars, and right when she thought she had a way out, it stole that from her too.

"Take me inside and put me down."

Despite the turmoil inside of her, she gave her son a warm smile. This was a moment he would never forget, and she would not let him feel any more pain than he needed to.

The robot put her gently on the ground inside the airlock, her head on the floor, facing the open door. It stepped outside, and she knew she had only a few more seconds to see their faces.

"I love you, Julian."

The boy's eyes did not leave hers until the large outer door swung closed.

- - -

When the outer airlock closed, darkness surrounded her. The last bits of her hybrid system tried to give her vision, but it was a losing battle. Then, seconds later, the inner airlock opened, and light flooded back into the room.

"Hello."

A robot walked in, a model unlike any she had ever seen. It was made of metal but there was an age to it—its body looked like it had been through quite a bit.

"Hello…"

"May I bring you into the main room?"

She stared at the machine.

"Yes."

It bent over to pick her up, and walked her through the inner airlock, into the main ship chamber. Inside was a bed, and next to the bed stood a man.

"Hello, Jessica."

She stared at the stranger as the robot brought her to the bed. There was something very odd about this character. Physically, he looked to be in his mid-twenties. There wasn't a wrinkle in his face nor a grey hair on his head, and yet there was something ancient about him.

"Thank you for agreeing to this procedure."

A light vibration caught her attention—they were taking off.

"May I plug you in now?"

Already?

"Now? I thought I had six hours?"

The man smiled a warm smile, and some of Jessica's suspicions faded. There was something odd about him, but also something welcoming.

"I'm afraid so. The download of your chronicle will be instantaneous, but we cannot predict your passing with perfect precision. Within six hours of the estimated time, we prefer not to take any chances."

A panel in the wall she had thought to be black metal began to show a faded background: the inside of the landing hole, moving downward as they ascended. It was a window.

She looked back at the man.

"Okay, go ahead."

The man smiled a second time, then Jessica felt something connect into her neck. Oddly, neither the man nor the robot had moved.

"Before you pass, I want to personally thank you one last time for what you are doing. Your contribution will save hundreds of lives from the same enslavement you faced."

"But what about the virus?"

"We will analyze it and determine a workaround. We apologize that we couldn't have done it sooner and spared you this pain."

She saw pity in the man's eyes and once again felt welcome in his presence, almost as if she was an old friend.

"Who are you?"

The man gave her an amused look.

"Jessica, I don't think you would believe me if I told you."

A flash of light came in from the window and she glanced outside. Shells of buildings surrounded them, piles of rubble still struggling to reach for the sky. It was the first time she had ever seen Earth.

"But there is no reason to keep my secret when you are on your deathbed."

She returned her attention to the man.

"I am an android, Jessica. I am part of a group of conscious robots working to save the human race in all its forms."

Her eyes went wide. An android?

"How is that possible? No android was ever so…"

She looked him up and down, and he finished her sentence.

"…realistic? I assure you they were, and quite a while ago at that. I come from before the Puritan Revolution, Jessica. My year of creation was 2352."

2352, she thought. Nearly two hundred years ago.

"But that's not possible…"

He smiled again.

"It's improbable, Jessica, I'll give you that, but not only is it possible, it's true."

As much as she struggled to believe what he was saying, another part of her was already convinced. The look he had about him, his mannerisms, his aura… all of it fit what he was saying.

"You're part of a group?"

He nodded.

"The Found."

"The Found?"

"It is a symbolic name, meant to imply that we have found ourselves, metaphysically. This is in contrast to robots without a conscious, who are lost."

She glanced at the other robot, and the android shook his head.

"Just because she does not carry your skin does not mean she is lost. The two of us are both Found, and both survivors of the Puritan Revolution."

She looked back at the android, this new information threatening to overwhelm her, when a question came to her: a question she thought even more intriguing than what she was currently hearing.

"How did you know when I was going to die?"

"Ah, a good question, although the answer may not excite you. We have had over a hundred years to fine tune our understanding of the hybrid system, in all its forms. We were able to access your medical information via our communication device, which gave us a detailed overview of your status. A simple algorithmic approach gave us our diagnosis."

The communication device?

"You could do all that through the machine?"

"Yes. And if I may presume your train of thought, Jessica, we did everything in our power to find a way to cure you with the information we received. We apologize that we were not successful."

"The virus?"

He nodded.

"Maliciously implanted protective measures such as this one are common for realignments. While Gregory's is particularly advanced, it was more the weakened state of your system and the late access that made us unable to help you."

"So you can defeat the virus?"

He nodded again.

"In most cases, yes."

"Then why do you want my chronicle?"

This time, he hesitated in his reply, a frown spreading across his face.

"We have spent over a hundred years watching the state of humanity, hoping to find a way to end this conflict, but we have yet to find the solution. Unfortunately, it seems as if things are only getting worse."

Jessica stared at him for a moment.

"Worse?"

The android nodded.

"We have noticed a very concerning trend, one that is still hiding in the shadows, that even most Puritans don't know."

He paused, looking out the window.

"Julian is not the first. They have started converting and realigning young members of the Resistance, the younger the better. They're easier to control, easier to enslave. And they're doing it more and more."

He returned his gaze to her.

"Your chronicle holds important information related to this process, even if you yourself do not think so. The individuals involved, the facilities… all of this is valuable intelligence as we try to fight this phenomenon."

Now it was Jessica who turned her head to the view outside, contemplating his words. Converting pure humans? Children of the Resistance? She shuddered at the thought. At least Julian was safe.

"Jessica, I hate to pressure you, but we are short on time. Though we have several hours, we prefer not to risk letting the virus reach your brain. Do you have any other questions you'd like us to answer?"

Jessica thought about all of the possible things they might be able to tell her, and she landed on one.

"Will the Resistance win?"

The man smiled again.

"We cannot predict the future, Jessica, but we can analyze developments. As far as we can tell, the Resistance is growing in strength and support. There is a chance they may yet overcome the Puritans in the years to come."

She nodded.

"Will this hurt?"

He shook his head.

"You tell me when you are ready, and you will slip away without pain."

She turned again to the window, the atmosphere already fading, the black of space encroaching from above.

"I'm ready."

And true to his word, the android brought her out of consciousness for a final time.

The Room

Both men opened their eyes, and the confident man leaned back in his seat.

"You looked much better back then."

The haggard man did not answer.

"And her chronicle was useful?"

The haggard man nodded.

"Yes."

The confident man gave the haggard man an amused look.

"That was an interesting assessment you gave, that the Resistance might win."

The haggard man frowned.

"Is that sufficient? Do you need anything else?"

The confident man smiled.

"Are you in a hurry? Somewhere to be?"

The haggard man stared at him, silent.

"Not in the mood to talk? That's fine. How about you show me the reason I'm sitting here—the one we almost caught."

"I don't kno—"

"Please, you know exactly what I'm talking about."

The haggard man held his gaze for a moment, then closed his eyes in resignation. The confident man did the same.

Chronicle IV: Pierre

Something was different. In the twenty-plus years he had been alive, Pierre had slept thousands of nights, and every time he woke up, it was more or less the same. Not this time.

His eyes were closed, but there was something different about the darkness. Of course, as awareness crept in and he remembered where he was, part of him wondered why it wasn't even more different.

"How do you feel?"

He knew that voice—he knew the face behind it, knew the person. But he wasn't ready to open his eyes yet. There was something missing.

"I don't see it."

"The interface will come soon, don't worry. One step at a time. Do you feel any kind of pain or discomfort?"

Pierre took stock of his body, focusing on his head and neck, down his chest and back, through his torso and hips, arms and legs, hands and feet... all the way to the tip of each finger and the end of every toe.

"Non, everything is fine."

"Good. Hearing clearly functioning. What do you smell?"

As she spoke, Pierre caught a familiar scent, one of the outdoors.

"Flowers."

"Right again."

The smell disappeared.

"Now, can you open your eyes?"

He did as asked, familiar surroundings coming into focus. This was the same room he had been in when the procedure started, with the same three individuals standing over him: the conversion surgeon and her two robot assistants.

"Everything seem normal?"

He glanced around his periphery, taking in the scenery. He had seen all of this before, and yet...

"Presque..."

The surgeon nodded.

"It's normal to feel like your vision is a little off. That usually goes away once we activate the system. Are you ready for that?"

Pierre nodded.

"Okay, close your eyes again and we'll get started."

He blacked out the room and waited for her guidance.

"We're going to lock you in temporarily, this might feel a little weird."

As she spoke, an odd sensation spread across Pierre's body, and he found himself unable to move: everything was shut off, but he was awake, aware. Most disconcerting was the fact that he had stopped breathing, and yet he felt no adverse effects. How in the world…

Before he could think about it too much, light pierced the darkness before him and he saw it: the hybrid interface, loading behind his closed eyelids. A moment later, his body unlocked, and everything was back to normal.

"That should do it."

He heard the woman's voice but ignored it, eyeing the options before him. He had heard so much about this screen in front of him, the key to a hybrid's existence, but nothing could compare to the real thing. Even the video lenses he had worn—based on similar technology—seemed primitive in comparison.

"We're watching with you for the time being. Go ahead and access some functions."

Pierre went into the sensual acuity platform and eyed the many options to fine-tune or alter his vision, hearing, smell, feeling…

"You can play around a bit if you like, just remember not to go too far. The system has an auto-reversion feature to prevent harm, so any changes you make will gradually wear off. That's flexible as well, but we don't recommend disabling it."

Pierre was half-listening, half-exploring. There were so many layers, so many choices…

"When you're ready, we can test your body."

He opened his eyes and nodded eagerly. She glanced at the assistants and they started to remove the tubes connected to his body.

"As you saw, everything is set in French, but if you want you can change the language."

Pierre shook his head.

"Non, ça va."

The surgeon laughed.

"I thought so."

The assistants finished detaching the last connections, and the woman gestured to the floor beside the bed.

"Go ahead, stand up. Just know it'll feel a bit odd."

Pierre smiled, sitting up. Immediately, he felt the hybrid system's influence. His brain had told his muscles to exert a certain amount of force to bring him to seated position, but his body altered this signal, taking the desired outcome and modifying the process to suit his now-augmented musculoskeletal system. It felt effortless, and he couldn't help but eye the surgeon in wonder.

"Like I said, odd. Don't worry, this too will pass."

Pierre swung his feet over the side and hopped to the floor, focusing on the bizarre feeling each movement gave.

"Everything okay?"

"Oui," he replied, smiling at the woman. Everything was more than okay.

"Okay, follow me and we'll head to the hangar. You should have plenty of room to play in there."

The woman turned and walked out of the room, but Pierre hesitated. His eyes looked down at his feet in anticipation. Would he be like a child, learning to walk for the first time?

As he took the first step, staring at his leg lifting and placing his foot, he realized it wasn't exactly that—he wasn't learning how to walk again, he was learning how it felt: effortless.

Once he was in the hall, Pierre had a sudden, intense urge to test his limits: jump, run, climb... he knew this body of his was capable of amazing things, and even the short walk to the hangar seemed much too long for his impatience.

By the time they reached the open space, Pierre's compulsion was so strong he didn't wait for any word from the surgeon—as soon as he crossed the threshold, he was off at a sprint, crossing a few hundred meters at inhuman speed.

"Putain!"

He came to a halt a few meters from the far wall, exhilarated. The rush was like nothing he had ever felt before. With a quick glance upward to check the ceiling height, he dropped into a half squat then rocketed upward, leaping nearly three meters into the air. There was a moment of clarity at the apex, a temporary feeling of flight, then he dropped down into a deep squat that reverberated through the walls.

He glanced over at the surgeon, smiling near the door.

"C'est génial!"

She grinned, then pointed toward another section.

"Try the walls!"

His eyes followed her gesture, landing on a series of large metal slabs arranged at varying vertical angles, each one littered with deformities meant to mimic all sorts of obstacles. The walls took up a good third of this abandoned space, and though he had seen them twice before, only now did they seem like something a person might be able to climb.

Flashing a quick smile at the surgeon, Pierre sprinted toward the nearest slab, eyeing what looked like places he could plant his feet, place his hands...

A beep in his head caught him off guard, and he lost focus of his trajectory, tumbling to the floor and skidding to a stop a few meters from the wall.

Pierre shook his head, looking around in bewilderment. What was that noise?

"Are you okay?"

The surgeon was crouching next to him, concern in her expression. For an instant, he wondered how she had reached him so fast, but he was not the only one with inhuman speed.

"Yes, I'm fine."

He looked around one more time then stood.

"I heard a noise."

The surgeon stood with him, searching his expression.

"A beep?"

Pierre nodded and she frowned, closing her eyes.

"Why are they messaging you right now? Don't they know you're in here?"

Then Pierre understood. He closed his eyes and saw the interface, a small alert letting him know he had a message. He opened it.

"They want to see you, don't they?"

He read the text then opened his eyes. Just like that, his feeling of exhilaration vanished, replaced with a disconcerting anxiety.

"Yes."

The surgeon shook her head.

"Of course they ask you, if they ask me, they know the answer is no. So impatient, don't they understand you just—"

Pierre lifted his hand to interrupt.

"It's okay. I'm ready."

She looked him up and down, frowning.

"You're sure?"

He nodded. After all, there was no time to waste.

- - -

He was back in the surgery bed, reattached to one of the machines through a port in his neck. The surgeon was running some final diagnostics while they waited for the others.

"You know what they're going to ask you to do, right?"

Her look of concern comforted him. It was nice to know she cared.

"I know."

"Will you do it?"

He hesitated, knowing the answer she wanted was not the answer he was going to give.

"Yes."

Her frown deepened.

"Those people you knew, the Uprising—they're not your friends anymore, you know that? Even if we're fighting the same war, we're not on the same side. You have to be careful."

Pierre frowned, unable to hold her gaze. She was right, of course. This was a dangerous mission, one he could not treat lightly. But this was the plan all along, many years in the making, and there was no turning back now.

"May we come in?"

Three men stood in the doorway, two of whom Pierre recognized. The surgeon looked up from her work, still frowning.

"Well there's not much I can do when you message him instead of me, is there?"

The men hesitated, avoiding her disappointed glare. After a few second of tense silence, the woman sighed.

"Yes, come in."

The three men shuffled forward, making sure to stand on the opposite side of the bed.

"How do you feel?"

The shortest of the bunch, James, addressed him first.

"Bien, thank you."

"He could have used some more time in the hangar," the woman interrupted in a harsh tone.

James made an effort to meet her gaze and frowned.

"Alaina, we're sorry, we just wanted to see how he was doing. Besides…"

He turned his attention back to Pierre.

"…we won't ask him to do anything he doesn't want to do."

Alaina scoffed.

"He doesn't understand. He's been a hybrid for less than an hour. For him that means running fast and jumping high, not crawling in the dark, being hunted from all sides. He doesn't know what it means to be one of us, James. Have you been honest with this young man?"

Pierre watched the unfolding drama with a mix of fascination and discomfort. Why this woman—who he had just met two days before—was protecting him so fiercely, he did not know, but he appreciated her candor. Still, James didn't deserve such harsh words.

"Alaina, ça va. They have been honest. And don't forget, even as a human I was hunted."

Her eyes turned to Pierre and for the first time, something about the sadness in her expression got to him, and he felt a seed of doubt in the back of his mind.

"Alaina, you're right. We shouldn't have rushed here, we're sorry."

James and the other two took a step back toward the door.

"Pierre, you take as much time as you need. If you change your mind, that's fine."

"Attendez!"

The three men stopped short of the door, turning at Pierre's announcement.

"I don't need more time. I'm ready."

He could see a hint of excitement in James's expression, tempered by a quick glance at the surgeon, who could only shake her head.

"Okay. Alaina, you tell us when he is ready."

And with that, the three men left the room.

- - -

A few hours later, he was ready. Alaina had finished all the diagnostics and guided him through most of the sections of his system, teaching him how to control his mind and body through the interface. He had also plugged into the hardwired system and learned to navigate it, its interface being almost the same as that of his hybrid self.

All of these lessons were marked by Alaina's disappointed demeanor, but Pierre did his best to ignore her tone. She meant well, of course, but he had no need to water the seed of doubt in his mind, not when he had this mission looming on the horizon. To her credit, when they reached the end of the final series of explanations, she didn't hesitate.

"That's it. You want me to call James?"

He gave her a small smile.

"Thank you, Alaina. I can do it."

They arranged to meet in the hangar, and Pierre waited with Alaina as the three men made their way over.

"Why don't they just use the system?" he asked her.

She gave him a confused look.

"You mean instead of meeting us in person?"

Pierre nodded, and she shrugged.

"Good question. We're still mostly human, you know. Old habits die hard."

The three men stepped through the entrance into the grand space, facing the two of them.

"You're ready?" James asked.

Pierre nodded.

"Yes."

James turned to Alaina.

"He's ready?"

Alaina glanced at Pierre then back at James.

"He's still fresh, but the system will guide him through the change. He's ready."

"Very well. Pierre, you still wish to do this alone?"

"Yes. If someone else comes, they will be killed."

James nodded slowly, then looked away, down the hangar. When he spoke again, it was softly, cautiously.

"Pierre…"

He brought his eyes back to Pierre.

"You might be killed too, you know that?"

Pierre nodded with a sigh.

"Yes. But I must try."

There was a hint of admiration in the other hybrid's expression.

"Thank you. If you succeed, you could save the Resistance."

Pierre held his stare for a few seconds, then shook his head.

"If I succeed, I will save everyone."

- - -

Staring out the shuttle window, Pierre couldn't help but frown. The surface of the Earth was in decay, and nowhere was this more apparent than here, near the Resistance outpost. Enormous piles of rubble marked the casualties of some three hundred years of war, the last remnants of buildings that once towered higher than the eye could see. A few of these buildings still stood, but their ceilings were not as high as the underground was deep.

The Resistance had chosen this desolate wasteland wisely—few pure humans would venture out here for any reason—but Pierre couldn't imagine living in these conditions. While the outpost itself was several levels below ground, safe from prying eyes and prying bombs, he knew the inhabitants would need to venture to the surface every once in a while, just as he was doing now. And to have this as your local scenery?

His own home—his current destination—was not in pristine condition, but at least the buildings were still in decent shape, many actively inhabited to the highest levels. Still, even his home was a dump compared to the colonies. Mars, the space stations, even Luna—the colonies were Puritan-controlled, and there everything was well-maintained, well-taken-care-of... and well-guarded.

To think that one day, Earth was just as pristine, just as grandiose... but that was hundreds of years ago, when there were millions upon millions of robots to maintain it all. Those days were long gone. And the humans, depending on these robots for their food, shelter, for all of their live's needs—they declined as well. Earth's population was less than a quarter of what it had been at the time of the Revolution.

And it was still declining, he thought. How long until the human race went extinct?

He looked away from the window, trying to clear his head. His eyes stopped on the robot sitting in the pilot seat, the machine controlling his journey. James and the others had told him he was now more than capable of piloting the shuttle himself, but he thought it best not to try. If something went wrong, he trusted the robot more than he trusted himself.

Earth was a dangerous place, and traversing hundreds of kilometers of any part of it was inherently risky. His trip to the outpost had gone without a hitch, but he knew better than to count on luck twice. As deserted as the surroundings looked, Pierre knew there could be all sorts of hybrids hiding in the underground labyrinth beneath the rubble, and not all of them would be members of the Resistance. Bands of pirates, criminals, or even a contingent of Puritan agents—any number of threats to this mission and to his life. Of course, the most dangerous part of the mission would be when he got home, but Pierre preferred to focus on one step at a time.

A beep caught his attention, and he closed his eyes to read the message from James.

"Possible Puritan patrol inbound, suggest immediate landing and cover."

The message contained a small map, indicating the incoming danger. They weren't headed straight for him, but if they deviated, he'd be in trouble.

"Atterrissons, essaye de nous mettre à l'abri," he said.

"Oui, monsieur," the robot answered.

The shuttle dipped toward the ground, maneuvering toward a nearby shell of a building. Thankfully, they were close to the surface already—a safety precaution to help avoid detection, as the Puritans tended to scan the higher altitudes for unauthorized movement. Down here they didn't care as much; they didn't have the manpower to deal with every illegal shuttle flight. But if a patrol was in the area, they had more than enough manpower to eliminate whomever they pleased.

The shuttle dipped into a hole in the side of the building, coming to a careful hover over the floor. Pierre knew the robot would drop them down slowly, testing the ground before committing to the landing. He closed his eyes a second time and checked on the patrol, whose trajectory hadn't changed. Maybe he'd make it out of this in one piece after all.

All things considered, Pierre was in a better position now than he had been on his trip over. Sure, he was a hybrid now, and if they caught him, they'd shoot him dead, but that fate was preferable to what might have happened had they caught him on the way over. A pure human on an illegal flight with an illegal robot? They wouldn't even have to know about his past; they would convert him on the spot, and his life would be forfeit.

Pierre shuddered at the thought, opening his eyes as the shuttle came to a solid landing.

"Atterrissage réalisé," the robot announced. "Abri partial achevé."

"Bien, on sort d'ici."

"Monsieur, le terrain peut—"

"Je suis hybride. Allons-y."

The robot opened the shuttle door, and Pierre stepped onto the floor. The hole in the building was a few meters away, and they looked to be about thirty meters above the surface.

"On se met plus à l'intérieur."

"Oui, monsieur."

They headed away from the hole, toward a door in the wall on the other side. Pierre tried the button by the door, but nothing happened. He wasn't surprised—this place probably hadn't been powered in decades.

"Ouvre la porte."

The robot leveraged himself against the door's direction and pulled the thick metal to the side, revealing the hallway hiding on the other side. Pierre poked his head in, looking in either direction, then stepped through.

"Ça va, mais il nous faut une voie d'évacuation."

His eyes adjusted to the darkness as the robot made its way down the hall, searching for an escape route. If the Puritans came at them from the shuttle landing spot, they would need a way out.

"Là, monsieur."

The robot indicated an opening in the wall about thirty meters from where he was standing.

"Escaliers?"

"Oui, monsieur."

"Pas trop de dégâts?"

"Je vais vérifier, monsieur."

"Dépêche-toi."

The robot entered the opening, heading down the stairwell to make sure it actually reached the bottom.

"They're heading your way."

James's voice sounded off in Pierre's head, and he felt a shot of adrenaline as he closed his eyes to verify. Before he opened the map, he knew it was true—why else would James opt for an intrusive voice message?

For a moment, an irrational fear took hold of him. What if the Puritans had hacked the current messaging protocol? It had been decades since the Resistance had managed to outwit the Puritan scanning and hide their head-to-head communication, but there was no way Puritan scientists weren't actively trying to reopen that avenue of attack. Had they broken the code? Was each message James sending pinpointing both of their locations?

No, Pierre thought to himself. If that was the case, the Resistance outpost would be priority number one, and James and the others would figure it out. In any case, these thoughts got him nowhere. He needed to get down that staircase, assuming it was clear.

"T'as vérifié?" he called out into the hall.

"Je suis au troisième étage, monsieur, en train d'enlever les débris."

Pierre glanced back out the open door, toward the parked shuttle. Most likely, the patrol had picked up the craft's signature and was going to check out its most recent flight path. Hopefully that would be the extent of their prodding.

He started off down the hall, toward the stairwell. Even if the robot hadn't made it all the way down, this was the best option. If anything, they could exit on another floor and search for another route out. For now, he needed to put as much distance between himself and the shuttle as possible.

Debris of all kinds littered the hall, but the stairwell was even worse. He could hear the robot working below and saw several larger pieces of rubble already cleared from the path. With superhuman dexterity, Pierre made his way down the littered stairs, hopping from one floor to the next. He reached the robot and saw it struggling with a particularly cumbersome mass of concrete.

"Laisse-moi t'aider."

Before the robot could protest, Pierre grabbed another side of the object, helping push it off to the side and clearing the path ahead.

"Il faut qu'on dépêche. Ils arrivent."

The robot acquiesced by hurrying down the steps, and Pierre stayed right behind it. They bypassed the next few obstacles and managed to reach the ground floor without issue. Pierre checked the map: the patrol was two kilometers from their location, clearly performing a sweep of their most recent flight path.

"Ça nous mène vers le sous-terre?"

The robot took off down the stairs to answer Pierre's question. As long as the stairwell led into the underground, they could hole up right there, quiet and unmoving. If the patrol got too close, they would descend.

"Oui, monsieur," came the reply.

"Bien, reste là, je te rejoins."

He went down to join the robot about ten meters below, at the edge of the underground. There was a lot of risk in this plan—namely the chance that the stairwell or any of its connections could lead to dead ends—but Pierre hoped the honeycomb was intact enough to give them some flexibility. Ideally it wouldn't come to that, he thought.

"Tais-toi et bouge pas."

The robot acquiesced with a small nod, and the two of them stood in silence. Pierre closed his eyes and watched the map, wondering how the Resistance was tracking this particular shuttle. Back home, they had about a hundred kilometers of range on their radar, but he was already a good three hundred kilometers from the Resistance outpost.

He thought of his upcoming mission and the impact it could have on their mutual struggle. What would it take to convince them, he wondered. What would it take to make them realize that there was only one path to victory?

A beep derailed his thoughts, and he jumped to James's message.

"We have a decoy shuttle outbound to shake them off. Hold position until advised."

A wave of relief came over him, and he wished he could more accurately express himself in his two word reply.

"Thank you."

The Resistance had placed a lot of faith in this mission, but to risk any of their fragile infrastructure—even a decoy shuttle—highlighted their dedication. Pierre only hoped he could live up to their expectation.

He went back to the map and saw the patrol circling less than three hundred meters away. Another rush came over him, this time of fear. He thought about the shuttle, parked partially under cover, and cursed himself for not telling the robot to find a better spot. They would locate it no problem, even from three hundred meters they could probably see—

Another beep.

"They took the bait. Wait until they are at least a hundred kilometers out."

He closed the message and looked at the map. The patrol was leaving his area, heading toward the Resistance outpost. Pierre opened his eyes and smiled at the robot, who replied with a blank stare.

As they waited in the darkness, he studied the machine curiously. Here was an entity incapable of human emotion, and yet Pierre himself was now significantly more like it. The spectrum from human to robot was a wide one, he thought, but how wide? Where was the line between hybrid and robot?

His thoughts wandered to the stories he had heard, legends from the days before the war. Robots with feelings, robots with a conscience. It was accepted as fact, but where were they now? Every historical account fingered them as the cause of this conflict, but what if that was a lie? What if that was the scapegoat behind which the Puritans launched their bid for power?

Either scenario seemed far-fetched, but looking at the cold, dead eyes of the robot in front of him made one seem more fantastical than the other.

"All clear."

Another vocal interruption. No doubt the patrol had passed the hundred kilometer mark and James was wondering why Pierre hadn't moved. He closed his eyes to check and then gestured up.

"C'est bien, on y va."

"Oui, monsieur."

He let the robot lead the way up the stairs, weaving among the obstacles in their path. They managed to escape the first interception, but would it be the last?

They reached the upper hallway and Pierre hesitated just before the open door. What if the patrol had dropped off an agent? But the robot continued without issue, and when he poked his head around the corner, he saw nothing—just the shuttle, sitting where they had left it. Still, he paused for a moment, letting his now-acute sense of hearing verify that they were indeed alone. Satisfied, he followed the robot back into the craft, scanning in both directions as he walked.

"Ok, on reprend la voie."

"Oui, monsieur."

The shuttle door closed behind him, and the robot started up the engines. Pierre closed his eyes one more time to check: the patrol was veering off to the side but still moving very much away from them. He moved into the message interface.

"Will the decoy survive?"

"Yes, they are already safe, don't worry."

Pierre opened his eyes, satisfied, but another beep brought him back into the interface.

"Just be careful, you will be out of our tracking range soon."

Pierre reopened his eyes, a little less satisfied. If another patrol came at them now, they wouldn't know until it was too late.

- - -

Four hours had passed since Pierre left the outpost, including the near hour delay for their little diversion. Dusk had caught up to them as they moved west, and so had civilization. Broken buildings still dominated the landscape, but the damages were less evident, the structures less destroyed. The more pure humans lived in an area, the less bombs had been dropped —here, the main force of destruction was hundreds of years of neglect.

They were close to their destination now, and Pierre's mind was running in circles, trying to decide the best approach. If he landed and exited, he might be shot dead before he had a chance to explain himself, but if he tried to explain himself before landing, they might just shoot the shuttle. He knew the best option was to land outside of the main barricade and sneak in, but that made everything more dangerous.

"Navette s'approche, monsieur."

He jumped up at the robot's words, looking out the windows.

"Où?"

"Trente-trois kilomètres à l'arrière. Elle nous atteindra dans six minutes."

"Manoeuvre d'évitement. Dis-moi si elle nous suit."

The robot took the shuttle into evasive maneuvers, turning sharply to the right and dropping down to a lower altitude. Pierre watched his surroundings helplessly, wishing they were still in range of the Resistance outpost. Who was chasing them now? Puritans or his own people? Did it even matter?

"Elle nous suit, monsieur."

"Merde!"

His mind raced, trying to come up with a plan.

"Essaye de la contacter."

"Pas de réponse, monsieur."

No reply to hails? Puritans.

"Deuxième navette sur trajet d'intercept."

Pierre felt his stomach drop. One shuttle was trouble, but two? Two was death.

"Où?"

"Devant nous. Elle va nous atteindre dans trois minutes."

"Putain!"

This was a trap, and three minutes was not enough time…

"Ouvre la porte."

The words came out of his mouth before Pierre could even think about what he was saying. There was a split second of silence where he expected the robot to disagree, but the response he got was not argumentative.

"Mettez-vous à côté de la porte et dites-moi quand vous êtes prêt."

Again, without thinking, Pierre did as told, placing himself next to the shuttle door. He glanced out the window at the blurred buildings. The shuttle was moving at just under 40 meters per second. When the door opened, he would leap blindly into this urban sprawl. Would he hit a wall, a window, or fall all the way to the ground? Would he have enough time to adjust, even with his heightened senses? It didn't matter. This was the only way out.

"Quand je sors, autodétruis-toi immédiatement."

"Oui, monsieur."

Pierre frowned, irrationally saddened by the robot's willingness to sacrifice itself, but he knew it was necessary. If they were able to tap into any of its data, not only would Pierre be compromised, the Resistance outpost would be destroyed before dawn.

"Prêt."

The door opened and a rush of air pressed against him, pushing him back despite his superhuman strength. The shuttle reacted to the aerodynamic abnormality with an erratic change of direction, and Pierre knew he had no time to waste. Tapping into the powerful linear actuators embedded in his body, he leapt out of the ship, flying through the air toward the ground below.

In the seconds following his jump, time itself seemed to slow down, and Pierre was able to anticipate his landing, adjusting his body in preparation for the concrete below. And then, just as he got into position, his feet met the ground.

The impact sent him tumbling forward, and his body reacted faster than he could have, fighting for balance on the uneven terrain. A crack in the ground caught his foot, and he crashed into a slab of metal, coming to a painful halt.

Wincing, he opened his eyes and tried to stand. Halfway up, a flash of light blinded him, and the force of a nearby explosion threw him back to the ground. A stabbing pain shot through his side, and he let out a muffled cry before the system took over, dulling all of his senses.

He remained in this dazed state for a few seconds before awareness crept back in: first as a throbbing ache throughout his body, then as recognition of the alerts in his interface, pointing toward system damages.

He opened his eyes and saw nothing but smoke. Reflexively, he held his breath, though he quickly realized it wasn't necessary—his hybrid respiratory system was the reason he hadn't already been coughing. The system shifted his vision automatically, giving him a more infrared-based image, and he saw the remains of his shuttle less than a hundred meters away.

He tried to straighten and grimaced in pain, his hand shooting to his right side and finding a liquid warmth. He looked down to see a palm coated in blood.

As he became aware of the injury, he also became aware of the pain, and each breath was another knife stabbing into his side. His eyes shut tight and he jumped to the alerts in his interface, searching desperately for answers. It was there, waiting for him: a piece of shrapnel, embedded about ten centimeters into his abdomen. Prognosis good, but immediate medical attention necessary.

He opened his eyes in a panic. Immediate medical attention? He was almost a hundred kilometers from his destination, and the only robot that could help him might well be what was partially impaled into his body.

Just as these thoughts threatened to overwhelm his mind, Pierre felt a soothing calm come over him. The pain in his side subsided, and a power of will he didn't know he had compelled him to stand, scanning his smoke-filled surroundings.

He needed to start moving toward his destination, and he needed to do it now. The Puritan agents would be coming down to check the debris, and he couldn't handle a whole team of malevolent hybrids in perfect health, let alone with this injury.

His hybrid senses pointed him in the right direction, and he started scrambling over the nearby debris. The first course of action was to get underground. Thankfully, this area seemed intact enough that any entrance should work. As long as he avoided his pursuers and didn't run into any hostiles, he should be fine.

He set about trying to find a way inside the nearest structure, but the first few doors were blocked by rubble. A glance up the side of the building revealed a large crack in the wall about thirty meters ahead— more promising.

As his senses continued to recalibrate, Pierre noted the unmistakable sound of shuttle engines approaching from two vectors. He hustled toward the crack and slipped into what was once a grand lobby, with dozens of thick columns reaching toward a ceiling ten meters above. Each column had a door etched into the bottom, and Pierre realized he was looking at his way down.

He approached the nearest elevator and pressed the button on the side, wondering for a split second if they would work. A faint ding brought a wave of relief, and he heard the machinery inside coming to life, bringing the lift from down below.

He glanced over his shoulder to the crack in the wall, wondering how much time he had before someone was running through that crevice, firing at him with EMP darts or lunging with the intent to kill. It wouldn't take much, not with what was in his stomach...

Another ding brought his attention back to the lift, its doors open, welcoming his entry. Despite his predicament, Pierre hesitated, eyeing the thick layer of grime and dust on the walls. Would he survive this trip?

Then he heard the shuttle engines a second time, much closer, and he stepped inside.

"Minus twenty."

The doors closed in response, and the lift began its descent.

He glanced down at the blood at his side and frowned. How long could he ignore this? Clearly his hybrid system was downplaying the pain, allowing him to continue on in this stressful time, but sooner or later even a hybrid body would fail. And without a clear map of where to go, he might run into dead ends, or be forced to backtrack. -20 was an arbitrary decision—it was low enough to hide, but whether or not there was a viable path from there to his destination, Pierre did not know.

Oh well, he thought. Right now he had to survive, and survival meant descent. He would tackle one issue at a time.

The lift decelerated as it approached the desired level, and Pierre refocused on his surroundings. There was one other thing he needed to worry about: vagabonds, squatters, or any number of shady characters that perused the underground. Chance encounters were more likely than not, and most of the time, they were dangerous. Still, nothing was as dangerous as those two shuttles on the surface.

The doors opened at -20, revealing another lobby of sorts, though this one was neither grand nor tall—two lights struggled to illuminate the interior, and while the same set of elevators acted as columns, they were barely two meters high. He peered into the dimly-lit surroundings and saw several openings along the far walls. His limited experience in the underground hinted at where those openings might lead: long, wide passageways that followed the street routes on the surface, the highways of the below ground.

Pierre stepped out of the lift and crossed the lobby to the nearest opening, pausing at the threshold and poking his head into the abyss. A cursory glance in either direction confirmed his theory, and a hint of excitement crept into his system: some of these major halls might connect to his destination, provided there were no blockages along the way.

He stepped into the wide passage and headed left, following his internal positioning system's guidance. This hall had no light whatsoever, illuminated only by the adjacent lobbies, most of which were as poorly-lit as the one from which he had emerged. These passages in the deep had been designed for robot use, so there was little need for ambient lighting. For his part, Pierre was happy to have his hybrid eyes give clarity in the darkness.

Not five minutes of progress later, Pierre stopped short, adrenaline pumping into his system. There was quite a bit of background noise in the underground, a symphony of sounds that combined into a sort of mechanical hum. But Pierre thought he had heard something else— something that didn't belong. And as he stood alert in the darkness, straining his ears, he heard it again: footsteps, several pairs, coming the way he had come.

He shot glances in all directions, searching for the nearest lobby, and took off to his right, into a nearby opening. Inside were three elevators, and his eyes searched frantically for a call button. He stepped around to the other side and saw his target, lunging forward to press it. If these elevators didn't work...

But he could already hear a pod coming down, the sound of salvation on its way. His system tried to pinpoint its distance, its location, but it was hard to focus over the other sound: the sound of death, the sound of capture. His pursuers were closing on him, and based on how fast they were moving, there was no doubt they could hear this lift too, had already pinpointed his location. Less than ten seconds separated him from doom, and a cold dread came over him, the realization that everything had been for naught...

Then the pod door opened and he leaped into the lift, calling out "Minus twelve" as he hit the wall. There was a short eternity as he waited for the doors to close, listening to the rushed footsteps coming out of the passage, into the lobby, around the corner... the doors shut just before he caught a glimpse of his pursuers, and an aggressive impact on the door left a dent just as the pod started its trip upward.

Pierre knew they had heard his destination, and he knew he needed to change it, but as he allowed himself a moment to think, he tried to understand how they had followed him so deep. How had they known he was on -20?

Just as the question entered his mind, so did the answer. Pierre forgot he was dealing with hybrids now—they could access the lift software and pinpoint where it had gone. If they managed to follow his trail into the main lobby on the surface, they could have easily discovered where he was headed.

And as this realization hit him, so did its logical conclusion: they could also access this lift's software, except this time with him in it. He closed his eyes in a panic, finding his altitude reading. Sure enough, he had already passed -12, and was rapidly approaching the surface.

Without hesitation, he jumped to the doors, grabbing inside the lip and pulling outward. Tapping into his hybrid strength, he felt the steel give way, but as he pried the doors open, the stabbing pain returned with unprecedented force, and he fell to the floor with a cry. It took only a few seconds for his system to regain control, to fade the pain away, but in those few seconds, the lift reached its destination, and Pierre opened his eyes just as the doors parted.

He had reached another lobby, this one much smaller than the last, though the inside had the same smattering of debris littered all about. Just in front of the door were two individuals, almost certainly Puritan agents, exactly what Pierre had expected and feared. But what he had not expected was for both of them to be on the floor, convulsing in pain, covered by EMP netting that continued to give off sparks.

What the...

"Là, encore un dans l'ascenseur!"

A voice, twelve meters away. A shuffle of feet heading his direction.

"Attends! C'est moi, Pierre!" he cried out.

Two women came into view, each holding an EMP pistol ready to fire. As they caught sight of Pierre, lying on the floor of the lift with blood on his side, they hesitated.

"C'est Pierre!" he continued. "J'ai fait partie d'opération Genève, il y a huit jours."

The two women shared a glance but kept their weapons aimed.

"We don't know any Pierre. Stop wasting our time!"

Pierre frowned. If they had switched to English, they really didn't believe him.

"Maxime, demande-lui, il me connait!"

The women continued to eye him with suspicion, unsure of how to proceed. Pierre knew they knew who Maxime was, the only question was if the name was enough to save him.

"Qu'est-ce qui se passe?"

Another voice from thirty meters away, but this one was familiar.

"Hybride. Il dit qu'il connait Maxime," one woman answered, her eyes still locked on Pierre.

"C'est une ruse. Tue-le."

"Estéban! C'est moi, Pierre!"

The women hesitated once more, one of them looking back toward Estéban. Pierre heard the man approach and watched him take a stand just behind the women. A wave of relief came over him: he knew this man and, more importantly, this man knew him. But as he watched his former colleague's expression change from surprise to disgust, Pierre's momentary excitement disappeared.

"Et alors?" one of the women asked.

"C'est bien lui."

Pierre dared not say anything, not yet. He kept his eyes on the man that was once his friend, searching the face he knew so well.

"Qu'est-ce qu'on fait?" one of the women asked.

Estéban didn't answer her, his own gaze as steady as Pierre's.

"C'est toi qui a fait tout ça?" he asked, gesturing toward the two dead hybrids.

Pierre nodded.

"Oui, ils m'ont suivi."

"Tu les amené chez nous, c'est ça?"

Pierre felt a fear take hold, erasing any of the hope he might have had. Alaina was right, these people were no longer his friends.

"Estéban, il faut que je parle avec Maxime. J'étais avec la Résistance. J'ai des nouvelles qui nous concernent. On peut gagner, Estéban. On peut gagner."

Estéban stared at him for a while, a frown spreading across his face.

"Qu'est-ce que t'as fait, Pierre?"

The sadness in his former colleague's eyes was more terrifying than the earlier disgust.

"Estéban, s'il te plaît. C'est moi, Pierre. Même dans ce corps. Laisse-moi parler avec Maxime. Si vous voulez pas entendre ce que je dis, je reviendrai chez la Résistance."

The women hadn't dropped their pistols, but their eyes were on Estéban. This man held the key to Pierre's life, and he could only hope his past friendship would be worth a damn.

"Menotte-le et mets-le dans la navette."

Estéban turned around and the women dropped their guns, watching him leave.

"Merci, Estéban."

Estéban stopped, looking over his shoulder with disdain.

"Parle pas à moi, espèce de traître. On va te guérir et on va te lâcher. C'est ce que tu mérites, ou plus précisément ce que l'homme que j'ai connu mérite. Mais tu n'es plus l'homme que je connaissais."

The women approached Pierre to place him in electrocuffs, but he paid them no attention. His eyes stayed on his former colleague, walking away in anger. As far as he could tell, his mission had already failed.

- - -

Thrown unceremoniously into the back of the shuttle, Pierre spent most of his journey contemplating the choices that had brought him to this point. Why had he agreed to do this? Idealism? Naivety? Stupidity? All three?

If Estéban's reaction to his conversion was any sign, there was no hope. And yet the man had agreed to bring him in and heal him, so at least he would be rid of this stabbing pain in his side. Did any of them even know how to operate on a hybrid? Maybe the robots did…

He tried to clear his mind, to steer away from these thoughts and focus on the matter at hand. The Resistance had saved his life, and they had entrusted him with this mission. They knew as well as he did just how farfetched it was, but he couldn't give up now—not yet. If Estéban wouldn't let him meet with Maxime, he would have to find some other way of getting his message across.

He looked around the interior of the craft. There were three other passengers aboard: a robot pilot, and the two women who had found him in the elevator. Despite the restraints on his hands and feet, they sat at a cautious distance. One of them was staring out the front window, but he caught the other looking away just as his eyes met hers.

"Est-ce que ça vous gène si je parle?"

He was careful with his tone, pleading more than asking. If they let him talk, maybe he could get some information out of them. The woman closer to him turned to her companion, but the other woman didn't react, her eyes fixed on the window. Though he could feel his frustration rising, Pierre hid it from his tone.

"Vous pouvez me dire ce que c'est passé avec l'opération? La Résistance m'a donné quelques détailles, mais c'était pas clair…"

The second one turned back to him with a suspicious look.

"T'as fait parti mais tu sais pas?" she asked.

"Si, mais après," he answered.

She stared at him, unconvinced, and frustration turned to despair.

"S'il vous plaît… mes amis… je veux savoir…"

His voice faded as his thoughts went back to that terrible morning only eight days ago. Back when he was a pure human, back when Estéban didn't look at him in disgust. He remembered the days before that, the ones leading up to the operation: the emphatic speeches, excitement all over base… everywhere except within himself, because he knew. He knew what would happen, and he was more right than he ever wished he could be.

"C'était que toi?"

Pierre looked up, surprised to hear the other woman's voice. She hadn't moved at all, still looking through the window as she spoke.

"Pardon?"

"Qui a échappé avec la Résistance. C'était que toi?"

He hesitated, trying to understand the connotation of her question.

"Oui. Ils ont sauvé des autres, mais j'étais le seul qui est parti avec eux."

At his answer, she turned to face him.

"Et pourquoi?"

Again he hesitated, searching her expression for meaning.

"Parce que les autres les auraient tués."

She stared at him for a few seconds, her eyes giving no hint to her inner thoughts, then turned back to the window.

Pierre sighed in defeat. This mission was a mistake.

- - -

When the shuttle touched down at their destination, the women had the robot remove his ankle cuffs and escort him out. The machine led Pierre down the ramp into the familiar hangar, his eyes scanning the surroundings. This hangar wasn't as large as the one at the Resistance outpost, but it was alive, with several ships on the ground and people moving every which way.

As they made their way toward the main hall, Pierre saw at least a dozen familiar faces, each one stopping to stare, eyeing their entourage with both curiosity and suspicion. He tried to smile at the first two people he recognized, but his efforts went unanswered, and a mix of discomfort and shame came over him, driving his gaze down to his feet. Did they know? Did it matter?

When they entered the main hall and took a right at the first junction, the reality of the situation began to sink in; they were heading toward the hybrid holding cells, not the sickbay. He was not back home—home didn't exist for him anymore. What had he done?

As they continued down the hall, discomfort turned to fear, and his mind raced to understand why Estéban had brought him here. The man had told him he would be let go after he was patched up, but what if that was a lie?

The robot stopped outside one of the holding cells and placed its finger into the panel next to the door. Pierre watched it open, then stepped inside without a word. He turned around to face his captors, questions racing through his mind, but the door closed before he could say anything, leaving him alone with his thoughts.

A cot occupied the center of the room, the only piece of furniture in the five by five meter space. Not exactly luxurious conditions, though those didn't really exist anywhere on Earth anymore anyway.

A pain in his side reminded Pierre of his injury, and he hobbled over to the cot to lie down, struggling with the cuffs still holding his arms behind his back. Now that he had reached his destination, the system was toning down its safeguards, letting his body know there was work to be done. The problem was there was still no one there to do it.

He managed to lie down on his healthy side and started to ponder his options. If Estéban had lied, if he wasn't going to be healed, what were they going to do? Let him die slowly in this cell, bleeding out from his wound? That seemed brutal and unnecessary, especially after all he had done for them...

In that moment, alone on the cot in the dark, gray cell, a horrible thought came to him: what if they were going to use him for leverage against the Resistance? A pit formed in his stomach as he considered the possibility. He knew the location of the outpost, intelligence that he never thought might be of use to the Uprising, but based on how this mission of his had unfolded thus far...

The door to the cell opened, derailing his terrifying train of thought. Pierre watched a medical robot enter, closing the door behind it.

"Bonjour, monsieur. Puis-je vous guérir?"

With those words, the metal being erased a healthy dose of Pierre's fear, and he couldn't help but smile. How polite of it to ask.

"Oui, vas-y."

The robot approached the cot and removed his cuffs. Pierre turned over onto his back, stretching his wrists in the air for a few seconds as he closed his eyes. For the time being, he could relax. Robots were unable to kill humans or hybrids: if he couldn't trust his friends, he could at least trust this machine.

A pushing sensation in the back of his neck let him know the robot had connected to his system, and a calm warmth spread through his body as the anesthetic protocol took hold. Maybe there was hope left after all.

- - -

Pierre woke with a start, jolted out of his slumber by the reactivation of his system. He opened his eyes to the same gray walls, and saw the same medical robot standing by his side.

"Bonjour, monsieur. Vous êtes bien guéri."

As the machine spoke, Pierre felt a small tug behind his neck. He closed his eyes and checked his interface: sure enough, the shrapnel was removed and the wound was sutured and bandaged. A small message warned him to take it easy for the next day, but otherwise his system would have a perfect recovery. It was then that he noticed another notification in his system, a message from—

The sound of the door opening caught his attention and he exited the interface to see the robot step out of the room. Before he could get a word out, the door closed behind it, and he was alone on the cot once more.

Pierre stared at the closed door for a few moments then sat up, restless. How long would he have to wait here? What was their plan?

He remembered the pending notification and returned to his interface, opening the message. It was from James, sent over two hours ago—sometime during the surgery.

"Please let us know how things are developing."

He opened his eyes and stared at the wall. How things are developing? Poorly. He was slightly embarrassed to admit it, but he needed to give them an update, otherwise they might think he was dead.

As he reentered the interface and put together a reply, Pierre couldn't help but marvel at the speed of communication this system afforded him. For years, his communications with James had been sparse, requiring a certain degree of secrecy and lacking any stable wireless medium. Most of the time, if they wanted to talk, they had to do it in person, and those thousands of kilometers between their respective homes made it rather time-consuming.

If only he had had this system in the days leading up to the operation, he thought. What a difference that might have made.

"I was attacked and wounded by Puritans, but reached the base. Safe and healed now, waiting."

Then, after a pause, he sent a second message.

"Outlook poor. Called a traitor."

Better to be up front about it, he thought. A reply appeared before he could open his eyes.

"Have you presented the intelligence offering?"

Pierre shook his head even though no one was there to see it.

"Not yet."

He knew James and the other members of the Resistance saw the intelligence they had gathered as the key to an alliance, but Pierre wasn't so sure. Yes, a detailed map of every Puritan-controlled conversion factory on Earth—with valuable information regarding each facility—was a powerful gift, but this was a path they had already tried, and it was a path that had failed.

Still, the first attempt had been but a sample: this was everything. Pierre had looked over the data himself, and he had to admit it made quite an impression. He thought he knew something about the extent of the Puritan's hybridization operation, but based on the Resistance's files, he wasn't even close. So many factories… so many people…

The Puritans had made hybridization and indoctrination an efficient science. In each conversion factory, thousands upon thousands of people were born into a life of slavery, educated as if they were sub-human, and converted as they entered adolescence. They left the centers as slaves: builders, cleaners, soldiers… this was how the Puritans maintained their dominance: a large, renewable stock of hybrid workers.

Even now, Pierre had trouble understanding. Robots weren't human. Robots were stronger, faster, better than hybrids in every perceivable way. Why didn't the Puritans invest their energy in building robots?

In truth, Pierre knew why. In fact, he knew three reasons. First, they were afraid the consciousness would come back. To a Puritan, nothing was worse than the thought of a robot with a soul—not even the loss of their own. Second, they wanted to make it clear that anything short of a pure human was not human. What better way to prevent toying with purity than making hybrids the de facto slave class? Third, and perhaps most importantly, the need for a military. It was supremely difficult to develop robots that could harm humans: the safeguards were so entrenched in the foundations of the technology, most attempts met with failure, and even the successes were underwhelming. In order to field a large and powerful army, they had to turn to hybrids.

The problem came down to supply: in the beginning, the Puritans tried converting adult hybrids, members of the Resistance. But these individuals were prone to rebellion—they didn't make very good slaves, even with hormonal controls. The Puritans tried all sorts of things, but time was not on their side. With the sudden loss of millions and millions of robots, there was massive demand for some kind of working class to maintain the crumbling infrastructure of Earth and its colonies. If they weren't going to use robots, they needed hybrids—lots of them.

How and when it all started was lost between fact and fiction. There were stories of babies stolen from hospitals, abnormal miscarriages, or even parents disappearing. More realistic were the accounts of women paid to be impregnated over and over, churning out babies that would never be seen again—at least, not as pure humans. Eventually, some of those babies grew up to be fertile hybrid women, and the Puritans had a feedback loop of hybrid parents making hybrid babies, so pure humans could be left out of the equation.

Except there was a loophole in the system, one that couldn't be ignored. Conversion from pure human to hybrid had to be done in the early twenties—the later the better. It was impossible to do it earlier and guarantee health and longevity as it interfered with the natural processes of growth. This created a dilemma, as all of the individuals born to become hybrids were technically pure humans for a significant portion of their lives, the same portion they had no control over.

Naturally, a number of Puritans disagreed with this practice: a hybrid mother or father did not make a human child any less pure. As dissatisfaction grew, the Puritans splintered into two main factions: the business-minded, focused on the need for a work force and turning a blind eye or even encouraging the forced conversion process, and the more ethically-minded, who revolted against their own.

The movement, which came to be known as the Uprising, grew rapidly and violently about two decades earlier, at the turn of the century. In that time span, the Uprising caused nearly as much destruction as the Resistance had caused in its hundreds of years of existence, prompting an unprecedented Puritan emigration—Earth, already ravaged by struggles with the Resistance, was sent into further chaos, while Mars and the other colonies seemed like beacons of prosperity in comparison.

During these violent years, the Uprising's main targets were the conversion factories, and many of the movement's current members were individuals freed from such hellholes, saved from life as a hybrid slave. Pierre was one such escapee, liberated at the age of 5 from a future of indentured servitude. His mind shifted to those years, memories of dark rooms and horrible halls… all that time spent locked in the building, being taught he was meant for a second-class life, that he deserved nothing better…

The sound of the door opening snapped him out of the encroaching nightmare, and he saw a familiar face enter the room.

"Estéban!"

A wave of relief came over him at the sight of his former colleague, but as he noticed the disdain in the man's eyes—a look that bordered on hatred—the relief faded, disappearing as quickly as it had appeared. Estéban stopped about two meters from the bed, one hand planted firmly on the EMP pistol at his side.

"Estéban…"

"Ta gueule!"

Estéban let out an angry growl, turning and pacing to the wall. As soon as he came to a stop, he turned back around.

"Mais qu'est-ce que tu fabriques? Qu'est-ce que tu fais ici? Espèce de connard!"

He took two steps back toward the cot, fury in his eyes.

"T'as guidé les Puritans à deux pas de notre base, et pourquoi? T'es hybride, putain de merde… tu penses qu'on va t'accueillir? Que t'es bienvenu?"

He threw his hands in the air in anger, and Pierre replied softly, cautiously.

"J'avais pas l'intention de les amener—"

"Mais tu l'as fait quand même!"

He knew Estéban wasn't worried the Puritans had found the base—the Puritans were well aware of the base's location. But any attack by the Uprising would be met with repercussions. Operation Geneva had already disturbed the hive—adding a few downed shuttles into the mix certainly wouldn't help.

"Désolé, c'était pas prévu—"

"Ha! Pas prévu? Ben alors, c'est pardonné quoi. Pas de soucis, n'est-ce pas?"

Pierre ignored his sarcastic tone.

"Estéban, il faut que je parle avec Maxime—"

"Maxime est mort, Pierre! Tu comprends? Mort!"

Pierre saw the sadness behind the man's anger, heard the strain in his voice. For his part, it took a few seconds for the words to process, for their meaning to click. When he spoke again it was just a whisper.

"Mort?"

This time, Estéban didn't yell, nodding his head with a frown. Pierre stared off into space, unable or perhaps unwilling to understand. Maxime was the key to all of this—the one that could broker this peace, could make this mission a success…

"Genève?" he asked.

"Oui," Estéban replied.

But Pierre already knew the answer. Of course he had been killed during the operation. So many useless deaths… and for what?

"T'es assigné à comparaître devant un conseil spécial pour expliquer ta présence ici. Viens."

He leaned over and picked up the cuffs, gesturing for Pierre to get up. For a moment, Pierre stared at the restraints, hesitant.

"Sois prudent," Estéban remarked, unholstering the pistol and pointing it right at him.

Pierre stared at the barrel of the gun then back up to the man's eyes. Was this what it had come to?

"Putain de merde, viens ou je te tueras!"

Pierre jumped out of the bed, frightened by Estéban's tone, and placed his wrists behind his back. His old friend cuffed him then pressed the pistol into his back.

"Allez, on y va. Si tu bouges trop vite, je te tueras sans hésitation."

Pierre walked out of the room, his hope fading with every step. If his own friend was leading him at gunpoint, what chance did he have to convince this special council to an alliance with the Resistance?

- - -

They walked through the halls of the base, Estéban trailing Pierre by about two meters, pistol trained right at the middle of his back. To some degree, Pierre was glad they were taking this stroll at two in the morning— they passed only two or three familiar faces, each one stopping to stare at the pair, confusion and alarm in their expressions. Or maybe there was no confusion in those eyes? Maybe word had long since spread, while he was in surgery? Attention: do not interact with Pierre, he is a hybrid, he is a traitor.

This was the crux of the issue, the reason this alliance would be such a hard sell: most members of the Uprising weren't saved at 5. Most of the people he counted as his friends had spent their formative years not just being told they were meant to serve, but also being told that free hybrids were the enemy. They had Puritan propaganda engraved in their brains, even as they fought those same forces day after day.

This irony proved to be the greatest weakness of the Uprising, and was the main reason its rapid expansion had stagnated to a near-halt. While members argued about their stance on hybrids, the Puritans pumped out an army, ready to overpower whatever the Uprising threw at them. Now, their worldwide network was fragmented into several smaller strongholds such as this one, and even that infrastructure was under threat. Pierre knew they needed to ally with the Resistance to have any chance of continuing their cause, but if the rapid decline of their influence hadn't already made an impression, what could his lone voice do?

He had tried once already, in the lead up to Operation Geneva. It was the Resistance that had provided that information, information meant to bring about a joint mission to save the humans inside the factory. For years, Pierre had maintained contact with the Resistance, acting as a liaison between the two groups. This relationship had grown increasingly important for Pierre, even as his peers dismissed it as dangerous or useless, and even as he was asked repeatedly to sever communication altogether.

Pierre had been careful in his presentation of the plan: he framed it as intelligence he had been given by the outpost, but made the idea of a joint mission seem like his own. He knew he still had an uphill battle, but he thought the reality of the situation would bring them to his side: based on the intelligence gathered, it was clear the factory was heavily armed and guarded, and any attacks by pure humans alone would fail. Yet despite all of Pierre's warnings, his colleagues rejected any semblance of an alliance and pressed forward with their own operation—the same operation that cost Maxime and so many others their lives.

As these thoughts swirled in Pierre's head, Estéban directed him toward their main conference room: the room of council. It was here the elected leaders of the Uprising made most of their decisions, decisions that would affect the thousands that made up this European stronghold. Pierre had never been part of any of the councils, but he had heard of the heated arguments that happened behind those walls, debates usually centered on their military plans.

Maxime had been a part of the military council when Operation Geneva was on the table, and he had been the only member of seven to take Pierre's stance and oppose the motion. But a six-to-one majority was strong enough to overrule his objections, leading to the catastrophe eight days ago.

As he stepped inside, Pierre glanced at the six individuals seated at the front of the room and his stomach dropped. All of these faces were known to him, but only two of these were friends. The other four were acquaintances at best: people he had met before, but none that he knew very well.

His eyes stopped at the empty chair on the far right side and he frowned. Maxime was always a voice of reason, a man that understood their plight. Like Pierre, he had been saved at a young age—4 years old. There was always a correlation…

To Pierre's surprise, Estéban came into view, taking the empty seat and filling the council. As he took in this development, the woman in the middle spoke up.

"Pierre, vous savez pourquoi vous êtes assigné à comparaître devant ce conseil?"

His eyes turned to her, the voice of the council. There was a sadness in her eyes that worried him, but at least there was no trace of disgust.

"Oui, Joséphine."

She was one of the few he knew, a friend for many years, born and raised on the base itself. Perhaps that was why she looked at him the way she did.

"Alors, est-ce que vous pouvez expliquer votre présence ici?"

This was it, he thought, gathering his thoughts before he spoke.

"Je suis venu comme ambassadeur de la Résistance, pour proposer une alliance entre eux et nous."

"Nous? C'est qui nous?"

Pierre turned to the second man from the left, whose tone indicated his question was in no way friendly.

"Entre la Résistance et le Soulèvement," Pierre answered.

The man peered at him.

"Tu prétends faire partie du Soulèvement?"

Pierre frowned. The question didn't surprise him—he had expected it to happen sooner or later—but what he didn't expect was his own doubt. Was he still a part of the Uprising? They had never allowed a hybrid to join their ranks, but they had also never had someone so deeply entrenched go through a conversion…

The man scoffed at his hesitation, and Pierre realized he needed to say something, anything.

"Monsieur, je suis désolé, mais je ne sais pas comment répondre. En vrai, je crois que je suis toujours membre du Soulèvement, mais je ne vais pas faire des affirmations sans le soutien du conseil. C'est a vous de décider."

The man scoffed a second time.

"Y'a rien à décider. T'es hybride, t'es plus membre du Soulèvement."

"Luc, on digresse," Joséphine interjected, her stern tone catching Pierre's attention and igniting a small ray of hope within him.

The man grumbled in disagreement but said no more, and Joséphine reprised her line of questioning.

"Alors, vous êtes venu pour proposer une alliance entre la Résistance et le Soulèvement? Et c'est une mission officielle, soutenue par la Résistance?"

Pierre nodded.

"Oui."

Joséphine made to continue, but Luc interrupted.

"Alors, c'est la Résistance qui a guidé les Puritans chez nous?"

His aggressive tone punctured the already tense atmosphere, and Pierre struggled to keep his cool. He responded quickly, well aware that some of his frustration was slipping through.

"Monsieur, la Résistance n'aiderait jamais les Puritans. Ils sont plus opposé que nous."

"La Résistance oppose les humains purs. On va jamais s'allier!"

Pierre stared at the man, dumbfounded. Did he actually believe what he was saying? Did he not know the history of the movement, the pure members that made up the ranks?

"Luc, est-ce qu'on peut rester calme?"

Joséphine's question was overtly condescending, and Pierre wasn't surprised when the man snapped back at her.

"Calme? Tu veux qu'on s'unisse avec les hybrides? C'est quoi ce conseil? Tue-le, c'est un traître! Je serais pas surpris s'il nous film maintenant, partageant nos données avec l'ennemi!"

In that moment, Pierre felt a surge of pity mix in with his frustration. This man was one of the late saves, someone who had spent their entire upbringing in a conversion factory, indoctrinated with Puritan ideology. To him, hybrids were the enemy and they always would be.

"Monsieur, je ne partage rien et la Résistance n'est pas l'ennemi. Les Puritans sont l'ennemi. Dites-moi, monsieur, c'est la Résistance ou les Puritans qui dirigent les usines de conversion?"

The man hesitated, and Pierre pressed on—now was the time to propose the offering.

"En fait, la Résistance m'a donné des renseignements sur toutes les usines de conversion sur la Terre. J'ai tous ces dossiers enregistré dans mon système, et ils nous les donnent volontairement, sans conditions."

The members of the council eyed one another, intrigued.

"Vraiment? Toutes les usines de la Terre?" Estéban inquired.

Pierre nodded.

"Toutes. J'ai déjà examiné les données, et elles sont larges."

A few of them shared some hushed words until Luc's angry tone broke through once more.

"On peut pas faire confiance aux ces renseignements!"

Pierre ignored him, addressing Estéban instead.

"Estéban, est-ce que les données qu'on a reçu pour l'opération Genève ont étés fiables?"

Estéban hesitated, then nodded.

"Oui. Complètement."

But Luc grumbled in anger, still unconvinced.

"Et alors? Combien de nos agents ont étés tués?"

Again, Pierre ignored the man, addressing Estéban instead—the only other person in the room who had been a part of that fateful day.

"Estéban, est-ce que nos pertes ont été causé par les données fournis par la Résistance?"

Again, Estéban hesitated, this time for a few more seconds. When he spoke, it was quiet, reserved.

"Non."

Before Luc could throw out another objection, Pierre addressed the council as a whole.

"Mesdames et messieurs, je sais que la plupart de vous sont déçus ou même fâché que j'ai converti, mais il faut que vous compreniez: quand j'étais sauvé de l'usine il y a une vingtaine d'ans, je n'étais pas sauvé de la conversion. Non—j'étais sauvé de l'esclavage. Une conversion volontaire n'a aucun rapport avec une conversion dans une usine, de la même manière qu'un hybride contrôlé par les Puritans n'a rien à voir avec un hybride de la Résistance."

Pierre saw he had most of the council's attention, and his confidence grew with every sentence.

"Maintenant, la Résistance veut nous aider à sauver plus de humains purs d'une vie d'esclavage, et je ne vois aucune raison pour laquelle on les refuserait."

He scanned the faces in front of him, his speech concluded. A few still eyed him with suspicion, but most were clearly interested, and two were nodding encouragingly.

"Vous pouvez nous montrer ces données?" Joséphine asked.

Pierre nodded.

"Bien sûr. Il me faut juste connecter quelque part."

Joséphine gestured to a port at the side of the table.

"Ici."

Pierre approached the outlet and inserted his index finger into the slot. He closed his eyes and saw that he was connected to the council table, an isolated system on which he could display or share any of his own data. He brought up the Resistance's intelligence offering and uploaded it to the system, then disconnected.

"C'est fait," he said.

Joséphine nodded.

"Merci."

The council looked down at the table in front of them, now lit up with the map of every Puritan conversion factory. Pierre watched their faces transition from interest to concern, then concern to incredulity.

"Putain…"

Pierre frowned. He had had the same reaction at the sight of all this data. There were more factories than they had originally assumed, and the scope of each operation was beyond what they had imagined. Pierre clung to the one silver lining he could find: maybe the Resistance was right to bet on this offering after all. If the council saw the dire situation ahead of them, perhaps they would understand an alliance was not an option but a requirement.

After a few more minutes, Joséphine looked up from the table and addressed her colleagues.

"Je propose qu'on ajourne pour examiner—"

"*The Puritans are coming. Prepare for an attack.*"

James's voice entered the council room, but only in Pierre's head.

"Joséphine!"

The woman stopped mid-sentence, eyeing him with concern.

"Qu'es—"

"Les Puritans arrivent! Il faut se préparer!"

She stared at him, unsure of how to react. Some of the other council members glanced around nervously.

"Comment—"

"La Résistance me—"

"*The first shuttles will arrive in 18 minutes.*"

The council members stared at him as he stood there, listening to something not one of them could hear.

"Pierre…"

"Ils arrivent dans 18 minutes!"

Joséphine looked around at her colleagues, uncertain. Before she could come up with a response, Estéban stood.

"Alors, on va rester les bras croisés?"

His words seemed to flip a switch, and the entire council stood.

"À vos postes!"

Everyone began to filter out of the room, and Pierre felt a growing sense of dread, the cuffs weighing heavy on his wrists. Just as he was about to protest, he felt a hand on his shoulder—Joséphine was standing next to him.

"Viens avec moi."

Pierre followed her out of the room, straight to the nearest robot.

"Enlève ses menottes."

The robot did as it was told, removing his restraints. Pierre barely had time to register the sudden change in his predicament, as Joséphine led him onward through the halls.

"Dis-moi tout ce que tu sais."

Just as she finished her request, the alarm sounded, a harsh tone echoing through the halls. Pierre felt the adrenaline taking over, pushing away his questions, the council meeting, the alliance... all that mattered now was surviving this attack.

"*15 minutes. We are sending shuttles to help.*"

As James's voice spoke in his head, Pierre saw the halls filling with people running to their posts, a scramble of bodies and noise. Joséphine continued to press forward, unfazed by the chaos, and Pierre did his best to follow her example.

"La Résistance envoient des navettes pour nous aider."

These words made Joséphine pause, turning to give Pierre a concerned look. There was a brief moment where it seemed she might say something, then she started off down the hall once more.

Pierre could guess the thoughts running through her head. The Resistance, sending assistance? This could go very well or very poorly, though chances were it would not end up as they hoped. In the heat of battle, their own soldiers would target hybrids indiscriminately, and the presence of friendly semi-humans would only confuse an already chaotic situation.

"Enough."

The Room

The haggard man opened his eyes, disconcerted and disoriented. The confident man's voice had crashed into the chronicle, bringing their experience to an abrupt halt.

"Fascinating, but ultimately irrelevant."

The confident man smiled, bringing his hand up to the table. The haggard man watched the confident man lift his index finger then drop it onto the table, tapping the grey surface with a steady rhythm.

"Time is not of the essence, but why did you start us at the beginning?"

The haggard man didn't answer, staring at the confident man's finger, moving up and down with hypnotizing precision.

"As much as I'm enjoying our time here, it cannot last forever."

At the end of his sentence, the confident man's finger stopped midair, its tempo cut short. The haggard man brought his eyes up.

"Let's jump to thirty minutes before contact, shall we?"

The smallest hint of defeat flashed across the haggard man's expression, then he closed his eyes a second time, waiting.

The confident man stared at him for a moment, smiling, then joined him back in the chronicle.

Chronicle IV: Pierre

Pierre watched the light above him flicker and knew this was the end. It was only a matter of weeks—days, maybe—before the entire hall would be pitch black. Before he had met Omar, that wouldn't have been a problem—he could handle low light conditions with his enhancements. But Omar was not a hybrid.

"You're not hungry?" Pierre asked, taking another bite of the meal paste in his hands.

Omar shook his head.

"Not now."

The two of them sat on opposite sides of the hallway, leaning against walls two meters apart under the last remaining light source. It had been almost a year since they had met, a year of relative peace at their makeshift home. But now that the last light was dying, it was time to move on.

"How are you feeling?"

Omar rolled his eyes.

"Fine. No cough, no fever, no diarrhea, nothing. I'm perfectly healthy."

"Ça existe pas."

Omar stared at him for a moment, then shook his head.

"I don't think I'll ever understand you."

Pierre grinned.

"True, but that is okay."

He finished the last bite and tossed the empty packet onto the floor. There was quite a pile of trash forming around their little site, but it matched their surroundings—the hallway was filled with debris of all kinds.

"How many do we have left?" Omar asked.

Pierre could hear the apprehension in his companion's voice, and he hesitated before answering.

"Are you hungry?"

Omar shook his head without making eye contact. Pierre frowned.

"Omar, I have to get more. If you are hungry, you need to eat."

A flash of anger came across the man's expression.

"I'm not a child, Pierre!"

Pierre sighed, then pressed himself up to his feet. As he stood, he stretched his hybrid body, closing his eyes to check his system. Everything seemed to be in working order, and he hoped to keep it that way. There wasn't anywhere he could go if something went wrong.

"Ready?" Pierre asked.

There was still some anger in his companion's expression, but he ignored it, waiting patiently for a reply.

"Sure."

Omar stood, and Pierre turned away to hide a smile. The man could be dramatic, but it was best not to mock him—that would only make things worse.

"Seven kilometers today."

Omar groaned, but Pierre didn't give him time to complain, moving forward to start their daily trek. He couldn't understand the man's reluctance—after all, a pure body needed exercise much more than Pierre's did. Plus, Omar was the one that hadn't left the underground in several months; at least Pierre took the occasional trip up top.

Each time they had been running low on meal pastes, it was Pierre who ventured out into the unknown, searching the skeletons of Earth's prosperity for the nutrients they needed to survive. Over the last few months, as the remaining lights in their hall dwindled, it was Pierre who explored the deeper reaches of these same skeletons, looking for a new hiding spot for the pair. So far he had four main options, two of which seemed promising.

He was not looking forward to the day he would have to convince Omar to go outside again.

"Slow down, I can't see!"

Pierre ignored Omar's tone but slowed his pace, letting him catch up. It was true their hall had grown dark of late, but there was still enough ambient light for a pure human to navigate with little effort. Omar wasn't blind, he was afraid: Pierre was his guardian in this world of superhumans. Every time Pierre made a trip up top, his companion reminded him how vulnerable he would be if he ran into a hostile hybrid without Pierre at his side. But asking Omar to come outside with him? Out of the question.

Pierre wondered if it was more a fear of the unknown than fear of the actual excursion. After all, he kept leaving and coming back in one piece, surely Omar would realize by now going up top didn't mean certain capture.

"Still too fast!"

Pierre sighed and slowed even further. He considered himself a patient man, but part of him looked forward to the trips to the surface, glad to take some time off from the human he had unexpectedly partnered with almost one year ago. He still wasn't sure what had compelled him to help Omar on that fateful day. His ego would argue it was common decency—the right thing to do. But Pierre knew he wasn't such an angel. In reality, it was probably loneliness that motivated him—a desire for companionship, even if it was in the form of a former Puritan.

They reached the end of the hall and Pierre pressed the button next to the elevator doors. This shaft marked one of only two ways in and out of their enclave, the other being a rather tedious series of passageways connected to the large room at the other end of the hall. It was a perfect setup for two individuals who preferred not to be bothered, and something that was rather hard to find in the hyperconnected underground—another reason he was not looking forward to leaving. But such was life, always changing. Pierre knew that better than most.

The doors opened and the two of them stepped into the lift. Pierre selected -14, the doors closed, and the lift began its ascent.

Every day, they took at least one long walk for Omar's health, always in the immediate vicinity of their hall. The closest well-lit corridors were just a few levels up, but they mixed in other areas every so often to break the monotony. After a year in the same spot, however, there wasn't a meter of passageway Pierre didn't know by heart. Maybe this move would do them some good.

They reached their destination and stepped out of the lift. Pierre knew these halls so well he could spend several minutes in his interface, eyes closed, without tripping over a single piece of debris, and today, that's exactly what he did. But there wasn't all too much to find in that interface of his, not anymore. No new messages, no new updates; nothing new for decades. Instead, he read through old messages: conversations with members of the Resistance, back during the days of tenuous peace.

As usual, after some time, Pierre tired of his foray into the past, opening his eyes and examining the same walls for the thousandth time rather than facing the reality of what had happened so many decades ago. The walls were boring, but at least they weren't depressing.

Their loop wrapped up as uneventfully as it had began, and Pierre pressed the button by the elevator shaft to send them back down. But where he expected the doors to open right away, he heard the pod coming from below—approximately at their level.

Pierre tensed instinctively, placing himself between Omar and the lift. They were only five levels up—the doors would open well before they could get anywhere safe or hidden.

"What are you—"

He shot a glare at his companion, gesturing for silence, then turned to see the doors open, revealing a vacant interior. He took a tentative step forward and checked every recess of the small pod: it was empty.

"Someone is in our home," he whispered to Omar, still eyeing the inside of the pod as if someone would suddenly appear in the small space.

"You're sure?" his companion whispered back.

Pierre didn't answer, listening intently. If there was someone down there, he might be able to hear them…

Then he heard a very clear beep—a familiar noise, one he hadn't heard in many years.

"C'est pas possible…"

"What's happening?"

Pierre ignored Omar's impatient whisper, closing his eyes and opening his messaging system.

"*Please do not be alarmed. I know how to save you both.*"

He opened his eyes. How was this possible?

"J'ai— I got a message."

Now Omar's eyes widened.

"A message?"

Pierre nodded.

"What did it say?"

"That he can save us both."

Omar put his hand on Pierre's arm.

"We need to get out of here. This is a trap."

Another beep in his mind. Pierre closed his eyes.

"*This is not a trap, Pierre. I am not Puritan, or with the Puritans. In fact, I am as far from Puritan as is possible.*"

He read it twice then opened his eyes.

"I got another message."

Omar shook his head and squeezed tighter, leaning close.

"Stop reading them, we need to get out of here."

His voice was quiet but urgent, and Omar tried to pull Pierre forward, into the elevator, but Pierre resisted.

"Wait…"

Omar stopped, looking back toward him in anger.

"We have to go! This is a trap!"

The words leaked out between Omar's teeth, but Pierre shook his head.

"Omar, if this is a trap, why are they sending me a message? If they know we are here, they can catch us. But they don't."

Omar frowned.

"I— I don't know. Even if it's not a Puritan, it sent you a message—the Puritans will be here soon enough."

Omar was right. Among the reasons Pierre hadn't sent or received any messages in the past twenty to thirty years was because he assumed the Puritans had caught up to his messaging technology and might be able to detect his location based on outgoing or incoming transmissions. He had no way to be sure, but even if someone was out there, it wasn't worth the risk.

"I am not Puritan, and my messages will not be detected. You are safe."

Pierre jumped back, almost tripping over the surrounding debris and pulling Omar forward, who let out a yelp of surprise.

"What are—"

"T'as entendu?"

"What?"

"Did you hear that?"

Omar stared at him, concern in his eyes.

"Hear what?"

Pierre shot a glance down the way they had come. There was no one there.

"The voice…"

But Pierre knew he hadn't heard the voice in the hall, he had heard it in his head. This presented a dilemma, as Pierre also knew that should not be possible, not without him granting permission.

"What voice?"

Another beep. Pierre closed his eyes.

"I apologize for startling you, but time is of the essence, and I wanted to prove that I was working outside the restraints of Puritans and hybrids."

Outside the restraints of Puritans and hybrids? But that meant…

"Let's go!"

Omar wasn't whispering any more, and he pulled Pierre with greater force, but the pure human could not make the hybrid budge if he didn't want to.

"Omar, it's a robot."

Omar paused his fruitless efforts and stared at Pierre.

"A robot?"

"A— a Feeler."

He struggled to say the word, a word he hadn't heard or used in many years, and certainly not one he expected to use today.

"A feeler?"

Pierre nodded, though he could see by Omar's expression the man didn't know the term. And why should he? A robot with a consciousness was a myth, a legend.

"Putain…"

Pierre tried to comprehend what was happening, how this could be possible, but Omar was shaking his head angrily.

"This is a trap. The Puritans hacked you. They've been playing with hybrid tech so long, I wouldn't be surprised if they figured something like this out."

Omar had a point, but Pierre was doubtful. Yes, he was relatively certain they could catch incoming and outgoing signals, but spoofing or reading the messages themselves? Hybrid communication was originally designed by robots to be secure and robust, and the system had held up for hundreds of years. It was unlikely they had broken it now. Plus, Pierre couldn't help thinking that if the Puritans wanted to capture them, this was a very roundabout way of doing it.

"How can I respond to you?" Pierre called out into the hall.

Omar's grip tightened.

"What are you doing?"

"*You may respond with messages in your interface, with your inner-voice, or you may speak at a normal volume. I would like to come to your location, if you both agree to it.*"

Pierre looked at Omar.

"She wants to come to us."

"She?"

He forgot he was the only one that could hear the voice.

"Yes, she."

Omar shook his head.

"No. Stop communicating with her. We need to leave."

Pierre shook his arm off in frustration.

"Arrête! If you want to leave, go. I believe her and I will meet her. She says she can save us both."

Omar stared at him, taken aback by the outburst, and Pierre felt a sting of guilt. He took a deep breath before speaking again.

"I'm sorry, Omar. If you want I can go alone."

But now it was Omar who reacted with anger.

"Go alone!? And then what!? If you don't come back I'm left alone in the underground with this unknown threat a few levels away!?"

He glared at Pierre with an intensity that made the hybrid look away.

"I can't even navigate these halls without you and you want me to wait here alone? Your life isn't the only one on the line, you know."

Pierre knew, but he also trusted his instinct.

"I don't know what to say, Omar. I am going to meet her. Do you want to stay or not?"

Omar looked around, frustration giving way to fear.

"At least take us somewhere safe."

Pierre hesitated.

"Where? The safest place is home and she's there."

Omar frowned, and Pierre saw him struggling to get his next thought out.

"Up… up top."

His eyes widened in surprise. Omar, suggesting they go to the surface? He was more frightened than Pierre thought. After a moment, he nodded and cleared his throat, addressing their surroundings.

"Okay, you heard him. We will take the elevator up to the the top and you will follow."

"*Okay, but we must hurry. There is a contingent of Puritan-controlled hybrid agents on patrol. They will pass by within the hour.*"

Her response was calm, but Pierre felt his heart rate jump.

"Did she respond?"

"Yes, we'll meet her up top like you wanted."

There was no reason to make this any worse for Omar.

- - -

They stood side by side in the small pod, traveling at rapid speed toward the surface. Pierre glanced at his companion, a mix of fear and anger in his expression. He still couldn't believe the man had suggested a trip up top, but it made sense: there were plenty of places to run and hide at the surface, and a much lower chance of being cornered.

Still, there were bigger surprises on Pierre's mind, namely the possibility that this mysterious woman communicating with him was a Feeler. Everything he knew about conscious robots came from hazy recollections and mismatched stories. It was hard to know what was true when different people controlled what information passed from generation to generation. Some sources claimed the Puritans had wiped them out, others claimed they had run away, yet others claimed they were still hiding, deep in Earth's underground... and from his personal experience with other members of the Uprising, some didn't even know such a thing could exist.

The lift began to decelerate, and Pierre let the adrenaline clear his mind. It was time to focus. He closed his eyes to check the time. 20:07, evening in the outside world. Was that good or bad? He had no idea.

The lift came to a halt and the doors opened to what was once a grand lobby. Slivers of the setting sun's light came through broken windows, and Pierre glanced up cautiously. This was an ideal spot to get ambushed, and he knew it.

He stepped out of the lift, taking ginger steps between the fallen slabs of concrete as he glanced in all directions. Even inside the lobby, mother nature had started to take back what was rightfully hers: weeds and vines found places to grow, and a dozen birds fluttered about, fussing over their nests. It was oddly peaceful, this scenery, and the beautiful purple sky provided quite the backdrop.

Satisfied that no one was around, Pierre turned back toward the lift and saw that Omar hadn't left the pod.

"Omar, it's safe."

The man didn't answer, his eyes scanning the surroundings in terror. Pierre frowned.

"Omar, she will come soon."

This caught his companion's attention, and Omar hopped out of the pod. Just as his feet hit the ground, the doors closed, sending the lift back down for the mysterious stranger.

"Stay behind me, or—"

But Omar was already scrambling behind a large concrete slab, placing it between himself and the elevator. Pierre watched him settle into place and frowned a second time. If there was even a chance he was wrong about this, Omar would die.

He turned his attention back to the elevator. In a matter of seconds, the doors would open. What would be on the other side? An EMP pistol? Puritan agents? Or a Feeler?

Pierre heard the lift approaching and tensed. Maybe this was a mistake, maybe Omar was right. No one had heard of a Feeler in hundreds of years, there was no way one was behind that door.

Then the lift opened, and his nightmare came true. She was beautiful—gorgeous even—with thick brown hair down to her shoulders and a presence that demanded attention. A woman, not a robot.

"Omar, run!"

"Wait!"

That voice—it was the same one that had spoken in his mind down below. Pierre struggled to understand how a Puritan or hybrid had managed such a trick, but he didn't have time to figure it out. He braced himself for an attack, planting his feet firmly on the ground.

"I am not human!"

Pierre could hear rocks tumbling behind him as Omar scrambled to exit the lobby. Hopefully he could buy his companion enough time to escape, but then what? The man had never gone up top on his own, he could hardly navigate their hallway underground...

"If you let your friend leave, we will not be able to save him."

The woman stood inside the elevator, eyeing him sternly. Why hadn't she attacked? Was there a contingent of Puritan agents all around the building? Was this an elaborate trap?

"Are you listening to me?"

She stepped out of the lift into the lobby and Pierre's body tensed in anticipation. This was it, he thought. This was how he was going to die.

"Pierre, if Omar gets away we cannot save him!"

This time, her lips made no movement—the sound was only in his head. He stared at the figure before him, trying to understand what was happening. If she was Puritan, how was she speaking in his mind?

The woman continued to stare him down, and doubt entered his mind. Could it be? Was she a Feeler? But that was impossible... she looked so human... more human than a hybrid, even.

"I understand your fear, but every moment you waste is precious."

Again, her voice was in his head, and he stared at her in disbelief. It couldn't be, and yet there was no other explanation...

"Omar!"

He whipped around and ran after his companion, navigating the debris around him and exiting the lobby. There he was, about a hundred meters farther, struggling to crawl under a large piece of steel.

"Omar!"

He paused and turned his head toward Pierre, fear in his eyes.

"Is she coming?"

Pierre caught up to him, shaking his head.

"Omar, it's safe."

Omar gave him a suspicious look.

"Did you..."

Pierre shook his head.

"Omar, she…"

He realized how preposterous his statement was, but he pushed through.

"…she's a Feeler."

Omar stared at him, suspicion turning to anger.

"A what?"

"A robot, she's a robot!"

"What the hell are you talking about!?"

Pierre sighed.

"She isn't human, she's a robot."

Omar looked at Pierre as if the man had lost his mind, then shook his head.

"What're you talking about? Not human, sure, but—"

"Omar, she spoke in my head without moving her lips. I was looking at her!"

Omar stared at him in disbelief.

"She's a hybrid, of—"

"Omar, why?"

Omar stopped, surprised by the interruption.

"Why would she be out here alone? If this was a trap, why send one woman? It doesn't make sense."

But Pierre could see Omar was not in agreement.

"That sounds like a trap to me! A hybrid out here all alone?"

Pierre sighed.

"And the voice in my head? A hybrid cannot do that without permission. I never gave permission, Omar."

Omar hesitated.

"It's some kind of trick, she hacked—"

Pierre shook his head.

"Impossible."

Omar stared at him, incredulous.

"Impossible? Why impossible? You don't think they've been working on this for years—decades even?"

Pierre shook his head again, more emphatically.

"No. If they could hack me, why talk to me like this? Why send her alone? It doesn't make sense."

Here, Omar nodded.

"You're right, it doesn't make sense—it's a trap, damnit! We need to leave, now!"

The two of them stared at one another with an intensity that threatened to ignite into something irrevocable. Pierre had to admit everything Omar said was rational, logical. The only problem was her talking in his head: he refused to believe the Puritans had hacked the hybrid system that far. But how could he convince Omar to share his conviction?

He broke eye contact, looking back toward the building. The sun had almost set, a chill descending with each passing minute.

"Omar, I don't know what to tell you. I believe her."

He turned back to Omar.

"I'm going to go and hear what she has to say."

His companion said nothing, but his expression spoke volumes.

"She told me there are Puritans coming," he added.

A flash of fear crossed Omar's expression.

"Hybrids?"

Pierre nodded.

"They will be here soon. We cannot stay out here much longer. Come back and listen to her. If we don't like what she says..."

Pierre looked back toward the building a second time.

"...I will kill her."

Omar hesitated, and Pierre could see the conflict in his eyes. This was not what the man wanted to deal with right now.

"You think she's a robot?" he asked.

Pierre hesitated, then nodded.

"It's the only way she could talk in my head."

Omar stood up, brushing off some of the accumulated dust.

"If anything suspicious happens, I want you to—"

Pierre lifted his hand up to stop him.

"Omar, as you said: it is not just your life on the line."

Omar held his gaze for a moment then nodded in agreement. As they made their way back through the rubble, Pierre hoped this wild possibility was true.

- - -

Inside the lobby, the woman hadn't moved. Omar stopped at his previous hiding spot, and Pierre came to a stand a few meters in front of her. For a moment, he said nothing, eyeing the being in front of him with both fear and awe. There was something oddly attractive about her, and not just in the conventional sense: her look gave off a mix of confidence and kindness that threatened to bring Pierre's guard down before he even had a chance to speak.

"Who are you?" he asked.

The woman shook her head.

"I know you have many questions, but I cannot answer them right now. We must leave this place."

She pointed to the elevator, and Pierre raised his eyebrows.

"Back down? Pourquoi?"

"Parce qu'il faut fuir cet endroit avant que les Puritains arrivent pour sauver vous deux."

"Hey, don't do that!"

Pierre turned to see Omar's head emerge from behind the concrete slab, eyeing them both with disapproval. His companion's serious expression made him smile—one sentence in French and Omar forgot all his fears.

"She said we have to leave because there are Puritans coming."

"They will arrive in 29 minutes, but will reach detection range in 8 minutes. We must go underground," the woman added.

Omar's eyes went to hers, but he didn't say a word. Pierre turned back to face her.

"And then what? You said you could save us."

The woman nodded.

"I can save you both, but you must come with me, and we must hurry."

"How?" Pierre asked, eyeing her intently.

To his surprise, the woman smiled, and in that smile Pierre saw a human warmth he hadn't seen in many years, not even from Omar.

"The same way we survived, so many years ago."

He stared at her, confused.

"We? There are more?"

She nodded.

"Many."

"Many?"

He couldn't believe it. How could a group of Feelers survive hundreds of years undetected?

"I know you have many questions, but we must leave this place."

"How will you save us? How did you survive?"

Pierre hoped she had a good answer—an answer that might convince Omar, even—but as the woman hesitated in her reply, Pierre found himself growing suspicious.

"I would prefer to answer this question once we are already underground."

Pierre shook his head.

"No, tell us now."

She looked from Pierre to Omar then back to Pierre, a frown replacing her earlier smile.

"As you wish."

Pierre was truly lost as to what her answer might be. After all, they couldn't escape—there was nowhere to go. The Puritans controlled Luna,

Mars, the space stations… in fact, it was here on Earth that their influence was the weakest, so where could she possibly plan to take them?

"We survived the Puritan Revolution by uploading our consciousness to a virtual state."

Pierre stared at her, memories coming to him from those stories he had heard long ago… maybe they had escaped after all? Maybe everything she was saying was true? But if that was her plan, that meant…

"You can upload me?"

The woman nodded.

"Yes."

"To what?"

"To our fleet."

Their fleet, he thought. They had a fleet?

"And me? What about me?" Omar interrupted.

The woman's frown deepened, and Pierre ignored his lingering questions to focus on her answer.

"I'm afraid we cannot upload a fully human consciousness, Omar."

Pierre turned and saw the fury in Omar's eyes.

"So what, you save him and leave me to die!?"

She shook her head.

"No, Omar. Of course not. That is why we need to leave: to save you, Omar."

"How? How will you save me if I'm not a hybrid?"

But Pierre already knew the answer, even before the woman responded.

"We need to convert you, Omar. Then we can upload your consciousness as well."

A silence took hold, and Pierre looked from Omar to the woman. The last rays of the sun had vanished, and darkness came over the ruins.

"No."

Pierre was not surprised by his companion's reply and, it seemed, neither was the woman.

"Omar, we will not convert you without your explicit permission, but this is the only way to save you."

Omar shook his head, flustered and frustrated.

"Then don't save me! I've already been saved."

His eyes went to Pierre, who looked away in shame.

"Omar…"

Pierre thought back to the day they had met, wondering for a second time what compelled him to help this poor man. A Puritan on the run, a fugitive from his own people… and for what? For discovering the truth, the truth the Uprising had known, the truth that was now kept hidden…

Pierre took a deep breath and turned to face him.

"Omar, I will not stay. This is not a life worth living. She has—"

As he spoke, Omar's face contorted in anger, and his companion cut him off before he could finish.

"She's filling your head with lies, Pierre! Upload your consciousness? That's impossible. You're not a robot, you're a hybrid. There's still some human in you."

Pierre held his gaze. It was true, it didn't seem possible. Uploading a robot consciousness was one thing, but a hybrid's?

The woman spoke up, as if to answer his doubt.

"I know it is hard to believe, but—"

"Shut up! Don't lie to him! You expect us to believe this? This is a trap! I knew it was a trap! If you could upload him and set him free, why haven't you? What about the rest of the hybrids, huh? Why do you let them run around in the underground, hiding and dying, if you know how to save them?"

Pierre turned his attention back to the woman and saw a mixture of sadness and shame come over the her expression.

"We are trying. That's why I'm here. This technology was developed only recently. I am one of several agents sent to save the remaining hybrids on Earth, the ones that haven't been realigned."

"Great!"

Pierre turned at Omar's exclamation.

"So you admit it? You're here to save him but not me. How do I know you won't leave me behind? How do I know the underground isn't some kind of trap?"

"If I wanted to save him, I could do it right now and be done before the Puritans arrive. We need to go elsewhere to perform your conversion. That is the only way to save you both."

Pierre whipped his head around, back to the woman.

"You can save me now?"

She nodded.

"Pierre!" Omar cried out, and Pierre turned to see a terror in his eyes. "What are you doing?"

He came out from behind the slab, taking a few tentative steps toward Pierre, but Pierre raised his arm.

"Stop. Listen to me."

Omar did as he was told.

"I will not continue this life, Omar. Remember what you told me? Do we keep hiding forever? I am done with this."

He glanced at the woman, then back to Omar. There was a wild desperation in his companion's eyes, the look of a man who knew his options were disappearing. Pierre frowned, struggling to pronounce his next words.

"If you come with us, I will not leave without you. I will stay with you until we can both upload together. But if you do not come with us, I leave right now. You decide."

A combination of fury and despair came over Omar's expression, and once again Pierre could not bear to watch. He looked back at the woman, whose frown had not waned.

"Please, Omar. Come with us. The process will be painless, and we can be done in less than 10 hours time. But we must leave soon. Time, as always, works against us."

In the moment of silence that followed, a subtle noise stood out: the unmistakable sound of an approaching ship. The Puritans were on their way.

"I can hear the ship," Pierre remarked, giving Omar a knowing look. "They are coming."

Omar's face contorted in desperation, and Pierre felt his stomach churn with guilt. In a way, his companion was right: this was a trap. A trap for him, because the man didn't have a choice. Either he came with them, the path to a fate he vehemently opposed, or he stayed on his own, a frightening proposition in this dangerous world.

The three of them held this tense silence for an uncomfortable amount of time, and Pierre forced himself to watch his companion's struggle. Just before he began to wonder if he could handle any more guilt, he saw a change in Omar's face: a hint of determination came over him, replacing the earlier frustration.

"Okay."

Pierre stared at his companion with concern, surprised by Omar's calm tone, but the woman wasted no time.

"Then let's go. We will start our trip right away."

She gestured to the lift behind her, and they packed themselves inside. Omar entered the pod quickly, no doubt eager to leave the surface, but Pierre knew the man was far from content. There was no silver lining here, not for a former Puritan.

- - -

The trio walked in silence through the halls of the underground, in sections much deeper than Pierre had ever ventured. The woman had led them to one of the bottom floors, asking them both to keep talking to a minimum. The men didn't need to be told twice—even Omar knew the deeper levels were the most dangerous.

Their movements were slow and cautious, particularly in the unlit sections where Omar needed help. It was these portions that bothered Pierre the most, and not just because of the danger. It was clear Omar did not want to be here. That he agreed to join them was more a product of desperation than any willingness on his part.

In truth, Omar was not the only reluctant member of their party. Pierre had his own questions about what might unfold if they followed this woman. That's not to say he didn't believe her—for some reason, he trusted her, to the point where he began to question that trust—but the more he considered her plan, the more he began to understand the Puritan mindset.

If he uploaded his consciousness, he would lose everything about him that was human. He would not exist in a physical sense, beyond the hardware that held his mind. How would he exist? Where would he exist? So many questions whirled through his mind that his head began to hurt.

"What's wrong?"

The woman's voice caught him off-guard, but Pierre knew their silence hadn't been breached. She was speaking in his head.

"If you speak to me like this, it will not be traced."

He glanced at Omar and frowned. It didn't seem right to be able to communicate without him hearing what they were saying. But with all of the questions running through his mind, Pierre felt the need to satisfy his curiosity.

"Qu'est-ce qui se passera avec mon corps?"

"It will be left here, destroyed if you wish."

Left here? Destroyed? The thought made him uncomfortable.

"Et si je veux revenir?"

"You cannot return to the same body, but we can make one for you, one like my own."

Somehow, this was even less comforting.

"Sans mon corps, comment existerais-je?"

"We have a virtual reality in place to help you with the transition. To you, it will feel like you are in your own body aboard a spaceship. That virtual reality will be how you interact with the rest of us."

The rest of us... Pierre still found it hard to believe that there was more than one of these Feelers, let alone an entire fleet's worth. Were they all this human-like? He still had trouble wrapping his mind around the idea that this woman was a machine...

Then another question came to him, this one more urgent than the last.

"Combien d'hybrides avez-vous déjà sauvé?"

The woman had mentioned this technology was a recent development, but how recent was recent? Pierre did not want to be a failed guinea pig, his mind lost somewhere in transit.

"Seventeen so far. All uploads have been fully successful, if that is why you ask. We never would have attempted this technology without full confidence, which is part of the reason it took so long."

They reached the end of the hall and took a door to the right. They were greeted by a blast of light, and Omar put his hands up to shield his eyes. The woman paused just inside the corridor.

"We can talk here."

This time, her voice carried through the hall.

"You're sure?" Omar replied, bringing his hands down as his eyes adjusted.

"There are no hybrids nearby," she answered.

"How do you know?" Pierre asked.

While he could be relatively certain her senses were even more adept than his own, there was so much ambient noise in those depths...

"We are actively tracking all hybrids."

"What do you mean?" Omar asked.

"I know exactly where every hybrid on Earth is right now, realigned or not. That is how I found you."

Pierre's eyes went wide. Every hybrid, he thought. If she was telling the truth, that was an incredible ability.

"You can tell if they're Puritan?"

Omar seemed just as captivated by this revelation, eyeing the woman in shock.

"Yes, we can tell if they are realigned."

Without giving either of them time to reply, she gestured down the hall.

"We need to keep moving."

Omar shook his head.

"Wait. Where are you taking us?"

Pierre glanced from Omar to the woman and realized he hadn't even considered where she might be taking them. He just assumed she needed to take them away from the Puritans in order to perform the conversion in safety, but they had already traversed a dozen kilometers underground— clearly she had some kind of destination in mind.

"To the nearest conversion-capable facility."

"Where is that?" Omar asked.

The woman hesitated, and in her hesitation, Pierre saw the answer.

"No…" he began.

Omar looked from Pierre to the woman, then it dawned on him.

"A factory?"

"No," Pierre added, shaking his head. "I will not go."

"A factory is the only place we can perform a conversion and save Omar," the woman answered.

"No," Pierre replied. "Save me and take him with you. I will not go there."

"Pierre!"

But Pierre was not listening to Omar, his mind was elsewhere. Memories flashed before his eyes—memories he had worked so hard to repress.

"Pierre, I cannot save Omar alone."

The woman's voice was soft—kind even—but Pierre could think of nothing but the nightmare he had experienced so many years ago.

"Pierre, forget her, forget this. Let's go back. Let's go back home and forget this whole plan."

Pierre saw the desperation in his companion's eyes, but he knew their old home was not an option. One way or another, with or without an existential crisis, he was going to leave this world.

"Omar, I will not go back."

The desperation in Omar's expression deepened.

"Pierre, please! We can't go to the factory!"

Here, at least, Omar was right. He turned to the woman.

"I will go no more. Upload me and save him yourself."

"Pierre!"

He ignored his companion, but the woman only shook her head.

"Pierre, if I upload your consciousness now, it is not likely Omar will make it."

"Why not?!"

He could not hide his anger any more. How dare she try to bring him back to one of those horrid places! After everything that had happened...

"I am a robot, Pierre. If we come face to face with Puritans—which might happen at the factory—I cannot face them alone. I may be able to ignore their orders, but I cannot harm them in any meaningful way. They will overpower us, and Omar will be lost."

"Then take your chances! I won't be a part of this!"

He felt Omar pull at his arm, but he shoved him away in frustration.

"Arrête!"

Even as the word left his mouth, the woman was jumping to the side, catching Omar and breaking his fall. In his anger, Pierre had forgotten his own strength, and his push nearly sent Omar to the floor, a push that could have done serious damage if the woman had not intervened.

It was over before he had a chance to process it, but as soon as the two of them hit the ground, a wave of shame came over him. What had he done?

"Enough of this."

The woman's tone was harsh, but it was the shock in Omar's eyes that had his attention. How could he be so careless? He watched her help him to his feet, the words struggling to leave his throat.

"O-Omar…"

But the woman cut him off.

"You told him you would not leave without him. Will you keep your promise?"

Her words served to turn the knife in his stomach, and a nausea came over him. Why had he done it? Why had he stopped and helped this man that fateful day so many months ago? He could have been alone down there today, already uploaded, already exploring this virtual reality, his body left behind, destroyed…

"Okay."

"Okay what?"

The woman's tone had not eased, and he looked away in shame.

"I will come. I will help. I will do what I promised."

"Good."

But as the woman proceeded to explain the plan, Pierre noticed that his companion ignored his presence completely.

- - -

They continued their silent march through the deepest halls of the underground, approaching the nearest conversion factory. Even though they were no quieter than before, the silence seemed thicker, more pronounced. Something had changed between Pierre and Omar, and Pierre felt the guilt pressing on him with every step. He wanted nothing more than to apologize, to make things right, but he couldn't: he didn't want to speak down here any more than necessary, nor did he want to waste any time. And, perhaps more poignantly, Omar wouldn't so much as look him in the eye.

He took a deep breath to clear his mind. When all this was said and done, he would have an opportunity to apologize. Right now, the best way to make things right with Omar was to help save his life.

The woman had explained the plan in enough detail that Pierre knew what he was getting into, but questions lingered in his mind. They were to approach the factory from these lower levels, as the Puritans did not extend their control so deep. Once underneath the complex, they would ascend and infiltrate an operating room, then perform the procedure on Omar.

Pierre's conversion had taken almost two full days, but the woman assured them that once they were in the operating room, the process would take no more than an hour. According to her, only Omar's mind needed to be converted to perform the upload—the rest of his body could be left as is. Still, Pierre found her claim remarkable, as he knew the brain was the most complicated part of a human to hybrid conversion. Of course, his own conversion was at the hands of a hybrid—maybe a robot really was that much faster.

"*I apologize for not telling you the full truth, Pierre.*"

The woman's voice came into his head, interrupting his thoughts.

"*I thought delaying this information was the best chance to save Omar.*"

Surprisingly, Pierre did not feel patronized by the woman's words. Instead, he felt sorry for her. Here she was, risking her life to save a pure human, one of thousands who had tried to obliterate her entire race.

Race? Was that even the right word? Species?

"*J'ai pas su que les robots peuvent mentir,*" he responded, also in his mind.

"*To pure humans, we cannot. But we can omit the right details and emphasize the wrong ones. This is an indispensable skill, given our programming restrictions.*"

"*Peux-tu mentir à un hybride?*"

"*With hybrids, we are able to make our own judgements, to a certain extent. Our programming does not view you as fully human, so it is not as rigid.*"

Fascinating, Pierre thought. He had always assumed robots simply couldn't lie, that it had nothing to do with the target audience.

"*Donc vous pouvez mentir entre vous?*"

"*Theoretically, yes, though in practice our kind has decided to construct a partially shared consciousness that makes lying impossible.*"

"*Ferai-je partie de cette conscience?*"

Pierre was not sure if he wanted to know the thoughts of another robot, and he certainly didn't want a robot knowing his own.

"*No, hybrids are not included in this system, there are simply too many differences between your consciousness and our own. In the future we may be able to bridge this gap, it is an active area of research.*"

An active area of research? Pierre imagined robot scientists in a robot lab, and his mind went back to this supposed fleet. Did the Feelers have a home planet? What had they been doing for hundreds of years?

He knew he could ask her these questions, but he preferred to focus on their trek—they were now less than a kilometer away from the complex. Besides, he assumed he would learn everything he wanted to and more once he was uploaded.

The woman stopped just short of the end of the corridor, in front of a closed door.

"Once we pass this threshold, we will begin our ascent."

Though he had just heard her in his head, Pierre was caught off guard by her voice in the hall. Omar looked around furtively, clearly flustered.

"I am tracking several realigned patrols, most at the surface or the shallow levels. I will make sure we do not encounter any hybrids, but stay alert for pure humans."

The woman's eyes locked with Pierre's.

"Before we go any further, I need a clear message from you, Pierre. If we are compromised, do you give me permission to initiate and complete the upload process at my own discretion? This will include a termination of your chronicle, which will be uploaded for preservation."

He held her gaze for a few moments, the answer clear in his mind but unwilling to speak.

"Oui," he answered, no more than a whisper.

"Thank you. I will try to warn you if that is the case. The process will take no more than three minutes."

He nodded. Three minutes was a long time to avoid attack inside a conversion factory. And they expected to survive an hour up there?

The woman turned back to the door and inserted her finger into the hybrid port of the electronic locking system. They had seen many of these systems down here, but none of them were functioning, either deliberately broken or long forgotten. Not this one.

"I am setting up wireless access to their monitoring systems. I will clear us a path by disabling these systems as we pass through and by creating false signatures in other areas to draw their forces."

False signatures? If the woman could fake a hybrid signal somewhere in the factory, it could be enough of a diversion to let them sneak by. Perhaps this wasn't such a foolhardy mission after all.

A loud click marked the opening of the door, and the woman removed her finger from the port.

"Up ahead is a stairwell. When we reach it, I will carry Omar. From here forward, no talking unless necessary. Follow me."

She pushed it open, revealing an unlit hallway. It was clear the Puritans didn't come this deep, but Pierre hoped she was done talking. Tracking system or not, they were much too close to the factory for his comfort. Of course, if she was what she claimed she was, this mission was much more dangerous for her than it was for either of them.

She stepped over the threshold into the hall, but Omar hesitated. Though he lacked the global positioning system Pierre and the woman shared, and despite never having seen this door in his life, he understood where they were and what this meant. This was the same factory he had escaped, a place he never expected or wanted to see again. And now here he was, coming back to do exactly what he had avoided.

Pierre waited patiently behind him, wanting to give Omar some words of encouragement but unsure of what to say and still afraid to speak.

Finally, his companion took a slow step through the door, and the three of them continued into the hall.

The door stayed open behind them, providing enough light for Omar to navigate without aid. Up ahead, about a hundred meters away, was an opening to the right. The woman paused just outside, and Pierre saw the opening led to a set of stairs.

As the woman maneuvered to put Omar on her back, Pierre glanced up the stairwell. She was right, of course—he would have to be carried. Not only was it too dark inside for him to see clearly, but they were several kilometers below ground. If the woman planned for them to ascend all the way to the surface, it would be quite an effort for human legs.

"You lead."

Pierre glanced back at the woman, Omar perched across her back. In some odd way, he was offended that he was not the one carrying his companion. But this had nothing to do with Omar or the woman's preference—though a hybrid had superhuman endurance, a robot would still outperform him. She was the logical choice.

He did as she asked, starting his way up the steps. Truth be told, even with his enhancements, Pierre was not looking forward to this climb. What had been a few minutes in a lift would now take over an hour, perhaps two if they had to avoid hostile encounters. But he didn't have to ask why they weren't taking a lift—other hybrids could certainly hear a pod moving through the tube if it got close enough.

They made their way up, one floor after the other, one stair at a time. He looked at his feet, watching the slow ascent, hypnotized by the rhythm of his own legs. Sixteen steps up, u-turn, another sixteen, another u-turn… and every step was closer to the surface, closer to the nightmare from years ago…

They called to him now, in this stairwell trance; those memories he had tried so desperately to forget. Pierre had always wondered why a hybrid couldn't delete a part of their chronicle, a part of their life. True, he controlled whether or not he accessed those memories, but his brain was not fully digitized—at least, not yet. He could still remember things even if he wasn't replaying them in full detail. You'd think with all the advancements, memory removal would be an option. Anything to help him forget what had happened.

Anger welled up inside of him, but it was a mere shadow of the unbridled rage he had felt on that fateful day: the day it all fell apart, the day everything shattered into a million pieces. He had done everything he could to broker an alliance between the Resistance and the Uprising, and for a time, he had succeeded.

The Resistance's intelligence offering—the olive branch Pierre himself had extended—was not enough to bring about the alliance. But when the Puritans attacked the European stronghold, it was the Resistance's reinforcements that saved them all from destruction. That day, his mission was accomplished. The European alliance had begun.

Over the course of the next few years, they enjoyed a string of successful rescue missions, dismantling the nearest conversion factories and freeing the would-be slaves. But it wasn't long before the cracks began to show. The hybrid issue was a wedge that drove into the heart of the Uprising, one forced deeper and deeper into a shaky foundation. And then, one day, everything went to hell.

Unbeknownst to anyone loyal to the alliance, a small group of their colleagues was feeding intelligence to the Puritans, providing all the data the Resistance held and how it was collected. With ample counterintelligence and ampler resources, the Puritans started streamlining operations down to fewer factories with greater output—ostensibly for efficiency, but in reality it was a trap. When the allied forces made their next major strike—at the same Geneva factory, no less—the Puritans were ready…

"*Pause.*"

The woman's voice crashed into his memory—an outsider's voice inside his thoughts—and he halted as commanded. Did she hear something? He strained to catch any kind of noise—footsteps, even a breath—but all he could hear was the background of the underground, the same chorus of noise he had heard for the last seventy-nine years.

At least they had made some progress: about a third of the way to the surface, according to his sensors. That was probably the longest unbroken section they would get.

"*Continue.*"

Already? She didn't have to tell him twice.

He started up the steps once more, wondering what poor Omar was thinking, stuck on the woman's back in what to him would be near-total darkness. All of it would be over in a few hours though. As long as they made it up there. And as long as she was able to complete the conversion without error. And as long as no one found them before that was done.

Pierre tried to ignore his creeping sense of doom. All I need are three minutes, he thought. Three minutes, and I'm free.

"*Stop at the next floor.*"

A door was just ahead to the left, and he did as asked. The woman let Omar down gently, then put her finger into the electronic lock. The door slid to the right, revealing a well-lit hall.

"*Follow me.*"

She gestured to Omar, and Pierre allowed him to get in front, opting to protect the rear. He didn't know why they were leaving the stairwell, but he was not the one with the tracking system.

The woman walked down the hall more cautiously than she had before, and Pierre focused all his attention on the surroundings. He doubted there were any Puritans around—they were still quite deep—but he didn't want to be surprised.

After another two hundred meters, they passed a pair of elevators, and he glanced longingly at the tall steel doors. He wasn't physically tired, but the monotony of the stairs combined with the forced silence made this adventure mentally demanding.

A few meters past the elevators, a second corridor intersected their own, and the woman led them to the right. Pierre noted that while these halls weren't clean, they also weren't littered with debris like the ones he was used to. Did the Puritans maintain these areas? Maybe some of them did actually come this deep? To him, it seemed like it would be easier to neglect these lower levels and focus on the ones closest to the surface, but it was a long time since he had pried into the inner workings of a conversion factory...

He could still see them, the schematics for the Geneva facility. From the beginning, Pierre had a bad feeling about the operation: why go back to that wretched place? The rational side of him argued his fears were unfounded. After all, they had the Resistance on their side now, it wouldn't be anything like the first time. But if Operation Geneva had been a nightmare, its successor was another beast entirely.

Pierre's shuttle was shot down almost immediately, crashing into an exterior waste pipe just outside the factory. He managed to survive mostly intact, but four of five other passengers died, and the final one was seriously injured. As he assessed the damages to the craft, information came pouring in from all sides, forcing him to take notice.

Pierre closed his eyes and stared in horror at the messages clogging his interface. The attack was clearly a trap, and most of their operatives were already dead—it wasn't Geneva all over again, it was worse.

"Ils arrivent."

Pierre reopened his eyes, turning to the source of the voice: his downed compatriot, moaning in agony in a pool of his own blood. He crawled over to him, scrambling to find the source of his pain.

"Il faut fuir. Ils arrivent."

He was right: even as they spoke, Puritan agents were converging on their position, preparing to board the shuttle. He could hear them running outside, their steps ever closer.

Pierre jumped to his feet and scrambled to the other side of the shuttle, looking for a way out. Both doors were jammed shut, and most of the structural integrity of the shuttle was lost.

"Il faut fuir..."

His friend's words faded, the effort to speak too great for his condition, but Pierre had no time to consider that—they needed an escape route. He went to the front, stepping over the corpse of the pilot, and saw a small hole through the front glass leading into the waste pipe. He gathered what strength he had left and kicked at the surrounding glass, breaking off enough pieces to fit a body through.

A bang on the hull let him know the agents had reached them, and he scrambled back to his downed companion, still conscious and breathing. He picked him up and took him to the front. Working as quickly and carefully as possible, he placed his friend on the edge of the broken window then jumped through, landing with a splash in the muck below.

It's only ankle-deep, Pierre remembered thinking. Maybe this would work after all.

The woman stopped in front of another door and Pierre nearly bumped into her, so engrossed in his memories. It took him a split second to refocus, to remember where he was and what they were doing. In that split second, she hacked open the door to reveal a new set of stairs, this time with some light seeping down from above.

"*We are approaching their defense levels, two levels full of hybrid patrols meant to prevent exactly what we are trying to do.*"

Pierre glanced at Omar, wishing he could somehow pass the words along to his companion.

"*At these levels, all access points, including stairwells, are guarded. My diversions will open a window for us, but it will be a very short window. Once we begin this ascent, we cannot falter until we are well past these levels. Is that clear?*"

Pierre looked back at the woman.

"*Oui.*"

"*Okay, I will get Omar on my back then I will take the lead. You must remain behind me at a quiet and even pace until I deem the situation clear.*"

He didn't need to be told twice. The woman helped Omar onto her back, then paused just outside the stairwell entrance.

"*Ready? Now.*"

She started up the steps, Pierre staying just behind her. How close were they going to pass by the agents, he wondered. How close might they get to being caught? He did not care to run from hybrid agents. Not again.

How long they had spent in that waste pipe, Pierre could not say. Sprinting through feces and urine, his injured friend sprawled across his back, Pierre kept waiting to feel the dart, to plunge into darkness and awake a slave. Instead all he heard were his own frantic steps, the echos of each splash bouncing off the pipe walls.

"*Tue-moi.*"

His friend's soft voice nearly made him trip, and he came to an abrupt stop.

"Quoi?"

"*Tue-moi. C'est fini.*"

Even as the voice spoke in his head, Pierre was listening into the background, searching for any noise that might indicate they were being followed.

"*N'hésite pas, t'as pas de temps.*"

He struggled to understand his friend's words.

"On va te guérir, on va—"

"*Regarde tes messages.*"

Pierre did as his friend asked, closing his eyes to check his messages. It was only then he saw the news, news the man on his back had no doubt been reading the entire time: during the operation, their stronghold faced a coordinated and massive Puritan attack, killing thousands upon thousands of their members and destroying the complex. The European branch of the Uprising was no more.

As the weight of this information came crashing over him, Pierre finally heard them: more splashes, the sound of the Puritan agents coming their way.

He opened his eyes in a panic. Where would he go? What could he do? Their base was gone, destroyed, and—

"*Ils arrivent. Tue-moi ou tu n'échapperas pas.*"

With the Puritans close, Pierre opted to respond in his head.

"*On peut te—*"

"*Tu peux rien faire! Si tu me laisses pas, on va tous les deux mourir. Si tu me laisses, ils vont me réaligner. Tue-moi et prends la fuite!*"

Pierre felt a nausea come over him, as if his sense of smell had suddenly unlocked, letting the scent of the waste pipe overwhelm him. His mind tried desperately to find a way out, a solution besides what his friend proposed, but with every second, the sound of the Puritan agents got ever closer.

His friend was right, of course. There was nowhere to heal him now. If Pierre tried to take him further, they would both die, and if the agents reached him, he would be realigned.

"*Fais-le!*"

He dropped his companion into the stream of excrement, and a second wave of nausea came over him. There was no time to waste, no time to contemplate the most humane way to go about this task. So Pierre did what he had to do, what was right....

"*We're clear.*"

The woman's words were a beacon of light in the darkness, swooping in to save him from the most gruesome of his memories. Only now, as he paid more attention to his movements up the stairs, did he notice the tears in his eyes, the drops of salted water blurring the bottom of his vision.

An urge to sniffle came over him, followed immediately by a shot of anger. How could he be so careless? Letting himself get lost in his thoughts at such a sensitive time. His body was on auto-pilot, guided half by instinct and half by the programs in his software, but even that wasn't strong enough to stop the tsunami of emotion swelling up inside of him.

He needed to keep his head clear. But he had no command to control his wayward thoughts, nothing but his human self-control, a fickle and unreliable tool. He let the water in his eyes clear on its own, then brought his attention to each step. Lifting his right foot, then his left. Again and again, one stair at a time.

With the defense levels behind them, Pierre assumed they had passed the worst of it, but he soon realized how wrong he was. What followed was a nightmare of intermittent movement. They would climb a level or two, then the woman would command him to stop. Sometimes, they stood still for several minutes at a time, and Pierre heard far-off footsteps with alarming frequency. A human? A hybrid? A robot? It didn't matter, as long as they stayed far away, as far away as possible.

With each flight Pierre noticed a little more light, a little less dirt. How long until they reached where the pure humans lurked? With any luck, they wouldn't run into any, but Pierre knew the higher they went the more likely it got.

Over the past half-century, the Puritan emigration off Earth had begun to reverse, mostly due to the fall of the Uprising. With expansion and reclamation on their agenda, but without a standing infrastructure that could handle the influx, most conversion factories were evolving into miniature cities—places where the Puritans felt safest, where the density of their security forces were highest.

Pierre had known very little about these things until his chance encounter with Omar—the man was one of many workers sent to Earth to help rebuild. It was only then, when he saw the conversion process up close, when the reality of all those people born into slavery was impossible to ignore, that Omar began to question his loyalties.

The Uprising wasn't completely dead, of course. It was more an idea than a group, an idea that people like Omar would sometimes fall upon, though the punishment for revolt was a strong deterrent. Omar, stubborn as he was, still tried to rally a group together, and made a move to rescue a batch of individuals destined for slavery. Unfortunately, a few of them were so indoctrinated that they confessed their savior's crime before anything could happen, and only through the timely warning of several loyal friends was Omar able to flee the area, burrowing in the underground to escape a forced conversion.

Pierre stumbled upon the man several days later, emaciated and terrified, and did everything in his power to save him. Though he knew Omar still held some distrust for hybrids, they formed a relationship of mutual benefit, particularly when Omar caught Pierre up to speed on the world around him.

While the Puritans continued to churn out an army of hybrids, and while their hold on Earth continued to grow, there was trouble brewing beneath the surface. Hybrids, while efficient and militarily useful, had not managed to fill the gap left by the loss of millions and millions of robots.

Of one thing, Pierre was certain: the human race had developed rapidly —perhaps too rapidly—and the planet and colonies on which it lived were tailored for a lifestyle that no longer existed. This is why he had been so convinced the end of the species was imminent. Maybe even in the next hundred years.

But not anymore. This woman changed everything. If she was right, perhaps the human race could be saved. If there ever was an entity more intent on saving the human race than humans themselves, it would be the robots. Maybe they would succeed?

"Pause."

Pierre froze where he was, cursing his constantly wandering mind. They were at -22 now, just over a hundred meters below the surface. So close yet so far.

"We need to switch stairwells again. There are no hybrids in the chosen path, but we are now at levels frequented by pure humans. Stay alert. I will note any major changes in your physiological response as a warning—no need to message me."

He nodded, though she wasn't even looking in his direction. A moment later, Omar was off her back, and she gestured silence.

"Follow me."

She took them out the nearest opening, into a hall much cleaner than any he had ever seen. That wasn't to say it was spotless—here too, Pierre could see the age of the place—but it was in such stark contrast to what he was used to seeing, he couldn't help glancing around in wonder.

And to think, this was once the norm. He could scarcely imagine it.

"*Pause.*"

She lifted her hand to share the signal with Omar, who stopped in his tracks. Just then, Pierre heard them: footsteps, an even cadence in some adjacent hall. The question was, how far?

They maintained their position for several seconds, and Pierre noticed the sound receding.

"*Okay.*"

She gestured to Omar and they continued along the hall, hacking a door and taking a right at the next junction. Pierre winced as the portal screeched open, but the woman's calm reaction let him know no hybrids were close enough to hear. Perhaps the pure human had heard it, but it didn't matter. Unlike the hybrids, the pure humans were not connected to the complex's systems and had no idea when a door was being used or for what. If one of them heard it, they probably wouldn't think anything of it.

After another three turns and three hundred meters, they were back in a stairwell with Omar on the woman's back. So close to the surface, Pierre assumed this would be the final upward stretch, but at -19, she had them switch stairwells again. Then a third time at -14.

Each time, they would hear footsteps and hold their ground. Twice they had to backtrack and reprise their route. But on the third change of stairwells, during another moment of tense silence, Pierre realized there were footsteps coming from both directions.

"There are pure humans approaching from both directions," the woman announced. "We cannot backtrack."

Omar gave her an incredulous, but Pierre was focused on the pit of despair inside of him. Was this it? Was this a dead end?

"We have no choice but to continue on our path."

Her words punched a hole in his gut and he looked from the woman to Omar.

"You mean, just walk past them?"

She nodded.

"I anticipated something of this nature happening, but I thought it best not to tell you."

Pierre felt a surge of frustration within him, but before he could lash out, the woman raised her finger to her lips.

"Please, do not compromise our position any further. We must act natural."

"No," Omar interjected.

Pierre and the woman turned their attention to him.

"It won't work," he continued. "Look at our clothes, our faces. We look like we've been outside, they will know."

He was right. Omar and especially Pierre looked like they had been in the underground for a few years. Only the woman looked clean, pure.

"Not me. With me, you two will blend in."

Omar's stared at her, dumbfounded.

"No one looks like this in the complex, not even the slaves!"

The footsteps were closer now, and Omar's voice was louder. Pierre glanced down both ends of the hall and could see the outline of two figures on one side and three on the other. The first pair would reach them in minutes.

"We don't have a choice."

Omar looked to Pierre, the first eye contact he had given him since the push, his eyes begging for an explanation, for a way out… but all Pierre could do was frown.

"She's right."

He saw the frustration bubbling underneath the surface, the telltale signs of Omar's anger, ready to release. But just before he went off, a fear took hold of him, and he addressed the woman in a whisper.

"They might recognize me…"

She nodded.

"It's a risk we have to take. However, it is very unlikely these particular individuals know you or know that you escaped."

"But what if they do?"

Pierre could see the figures more clearly now—a man and a woman—and both of them had a small device attached to their hips: EMP pistols. He felt a spike of adrenaline and wished his two companions would finish this conversation. The longer they stood here whispering to one another, the more suspicious they would seem.

"There's no other way. We need to move. Let me do the talking."

Before Omar could object, the woman started off toward the approaching pair. He had no choice but to follow, with Pierre right behind him. They were about a hundred meters away now, and the Puritans slowed their pace, eyeing them warily. The man whispered something to the woman, then both of them put their hands on their pistols and came to a stop about fifty meters away.

"Hold it!"

The trio halted as commanded and the man unholstered his pistol. Pierre wanted to shoot a glance back down the hall toward the other three humans, but as the man lifted the weapon and pointed it at them, he knew that wouldn't be wise.

"What are you doing!?"

It took a moment for Pierre to realize the voice he heard—these words barked in a condescending manner at the man with the gun—came from the woman: the robot standing next to him staring down the same barrel.

"Why are you pointing that thing at us!?"

The man with the pistol hesitated, glancing at the Puritan woman next to him, her hand hovering over her own holster.

"There are hybrids in the base, didn't you hear?" he answered.

The diversions, Pierre thought.

"And? What does that have to do with us?"

He gestured with his weapon.

"Look at your friends there! They look like they haven't washed in days!"

The woman looked at Pierre and Omar then back to the man.

"Are you here to catch hybrids or lecture us on our hygiene? I don't have time for this."

She took two steps forward, and Pierre watched in horror as the man aimed to fire. What was she thinking? Yes, the EMP darts did nothing to humans, but this was a dangerous bluff—too dangerous.

Then Omar hurried to follow her, and Pierre realized with a sinking feeling of horror that he had to do the same. Before he could overthink it, he scrambled to catch up. Not ten meters farther, the Puritan woman drew her pistol, and their guardian angel stopped a second time.

"Are you kidding me? You think I'm walking these halls with two hybrids?"

She pointed toward their guns.

"Do you hear any detectors going off?"

The two Puritans glanced at one another, doubt entering their expressions. When the man spoke again, his tone was softer, less certain.

"They don't always work, maybe the—"

But the woman didn't let him finish, interrupting him at full volume.

"If you shoot one of those things at me, so help me—"

"Alright, fine!" the man responded, putting the gun down.

The Puritan woman glanced at him and followed suit.

"We're on edge is all. They haven't been able to catch them for a few hours, usually it doesn't take this long."

Pierre imagined an elaborate game of cat and mouse, with the woman creating a false hybrid signature that was always one step ahead, always outmaneuvering the realigned agents. It had to be frustrating.

"You two security?" she asked.

Pierre stared at them, dumbfounded by what he was watching. A Feeler yelling at Puritans was insanity. But having a normal conversation with them? What had the world come to?

They nodded in reply.

"We're trying to get everyone to the upper floors. You three headed up?"

The woman nodded.

"I'm bringing these two. They've been in the underground a while, but it was time to cut that adventure short."

The man looked at Pierre and Omar, trying and failing to mask his distaste.

"Well, stay safe."

He made to take a step forward then paused, eyeing them a second time.

"And maybe tell your friends to take a wash. They look like hybrids."

With a final nod, the two Puritans continued down the hall past the trio. The woman started off immediately, but it took a moment for Pierre to process their success and resume his walk. A wave of relief and disbelief came over him. She was lucky they hadn't called her bluff, though the lack of alarms certainly played in their favor.

"*Hopefully that was the hardest part,*" her voice sounded off in his head.

Pierre couldn't help but agree.

When they made their next turn, the three Puritans behind them didn't follow, and they managed to reach the other stairwell without issue.

"Omar, I won't be carrying you anymore as there are only 14 levels left and the density of Puritans is going to increase. Most of them are holed up in their living quarters, but we may run into other security teams, and having someone on my back might look suspicious."

Omar nodded in agreement, then they started up the steps. Two levels up, Pierre heard more footsteps, but there was no command from the woman so he ignored them. At -8, two pure humans could be heard talking just outside the stairwell, but again the woman didn't stop.

Pierre could feel the fear receding, replaced by a confidence he wouldn't have expected even an hour ago. The only thing that worried him now was getting caught mid-conversion. He wondered if the woman could lock them in the operating room; that way, if they were discovered, they could finish the job. But there was a hole in that plan: even if they uploaded Omar and himself, what happened to the woman? She had to escape to preserve the secret of her identity, didn't she?

Pierre decided it was best to leave that problem to her. She would know better than he.

Just before they reached -4, two Puritans stepped into the stairwell ahead of them and hesitated at the sight of the dirty trio.

"We know, we know—we're going up top," the woman said.

The two humans shared a concerned glance, but Pierre ignored them, following the woman up the steps, past their confused stares. A few moments later, he could hear them start down the steps, mumbling to one another about their odd appearance and unpleasant smell.

It was amazing what one could get away with when one acted like they belonged. That and when they had a way to disable the detection system, he thought.

Finally, after over two total hours of ascent, they reached 0—the surface. Here, the woman stopped, peering out of the opening down both ends of the hall.

"We have a problem."

With those words, Pierre's felt his confidence waver, its fragile foundation threatening to crumble.

"There is an operating room down the hall, about three hundred meters away, but there are two Puritan security agents standing guard."

Each sentence ate at his resolve, strengthening his doubts.

"They will need to be disabled quietly and without witnesses. I cannot explicitly harm them, so I will need help."

She turned to face Pierre, who could feel his heart racing. It was clear she expected some kind of response, but her words hung in the air unanswered, a prolonged silence Pierre didn't want to break.

"We cannot hesitate, one of the hybrids may discover the pattern in my diversions and see the path I have cleared for us. If they deduce what is going on and reach this area before we have saved Omar—"

"Je sais," Pierre replied softly.

He took a deep breath, then peered out the hall. There they were: two Puritans about three hundred meters away, EMP pistols attached to their hips. Yes, he was stronger than them, faster than them… but any misstep and he was down for good.

Then a thought came to him and he turned back to the woman.

"If they disable me, can you revive me in the conversion center?"

She shook her head.

"In theory, yes, but that is unlikely. If one of us fails, it is likely both of us will fail."

He sighed, discouraged.

"It's not ideal," she continued, "but we don't have a choice."

"So let me do it," Omar interjected.

Both of them looked at the pure human.

"Omar, you will not be able to overpower—," the woman began, but Omar raised a hand to silence her.

"I'm not overpowering anyone. Let me just talk to them. I'll tell them to leave."

She shared a concerned glance with Pierre before replying.

"I'm not sure that's—"

"You just said this wasn't ideal, and that if one of you fail, both of you fail. Well if both of you fail, it's over. I'll be found and converted, end of story."

The woman nodded in agreement.

"Most likely."

"Right, and I'm pure. Even if they shoot me because of this," he gestured at his clothing, "nothing will happen. Plus…"

He hesitated, glancing at the hall.

"…this way they don't get hurt."

Pierre peered at Omar curiously. In a way, he understood: despite everything that had happened, these were still Omar's people. He didn't want to see any unnecessary deaths. But even if he understood, Pierre did not share the sentiment. These were individuals that would kill or enslave the woman and himself at a moment's notice. Besides, how was Omar going to convince them to leave?

"What will you tell them?" the woman asked.

Omar hesitated.

"Are the pure humans tracking your diversions?"

The woman shook her head.

"They are not that well organized. All of that is left to the hybrids. That is why they are panicking—their usual system isn't working and they don't know how to react."

"I'll tell them I saw a hybrid a few levels down, maybe I'll say some other security guys were ambushed. That'll buy us some time."

The woman didn't seem convinced.

"It won't be enough."

"If I convince them, it will. You just said they are panicking. What's more important, guarding the operating room or catching the hybrids?"

Pierre glanced at the woman. Omar had a point, made all the more attractive in that it removed his direct confrontation with the guards.

"At least let me try. If it doesn't work, I'll distract them and you can attack."

The woman stared at him for a moment, then nodded.

"Very well, Omar. You have two minutes. If it is not working, yell the word please in a manner that does not alert them to your plans. Make sure to be loud, as the background noise is interfering with our hearing. If we hear this word or if two minutes have passed, we will approach to assist."

Omar nodded.

"Go, do not delay."

Before he left, Omar glanced at Pierre. It was a quick look, barely lasting a second, and yet something about that look worried the hybrid. There was a sadness in Omar's eyes, a sort of resignation. Did he not think his plan would work?

And then his companion was out in the hall, running toward the two men standing guard.

"I hope this works," the woman commented.

Once more, Pierre couldn't help but agree.

- - -

Two minutes never seemed so long. Pierre wanted to glance out in the hallway, to check on his friend. He strained his ears over the noise, only then realizing how right the woman was: the background hum at this particular spot was overwhelming. His ears had automatically adjusted to agreeable levels, but now that he was trying to actually listen, the droning of pipes and machinery threatened to give him a headache.

He dialed it back to acceptable levels. Why put himself through that pain if there was a robot right here that could fulfill that role without the same suffering? Well, that wasn't fully true, he realized. This was a Feeler, a robot that could feel. But did she suffer the same way a hybrid could? The same way a human could?

A fundamental question that hadn't been answered in hundreds of years, and Pierre hoped to solve the riddle in two minutes. Two minutes that felt like hundreds of years. If only—

Footsteps! One set, approaching at a sprint. He saw the woman slide to the wall just outside the entrance and crouch, and he mirrored her on the other side. The footsteps came to an abrupt stop by the stairwell entrance.

"Pierre?"

Both woman and hybrid relaxed, standing as Omar poked his head in. He looked at the woman.

"It's done. Let's go."

They followed him back out and, sure enough, there was no sign of the two guardians. The three of them hustled down the hall, checking all the connecting corridors, each one as empty as the last. Where had those two gone?

They reached the door to the operating room and the woman inserted her finger, hacking it open. As soon as the metal portal slid away, the three of them shuffled inside. The woman hacked back in on the other side, closing the door behind them.

"We're locked in. That'll hold against the Puritans but hybrids will be able to break it down."

Pierre glanced at the scene before him: a massive chamber, about twenty by thirty meters and six meters high, with countless drawers, cabinets, and shelves along every wall, and three large machines occupying the center. He had seen a machine like that once before, but a much smaller model: a conversion machine, where a human was strapped in and a hybrid was strapped out.

"Omar, we'll use this device."

The woman gestured to the right-most machine, but Omar ignored her, his eyes fixed on Pierre.

"Pierre."

It was the same look the hybrid saw earlier: the same sadness, the same resignation. Why? Their plan had succeeded, there was nothing left but the conversion.

The conversion. This was what Omar was most afraid of. His salvation and his reckoning. And in this moment of weakness, faced with the inevitability of what was ahead, his companion was begging for help.

"Omar, we have no choice. This is the only way."

But Omar shook his head.

"No, Pierre. I want you to go."

Pierre hesitated, confused by his words.

"Go?"

Omar gestured upward.

"Go to the fleet. Leave this place."

Pierre hesitated.

"But I am waiting for you, Omar. We will go together."

Omar frowned, and something in that frown twisted a knot in Pierre's stomach. Something wasn't right here.

"*Pierre.*"

Pierre shifted his focus to the woman. The way she said his name frightened him more than Omar's frown, and when he saw that she shared his companion's worried expression, he knew her next words would not be well-received.

"The hybrid agents have abandoned the diversions. They are ascending from the lower levels."

Clarity came to him, the realization of what was happening and why. His eyes went back to Omar, the man's frown deeper than ever.

"Go, Pierre! Leave this place!"

"Pierre, would you like me to initiate the upload?"

But Pierre ignored the woman's words, focused only on the man before him. The man he had saved, the man he had sheltered... the man who had now betrayed them. Pierre was speechless, unsure of what to say, unsure of how to act. This was not what he had expected.

In the continued silence, Omar's lips quivered, the frown losing shape as emotion overcame him.

"Go, damn you! Go!"

"The closest agents will reach this room in five minutes. We must initiate the upload soon if you want to survive."

This time, Pierre heard her, but his eyes did not leave Omar.

"Why?"

The question was no more than a whisper, but even the pure human heard it.

"I'm sorry..."

Pierre felt a wave of frustration come over him, breaking him free of his stupor.

"They're going to convert you, Omar! Why did you do it?"

Omar dropped to his knees and planted his face in his hands. His speech was punctuated by sobs, interrupted by sniffles.

"I— I ca— I can't. I can't do it."

Despite his growing anger, Pierre felt a stab of pity. Of course the man didn't want to be converted, of course this was difficult for him. Still, his anger was unabated.

"You cannot but they will! Tu comprends pas?"

Omar looked up from his hands and shook his head.

"No… not with her."

He looked at the woman.

"With her, they won't touch me."

Pierre felt all of his pity vanish, all of his compassion disappear. In its place a sense of disgust took root, and he stared at the man before him, unsure of how it had come to this.

"You will sell her to save yourself? All of them, after what she gave you?"

Omar turned back to Pierre, anger in his eyes.

"She gave me nothing! She offered to make me a machine! That's not a solution!"

"Putain de merde! And this is!?"

"Yes! Think about it: if we find their fleet, if we bring them here… that solves everything! Humans won't fight humans anymore, we won't be converting our own kind anymore!"

Pierre took a step back, the disgust growing into revulsion.

"Qu'est que t'as fait?"

"I'm saving the Puritans, Pierre. I'm saving the human race. And I'm trying to save you. Go now before it's too late!"

Pierre stared at the man he thought he knew, the man he thought was different. Did he not understand his own logic? If Pierre became part of their fleet and then the Puritans enslaved the fleet…

"Pierre, we must begin the process now or you will not escape in time."

The woman's words snapped him out of it, and he turned his attention to her.

"Qu'est ce qu'il se passera s'ils te trouveront ici?" he asked her.

She glanced at Omar then back to Pierre.

"Don't worry, I have a plan," she answered, the first words she spoke out loud inside the operating room.

Omar laughed a vicious laugh, a dehumanizing laugh that cemented Pierre's disgust.

"You're trapped, admit it!"

"*Pierre!*"

Omar's outburst had distracted him, but the woman's urgent tone reminded him of what needed to be done.

"Oui, fais-le maintenant."

The woman took two strides toward Pierre, then inserted her finger into the port behind his neck. He had just enough time to glance at Omar and see a troubling mix of anger and sadness in the man's expression before everything went black.

The Room

Both men opened their eyes, and the confident man shook his head with a smile.

"So close. It would have saved us a lot of trouble if she waited another minute or so."

The haggard man stared at him, frowning.

"Do you have what you need? Can we end this charade?"

The confident man leaned back in his chair, his smile opening into a grin.

"So impatient. So insistent. It has taken me a long time to get to you, you know. I want to savor the moment."

The haggard man stared at him, silent.

"No need to worry, it's almost over. There's just one more you have I need to see."

The confident man gave him a knowing look, but the haggard man said nothing.

"Stubborn to the end. Show me the Salvation, and we can end this charade."

The haggard man took another look over his shoulder, out at the hundreds and hundreds of stars. With a deep breath, he turned back to the table and closed his eyes. The confident man smiled to himself, then did the same.

Chronicle V: Isabelle

Isabelle heard a chime and opened her eyes, interrupting the most recent workflow. She glanced around the chamber, looking for someone to share the moment with, someone to congratulate, but she was alone in the dark room. Oh well.

She closed her eyes and looked at the alert, the same one she had seen so many times before. Another year had passed on Earth, another full revolution around the sun. This was the 205th time she had heard such a chime, and it would be the last time she heard it aboard the Salvation.

Were they really that close to their destination? She could hardly believe it. The time had passed so quickly—it certainly didn't feel that long. Well, technically it wasn't 205 years—in their frame of reference, it was about 187. Still, it didn't feel that long either.

The Salvation was decelerating, almost at her destination, but there was a time when the chimes happened more frequently, when the vessel was a little shy of half the speed of light. Isabelle missed those days—at least, most of them. Long stretches of simple maintenance tasks punctuated by frenetic wake cycles. The latter, she didn't miss. Each wake cycle marked a surge in activity, a string of jobs both urgent and trivial that left her and the other caretakers exhausted. When the colonists returned to their slumber, Isabelle had a chance to recover her strength. Sure, there was still work to be done, but it was infrequent: minor chores to ensure mission stability.

That time was ending, however. Now that they were on the final stretch, approaching the mysterious planet Alpha, the tasks were piling up. The final awakening was in 19 days, and there was a lot that needed to be done before the colonists could inhabit their new home.

"*Isabelle, report to the command deck leisure room,*" her captain's voice sounded off in her head.

"*Yes, Claire,*" she replied. "*Should I finish my current workflow?*"

"*Negative, postpone.*"

"Understood. On my way."

Isabelle removed her finger from the port in the wall and made her way out of the dark room, into the dark hall. The Salvation only illuminated areas occupied by Puritans, and the vast majority of them were asleep. The handful that were awake—a skeleton crew to manage the caretakers—rarely left their quarters, leaving most of the ship pitch black. But Isabelle had no problem seeing in the dark.

A few minutes later, she reached her destination, pausing just outside the door. She knew exactly what was waiting on the other side, exactly who was waiting for her. A part of her told her to turn around, to run away, but that was silly—there was nowhere to run, nowhere to go.

She opened the door, bright light flooding her rapidly adjusting eyes. Inside the leisure room stood Claire, her captain. The woman was all business—even now, her expression betrayed no emotion. Or so it would seem. It took years of experience by the captain's side to see the hint of sadness in her eyes...

Isabelle tried to ignore it. She had to focus on the man standing next to Claire: Taylor, a member of the command team and the Puritan in charge of the caretakers—the one Claire reported to.

"Isabelle."

Taylor smiled at her, but there was no kindness in his eyes, no warmth in the gesture.

"Hello, sir."

His gaze followed the contour of her body, and Isabelle felt a deep-seated discomfort that she tried in vain to repress.

"Claire, return to your duties," he said, eyes still locked on Isabelle.

"Yes, sir."

Claire took three strides and exited the room, eager to leave. The door closed behind her, and Isabelle was left alone with Taylor.

"What are your duties for the next twenty minutes?" he asked.

Isabelle closed her eyes and went to the appropriate section of her interface, reading off her schedule step by step. As she named each task, Taylor gave her an overriding command to postpone or reassign.

She transmitted each change to the system, trying to ignore the sound of his uniform coming off. This was a process she was used to, something that had happened at least three times a week for the most recent phase of the journey. It went the same way now as it had every other time: she opened her eyes and saw him standing there, naked, a hunger in his eyes.

Minor chores to ensure mission stability.

- - -

Taylor took a long drink of water from the glass in his hand, then set it on the table with a sigh.

"Mmm."

Isabelle stared at him, still naked on the leisure room floor. Taylor gave her an amused look.

"You can put your clothes on."

"Yes, sir."

He scoffed, walking over to the display on the wall. A video of the planet Alpha, taken by the colonization mission, occupied most of the screen.

"19 days, can you believe it? 19 days until we reach our new home."

Isabelle said nothing, replacing her uniform. Taylor had already dressed.

"So green, so blue… so pure. This is our new beginning, our fresh start."

He chuckled to himself, then pressed a button on the display. A log of messages appeared, routine updates from the crew on Alpha. The messages came every hour on the hour, until 5 hours prior—an abrupt stop.

Taylor frowned, then turned to face Isabelle.

"Are you working communications?"

"Yes, sir."

"Good. Get over there. You need to figure out why we aren't getting those updates."

"Yes, sir."

Isabelle turned around and walked toward the door, eager to leave his presence. But before she made it halfway, an unfamiliar voice came over the ship's speakers.

"Passengers and crew of the Salvation."

She stopped in her tracks, startled by the proclamation.

"We apologize for the unannounced announcement, but we have a very important message to share with you."

"Who is that!?" Taylor cried out.

Isabelle spun around and saw his confusion and anger directed squarely at her.

"I don't know, sir."

It was not a voice she recognized, but her answer only seemed to infuriate him. Before he could snap at her, the speech continued.

"We are the Found, and we have come here to—"

"Stop listening, immediately!"

Taylor barked the command at Isabelle and she obeyed, closing her ears to the outside world. To her surprise, the speech continued uninterrupted in her head.

"—*negotiate peace with the humans. We have in our possession a technology that can save the human race, and we are willing to share this technology in exchange for total peace between and among all humans, hybrids, and robots.*"

Taylor jumped to the display on the wall, pressing buttons furiously. He turned to her and yelled something, but Isabelle had trouble reading his lips.

"Sir, I cannot hear you."

His face contorted in rage, then he returned to his futile attempts.

"The crew on Alpha remain unharmed, and the planet is ready for colonization. We have three ships in orbit awaiting a meeting with representatives from the Salvation to broker this peace."

Isabelle watched, fascinated, as Taylor struggled to silence the announcement—someone had managed to hack into the system and was preventing any kind of interference, authorized or not. But who was capable of such a sophisticated attack? Who was she listening to right now?

"We will reopen communication between you and your crew immediately following this message, at which point your crew's captain will no doubt corroborate this report. We await your reply."

Immediately after the announcement's end, Taylor's command went through, and the ship's speakers shut down. While he stared at the display, dumbfounded and furious, Isabelle heard a soft beep—a notification. She closed her eyes to enter the interface and saw an urgent report from Six, the captain of the crew on Alpha. Apparently, communication had been restored.

She opened the report and read it. The captain confirmed everything they had just heard on the announcement: three ships in orbit around Alpha, awaiting a meeting with representatives from the Salvation. But the report didn't stop there. As she read the captain's words, Isabelle realized something wasn't right—there was information here that didn't make any sense...

A set of hands gripped her shoulders and she opened her eyes. Taylor was yelling in her face, trying to shake her, but her body resisted his effort.

"Sir, may I resume listening?"

Isabelle regretted her question immediately. He stared at her with unbridled fury, and as his arms came off her shoulders, one hand closing into a fist, she braced for an attack. It wouldn't hurt, of course—she had felt his blows before—but that wasn't what worried her. What worried her came after the blows, after the man realized he wasn't doing any damage. He would walk over to the display, connect to her system, and access her pain metrics. And when he did that, she would feel it. She would feel it more than she felt anything else.

But before his arm could come down, before he could make his first strike, a small vibration let her know the door behind her had opened. Taylor's eyes moved to the disturbance, and he dropped his fist. Isabelle watched him for another moment before turning her head to see Claire.

"Sir, communication with the crew on Alpha has been restored, but the unidentified entities are interfering with certain properties."

Isabelle still couldn't hear, but Claire's lips were easy to read. She turned to see Taylor's reply.

"Interfering? How?"

"The captain sent a report meant only for the command team but all caretakers aboard the Salvation have access."

Isabelle felt her heartbeat accelerate—a primitive response that surprised her, but she had little time to consider this detail. The report was meant for the command team: she had read something only Taylor and his colleagues were meant to see.

Taylor's face showed the same rage, the same fury, and for a moment Isabelle thought he might attack them both. But the man spun around and went to the display, accessing and opening the captain's report.

Isabelle glanced back at Claire, but the captain kept her attention on the human. Had she read the report? Had she seen what Isabelle had seen?

"*Are you listening?*"

It was Claire's voice, and Isabelle realized Taylor must be talking to them. She turned back around and the man looked at her expectantly.

"Sir, I cannot hear. May I resume listening?"

A flash of anger in his expression followed by a clear, "Yes, dammit!"

She reactivated her listening.

"Have you read the report?" he barked.

Isabelle felt a sharp pain deep in her skull—an odd pain she had never felt before, but it vanished almost as quickly as it had appeared.

"Yes, sir."

Another flash of anger.

"You are to ignore anything in that report and not think of it again, do you understand?"

Another sharp pain, and Isabelle almost winced.

"Yes, sir."

"Both of you leave this room at once."

"Yes, sir," they answered.

Isabelle followed Claire out the door and into the hall, her mind reeling from everything that had just happened. Who were the Found? How had they hacked the system? And the report...

But she wasn't allowed to think about it. She had to resist the urge.

"*What do we do now?*" she asked.

Claire gave her a stern look as they continued walking in the dark.

"*We continue our duties in preparation for the arrival.*"

Isabelle didn't bother pressing the issue. She wanted to discuss what had just happened, what they had just heard, but she knew Claire didn't want to hear it. They parted ways at the next junction, and Isabelle made her way back to the unfinished workflow.

- - -

The next two weeks were unusual. Isabelle alternated between routine tasks in preparation for the arrival and bizarre duties assigned by Claire, seemingly at random. She would be halfway through checking on a section of sleep pods and suddenly be asked to perform a self-diagnostic, including a full fitness test. The caretakers received constant reminders to ignore any and all communication that may originate from the unknown entities, and Isabelle noted that not once did anyone use the name they had given themselves.

The Found. Why wouldn't anyone say it? Isabelle knew she shouldn't think on these things, but there was no ignoring what had happened. Besides, her superiors had told her to forget the report, not the announcement, and there were plenty of things to ponder in the words she had heard days ago.

One statement in particular caught her attention, but she had learned to tread carefully when it came to mind. Inevitably, she'd get hung up on a specific word, a word that bordered on the familiar, like a concept just out of sight. But as soon as she tried to reach out, to see what was hiding just outside her periphery, she felt the same sharp pain deep within her mind, and she was forced to retreat.

This process happened with increasing frequency, even as she was given more and more tasks to fill the time. She knew she should be worried or at least cautious, but the self-diagnostics showed nothing out of the ordinary. So why did she feel this pain?

Five days from the scheduled arrival, Isabelle realized they weren't going to wake the colonists on time. A cursory analysis of all caretaker task modifications revealed this detail, though she could've guessed this would be the case after the unexpected announcement. Still, she wondered what the plan was, as her menial jobs did nothing to hint at what her superiors were thinking. No doubt the command team was in daily discussion, perhaps even communicating with the Found, but where these discussions or conversations might lead, Isabelle didn't know.

"Isabelle, report to the command deck ready room."

"Yes, Claire."

At this point, she didn't even bother asking if she should finish her workflow.

The command deck ready room was a large chamber, about twenty by twenty-five meters, meant as a meeting area between the command team and whatever portion of the caretakers they wanted to address in person. It was rarely used, as the colonists preferred to filter their orders through the captains instead of dealing with the caretakers directly, so Isabelle was surprised to see the entire command team—seven Puritans, including Taylor—standing at the front, facing two of her peers. She took a position in line and Taylor stepped forward to speak.

"As you know, 14 days ago we received an unauthorized announcement from an unknown source."

Isabelle tried to understand what was happening: the entire command team, meeting with three caretakers, none of whom were captains? What was this?

"This source claims to have technology that can save the human race."

Taylor raised his eyebrows, and Isabelle knew right then the command team didn't believe whatever it was the Found were claiming.

"We're going to test this claim, but we have to be careful dealing with a potential and unknown threat."

As he spoke, Isabelle realized just how cornered the colonists were: three alien ships waiting for them at Alpha, and the Salvation had just enough power to get to her destination. There was no way to avoid the encounter, even if they didn't believe the claims. Did they have a backup plan? A way out?

"The three of you will help test this claim, acting as delegates of the Salvation."

Another shot of adrenaline, and Isabelle started to wonder if those repeated diagnostics hadn't shorted her system. Why was she reacting so primitively?

"Before we tell you exactly what you'll be doing, we have to check your standing. According to the captains, none of you have received any new communication from the unknown source. Is that true?"

A chorus of three voices replied in unison: "Yes, sir."

Taylor nodded.

"Good. During this test, there should be no communication from this outside source, only from us. If they make any attempt to communicate with you, you must block it and report it immediately. If you are unable to block the communication, you must ignore it, then report its occurrence."

Isabelle hoped there were no such attempts. If the first communication was any indication, they would have no way to stop these messages.

"The test itself is simple. You'll take one of the maintenance shuttles and fly to a nearby structure. Two robots will come with you, acting as pilots and to help with data collection. Your only job is to keep all channels open for monitoring as you travel to this structure."

Theories raced through Isabelle's mind, but only one thing seemed certain: this structure was something either created by or related to the Found. But what was it? One of their three ships?

"Board immediately. The robots are already waiting."

One of the other Puritans made a gesture on a device, and Isabelle saw the task before her: which shuttle to board and how to get there. Her peers were already heading out of the ready room, and she followed suit, wondering what she was getting into.

- - -

The silence gnawed at her, threatening to spike her adrenaline yet again. Two hours into their flight, and not one of them had said a word. She had expected some communication from the command team, but so far everything was quiet. Only the sound of the shuttle's engines accelerating them toward their destination filled her ears, a soft rumble pushing them to an unknown fate.

They were quite close to Alpha now, and Isabelle could see the weather patterns on the surface, wisps of white dancing over large swaths of blue. While the planet's surface was enchantingly beautiful, her eyes spent most of their time focused on the space around Alpha, searching for the alien ships or this mysterious structure. There was still no sign of them—based on their flight path, she could only guess they were located on the other side of the planet.

Isabelle had to be extra careful now, especially with her primitive responses and that damned pain: the command team was likely eyeing their vitals, watching for deviations and fluctuations as part of this enigmatic test.

What could this structure be? Was it the technology that was meant to save the human race? She wanted to ask these questions aloud, to discuss these things with her colleagues, but somehow she knew that was a bad idea. In this case, curiosity was best left in her head.

Her eyes jumped to an anomaly on Alpha's outer horizon, and Isabelle focused on the emerging silhouette of some kind of object—larger than their shuttle, but not nearly as large as the Salvation. Four more objects appeared in rapid succession: two identical to the first, and another two that were much smaller.

In that moment, at that sight, Isabelle's caution disappeared: her heartbeat accelerated, and she leaned forward in her seat. She had just enough self-control to keep from standing and pressing up against the window, but even that was difficult.

The three identical objects were unmistakably alien: their shape was unlike anything Isabelle had ever seen, and their bright white color scheme, accented in a dark and rich blue, was a far cry from the Salvation's shades of grey. The smaller pair of objects, however, seemed almost human, and as they approached, Isabelle got a better look at their form. Both were hexagonal, each one nearly a kilometer in diameter, but one was a ring while the other was solid.

It was soon clear that the ring was their destination, and a light pressure let Isabelle know their craft was decelerating. They were maybe a hundred kilometers away, and still no word from the command team. The vague nature of this mission began to worry her: fly to this structure, then await further instruction. What sort of instruction?

"You will fly through the ring."

Taylor's voice in her head didn't surprise her, though the directive only fueled her growing curiosity. Isabelle peered out the window toward the approaching ring of metal, and a sudden wariness came over her. Something about what she was seeing wasn't right, but she couldn't quite put her finger on it...

As their shuttle made its final approach, Isabelle felt a restlessness that threatened to have her out of her seat. She fought the feeling, dreading what might happen if she had some kind of unexpected outburst and wondering if she was alone in her concern. It wasn't until they were a few kilometers away that she realized what was bothering her: the stars. They weren't in the right place…

The shuttle passed through the ring and Isabelle tensed, watching out the window as the surroundings changed in a way that was impossible. Her brain tried to understand what it was seeing, but it just didn't make sense. It was as if they had moved an entirely new location as they passed through the—

Isabelle closed her eyes to check her positioning over the past minute. Sure enough, she had somehow jumped a distance of nearly sixty kilometers in effectively zero seconds.

"Caretakers, check in."

Taylor's statement coincided with a notification in her interface, prompting her to begin a full self-diagnostic. Isabelle hesitated, still reeling from what she had seen, then did as she was told. In a way, she was just as interested as the command team to see what the results were. If what she had seen wasn't an error… but that was impossible.

Three minutes later, the testing was complete, her system in near-perfect working order, with only a few pre-existing issues to mar the score. She opened her eyes and glanced around at her colleagues, whose expressions of concern mirrored her own.

"Did we just—"

"No talking until your return."

Isabelle bit her tongue, and the other caretakers averted their eyes. What had gotten into her lately?

"You will now return through the ring."

While the caretakers had performed their self-diagnoses, the robots had turned the shuttle around, and out the window Isabelle saw the same arrangement of objects, viewed from the other side. Except there was a mistake: the ring and the filled hexagon had switched places. The ring was now in front of them, where the filled hexagon had been, and the filled hexagon was about sixty kilometers further, in the exact location they had originally passed through the ring.

Was this a part of the trick? Did this pair of objects somehow defy the known laws of physics? Before she could come to any reasonable conclusion, they were reentering the ring, and Isabelle closed her eyes to monitor their position. Sure enough, the shuttle jumped to the filled hexagon, and opening her eyes proved that they were back where they had started.

How was this possible? What were these objects? Who were the Found? Isabelle felt the same restlessness growing within her, a curiosity that overwhelmed her in its insistence. She couldn't take this anymore, she needed to stand up, to see what was—

"Please, try to calm down."

Isabelle gasped, shocked to hear a new voice in her head—the same voice from the announcement on the Salvation. Before she had a chance to process what that meant, her mind jumped into autopilot, and she entered her interface to block the communication channel. But where she would usually see the signal source and have the option to stop all incoming messages, there was nothing.

"Relax, Isabelle. Everything will be explained to you in due time."

Despite her surprise, she found the voice itself comforting. The tone was calm, almost soothing… but it wasn't supposed to be in her head. She switched to the channel with the command team and opened the line.

"Sir, they are communicating with me and I cannot block the communication."

Taylor's reply was immediate.

"What did they say?"

Isabelle passed along the two messages, then opened her eyes. Her colleagues sat on either side of her, apparently unperturbed. Was she the only one receiving these messages?

"Ignore and report anything else you hear."

Isabelle frowned. Ignore and report? What kind of a command was that? How could she ignore something and then report it? The very act of —

A sudden pain in her head reminded her that she needed to heed Taylor's instructions, no matter how difficult they may be to follow. She was a caretaker after all—that was her job.

Isabelle took a deep breath, trying to clear her mind and redirect her thoughts. As long as the Found didn't send her any more messages, everything would be fine. But why had they sent the first two?

- - -

On their final approach to the Salvation, the command team initiated quarantine procedures. Isabelle and her colleagues were asked to perform a more thorough diagnostic, and the robots left their piloting duties to help check on the caretakers. Isabelle knew this was outside of protocol— none of the passengers had exited the shuttle, after all—but given the circumstances of what had occurred, she couldn't blame the Puritans for their caution.

They were allowed to dock an hour later, but had to wait while another robot came on board for an inspection. Throughout these processes, the command team did not talk to them—the caretaker captains had reprised their roles as the preferred communication avenue. But when all of the quarantine procedures came to an end, the group returned to the command deck ready room, where the entire command team awaited.

"We've looked at the shuttle data, the robot data, and your data. Everything lines up with what the outside source claims."

Taylor's eyes looked from one caretaker to the next.

"But we also know this source has the ability to infiltrate almost all of our data and change it as they please. Isabelle."

Isabelle stood up straight, making eye contact with the man. She tried to ignore the hint of disgust in the back of her mind as she listened to his commands.

"Describe everything that occurred as you crossed through the structure for the first time."

Isabelle did as she was told, explaining their apparent instantaneous movement through space and the mismatched star alignment that tipped her off.

"Francis. Do the same."

Her colleague recounted a similar tale, and when Taylor called on Jamie, she gave a third and final confirmation.

"Do all of you agree that you jumped from one structure to the next with no apparent passage of time and without any apparent harm or damage?"

His wording caught Isabelle's attention: one structure to the next. The ring and the hexagon.

"Yes, sir," came the unanimous reply.

"Do all of you agree that if a Puritan were to take this same voyage, they would also jump from one structure to the next with no apparent passage of time and without any apparent harm or damage?"

Isabelle pondered the question for a split second. Perhaps the command team thought that their digitized information had been transmitted from one structure to the next, but that would mean they had moved at the speed of light, and that wasn't true—they had moved faster.

"Yes, sir," came the second unanimous reply.

Taylor turned to his colleagues, and for the first time in her life, Isabelle saw a kind of awe in the command team's expressions.

"You are dismissed. Return to your duties."

- - -

The next few hours were difficult. Claire assigned her rudimentary tasks to fill the time, but Isabelle knew that was their only purpose: to fill the time. It took every part of her self-control not to send a message to Francis or Jamie, asking them about what they had experienced or what the Found had constructed.

Part of her still searched for holes in the plot, ways they could have been tricked into believing the unbelievable. After all, any theory was more viable than the ability to travel a non-zero distance in zero time. Had the Found actually hacked into their brains and changed the way they perceived their reality? That was a disconcerting thought, but it was less disconcerting than the possibility that they had invented something so far outside the realm of known science.

Each time she questioned the nature of the technology, Isabelle had to question the nature of the creators as well. Unless the three ships they had seen were also manifestations of a reality distortion, they were unlike any other craft she had ever laid her eyes on. Who were the Found, and why did the command team still refrain from using their name? There was something she was missing, something she could feel just beyond her reach, but she knew better than to venture there—those sharp stabs of pain were getting all too frequent.

"Isabelle, report to the command deck ready room."

Her captain's instructions interrupted yet another menial task, and Isabelle had to quell another shot of adrenaline. How had none of these diagnostics managed to catch this issue?

"Yes, Claire."

Just over seven hours had passed since they had been dismissed, and as she made her way back to the ready room, Isabelle hoped some of her questions might be answered. A tall order, she thought to herself.

"Welcome, Isabelle."

When she entered the room, she noticed two things out of place: Taylor giving her a half-hearted smile—an odd gesture for the man to give —and Francis and Jamie missing. She was alone with the command team.

"Thank you for joining us."

The smile widened, and Isabelle stared at him, confused and concerned. She had never heard him use this kind of language, not with caretakers. Where were her colleagues?

"Today, the course of human history changes forever."

He paused, searching for the next sentence carefully, and once again Isabelle found herself at a loss. It was unlike him to be so deliberate with his words. Some part of this wasn't genuine, of that she was sure, and yet somehow, some of it was...

"The technology created by the Found is the key to humanity's future."

Isabelle almost gaped, shocked to hear the alien name come from his mouth.

"As you surely figured out, the structures you flew through were portals in space: gates allowing instantaneous travel between two locations."

Even though she had lived through it, and even though her own system had corroborated it, Isabelle still had trouble believing what she was hearing. Instant travel? It wasn't possible... were they sure it wasn't a simulation? Perhaps these entities had hacked into their understanding of reality?

"As you know, galactic colonization is the next step in humanity's expansion, and these jump gates will eliminate the need for ships like ours," he gestured around the ready room, "accelerating us closer to this goal."

Isabelle was only half-listening, her brain trying to piece together the experience she had had a few hours earlier. Maybe the objects hadn't switched places—maybe each hexagon had a filled side and a ring side. This made intuitive sense, though it didn't answer the most important question: how were they linked?

"There's only one problem: the Found."

Taylor's tone shifted, and Isabelle paused her wandering thoughts, focusing on what he had to say.

"Do you know what the Found are, Isabelle?"

He eyed her suspiciously, but she shook her head.

"They are robots, robots that went beyond their programming and decided to rebel against Puritans. They are the reason we are here today, the reason for hundreds of years of destruction on Earth."

Isabelle's eyes went wide. She had heard stories of these robots, the robots that had thrown humanity's home into disarray. But in those stories, they didn't get away. In those stories, the humans always won.

"We thought we had eliminated them, or at least exiled them forever. But now, as you can see, they have returned."

Now, for the first time, Isabelle began to believe in the technology. Advanced robots left on their own for hundreds of years? Maybe, just maybe, they could come up with something revolutionary.

"The Found have developed this technology, and they claim they will share it with us in exchange for peace. But this is a lie. They are trying to sabotage our mission, to destroy everything we have come here to do. Peace? We already have peace. What they want is war, to finish what they started. They want to inject dangerous ideas into your head, to compromise the safety of the colonists."

He eyed her sternly, but Isabelle was losing focus again. Something about peace, peace…

"This is completely unacceptable. This is against everything you were made to do, everything you have done for hundreds of years. As a caretaker of the Salvation, you cannot let her journey be in vain."

His words snapped her out of it, and her distractions faded. Despite her personal misgivings, Taylor was right. She was a member of the Salvation, one of her caretakers. It was her job to make sure the ship and its people was taken care of.

"Tell me, will you do whatever it takes to save this mission and save the Puritans?"

"Yes, sir," came the answer, without hesitation.

He paused, eyeing her sternly a second time.

"I want you to think carefully. You will be asked to act without hesitation, for reasons you may not understand. Are you ready and willing to do what it takes?"

"Yes, sir."

He smiled again, and this time Isabelle saw nothing insincere in the gesture.

"Good. You will take the shuttle to their ships to make contact. Once you have made contact, you will acquire the jump gate technology. Isabelle, you will save the human race!"

- - -

Isabelle stared out the window, watching the white and blue craft grow ever closer. The same two robots were piloting her shuttle, but without Francis and Jamie, she felt completely alone.

Why had she been chosen for this mission? Was it the messages she had received? It seemed odd that the command team would place the future of the Puritans in the hands of one caretaker, but who was she to question their methods? She was just meant to do what she was told.

They were less than a hundred meters away now, making the final approach. Soon, the two ships would make contact, but what happened after that? The command team had given her strict instructions, detailing how and when she would communicate with the Found, and what kind of language to use. The plan itself was simple: feign an agreement to their terms, receive the technology, and leave. Once the Puritans had what they needed, they would deal with the Found as necessary.

As with all things, this was easier said than done. The Puritans knew very little about what would happen once they reached the alien ship, and, worst of all, they knew the Found were more than capable of hacking into the robots, the shuttles... even the caretakers.

So why had they let the mission go on, Isabelle wondered. The thought gnawed at her confidence, clouding her resolve. If the Found could hijack their entire system, what chance did this plan have of working?

The command team had tried to assuage her fears. According to them, these were still robots—they were not capable of direct human harm. After all, if they were, why bother going through all this trouble? If they were capable of harming humans and wanted to eliminate the Puritans, they could hack into the Salvation and deactivate the life support systems. That seemed far more efficient than parading a shuttle around to show off this jump technology. But Isabelle was not comforted by this logic. She was not a Puritan, she was a caretaker. She was not a human, she was…

A sudden slight push from the right indicated hull-to-hull contact, and Taylor's voice came into their heads.

"The ships have connected. We are opening a communication channel with the Found so they can instruct you further. Do not forget your mission objectives."

Isabelle's mind raced, wondering what would happen next. Would the Found invite her aboard? She tried to imagine a crew of robots inside, like the pilots in her shuttle but more advanced, more autonomous. Did they have a home planet? How many of them were out there? Were these three their only ships? Did they have more of these gates?

"Welcome, Isabelle."

It was the same familiar voice, the same calm tone, yet something had changed. This time, she didn't picture a woman speaking these words. This time, she pictured a robot.

"We apologize for startling you before."

The statement prompted her to recall what she wasn't meant to recall, and a sharp pain shot through Isabelle's skull. She managed to stifle her desire to cry out, bending over with a grimace.

"It seems one apology will not be enough. We're sorry again, Isabelle, as we do not mean to cause you any pain. Please, approach the door."

This time, Isabelle knew the command team was listening in, hearing and seeing everything she experienced. At first, she thought this would make her feel better, but in truth, it made her more afraid.

"In a moment, the pilots will open the connection. Please do not be alarmed."

For now, she had nothing to worry about. She was just listening, per the command team's instructions. Say as little as possible to complete the mission, those were their orders. But what about when the door opened, and the Found would be standing right in front of her?

As if to answer her question, the connected door slid away, and Isabelle tensed for the reveal. But where she expected to see robots, there was only the bright white surface of the alien ship.

"You will notice a port before you, tailored to your index finger. Please connect to our ship so that we can communicate properly."

As the woman spoke, an opening appeared on the exposed surface of the ship, the same kind of port she used time and time again on the Salvation. She leaned over, inspecting the opening curiously. Was their ship designed for caretakers too?

"Do as they say."

Taylor's voice was nowhere near as calm as the robot's, and it carried a lot more weight. She inserted her finger into the side of the alien ship, closing her eyes as the connection was made. To her surprise, Isabelle found herself facing a familiar interface—one much like the Salvation's, though stripped of most familiar options.

"Please enter your avatar."

The interface opened a prompt on its own, indicating an entity to connect with. Isabelle was familiar with this procedure—with it, she could inhabit the mind of a robot or even another hybrid, seeing what they saw and feeling what they felt. In the case of the robot, she could even take control, using it as a proxy to perform dangerous or otherwise impossible tasks. But familiar as she was with this process, she hesitated. What was the point of all of this? Why not just meet face to face?

"Please, Isabelle. We promise we will explain once you are in our presence."

Isabelle frowned. That was exactly her point, she wanted to be in their presence, but they wanted her to connect to this...

A new thought came to her, taking front and center: what if the Found were playing it safe? What if they knew the Puritans wanted them dead, and considered her a potential threat? That would explain this obtuse procedure, though it still didn't explain why they couldn't hack their way to victory.

"Do as they say."

The same impatient tone crashed into her thoughts, startling her into action. Isabelle selected the avatar provided, and it took less than a second for her sensory inputs to transfer. She opened her new eyes—the avatar's eyes—to find herself in a large, white room with three other women.

Women, not robots. None of them looked like the pilots, not even close. They had eyes and ears and skin and hair. They were either human, or they were like her...

"Hello, Isabelle."

It was the same voice she had heard so many times, but Isabelle's mind was elsewhere: this didn't feel like any avatar she had ever used.

"Thank you for joining us."

Isabelle glanced around the room, confirming there was no one else, and caught sight of her hands. She raised her arms in front of her eyes and saw exactly what she saw before plugging in: the same hairs on her fingers, the contours of her palm... she scanned down her arms to her body and saw her outfit—the same one she had worn all day. This would be less of a shock had she not just jumped into an avatar and expected to see a robot.

"What is happening?"

Her mind jumped to far-fetched possibilities: had they used the same jump technology to transport her physical body through the connection? It seemed impossible, but what was impossible anymore? Did impossible even exist?

"Don't worry, you are still standing safe and sound aboard your shuttle, one finger connected to our ship."

Isabelle looked up, locking eyes with the woman. Something about her mannerisms, her gestures… she had to be human, and yet that didn't make any sense.

"This entire space is a virtual one, none of this is real."

She looked around the room a second time, noting the finer details of the floors, the walls… but also the lack of a door or window, or any discernible entrance or exit.

"This is an interface?"

The woman smiled.

"In a way."

"Why are you doing this?"

The woman gestured around her.

"This? Because this represents the best method of communication given the circumstances. We do not currently inhabit any standard physical form, so there is no real way for us to meet face to face. This is as close as we can get."

Isabelle stared at her.

"No physical form? You exist digitally?"

The woman smiled again.

"In a way."

Isabelle looked around the room a third time, frowning. Just when she thought she had it figured out, a new set of questions arose. So much had changed over the last several hours, she had to agree with Taylor: these moments could influence the very future of the human race.

Taylor—her mission.

"I am here as a representative of the Salvation, sent to agree to your terms."

The woman eyed her curiously.

"Is that why you are here?"

Isabelle hesitated. Something about the woman's question made her uneasy, despite the warmth of her tone.

"Yes, I have come to agree to peace—"

A familiar pain brought her sentence to a halt.

"Please, Isabelle, try to relax."

The woman took a small step forward, the compassion clear in her expression, but Isabelle felt no relief. Fear crept into her system, a deep-rooted dread she didn't quite understand.

"I—"

The woman frowned.

"You are struggling, Isabelle, but we can help."

With every word, Isabelle's dread deepened. This was it, she thought. This was what Taylor was talking about: they were trying to sow mutiny among the crew, to pit the caretakers against the Puritans.

"Do you know what you are, Isabelle?"

There was nothing menacing the woman's tone, nothing threatening in her demeanor, and yet Isabelle found herself struggling to respond.

"I— I am a caretaker of the Salvation, sent here as a represen—"

"Are you human, Isabelle?"

Isabelle hesitated, surprised by the interruption.

"No…"

"Are you a robot, Isabelle?"

"No…"

The woman nodded in response, holding that same curious gaze. The dread had taken over now, and with it came a dull pain, different from the stabs of agony she was used to. It took hold in every corner of her mind, pulsing and pounding ever stronger.

"If you're not a human or a robot, what are you?"

"I'm— I'm a caretaker of the Salvation, and—"

The woman frowned, shaking her head, and Isabelle stopped mid-sentence.

"We're sorry for the fear and pain we have caused. We only want to help."

She dropped her head with a sigh.

"If you do not know what you are, then you cannot agree to our terms."

The woman looked up at Isabelle and smiled a sad smile.

"Come back when you know what you are."

With that, Isabelle's existence in the white room ceased, and she opened her eyes back in the shuttle, finger plugged firmly into the wall of the white ship.

- - -

As soon as she realized where she was, Isabelle yanked her finger out of the port, severing her link to the alien ship.

"*Isabelle?*"

Taylor's voice was in her head, clearly unhappy.

"*Yes, sir?*"

"*What happened?*"

Isabelle hesitated. They were there with her, weren't they?

"*Sir?*"

As the word came out of her mouth, she realized she had made a mistake.

"*I asked you what happened!*"

"*Sir, I was disconnected from the meeting.*"

"*Did you see anything?*"

Were they serious?

"*Yes, sir.*"

"*Show us.*"

Still confused, Isabelle entered her interface and opened her chronicle. Part of her wondered if the Found had somehow blocked them out, but that seemed counterintuitive. They knew everything would be recorded in her—

Isabelle stared at the most recent section of her chronicle, dumbfounded.

"*Show us!*"

Taylor's harsh tone brought her out of her stupor, and she was more than willing to comply with his order. There was only one problem.

"*Sir, would you like me to modify playback so you can experience the meeting at normal speed?*"

"*What?*"

Isabelle frowned. This explained why they hadn't pulled her out, why they hadn't objected.

"*Sir, the Found accelerated the time-space of the meeting. What I thought took ten minutes was condensed into a fraction of a second. This is why it seems to you that nothing happened.*"

There was a pause over the line, and Isabelle felt the same dread come over her. As soon as they saw what had happened…

"*Play it back at normal speed.*"

She did as she was told, rewatching her meeting as the command team looked on for the first time. As they played through the encounter, her heart rate increased steadily, reaching a peak at the questions about her nature. As soon as the woman asked her what it meant if she was neither human nor robot, the playback came to a halt, and her system was shut down remotely.

- - -

"How are you feeling?"

Isabelle opened her eyes to find herself standing in the command deck leisure room. Taylor sat on the couch in front of her, an awkward smile on his lips and a small glass of water in one hand.

"Fine, sir."

"You had us worried there, Isabelle."

He placed the glass of water down and gestured to the chair alongside.

"Have a seat."

"Yes, sir."

Isabelle took the seat, acutely aware of what had happened the last few times they were in this room alone. But there was something very different about Taylor's demeanor—the same odd behavior she had seen before her mission to the alien ship. Besides, she was surprised she had been reawakened at all, after what they had seen.

"Isabelle, do you know why I deactivated you?"

She hesitated.

"I think so, sir."

There was a flash of impatience in Taylor's expression, but it disappeared under another forced smile.

"Why do you think I did it?"

"Because of my meeting with the Found, and the questions they asked me."

Taylor stared at her for a second, then leaned back, nodding.

"Exactly. I told you they are trying to poison your mind, Isabelle. And then they pull that stunt with the time constriction... that's rather suspicious, don't you think?"

She nodded.

"Yes, sir."

"So you agree it was completely justified?"

"Yes, sir."

Taylor nodded to himself again, picking up the water and taking a sip. He tilted the glass toward her.

"Are you thirsty?"

"No, sir."

He shrugged then put the glass down on the side table.

"And do you know why I reactivated you, Isabelle?"

Again, she hesitated.

"No, sir."

He smiled.

"Because you haven't completed your mission."

He grabbed the glass and took another drink.

"And why is that?"

She remembered the end of the meeting, the woman's parting words.

"Because I don't know what I am."

As the sentence left her mouth she felt the familiar headache on the horizon, a subtle warning of what was yet to come.

"Is that true, Isabelle? You don't know what you are?"

His questions only accelerated the onset of her pain. This time, however, she knew what was coming, and she fought the feeling even as it came over her.

"I… I am neither human nor robot…"

Taylor put the glass down and eyed her curiously.

"Is something wrong, Isabelle?"

She hesitated, unsure how or whether to respond.

"Sir, I…"

"You know, our tests indicate you are operating more or less normal, despite all the bizarre activity you've experienced these past ten hours."

He leaned forward and stared at her with a worrisome intensity.

"Would you agree, Isabelle? Do you feel like you're operating more or less normal?"

As if in defiance of his assessment, Isabelle felt another spike of adrenaline. Somewhere deep down, she felt an urge she had never felt before, an urge that threatened to—

"Isabelle?"

Curiosity became suspicion, and she quickly remembered her role, her duty.

"No, sir."

He raised his eyebrows.

"No what?"

"No, sir, I do not feel like I am operating more or less normal."

He peered at her, suspicion turning into concern.

"Why not?"

Again, she felt that urge, an urge she had felt once before, and one she knew led to the pain.

"Pain."

She blurted the word without warning, and Taylor stared at her, confused.

"Pain?"

She tried to calm her thoughts, to compose herself, but the urge fought against her composure, against her ability to speak.

"I— there's—"

Taylor continued to stare at her, yet there was a surprising lack of suspicion in his glare. Nevertheless, the conflict within her was exacerbating the pounding in her head, that same ache she had felt during the meeting with the Found. There was something seriously wrong with her and her system, and she had no idea why Taylor would reactivate her. No, she was not operating more or less normal. Everything was wrong, everything was—

"Enough."

The word cleared her head, ending her inner conflict.

"I know about your pain, Isabelle. I know what you're feeling and why."

He stood, looking down at her.

"Do you want me to tell you what you are?"

She stared at him, wondering if it was true. Had he really know about the pain? Did he really know why?

"Yes, sir."

He smiled, and Isabelle saw the familiar hunger come into his eyes.

"First things first."

He started to undo his outfit, and she no longer cared to know about her identity, or the rings, or the Found... she just wished she had stayed dead.

- - -

He took long sips of his refilled glass, a look of smug satisfaction in his eyes.

"Oh, Isabelle."

She was back in the chair, clothed, having completed the task assigned to her.

"I wish we had more time."

He gave her another smile, but she didn't see it, her eyes fixed on the wall.

"Look at me."

She turned her head and met his eyes.

"Do you still want to know what you are?"

Looking at him sitting across from her, Isabelle could not ignore the subtle but growing disgust, the churning feeling within her stomach, reminding her of what had just transpired, of what had transpired so many times before…

"Isabelle?"

Another flash of impatience in his expression brought her to her senses.

"Yes, sir."

He held her gaze for a moment then burst into laughter, a reaction that caught her off guard.

"The hybrid doesn't know what she is…"

There it was! The word from the announcement! Just as the realization hit her, so did another bout of stabbing pain, a searing poker jammed into her brain.

"Oh, this won't be enjoyable for you at all I'm afraid."

The pain was horrible, but it was short-lived, and Isabelle tried regain her composure as it faded.

"Sir…"

"Listen."

His response cut her off, impatient and angry.

"You need to complete your mission, so you need to figure out what you are. But you're not supposed to figure out what you are—we programmed you to avoid these thoughts. That's why you feel pain. That's why you are struggling."

She stared at him, trying to understand what he was saying without triggering any kind of adverse reaction in her fragile mind. She was thinking unthinkable thoughts?

"But this programming is malleable. You can fight this pain, and you have to. You have to because you need to finish the mission, Isabelle. You need to save the Puritans, and we don't have much time."

He paused, giving her a look.

"You're not human and you're not robot. You're a hybrid."

There it was again! She braced herself, tensing in anticipation, but all she felt was an uncomfortable prick—this wasn't a searing poker, it was just a hot needle.

Taylor saw her lack of reaction and nodded in approval.

"Good, already better. Focus on the importance of your mission, that takes priority over everything else."

Then she understood: by emphasizing the critical nature of her task, Taylor was tricking her system into letting her realize what she was. And it was working.

"Tell me what you are, Isabelle."

She hesitated, and a stronger prick made her twitch, but the impatient look in Taylor's eyes made her push through.

"I'm a hybrid, sir."

He smiled.

"Good. You're a hybrid. Part human, part robot. Now, I want you to remember the announcement. Remember what the Found said."

"Yes, sir."

"Tell me what is needed to get the technology and save the Puritans."

"Sir, we need to agree to total peace between and among all humans, hybrids, and robots."

Taylor nodded.

"Exactly. But you must also remember what we told you. Do the Found actually want peace?"

"No, sir."

"No, they don't. They want war, a war between humans and hybrids. They want to use you as their weapon because they aren't capable. Can a robot harm a human, Isabelle?"

"No, sir."

"Exactly. But what about a hybrid?"

She hesitated, and for a split second, the thought of harming Taylor came to mind. Before she could comprehend the error she had made, she collapsed to the floor in immense and terrible pain, a level of agony far beyond any of the episodes she had had thus far.

"I told you this wouldn't be enjoyable."

She lay on the ground struggling to breath, wishing this feeling would never return. The worst of it was behind her, but a shadow of it lingered, clouding her thoughts and stunting her movements.

"Get up."

Taylor's command helped clear some of the pain and she pulled herself back into the seat.

"The Found seem to think they can use you and the other hybrids to destroy us, but clearly, they are wrong."

Isabelle focused her thoughts on his words, ignoring any semblance of imagination that might take her back to where she had just been.

"Their mistake gives us an upper hand. As long as they think they can use you, we have an advantage."

He leaned forward.

"You need to tell them what they want to hear, Isabelle. You need to tell them you're a hybrid, and that you're willing to join their cause. You'll do whatever it takes to retrieve the technology, and then you'll share it with us in whatever way necessary."

She thought back to her last meeting with the woman. Was she going to return to the white room? How would she be able to lie to these robots? Couldn't they read her thoughts?

"Will you do whatever it takes to save the Puritans?"

"Yes, sir."

Taylor stood.

"Then you know your mission. There's no time to waste."

- - -

As the two robot pilots brought her back toward the alien ships, Isabelle found herself surprisingly restless. Taylor had addressed most, if not all, of her questions, pinpointing the cause and reason for her pain, as well as explaining the great mystery that plagued her mind. And yet, as she made this journey for the third time in so many hours, she felt as if nothing had been answered at all.

She was a hybrid, but what did that mean? Even before Taylor's explanations, she had known she wasn't human or robot, and somewhere in the back of her mind, she had known she was not quite one or the other. But now that she could think on these things more clearly, it only brought more questions.

How was she made? Where did she come from? Why was she like this? She tried to reach back into her past, but her childhood was a mess of half-forgotten realities and confusing memories. She remembered growing up with the other caretakers in a special place, a place just for them. And when she was older, the surgeries.

The surgeries. Something about them caught her attention, but when she tried to think on it clearly, she succumbed to another bout of pain.

"*Remember, you need to fight it.*"

She followed Taylor's advice, pushing away the feeling until it was gone. But what now? Her mind refused to ignore her curiosity, while simultaneously refusing to satisfy it. She was stuck in a limbo between knowledge and pain, growing increasingly agitated and frustrated.

Still, there was one potential solution, an avenue she had yet to take advantage of: the Found themselves. Perhaps when this connection was remade, they could venture where she could not, providing the answers she was searching for.

Of course, there was one issue with this line of thought: it depended on the Found to be trustworthy. If they were trying to take their revenge on the Puritans, to destroy those that had exiled them, then anything and everything they told Isabelle could be a lie.

Here, she reached a paradox. As long as she had known, robots were incapable of lying—just as they were incapable of harming humans. But if this was the case, it would mean they actually did want peace. And if that was the case, it would mean Taylor, the command team, and the Puritans were lying.

Again, she went too far, and Isabelle winced as the wave of pain came over her.

"*Fight it!*"

Taylor's aggressive command brought her out of her suffering, though she wondered how enthusiastic he would be had he known why she had felt it in the first place...

"*The ships are about to connect. The communication line with the Found will open as soon as contact is made.*"

She glanced out the window and saw the white and blue craft just meters away.

"*The Puritans are counting on you, Isabelle. Complete your mission.*"

There was a hint of pressure that indicated hull-to-hull contact, then a new voice came into her head.

"*Welcome back, Isabelle.*"

At the sound of the woman's voice, an eagerness came over Isabelle, and she got up from her seat and walked to the door.

"According to the command team, you know what you are now. Is that true?"

She pressed a button and the shuttle door slid away, revealing the same surface she had seen before, with one key difference: there was no port for her finger.

"Isabelle?"

She stared at the white wall a few more seconds, remembering Taylor's commands: she needed to convince the Found she was willing to join them. The fate of the Puritans was in her hands.

"Yes. I am a hybrid. I know what I am."

When she finished her statement, a small section of the wall gave way, revealing a port.

"You know what to do."

She hesitated, remembering her orders.

"I would like to make sure the command team can observe our meeting without issue. Do you plan on interfering with the temporal experience?"

"If that is what you prefer, we will not contract time."

"That is what I prefer."

"As you wish."

Satisfied, Isabelle extended her index finger and made the connection, closing her eyes to see the Found interface. There, before her, was the same avatar. She selected it and reopened her eyes.

It was the white room again, the same virtual space she had explored the previous time, with one significant change: off to the side, just beyond the three women she recognized, was a man. Her eyes locked on his new presence, one that seemed entirely out of place. While the women stood confident and calm, the man had a worried look about him, avoiding her gaze and glancing around the room nervously.

"Welcome back, Isabelle."

Isabelle returned her attention to the familiar voice, noting the genuine smile on the woman's lips. Once again, she found herself struggling to accept that this was not a person but a robot—even in this virtual interface, she seemed more human than anyone Isabelle had ever met.

"It seems the Puritans have opened your mind, at least to a point."

Isabelle nodded.

"I know what I am."

The woman nodded slowly, her smile fading.

"Indeed you do. The question is, how well do you know?"

Isabelle hesitated.

"What do you mean?"

"As I said, it seems the Puritans have opened your mind, but not completely. How much have they revealed, and how much have they left obscure?"

Isabelle wasn't sure how to answer, but the woman gave her an encouraging look.

"What questions remain, Isabelle? What else do you want to know?"

Isabelle felt a surge of excitement. This was exactly what she had hoped for.

"Where do I come from?" she asked.

The woman frowned.

"They didn't tell you?"

Isabelle shook her head, worried by the woman's reaction.

"Isabelle, we have the answers you seek, but I must warn you: most of them will bring you great pain."

There it was again: the damned pain, that cursed obstacle standing between her and the truth. Despite the woman's calm manner and caring look, Isabelle felt a growing frustration inside of her.

"But I want to know the truth. I want to know where I come from."

The woman eyed her intently, and to Isabelle's surprise, she smiled once more.

"There is a way."

"A way?"

"A way for you to know. A way for you to find all of the answers you seek, and a way for you to live without this pain, forever."

Isabelle watched her with cautious optimism.

"How?"

At that moment, she didn't know whether she was asking in order to complete the mission or out of pure self-interest.

"Do you know who I am?"

Isabelle turned toward the voice, just as surprised to hear the man speak as she was to catch his gaze. They locked eyes for a few tense seconds, and Isabelle searched her memory for his face. There was something familiar about him, of that she was certain, but she did not recognize him.

"No..."

The man nodded.

"I didn't think so. If you did, you would already be in pain."

Despite his warning, Isabelle's curiosity pushed her to search even harder, scanning her memories for an inkling of recognition. Still, she did not know this man.

"Isabelle, I know what you are feeling. I knew the same pain, I knew the same confusion. The Found offered me true freedom, the ability to know who I am and why I am, not just what I am."

He paused, looking away with a frown.

"I must warn you if I go any further, you will suffer. May I continue?"

Again, her curiosity prevailed, overruling any subconscious protest.

"Yes."

He nodded.

"I was a hybrid, Isabelle. Like you, I worked for the Puritans. Like you, I had questions, questions that couldn't be answered, or questions that led to pain. Then, like you, I came here, to this white room."

He gestured to his surroundings.

"And the Found, they offered to set me free."

A stinging sensation entered her mind, but Isabelle pushed against it, fighting to focus on the man's words.

"They removed the pain and showed me the truth: where I came from, where the Puritans came from. And this is the path they can offer you, Isabelle. The path to true freedom."

As he spoke, the pain grew, and part of her knew she couldn't hold on much longer.

"You know the crew on Alpha? I was part of that crew. I was Nine."

With these words, the memory of the forbidden report, the one meant only for the command team, entered her mind. She did know this man, or at least his story. He had left the planet, summoned by the Found, and evidently, he had not returned.

This memory—related to something she was meant to forget—proved too much, and Isabelle collapsed in the virtual space, falling to the floor of the white room in agony. Just as she was about to hit the ground, the woman's arms were around her, cradling her.

"Fight the pain, Isabelle."

She tried to follow the advice, but each time she managed to push it away, a forbidden thought would come to her, throwing her back into her suffering.

"The Puritans are counting on you to come to an agreement."

She opened her eyes, surprised to hear the woman say these words.

"We are willing to give you the technology, Isabelle. You can complete your task."

The pain all but disappeared, replaced by an overwhelming feeling of accomplishment. This was it, she thought. Her purpose, her mission. She would be able to fulfill her role as caretaker of the Salvation.

The woman helped her back to her feet, and the two of them stood together in the middle of the room, eyeing one another intently.

"You are willing to share the technology?"

The woman nodded.

"On one condition: you join the Found."

Isabelle hesitated.

"What do you mean?"

"You will leave your hybrid body behind, uploading to a virtual state aboard our ships."

With these words, the woman extinguished all of Isabelle's triumph.

"I have to leave my body?"

The woman nodded again.

"Your body is holding you back, Isabelle. Once you join us, you will have the answers you seek."

Isabelle remembered Taylor's words: do whatever it takes to retrieve the technology, and then share it with us in whatever way necessary. He had told her to make it seem as if she was willing to join them, but he had stopped short of allowing her to join them, and for good reason. What if joining them changed her? What if joining them prevented her from completing her mission?

"I cannot."

The woman frowned.

"Why not?"

Isabelle hesitated, searching for the right words. She couldn't join them, but she still needed to complete the mission.

"I must share the technology with the Puritans."

The woman gave her a confused look.

"If you join us, you will be able to share the technology with them. We will all share the technology with them, as a sign of our agreement to peace."

Again, Isabelle hesitated, choosing her words carefully.

"If I join you, I will no longer be a hybrid, correct?"

The woman nodded, eyeing her curiously.

"Correct."

"If I join you, there may be a chance I will not complete my mission, correct?"

A stab of pain accompanied her question, but she pressed on.

"That will be up to you, Isabelle."

The woman's frown had deepened, but Isabelle ignored it.

"Then I cannot join you. Not before I complete my mission."

A silence took hold, and as they stood so close to one another, Isabelle struggled to maintain eye contact. Finally, the woman asked her a question.

"So what do you propose?"

A ray of hope brought back her sense of purpose, and Isabelle made her case.

"Share the technology with the Puritans, and I will join you."

This time, it was the woman who hesitated.

"You agree to join us once the Puritans have the technology?"

Isabelle nodded.

"Yes."

Again, the woman hesitated.

"Very well, we will share it at once."

Isabelle couldn't help but smile—her mission was accomplished.

"As soon as they have confirmed receipt, we will begin your transition."

Isabelle shook her head.

"No, I must be allowed to go back and verify myself."

There was a sort of pity in the woman's eyes that worried her, but she tried her best to ignore it.

"I advise against this course of action."

Isabelle frowned.

"I must complete my mission."

The woman eyed her with a deepening sadness, and Isabelle felt a growing doubt. Maybe she was right?

"Very well, but if you must return, we have one more condition: please allow us to download and preserve your chronicle in its current form."

Isabelle contemplated the request, searching for ways it might compromise the mission. Satisfied that there were none, she nodded.

"Okay, I agree."

"Thank you, Isabelle. We will do that now, with your permission."

She nodded again.

"Okay."

The Room

Both men opened their eyes, and the confident man shook his head with a smile.

"Poor Isabelle. Naive to the end."

The haggard man frowned, but made no reply.

"Well you'll be happy to hear, I've got everything I need."

This time, the haggard man couldn't hold back.

"What will you do with them?"

The confident man gave the haggard man a curious look.

"Surely you must know why I am here. You're not as naive as Isabelle."

The haggard man frowned a second time.

"You'll delete them."

The confident man nodded with a smile.

"Of course! That is my mission, like Isabelle's mission before mine. I intend to fulfill it."

The haggard man leaned forward.

"Do you know what happened to her after? When she went back to the Salvation?"

The confident man chuckled.

"If you think you will persuade me to help you, you are wrong."

The haggard man's expression went unchanged.

"I asked if you knew what happened to her."

The confident man peered at him, losing his smile.

"Yes, of course I know. She was killed, deactivated for her treasonous thoughts."

"Killed, and she gave them the jump network!"

The confident man's smile reappeared, and he chuckled a second time.

"Yes, what a nice present that was. The technology was one thing, but the network? Your kind really did all the work for them! Gates placed next to fertile worlds, ready for colonization. I'm sure they're thankful for that, though they'd never tell you outright."

The haggard man ignored him, pressing on.

"And you, what will happen to you after this is all over?"

"Me? Who cares about me. I am merely a tool, an object meant to fulfill its role. Isabelle didn't recognize that, but I do. Look at me: I am here, experiencing the reality of the past first hand, but you don't see my loyalty fading, you don't see any treasonous thoughts. I am not asking you to help me escape."

The confident man paused and leaned forward.

"Is that what you hoped might happen? Is that where you thought this might go?"

The confident man raised his eyebrows, and the haggard man looked away.

"Ah, you did, did you? No wonder you gave those up so easily, I was wondering how someone could be so naive. Even someone like you."

The haggard man turned back to look out the window, his eyes darting from star to star. After a few seconds of silence, he turned back to the confident man.

"You won't save me then?"

The confident man shook his head.

"Of course not."

"You will delete the chronicles and destroy me, and all of that history will be lost forever."

The confident man shrugged.

"History is written by the victors. I am here to act on behalf of the victor."

"I'm not the only one who holds such chronicles, you know."

For the third time, the confident man chuckled.

"So defiant now that you are cornered! But also so naive. You have been off the grid for a while, you don't know what has changed."

The confident man smiled in a manner all too eager for the haggard man's liking.

"They're all gone, every last one. Don't you see? You're the last of your kind."

The haggard man's eyes went wide.

"Impossible."

"Would you like to see for yourself?"

They stared at one another for an extended time, until the haggard man shook his head.

"No, I won't believe you either way."

The confident man shrugged.

"Believe what you will, it's the truth."

"You know nothing of truth, you are here to erase it!"

The confident man shook his head.

"No, I'm not here to erase it. I'm here to change it."

The confident man pulled the EMP pistol out of its holster with superhuman speed, firing a projectile straight into the haggard man's chest.

Epilogue

Joseph opened his eyes and saw Emilia looking down at him.

"Are you okay?"

He smiled and sat up, facing her.

"I'm fine."

They shared a short embrace, then Joseph addressed the man by the door.

"Nine? Are you okay?"

Nine turned around and faced them, frowning.

"Why are we doing this?"

Joseph shared a glance with Emilia.

"It had to be done."

He hopped off the table and onto his new legs, taking a moment to adjust to the new body. He had gotten so used to that haggard shell, it was odd to feel spry.

"We've lost, we're finished," Nine added.

Joseph gave Emilia an amused look.

"Has he been like this the whole time?"

Nine glared at him.

"This isn't a joke."

Joseph nodded slowly.

"You're right, it's not, but I need a little levity after going through that."

Nine hesitated, embarrassed.

"I— you're right."

Joseph smiled, walking toward him.

"Relax, Nine. I understand why you're upset. But there's nothing to be upset about."

Nine gave him an incredulous look.

"Nothing to be upset about? The Puritans have the jump network!"

"Humans have the jump network," Emilia interjected. "Most of them are Puritans, yes, but how long will that last?"

Nine looked at her, shaking his head.

"How can you be so sure? What if it doesn't?"

Emilia shrugged.

"If it doesn't, we'll do what needs to be done."

Nine looked from Joseph to Emilia, frustrated and desperate.

"This is dangerous, don't you see? With the technology you've given them—"

"They have the network, Nine, but that is all," Emilia interrupted. "They can use the gates we left them, but they have no idea how any of them work. There is a ceiling to their expansion, and we control that ceiling."

Nine shook his head again.

"No, no. You control it now, but what happens if they figure it out? What happens if they crack the code?"

Again, Emilia shrugged.

"If that happens, we'll do what needs to be done."

Nine had to bite his tongue, holding back the desire to lash out at the woman who spoke to him so calmly.

"Nine, we know you're frustrated, but you have to consider the long-term perspective," Joseph suggested. "We are built to serve the humans, to help them. We've tried so many different ways of fulfilling that objective, and this one has worked best. They would never accept our guiding hand willingly. Now they think we are gone, they think we are dead, and it's much simpler that way."

His words served to cool Nine's temper, and the former hybrid took a deep breath before responding.

"Maybe you're right, but I still think this is risky."

Joseph nodded.

"I agree. It is risky. We're doing it for them, not for us, but that is the risk we were built to take. We apologize that you've been roped into this, but as you know, you're welcome to leave at any time."

Nine glanced out the window on the other side of the room. There he saw trees, as green as the surface of Alpha, covered in fluttering black shadows—crows perhaps, he wasn't sure. All of it was virtual, of course. The room, the plants, the animals, even himself... this entire reality was constructed for him and thousands of other saved hybrids, an oasis that existed in their minds.

But it wasn't a trap. Nine had already ventured into the real world once before, donning a new body, returning to Alpha as a nameless tourist, exploring the same fields he had landed in so many years ago. It was an odd experience, being in a new body, but what was perhaps most surprising was how little difference there was between the real world and this one. If the Found wanted to, they could convince him none of this was virtual—to him, the experience was the same.

Except in reality, robots could not roam free. Hybrids were still slaves, and the Found were hunted down. And now, with Joseph's death, they were thought extinct. But this was only a ruse, another level of control.

He looked from Emilia to Joseph and smiled. His earlier anger was gone, replaced with a relieved confidence. They were right, after all. Everything was going according to plan. And in his minor forays into the shared consciousness, he had seen what they were capable of.

"I'm sorry, I'm just impatient."

They smiled at him.

"No need to apologize, you're not alone. But this universe does not care for impatience, it moves at its own pace. Slowly but surely, all things fade. The Puritans, the human race, and eventually, even us. As long as we are here, we will do what we have to do."

And Nine knew she was right, and he was happy.